*The PEN/O. Henry Prize Stories 2010*

# The PEN/O. Henry Prize Stories 2010

*Edited and with an Introduction by*
Laura Furman

*With Essays on the Stories They Admire Most*
*by Jurors*
Junot Díaz
Paula Fox
Yiyun Li

ANCHOR BOOKS
*A Division of Random House, Inc.*
New York

AN ANCHOR BOOKS ORIGINAL, MAY 2010

*Copyright © 2010 by Vintage Anchor Publishing, a division of Random House, Inc.*
*Introduction copyright © 2010 by Laura Furman*

All rights reserved. Published in the United States by Anchor Books,
a division of Random House, Inc., New York, and in Canada
by Random House of Canada Limited, Toronto.

Anchor Books and colophon are registered trademarks of Random House, Inc.

Permissions appear at the end of the book.

Cataloging-in-Publication Data for *The Pen/O. Henry Prize Stories 2010* is available at the
Library of Congress.

ISBN 978-0-307-47236-6

*Book design by Debbie Glasserman*

www.anchorbooks.com

Printed in the United States of America
10  9  8  7  6  5  4  3  2  1

*To Barbara Thompson Davis,*
*dear friend, author, supporter of writers*
*and the freedom to write*

The series editor wishes to thank the staff of Anchor Books for making each new collection a pleasure to work on and to read, and the staff of PEN America for giving new spirit to our collection. Without Cara Zimmer in Austin, the 2010 collection wouldn't have been possible. Thanks to Cara for her intelligence, taste, care, and patience.

*Publisher's Note*

## A BRIEF HISTORY OF THE PEN/O. HENRY PRIZE STORIES

Many readers have come to love the short story through the simple characters, easy narrative voice and humor, and compelling plotting in the work of William Sydney Porter (1862–1910), best known as O. Henry. His surprise endings entertain readers, even those back for a second, third, or fourth look. Even now one can say, "'Gift of the Magi,'" in a conversation about a love affair or marriage, and almost any literate person will know what is meant. It's hard to think of many other American writers whose work has been so incorporated into our national shorthand.

O. Henry was a newspaperman, skilled at hiding from his editors at deadline. A prolific writer, he wrote to make a living and to make sense of his life. He spent his childhood in Greensboro, North Carolina, his adolescence and young manhood in Texas, and his mature years in New York City. In between Texas and New York, he served out a prison sentence for bank fraud in Columbus, Ohio. Accounts of the origin of his pen name vary: one story dates from his days in Austin, where he was said to call the wandering family cat "Oh!

Henry!"; another states that the name was inspired by the captain of the guard in the Ohio State Penitentiary, Orrin Henry.

Porter had devoted friends, and it's not hard to see why. He was charming and had an attractively gallant attitude. He drank too much and neglected his health, which caused his friends concern. He was often short of money; in a letter to a friend asking for a loan of $15 (his banker was out of town, he wrote), Porter added a post-script: "If it isn't convenient, I'll love you just the same." The banker was unavailable most of Porter's life. His sense of humor was always with him.

Reportedly, Porter's last words were from a popular song: "Turn up the light, for I don't want to go home in the dark."

Eight years after O. Henry's death, in April 1918, the Twilight Club (founded in 1883 and later known as the Society of Arts and Letters) held a dinner in his honor at the Hotel McAlpin in New York City. His friends remembered him so enthusiastically that a group of them met at the Biltmore Hotel in December of that year to establish some kind of memorial to him. They decided to award annual prizes in his name for short-story writers, and formed a Committee of Award to read the short stories published in a year and to pick the winners. In the words of Blanche Colton Williams (1879–1944), the first of the nine series editors, the memorial was intended to "strengthen the art of the short story and to stimulate younger authors."

Doubleday, Page & Company was chosen to publish the first volume, *O. Henry Memorial Award Prize Stories 1919.* In 1927, the society sold all rights to the annual collection to Doubleday, Doran & Company. Doubleday published *The O. Henry Prize Stories,* as it came to be known, in hardcover, and from 1984 to 1996 its subsidiary, Anchor Books, published it simultaneously in paperback. Since 1997 *The O. Henry Prize Stories* has been published as an original Anchor Books paperback, retitled *The PEN/O. Henry Prize Stories* in 2009.

## HOW THE STORIES ARE CHOSEN

All stories originally written in the English language and published in an American or Canadian periodical are eligible for consideration. Stories are not nominated; magazines submit the year's issues in their entirety by May 1.

The series editor chooses the twenty PEN/O. Henry Prize Stories, and each year three writers distinguished for their fiction are asked to evaluate the entire collection and to write an appreciation of the story they most admire. These three writers receive the twenty prize stories in manuscript form with no identification of author or publication. They make their choices independent of one another and the series editor.

The goal of *The PEN/O. Henry Prize Stories* remains to strengthen the art of the short story.

## To Hortense Calisher (1911–2009)

*"What's a memoir? Ask the living. Hear the dead reply.*
*Not all of them yours, but some—*
*and that's what history is."*

—HORTENSE CALISHER, *TATTOO FOR A SLAVE* (2004)

HORTENSE CALISHER KNEW the importance of trusting the reader to understand both what is said on the page and what doesn't need to be said. Understanding the difference between the two is the life work of most writers, and was Calisher's in particular. Perhaps this was why she moved from short story to novel, from autobiography to memoir, from science fiction to mystery, from genre to genre, exploring the unknown in her majestic yet intimate voice. Although she greatly enjoyed what might be termed the stagecraft of writing, that is, the creation and expression of setting and character, atmosphere and background, Hortense Calisher's true goal was the secret and unsaid relationship with her reader through her prose. The play of language through literary forms and conventions was everything to her, and it served her well in the writing of twenty-three books of fiction and two of nonfiction, an autobiography and a memoir.

The idea of time as it reaches into the past and the future compelled her, and added a fascination to her observations of human beings and herself. In Hortense Calisher's long life, she shared a great deal of hospitality, laughter, style, and perspective with her many friends. She cherished her family. She did her work and enjoyed her life. She will be missed.

# Contents

Introduction • xvii
    Laura Furman, Series Editor

**Them Old Cowboy Songs** • 3
    Annie Proulx, *The New Yorker*

**Clothed, Female Figure** • 30
    Kirstin Allio, *The Iowa Review*

**The Headstrong Historian** • 60
    Chimamanda Ngozi Adichie, *The New Yorker*

**Stand by Me** • 78
    Wendell Berry, *The Atlantic Monthly*

**Sheep May Safely Graze** • 93
    Jess Row, *Threepenny Review*

**Birch Memorial** • 115
    Preeta Samarasan, *A Public Space*

**Visitation** • 139
    Brad Watson, *The New Yorker*

**The Woman of the House** • 158
William Trevor, *The New Yorker*

**The Bridge** • 174
Daniel Alarcón, *Granta*

**A Spoiled Man** • 206
Daniyal Mueenuddin, *The New Yorker*

**Oh, Death** • 231
James Lasdun, *The Paris Review*

**Fresco, Byzantine** • 246
Natalie Bakopoulos, *Tin House*

**The End of My Life in New York** • 266
Peter Cameron, *Subtropics*

**Obit** • 281
Ted Sanders, *Indiana Review*

**The Lover** • 289
Damon Galgut, *The Paris Review*

**An East Egg Update** • 337
George Bradley, *The Yale Review*

**Into the Gorge** • 351
Ron Rash, *The Southern Review*

**Microstories** • 364
John Edgar Wideman, *Harper's Magazine*

**Some Women** • 379
Alice Munro, *The New Yorker*

**Making Good** • 401
Lore Segal, *The American Scholar*

**Reading *The PEN/O. Henry Prize Stories 2010*** • 417
The Jurors on Their Favorites
Junot Díaz on "A Spoiled Man" by Daniyal Mueenuddin
Paula Fox on "Oh, Death" by James Lasdun
Yiyun Li on "The Woman of the House" by William Trevor

**Writing *The PEN/O. Henry Prize Stories 2010*** • 425
The Writers on Their Work

Recommended Stories 2010 • 443
Publications Submitted • 445
Permissions • 477

# Introduction

FOR THE READER, the short story is nothing less than a brief and intense residence in another world. This other place offers escape from yourself and your own world, as well as the rarest of gifts—the possibility of becoming someone else. Each crucial element of fiction—character, place, time, event—offers the opportunity for *intimacy* and *compassion*. These two words, so quiet and loaded, contain difficult and threatening emotions, but they are also the emotions that in the end make us feeling beings. The short story, while you're reading, includes you as a witness and imaginary participant, and allows you to suffer and rejoice.

The reader's entrance into the new world depends, mysteriously, on the language used to tell the tale. Unless the teller's voice is true, the reader won't have the courage to go to Pakistan, to a hollow or gorge or prairie, to a village in Malaysia, certainly not into the mind and heart of a character quite unlike the reader.

Read the statements of the authors in *The PEN/O. Henry Prize Stories 2010*. Some of the writers have impressive bodies of work, others are beginning, but none claims to be in complete control of a story or to say that it came out as planned. The impulse to write is not an impulse to control. It's more like an experienced sailor going to sea once more. Writing a short story is akin to being on a voyage to India and ending up in Indiana. There are discoveries to be made along the way, and the new land has its points of fascination, but it isn't where you thought you were going.

Ron Rash, one of our best living storytellers, lives and writes close to his Appalachian roots. "Into the Gorge," he tells us, came from a story he'd heard as a child. The story is emblematic of Rash's work and his precise, modest, often beautiful prose. His people are rooted to their landscape, and it in turn is at the mercy of its long-staying temporary residents. Rash seems at times to be writing about paradise, but his settings soon turn out to be the opposite for his characters. He examines through vivid, often morally complex situations both the dangers of nature to human beings and the danger human beings bring to nature. It's often a question of which suffers more.

James Lasdun's "Oh, Death" is set in a community of newcomers and the less privileged descendants of early settlers of Vanderbeck Hollow. The narrator, a newcomer, "games the system" for a living, as he tells Rick, who grew up in the hollow. To support his family Rick performs manual labor, doing whatever he can—chopping and delivering cords of wood, trimming trees, landscaping. Rick knows the nearby woods, and has seen a mountain lion up on state land, though the narrator knows for a "fact" that there are no longer catamounts in the area. By the story's end, a reversal has taken place, and the narrator, the stranger to the woods, learns new and truer facts.

Such reversals occur often in the short story; if the story is good, the reversal evolves from the combination of character and circumstance. Annie Proulx's "Them Old Cowboy Songs" is a meditation on an American belief—that if one works long and hard, one's sacrifices and pains will pay off in the end. The story begins with high spirits and an admirable and naive reliance on love's promise, and ends in abandonment and a bitter disappointment that resonates more truly than the success stories we'd like to believe. The story is remarkable not only for its penetration into another time but for its convincing portrayal of the cruelty and indifference of nature. In the world of Proulx's remarkable story, waking to see another day comes to seem miraculous.

When the narrator of Wendell Berry's "Stand by Me" uses the simple phrase "home place," we leap ahead from Annie Proulx's tale of western settlers to a country where nature has been tamed and named: ". . . the Dead Tree Path, I remember, and the Spring Path, and the Rock Fence Path." There's harmony between the people and the place they live, and a community watches over its children and elders, but nothing can keep loss and sorrow at bay. The narrator's evenhanded telling, more than what is told, speaks of the lifelong habit of turning over facts, like well-worn pebbles, by a man trying to understand the beginning of his own story so that he can bear the end.

In a story literally of a different shape than any of the others in this year's PEN/O. Henry, Ted Sanders uses the form of the obituary to sing the lives and deaths of his characters. The newspaper-column format is joined to the repetitious, charming storytelling cadence of a fairy tale, but "Obit" is a story for grown-ups.

One method of reading short stories, or at least analyzing them, suggests that the development and ending sections evolve entirely from the beginning. In Jess Row's "Sheep May Safely Graze," the development extends again and again, illuminating the more simple beginning, amplifying it, and then, in the ending, returning to it. The development has a large life of its own, with action enough for several short stories. Row manages the episodes in the cascading fashion of waves beating against the shore, until he quiets the story—and the reader—with the lyrics of the Bach cantata that give the story its name and lead into the slow, movement-by-movement action of the narrator's final cri de coeur.

"Birch Memorial" by Preeta Samarasan is a love story set in post-colonial Malaysia that encompasses several types of love. At a distance of twenty-five years, Kalyani tells of the time when she was twenty, orphaned and beautiful, supporting herself and her crippled brother by selling appam, a street snack, and trying to save money for an operation for her brother and a house for them both. She tells us of the foreign researcher Sebastian Mills, of the mad beggar Millionaire Komalam, of her disabled brother. Though she says she doesn't believe in God, she also tells us of God's disguises and appearances. She addresses the story to "you," both to us as readers and to the people of Ipoh town who witnessed her life and gossiped about her. The narrative both draws the reader in, as does the dialect in which it's told, and at the same time reminds us of the distance between us and the privilege we enjoy in hearing the secrets of Kalyani's life.

F. Scott Fitzgerald was a shrewd and romantic observer of the troubled relationship between Americans and their New World. In "An East Egg Update," George Bradley, shrewdly if not romantically, observes the changes time has brought to Gatsby's territory since Fitzgerald's masterpiece. The story includes the large changes as suburbs replace villages and estates, and of the inexplicable, memorable action of a dying woman. The intensity and strength of "An East Egg Update" lies in its perspective; it's a large view, seen up close.

Brad Watson's characters in "Visitation" inhabit an anonymous, familiar freeway landscape in California. Father and son are passing through, as are most of the other characters. Watson uses the commonplace situations of divorce and a father visiting his child as background to the story the father tells of his own failures: "He'd been painfully aware of his own despair for most of his life. Most of his troubles had come from attempts to deny the essential hopelessness in his nature." It seems for a long time in "Visitation" that there's not much to contradict the universal bleakness of the father's vision, a quality echoed in the constancy of the highway, the marginal motel, food, TV fare, even the other guests in the motel. Then a ripple appears in the even vision: a strange family—Gypsies, the father names them, frightening his son—whose oddness, poverty, and assertiveness break the hopeless politeness between father and son.

From the break comes something more difficult and rewarding for the narrator to bear than despair.

"But the ancient Dodge was part of Martina's circumstances, to be tolerated because it was necessary." Martina is the woman in William Trevor's "The Woman of the House," and there is much aside from an unreliable car she has to tolerate, as we learn little by little. Two brothers of uncertain nationality turn up and they're hired to paint the outside of the isolated Irish cottage where Martina lives with the crippled owner, a relative. The brothers have each other, a living to make, and the world to roam. The crippled man has his house and land, his benefits coming monthly in the mail, and Martina to torture. Martina has no one and nothing, only a Gold Flake tin crammed with money she's gotten by cheating the crippled man and selling herself. In other stories, some of William Trevor's characters free themselves from their own anxious delusions, such as Harriet in his memorable "After Rain," but he doesn't make a case for redemption or despair. As he once wrote, "My fiction may, now and again, illuminate aspects of the human condition, but I do not consciously set out to do so." In "The Woman of the House," there is plenty of incident—betrayal, the possibility of murder—but such excitement is secondary, deferring to the struggle by Martina and the brothers for their own survival.

Until its turning point, Daniyal Mueenuddin's "A Spoiled Man" seems to be the story of Rezak, a very poor, rather proud, and resourceful Pakistani who falls by luck into being the caretaker for an orchard owned by the wealthy Sohail Harouni and his American wife, Sonya. All goes well for Rezak, almost too well, the experienced reader senses; in the world of the short story, good fortune requires its opposite. Unwittingly, the well-meaning Sonya delivers Rezak to his doom. The story, richly told, is a complicated and rewarding reflection on an entanglement of power and helplessness.

"Many, even if they had not arrived as artists, would leave at least as craftsmen: they created things from delicate worry beads to nice sitting chairs to tables they could gather around. Something from nothing, something in nothing." So Natalie Bakopoulos describes life on a Greek prison island in 1970, an arbitrarily administered place, inhabited by political prisoners, many of them "artists and writers and the rank-and-file of the Left and Center." The newly arrived Mihalis and the long-serving Vagelis are old friends reunited on the island. Vagelis is so well acclimated to prison that he doesn't ask Mihalis about his wife and friends who are free. Soon we learn of a compelling reason for his immersion in prison life. In prison or free, citizens of a country run by a military junta or not, we're enclosed by our feelings and dreams. The story reminds us to look beyond the details of setting and background, even when they're as engrossing as they are in "Fresco, Byzantine."

The title of Peter Cameron's touching, witty "The End of My Life in New York" refers to a realization the narrator has in the course of the story. The notion of leaving New York is embellished by the perfectly chosen details of that life, and those who live in it, or try to. Cameron's narrator is unemployed (and perhaps unemployable), scarred, in chronic pain, and guilty. Years before, his drunk driving set off a terrible sequence of injuries to himself and others, and in the accident's aftermath he's removed not only from his companionable life with his partner but from his profession, his erotic life, and eventually his city. Throughout the story, as in Chekhov's classic "Misery" when the cabdriver tries all through a snowy night to find someone who'll listen to him, Cameron's narrator tries to tell an awful story he heard at a dinner party. His only listener is the reader. Hearing it, we can only wish him well and hope he can figure out whether New York's complications, demands, and ironies can be escaped in any life, anywhere.

John Edgar Wideman's "Microstories" can be read as separate stories, or meditations, or as one narrative distributed widely. One thing is certain: that the small pieces gain power when taken together, and that they add up to a fully realized work. The stories are varied and absorbing, about unbearable memories and the forms love takes as it leaves us or stays. However much "Microstories" dwells on separation, the strength of the writing brings warmth both to the characters and to the reader.

In Daniel Alarcón's "The Bridge," the narrator inherits his uncle Ramón's modest house and declares, "There was nothing of my family in this house and maybe that was the only attractive thing about it." Named after a failed connection, "The Bridge" is about a family engaged in a malicious civil war both in life and after death. The narrator, as executor of his uncle's estate, delves into his family's history as he searches for information about the one relative he liked, Ramón, a blind translator married to another blind translator. The story is full of puns and doubling, even down to a minor but crucial character, a truck driver, who shares a name with the renowned translator Gregory Rabassa. The jokiness of such literary devices only deepens one's sense of the infinitely complex and bridgeless gap that often defines family life.

The Russian nanny in Kirstin Allio's "Clothed, Female Figure" purposefully does not pick favorites among her families, another way of saying that she herself has no family. She is a deliberately distant observer of her employers, her stance a muddy reflection of her education as a psychologist. For better or worse, she's chosen her life, and at the end we discern her reasons for her exile from intimate relationships. As in other fine stories, we understand the first paragraph of "Clothed, Female Figure" only when we've reached the story's end.

The narrator of Damon Galgut's long and absorbing "The Lover" is troubled not so much by his past or present as by his future. As the story leads us across Africa from Zimbabwe to Tanzania and into Europe, the narrator demonstrates the experienced traveler's capacity to accept and appreciate what the present day brings. But he leans always toward the next thing, and he thinks that without love this will always be so. "All his few belongings are in storage and he has spent months wandering around from one spare room to another. It has begun to feel as if he's never lived in any other way, nor will he ever settle down. He can't seem to connect properly with the world. He feels this not as a failure of the world but as a massive failing in himself, he would like to change it but doesn't know how." A lovely Swiss man appears who might become his lover; a hesitant courtship begins. The engaging pull of Galgut's prose is such that we follow the narrator willingly not only from nation to nation and continent to continent, but from the country of first-person narrative to that of third-person, and back again. The main character, both narrator and character, must now be settled, one thinks, homeless no more, the troublesome mechanics and restless loneliness of youth behind him, because he is telling the tale. For the reader, the story is a chance to be uprooted, to go far from home and feel the chill of travel.

Chimamanda Ngozi Adichie's "The Headstrong Historian" takes us to another Africa altogether, to late nineteenth-century Nigeria and the life story of Nwamgba. She is a strong woman hemmed in by custom and circumstance, whose beloved son betrays her in an unimaginable way. Nwamgba is both the historian of the title and the grandmother of another headstrong historian. Nwamgba preserves and lives within her traditions but uses her will to cut her own path, marrying Obierika despite her family's disapproval—wise, as it turns out. Characteristically, Nwamgba "had believed with a quiet stubbornness that her chi and his chi had destined their marriage." In both her marriage and in raising her son when she is widowed, Nwamgba stays in conflict with her husband's greedy cousins and the whites who come to Nigeria as slavers and missionaries. Nwamgba holds firmly to her own sensible beliefs and in the story's surprising ending is more than vindicated. In her second prizewinning PEN/O. Henry story, Adichie mixes the magic of human character and that of spiritual belief, and takes her readers with her wherever she wishes to lead.

Among Alice Munro's many gifts is that of graceful compression; we can understand the whole of a life within the pages of a short story. Other writers do this also, each in her own way. But it's a hallmark of Munro's writing that in the shell game of storytelling it delights rather than annoys the reader when the true nugget of intention and heart is revealed. In "Some Women" there are many threads of meaning and heart for the reader to follow, but the narrator's understanding that time has passed is the story's warp. The reader feels the wonder of an old woman at the complications of human relationships and the varied personalities met in a long life, that she once had so much to learn, and did.

Some stories are meant to be written, and Lore Segal's "Making Good"—about a circle of reconciliation or "bridge building"—is such a story. Its wit and lightness hold the infinitely complicated and essential conundrum of forgiveness. Who has the authority to forgive a grave crime against humanity? Great public crimes cannot by their nature be forgiven, except by those most closely harmed and by the dead. Is forgiveness even possible? Lore Segal's particularity of diction, humor, and restraint of sentiment give her fictional disquisition on forgiveness its grace and fascination. To amend the folk saying that the devil is in the details, perhaps forgiveness is possible only when one knows all the details. Uncomfortable and sometimes absurd as the little circle seems in "Making Good," it's an honorable place to be.

In the end, what's striking about the characters in *The PEN/O. Henry Prize Stories 2010* is not so much the forces that divide them—war, death, nationality, race, plain bad luck, environmental depredation—as how hard they must try to keep themselves together.

*Laura Furman*
*Austin, Texas*

*The PEN/O. Henry Prize Stories 2010*

Annie Proulx

# *Them Old Cowboy Songs*

## ARCHIE AND ROSE, 1885

ARCHIE AND ROSE McLaverty staked out a homestead where the Little Weed comes rattling down from the Sierra Madre, water named not for miniature obnoxious flora but for P. H. Weed, a gold-seeker who had starved near its source. Archie had a face as smooth as a skinned aspen, his lips barely incised on the surface, as though scratched in with a knife. All his natural decoration was in his red cheeks and his springy waves of auburn hair, which seemed charged with voltage. He lied about his age to anyone who asked—he was not twenty-one but sixteen. The first summer, they lived in a tent while Archie worked on a small cabin. It took him a month of rounding up stray cows for Bunk Peck before he could afford two glass windows. The cabin was snug, built with eight-foot squared-off logs tenoned on the ends and dropped into mortised uprights, a size Archie could handle himself, with a little help from their only neighbor, Tom Ackler, a sun-dried prospector with a summer shack up on the mountain. They chinked the cabin with heavy yellow clay. One day, Archie dragged a huge flat stone to the house for a doorstep. It was pleasant to sit in the cool of the evening with their feet on the great stone and watch the deer come down to drink and, just before darkness, see the herons flying upstream, their color matching the sky so closely they might have been eyes of wind. Archie dug into the side of the hill and built a stout meat house, sawed wood while Rose split kindling until they had four cords stacked high against the cabin, almost to the eaves, the pile immediately tenanted by a weasel.

"He'll keep the mice down," Rose said.

"Yeah, if the bastard don't bite somebody," Archie said, flexing his right forefinger. A faint brogue flavored his sentences, for he had been conceived in Ireland and born, in 1868, in Dakota Territory, of parents arrived from Bantry Bay, his father to spike ties for the Union Pacific Railroad. His mother's death from cholera when he was seven was followed a few weeks later by that of his father, who had guzzled an entire bottle of strychnine-laced patent medicine that was guaranteed to ward off cholera and measles if taken in teaspoon quantities. Before Archie's mother died, she had taught him dozens of old songs and the rudiments of music structure by painting a plank with black and white piano keys, sitting him before it, and encouraging him to touch the keys with the correct fingers. The family wipeout removed the Irish influence. Mrs. Sarah Peck, a warmhearted Missouri Methodist widow, raised the young orphan, to the great resentment of her son, Bunk.

A parade of saddle bums drifted through the Peck bunkhouse, and from an early age Archie listened to the songs they sang. He was a quick study for a tune, and had a memory for rhymes, verses, and intonations. When Mrs. Peck died, caught in a grass conflagration she had started while singeing slaughtered chickens, Archie was fourteen and Bunk in his early twenties. Without Mrs. Peck as a buffer, the relationship became one of hired hand and boss. There had never been any sense of kinship, fictive or otherwise, between them, and Bunk Peck fumed over the hundred dollars his mother had left Archie in her will.

Archie McLaverty had a singing voice that once heard was never forgotten. It was a straight, hard voice, the words falling out halfway between a shout and a song. Sad and flat and without ornamentation, it expressed things that were unsayable. He sang plain and square-cut, "Brandy's brandy, any way you mix it, a Texian's a Texian any way you fix it," and the listeners laughed at the droll way he rolled out "fix it," the words surely meaning castration. He could sing every song—"Go 'Long Blue Dog," and "When the Green Grass Comes," "Don't Pull Off My Boots," and "Two Quarts of Whiskey," and at all-male roundup nights he had endless verses of "The Stinkin Cow," "The Buckskin Shirt," and "Cousin Harry." He courted Rose by singing, "Never marry no good-for-nothin boy," it being understood that the boy was himself, the "good-for-nothin" a disclaimer. Later, with winks and innuendo, he sang, "Little girl, for safety you better get branded."

Archie, advised by an ex-homesteader working for Bunk Peck, used his inheritance from Mrs. Peck to buy eighty acres of private land. It would have cost nothing if he had filed for a homestead twice that size on public land, or eight times larger on desert land, but Archie feared the government would discover he was a minor. Since he had never expected anything from Mrs. Peck, buying the land with the surprise legacy seemed like getting it for free. Archie, thrilled to be a landowner, told Rose he had to sing the metes and bounds. He started on the southwest corner early one morning and headed east. Rose walked along with him at the beginning and even tried to sing with him but got out of breath from walking so fast and singing at the same time. Nor did she know the words to many of his songs. Archie kept going. Late in the afternoon, he was on the west line, drawing near and still singing, though his voice was raspy, "an we'll go downtown, an we'll buy some shirts. . . ," and slouching down the slope the last hundred feet in the evening dusk so worn of voice she could only just hear him breathily chant, "never had a nickel and I don't give a shit."

. . .

There is no happiness like that of a young couple in a little house they have built themselves in a place of beauty and solitude. Archie had hammered together a table with sapling legs and two benches. At the evening meal, their faces lit by the yellow shine of the coal-oil lamp whose light threw wild shadows on the ceiling, their world seemed in order.

Rose was not pretty, but warmhearted and quick to laugh. She had grown up at the Jackrabbit stage station, the daughter of kettle-bellied Sundown Mealor, who dreamed of plunging steeds but because of his bottle habit drove a freight wagon. The station was on a north–south trail that connected hardscrabble ranches with the blowout railroad town of Rawlins after the Union Pacific line went through. Rose's mother was gray with some wasting disease that kept her to her bed, sinking slowly out of life. She wept over Rose's early marriage at barely fourteen but gave her a family treasure, a large silver spoon that had come across the Atlantic.

The stationmaster was Robert F. Dorgan, affable and jowly, yearning to be appointed to a position of importance and seeing the station as a brief stop not only for freight wagons but for himself. His second wife, Flora, stepmother to his daughter Queeda, went to Denver every winter with Queeda, and so they became authorities on fashion and style. They were as close as a natural mother and daughter. In Denver, Mrs. Dorgan sought out important people who could help her husband climb to success. Many political men spent the winter in Denver, and one of them, Rufus Clatter, with connections to Washington, hinted that there was a chance for Dorgan to be appointed as the territory's surveyor.

"I'm sure he knows a good deal about surveying," he said with a wink.

"Considerable," she said, thinking that Dorgan could find some stripling surveyor to do the work for a few dollars.

"I'll see what I can do," Clatter said, pressing heavily against her thigh, but tensed to step away if she took offense. She allowed him a few seconds, smiled, and turned away.

Back at the station in the spring, where her rings and metallic dress trim cast a golden aura, she bossed the local society and gossip, saying that Archie McLaverty had ruined Rose, precipitating their youthful marriage, but what could you expect from a girl with a drunkard father, an uncontrolled girl who'd had the run of the station, sassing rough drivers and exchanging low repartee with bumpkin cowhands, among them Archie McLaverty, a lowlife who sang vulgar songs? She whisked her hands together as though ridding them of filth.

The other inhabitant of the station was an old bachelor (the country was rich in bachelors), Harp Daft, the telegraph key operator. His face and neck formed a visor of scars, moles, wens, boils, and acne. One leg was shorter than the other, and his voice twanged with catarrh. His window faced the Dorgan house, and a black circle that Rose knew to be a telescope sometimes showed in it.

Rose both admired and despised Queeda Dorgan. She greedily took in every detail of the beautiful dresses, the fire-opal brooch, satin shoes, and saucy hats so exquisitely out of place at the dusty station, but she knew that Miss Dainty had to wash out her bloody menstrual rags like every woman, although she tried to hide them by hanging them on the line at night or inside pillow slips. Beneath the silk skirts, she, too, had to put up with sopping pads torn from old sheets, the crusted edges chafing her thighs and pulling at her pubic hairs. At those times of the month, the animal smell seeped through Queeda's perfumed defenses.

Rose saw Mrs. Dorgan as an iron-boned, two-faced enemy, her public sweetness offset by private coarseness. She had seen the woman spit on the ground like a drover, had seen her scratch her crotch on the corner of the table when she thought no one was looking. Believing that she was a superior creature, Mrs. Dorgan never spoke to the Mealors, nor to the despicable bachelor pawing his telegraph key, or, as he said, seeking out constellations.

. . .

Every morning in the little cabin, Rose braided her straight brown hair, dabbed it with drops of lilac water from the blue bottle Archie had presented her on the day of their wedding, and wound it around her head in a coronet, the way Queeda Dorgan bound up her hair. She did not want to become like a homestead woman, with skunky armpits and greasy hair yanked into a bun. She hoped that their children would get Archie's auburn waves and his red-cheeked, handsome face. She trimmed his hair with a pair of embroidery scissors dropped in the dust by some lady stagecoach passenger at the station years before. But it was hard, keeping clean. Queeda Dorgan had little to do at the station except primp and flounce, but Rose, in her cabin, lifted heavy kettles, split kindling, baked bread, scrubbed pots, and hacked the stone-filled ground for a garden, and hauled water when Archie was not there. They were lucky their first winter that the river did not freeze. Her personal wash and the dishes and the floor took four daily buckets of water lugged up from the Little Weed, each trip disturbing the ducks who favored the nearby setback for their business meetings. She tried to keep Archie clean as well. He rode in from days of chasing Peck's cows or running wild horses on the desert with a stubbled face, mosquito-bitten neck and grimed hands, cut, cracked nails, and stinking feet. She pulled off his boots and washed his feet in the dishpan, patting them dry with a clean feed-sack towel.

"If you had stockins, it wouldn't be so bad," she said. "If I could get me some knittin needles and yarn I could make stockins."

"Mrs. Peck made some. Once. Took about a hour before they was holed. No point to it, and they clamber around in your boots. Hell with stockins."

Supper was venison hash or a platter of fried sage hen she had shot, but not beans, which Archie said had been and still were the main provender at Peck's. Occasionally their neighbor Tom Ackler rode down for supper, sometimes with his yellow cat, Gold Dust, riding behind him on the saddle. While Tom talked, Gold Dust set to work to claw the weasel out of the woodpile. Rose liked the black-eyed, balding prospector and asked him about the gold earring in his left ear.

"Used a sail the world, girlie. That's my port ear and that ring tells them as knows that I been east round Cape Horn. And if you been east, you been west first. Been all over the world." He had a rich collection of stories of storms, violent williwaws, and southerly busters, of waterspouts and whales leaping like trout, icebergs and doldrums and enmeshing seaweed, of wild times in distant ports.

"How come you to leave the sailor-boy life?" Rose asked.

"No way to get rich, girlie. And this fella wanted a snug harbor after the pitchin deck."

Archie asked about maritime songs, and the next visit Tom Ackler brought his concertina with him, and for hours sea chanteys and sailors' verses filled the cabin, Archie asking for a repeat of some and often chiming in after a single hearing.

*They say old man your horse will die.*
*And they say so, and they hope so.*
*O poor old man your horse will die.*
*O poor old man.*

Rose was an eager lover when Archie called, "Put your ass up like a whip-poor-will," and an expert at shifting his occasional glum moods into pleased laughter. She seemed unaware that she lived in a time when love killed women. One summer evening, their bedspread on the floor among the chips and splinters in the half-finished cabin, they fell to kissing. Rose, in some kind of transport, began to bite her kisses, sharp nips along his neck, his shoulder, in the musky crevice between his arm and torso, his nipples, until she felt him shaking and looked up to see his eyes closed, tears in his lashes, face contorted in a grimace.

"Oh, Archie, I didn't mean to hurt, Archie—"

"You did not," he groaned. "It's. I ain't never been. Loved. I just can't hardly STAND IT—" And he began to blubber, "Feel like I been shot," pulling her into his arms, rolling half over so that the salty tears and his saliva wet her embroidered shirtwaist, calling her his little birdeen, and at that moment she would have walked into a furnace for him.

On the days he was away she would hack at the garden. She shot a hawk that was after her three laying hens, plucked and cleaned it, and threw it in the soup pot with a handful of wild onions and some pepper. Another day she gathered two quarts of wild strawberries, her fingers stained a deep red that would not wash away.

"Look like you killed and skinned a griz bear by hand," he said. "It could be a bear might come down for his berries, so don't you go pickin no more."


The second winter came on and Bunk Peck laid off all the men, including Archie. Cowhands rode the circuit, moving from ranch to ranch, doing odd jobs in return for a place in the bunkhouse and three squares. Down on the Little Weed, Archie and Rose were ready for the cold. He had waited for good tracking snow and shot two elk and two deer in November when the weather chilled, swapping a share of the meat with Tom Ackler for his help, for it could take a lone man several days to pack a big elk out, with bears, lions, and wolves, coyotes, ravens, and eagles gorging as much of the unattended carcass as they could. The meat house was full. They had a barrel of flour and enough baking powder and sugar for the city of Chicago. Some mornings the wind stirred the snow into a scrim that bleached the mountains and made opaline dawn skies. Once the sun below the horizon threw savage red onto the bottom of the cloud that hung over Barrel Mountain, and Archie glanced up and saw Rose in the doorway burning an unearthly color in the lurid glow.

By spring, both of them were tired of elk and venison, tired of bumping into each other in the little cabin. Rose was pregnant. Her vitality seemed to have ebbed away, her good humor with it. Archie carried her water buckets from the river and swore he would dig a well the coming summer. It was hot in the cabin, the April sun like an oven door ajar.

"You better get somebody knows about well diggin," she said sourly, slapping the bowls on the table for the everlasting elk stew, nothing more than meat, water, and salt, simmered to chewability, then reheated for days. "Remember how Mr. Town got killed when his well caved in and him in it?"

"A well can damn cave in and *I* won't be in it," he said. "I got in mind not diggin a deep killin well but clearin out that little seep east a the meat house. Could make a good spring, and I'd build a spring-house, put up some shelves, and maybe git a cow. Butter-and-cream cow. Hell, I'm goin a dig out that spring today." He was short but muscular, and his shoulders had broadened, his chest filled out with the work. He started to sing, "Got to bring along my shovel if I got to dig a spring," ending with one of Tom's yo-heave-hos, but his jokey song did not soothe her irritation. An older woman would have seen that, although they were little more than children, they were shifting out of the days of clutching love and into the long haul of married life.

"Cows cost money, specially butter-and-cream cows. We ain't got enough for a butter dish even. And I'd need a churn. Long as we are dreamin, might as well dream a pig, too, give the skim and have the pork in the fall. Sick a deer meat. It's too bad you spent all your money on this land. Should a saved some out."

"Still think it was the right way to do, but we sure need some chink. I'm ridin to talk with Bunk in a few days, see can I get hired on again." He pulled on his dirty digging pants, still spattered with mud from the three-day job of the privy pit. "Don't git me no dinner. I'll dig until noon and come in for coffee. We got coffee yet?"

Bunk Peck took pleasure in saying there was no job for him. Nor was there anything at the other ranches. Eight or ten Texas cowhands left over from last fall's Montana drive had stayed in the country and taken all the work.

He tried to make a joke out of it for Rose, but the way he breathed through his teeth showed it wasn't funny. After a few minutes she said in a low voice, "At the station they used a say they pay a hunderd a month up in Butte."

"Missus McLaverty, I wouldn't work in no mine. You married you a cowboy." And he sang, "I'm just a lonesome cowboy who loves a gal named Rose, I don't care if my hat gets wet or if I freeze my toes, but I won't work no copper mine, so put that up your nose." He picked a piece of turnip from the frying pan on the stove and ate it. "I'll ride over Cheyenne way an see what I can find. There's some big ranches over there and they probly need hands. Stop by Tom's place on my way an ask him to look in on you."

Despite the strong April sun, there was still deep snow under the lodgepoles and in the north hollows around Tom Ackler's cabin; the place had a deserted feeling to it, something more than if Tom had gone off for the day. His cat, Gold Dust, came purring up onto the steps, but when Archie tried to pet her she tore his hand and with flattened ears raced into the pines. Inside the cabin he found the stub of a pencil and wrote a note on the edge of an old newspaper, and left it on the table.

> Tom I looking for werk arond Shyanne.
> Check on Rose now & than, ok?

## KAROK'S COWS

In a saloon on a Cheyenne street packed with whiskey mills and gambling snaps, he heard that a rancher up on Rawhide Creek was looking for spring roundup hands. The whiskey bottles glittered as the swinging doors let in planks of light—Kellogg's Old Bourbon, Squirrel, Great Gun, G. G. Booz, Day Dream. He bought his informant a drink. The thing was, the man said, a big-mustached smiler showing rotten nutcrackers, putting on the sideboards by wrapping his thumb and forefinger around the shot glass to gain another inch of fullness, that although Karok paid well and he didn't hardly lay off men in the fall, he would not hire married men, because they had the bad habit of running off home to see wife and kiddies while Karok's cows fell in mud holes, were victimized by mountain lions and rustlers, drifted down the draw, and suffered the hundred other ills that could befall untended cattle. The bartender, half listening, sucked a draft of Wheatley's Spanish Pain Destroyer from a small bottle near the cash register.

"Stomach," he said to no one, belching.

Big Mustache knocked back his brimming shot of Squirrel and went on. "He's a foreigner from back East, and the only thing counts to him is cows. He learned that fast when he come here back in the early days, cows is the only thing. Grub's pretty poor, too. There ain't no chicken in the chicken soup."

"Yeah, and no horse in the horseradish," said Archie, who'd heard all the feeble bunkhouse jokes.

"Huh. Well, he rubs some the wrong way. Most a them quit. What I done. Some law dog come out there once with his hand hoverin over his shooter, and I could see he was itchin to dabble in gore. I felt like it was a awful good place a put behind me. But there's a few like Karok's ways. Maybe you are one a them. Men rides for him gets plenty practice night ropin. See, his herd grows like a son of a bitch, if you take my meanin. But I'll give you some advice: one a these days there'll be some trouble there. That's how come that law was nosin round."

Archie rode up through country as yellow and flat as an old newspaper and went to see Karok. There was a big sign on the gate: "NO MARIED MEN." When the dour rancher asked him, Archie lied himself single, and said that he had to fetch his gear and would be back in six days.

"Five," said the kingpin, looking at him suspiciously. "Other fellas look for work, they carry their fixins. They don't have to go home and git it."

Archie worked up some story about visiting Cheyenne and not

knowing he'd been laid off until one of the old outfit's boys showed up and said they were all on the bum.

"Yeah? Get goin, then. Roundup started two days ago."

Back on the Little Weed with Rose, he half explained the situation, said she would not be able to send him letters or messages until he worked something out, said he had to get back to Karok's outfit fast and would be gone for months and that she had better get her mother to come down from the station to help with the baby, expected in late September.

"She can't stand a make that trip. You know how sick she is. Won't you come back for the baby?" Even in the few days he had been gone, he seemed changed. She touched him and sat very close, waiting for the familiar oneness to lock them together.

"If I can git loose I will. But this is a real good job, good money, fifty-five a month, almost twice what Bunk Peck pays, and I'm goin a save ever nickel. And if she can't come down, you better go up there, be around womenfolk. Maybe I can git Tom to bring you up, say in July or August? Or sooner?" He was fidgety, as though he wanted to leave that minute. "He been around? His place was closed up when I stopped there before. I'll stop again on my way."

Rose said that if she had to go to the station, early September was soon enough. She did not want to be where she would have to tend her sick mother and put up with her drunk father, to see the telegraph man's face like an eroded cliff, to suffer Mrs. Dorgan's supercilious comments about "some people" directed at Queeda but meant for Rose to hear. She did not want to show up rough and distended and abandoned, without the husband they had prophesied would skedaddle. September was five months away, and she would worry about it when it came. Together they added up what a year's pay might come to, working for Karok.

"If you save everthing it will be six hundred fifty dollars. We'll be rich, won't we?" she asked in a mournful tone he chose not to notice.

He spoke enthusiastically. "And that's not countin what I maybe can pick up in wolf bounties. Possible another hunderd. Enough to git us started. I'll quit this feller's ranch after a year an git back here."

"How do I get news to you—about the baby?"

"I don't know yet. But I'll work somethin out. You know what? I feel like I need my hair combed some. You want a comb my hair?"

"Yes," she said, and laughed just when he'd thought she was going to cry. But for the first time she recognized that they were not two cleaving halves of one person but two separate people, and that because he was a man he could leave any time he wanted, and because she was a woman she could not. The cabin reeked of desertion and betrayal.

## ARCHIE AND SINK

Men raised from infancy with horses could identify salient differences with a glance, but some had a keener talent for understanding equine temperament than others. Sink Gartrell was one of those, the polar opposite of Montana bronc-buster Wally Finch, who used a secret ghost cord and made unrideable outlaws of the horses he was breaking. Sink gave off a hard air of competence.

Sink thought the new kid might make a top hand with horses if he got over being a show-off. The second or third morning after he joined the roundup, Archie had woken early, sat up in his bedroll, and let loose a getting-up holler decorated with some rattlesnake yodels, startling old cookie Hel, who dropped the coffeepot in the fire, earning curses from the scattered bedrolls. The black smell of scorched coffee knocked the day over on the wrong side. The foreman, Alonzo Lago, who had barely noticed him before, stared hard at the curly-haired new hand who'd made all the noise. Sink saw him looking.

Later, Sink took the kid aside and put the boo on him, told him the facts of life, said that the leathery old foreman was well-known for bareback riding of new young hires. Archie, who'd seen it all at

Peck's bunkhouse, gave him a look as though he suspected Sink of the same base design, said that he could take care of himself and that if anyone tried anything on him he'd clean his plow good. He moved off. When Sink came in from watch at the past-midnight hour, he walked past the foreman's bedroll but there was only a solitary head sticking out from under the tarpaulin; the kid was somewhere far away in the sage with the coyotes.

For Archie the work was the usual ranch hand's luck—hard, dirty, long, and dull. There was no time for anything but saddle up, ride, rope, cut, herd, unsaddle, eat, sleep, and do it again. On clear, dry nights, coyote voices seemed to emanate each from a single point in a straight line, the calls crisscrossing like taut wires. When cloud cover moved in, the howls spread out in a different geometry, overlapping like concentric circles from a handful of pebbles thrown into water. But most often the wind surging over the plain sanded the cries into a kind of coyote dust, fractioned into particles of sound. He longed to be back on his own sweet place, fencing his horse pastures, happy with Rose. He thought about the coming child, imagined a boy half grown and helping him build wild-horse traps in the desert, capturing the mustangs. He could not quite conjure up a baby.

As the late summer folded, Sink saw that Archie sat straight up in the saddle, was quiet and even-tempered, good with horses. The kid was one of the kind horses liked, calm and steady. No more morning hollers, and the only songs he sang were after supper when somebody else started one, where his voice was appreciated but never mentioned. He kept to himself pretty much, often staring into the distance, but every man had something of value beyond the horizon. Despite his ease with horses, the kid had been bucked off an oily bronc that had been ruined beyond redemption by Wally Finch, and, instinctively putting out one hand to break his fall, had snapped his wrist. He spent weeks with his arm strapped to his body, rode and did everything else one-handed. Alonzo Lago fired Wally Finch, refused to pay him for ruined horses, even if they were mustangs from the wild herds, and sent him walking north to Montana.

"Kid, there's a way you fall so's you don't get hurt," Sink said. "Fold your arms, see, git one shoulder up and your head down. You give a little twist while you're fallin so's you hit the ground with your shoulder and you just roll right on over and onto your feet." He didn't know why he was telling Archie this and grouched up. "Hell, figure it out yourself."

## ROSE AND THE COYOTES

July was hot, the air vibrating, the dry land like a scraped sheep hoof. The sun drew the color from everything and the Little Weed trickled through dull stones. In a month, even that trickle would be dried by the hot river rocks, the grass parched white, and preachers praying for rain. Rose could not sleep in the cabin, which was as hot as the inside of a black hatbox. Once she carried her pillow to the big stone doorstep and lay on its chill until mosquitoes drove her back inside.

She woke one morning exhausted and sweaty, and went down to the Little Weed hoping for night-cooled water. There was a dark cloud to the south, and she was glad to hear the distant rumble of thunder. In anticipation, she set out the big kettle and two buckets to catch rainwater. The advance wind came in, thrashing tree branches and ripping leaves. The grass went sidewise. Lightning danced on the crest of Barrel Mountain, and then a burst of hail swallowed up the landscape in a chattering, roaring sweep. She ran inside and watched the ice pellets flail the river rocks and slowly give way to thrumming rain. The rocks disappeared in the foam of rising water. Almost as quickly as it had started the rain stopped, a few last hailstones fell, and against the moving cloud the arc of a double rainbow promised everything. Her buckets were full of sweet water and floating hail-stones. She stripped and poured dippers of goose-bump water over her head again and again until one bucket was nearly empty and she was shaking. The air was as cool and fresh as September, the heat broken. Around midnight the rain began again, slow and steady. Half awake, she could hear it dripping on the stone doorstep.

The next morning, it was cold and sleety and her back ached; she wished for the heat of summer to return. She staggered when she walked, and making coffee didn't seem worth it. She drank water and stared at the icy spicules sliding down the window glass. Around midmorning the backache increased, working itself into a slow rhythm. It dawned on her very slowly that the baby was not waiting for September. By afternoon the backache was an encircling python and she could do nothing but pant and whimper, the steady rattle of rain dampening her moaning call for succor. She wriggled out of her heavy dress and put on her oldest nightgown. The pain increased to waves of cramping agony that left her gasping for breath, on and on, the day fading into night, the rain torn away by wind, the dark choking hours eternal. Another dawn came, sticky with the return of heat, and still her raw loins could not deliver the child. On the fourth day, when Rose was voiceless from calling for Archie, her mother, Tom Ackler, Tom Ackler's cat, from screaming imprecations at all of them, at God, any god, then at the river ducks and the weasel, to any entity that might hear, the python relaxed its grip and slid off the bloody bed, leaving her spiraling down in plum-colored mist.

It seemed to be late afternoon. She was glued to the bed, and at the slightest movement felt a hot surge that she knew was blood. She got up on her elbows and saw the clotted child, stiff and gray, the barley-rope cord, and the afterbirth. She did not weep, but, filled with an ancient rage, knelt on the floor, ignoring the hot blood seeping from her, and rolled the infant up in the rough sheet. It was a bulky mass, and she felt the loss of the sheet as another tragedy. When she tried to stand, the blood poured, but she was driven to bury the child, to end the horror of the event. She crept to the cupboard, got a dishtowel, and rewrapped the baby in a smaller bundle. Her hand closed on the silver spoon, her mother's wedding present, and she thrust it into the placket neck of her nightgown, the cool metal like balm.

Clenching the knot of the dishtowel in her teeth, she crawled out the door and toward the sandy soil near the river, where, still on hands and knees, she dug a shallow hole with the silver spoon and laid the child in it, heaping it with sand and piling on top whatever river stones were within reach. It took more than an hour to follow her blood trail back to the cabin, the twilight deep by the time she reached the doorstep.

The bloody sheet lay bunched on the floor and the bare mattress showed a black stain like the map of South America. She lay on the floor, for the bed was miles away, a cliff only birds could reach. Everything seemed to swell and shrink, the twitching bed leg, a dank clout swooning over the edge of the dishpan, the wall itself bulging forward, the chair flying viciously—all pulsing with the rhythm of her hot, pumping blood. Barrel Mountain, bringing darkness, squashed its bulk against the window, and owls crashed through, wings like iron bars. Struggling through the syrup of subconsciousness in the last hour, she heard the coyotes outside and knew what they were doing.

## THE LINE SHACK

As the September nights cooled, Archie got nervous, went into town as often as he could, called at the post office, but no one saw him come out with any letters or packages. Alonzo Lago sent Sink and Archie to check some distant draws, ostensibly for old renegade cows too wily or a few mavericks too young to be caught in any roundup.

"What's eatin you?" said Sink as they rode out, but the kid shook his head. Half an hour later he opened his mouth as if he were going to say something, looked away from Sink, and gave a half shrug.

"Got somethin you want a say," Sink said, "Chrissake say it. I got my head on backwards or what? You didn't know we was goin a smudge brands? Goin a get all holy about it, are you?"

Archie looked around.

"I'm married," he said. "She is havin a baby. Pretty soon."

"Well, I'm damned. How old are you?"

"Seventeen. Old enough to do what's got a be did. Anyway, how old are you?"

"Thirty-two. Old enough a be your daddy." There was a half-hour silence, then Sink started again. "You know old Karok don't keep married fellers. Finds out, he'll fire you."

"He ain't goin a find out from me. And it's more money than I can git on the Little Weed. But I got a find a way Rose can let me know. About things."

"Well, I ain't no wet nurse."

"I know that."

"Long as you know it." Damn fool kid, he thought, his life already too complicated to live. He said aloud, "Me, I wouldn't never git hitched to no fell-on-a-hatchet female."

The next week, half the crew went into town and Archie spent an hour on the bench outside the post office writing on some brown wrapping paper, and addressed the tortured missive to Rose at the stage station where he believed her to be. What about the baby? he wrote. Is he born? But inside the post office the walleyed clerk with fingernails like yellow chisels told him the postage had gone up.

"First time in a hunderd year. Cost you two cents a send a letter now." He smirked with satisfaction. Archie, who had only one cent, tore up his letter and threw the pieces in the street. The wind dealt them to the prairie, its chill promising a tight-clenched winter.

Rose's parents moved to Omaha in November, seeking a cure for Mrs. Mealor's declining health.

"You think you can stay sober long enough to ride down and let Rosie and Archie know we are going?" the sick woman whispered to Sundown.

"Why, I am goin right now soon as I find my other boot. Just you don't worry, I got it covered."

A full bottle of whiskey took him as far as the river crossing.

Dazedly drunk, he rode to the little cabin on the river but found the place silent, the door closed. Swaying, feeling the landscape slide around, he called out three or four times but was unable to get off his horse, and knew well enough that if he did he could never get back on.

"They're not there," he reported to his wife. "Not there."

"Where could they be? Did you put a note on the table?"

"Didn't think of it. Anyway, not there."

"I'll write her from Omaha," she whispered.

Within a week of their departure a replacement freighter arrived, Buck Roy, with his heavyset wife and a raft of children. The Mealors, who had failed even to be buried in the stage station's cemetery, were forgotten.

There were no cattle as bad as Karok's to stray, and ranchers said it was a curious thing the way his cows turned up in distant locations. December was miserable, one storm after another bouncing in like a handful of hurled poker chips, and January turned cold enough to freeze flying birds dead. Alonzo Lago sent Archie out alone to gather any bovine wanderers he could find in a certain washout area, swampy in June but now made up of hundreds of deep holes and snaky little streams smoothly covered with snow.

"Keep your eyes peeled for any Wing-Cross leather-pounders. Better take some sticks and a cinch ring." So Archie knew he was looking for Wing-Cross cows, to doctor their brands. But the Wing-Cross had its own little ways with brand reworkings, so he guessed it was more or less an even exchange.

The horse did not want to go into the swamp maze. It was one of the warm days between storms, and the snow was soft. Archie dismounted and led his horse, keeping to the edge of the bog, wading through wet snow for hours. The exercise sweated him up. Only two cows allowed themselves to be driven out into the open, the others scattering far back into the coyote willows behind the swamp. In the murky, half-frozen world of stream slop and trampled stems there was no way a man alone could fix brands. He watched the cows circle around to the backcountry. The wind dived, pulling cold air with it. The weather was changing. When he reached the bunkhouse, four hours after dark, the thermometer had fallen to zero. His boots were frozen, and, chilled to the liver, he fell asleep without eating or undressing beyond his boots.

"Git back and git them cows," hissed Alonzo Lago two hours later, leaning over his face. "Git up and on it. Rat now! Mr. Karok wants them cows."

"Goddam short nights on this goddam ranch," Archie muttered, pulling on his wet boots.

Back in the swamp it was just coming light, like gray polish on the cold world, the air so still that Archie could see the tiny breath cloud of a finch on a willow twig. Beneath the hardened crust the snow was wallowy. His fresh horse was Poco, who did not know any swamps. Poco blundered along, stumbled in an invisible sinkhole, and took Archie deep with him. The snow shot down his neck, up his sleeves, into his boots, filled eyes, ears, nose, matted his hair. Poco, in getting up, rammed Archie's hat deep into the bog. The snow in contact with his body heat melted, and as he climbed back into the saddle the wind that accompanied the pale sunlight froze his clothes. Somehow he managed to push eight Wing-Cross strays out of the swamp and back toward the high ground, but his matches would not light, and while he struggled to make a fire the cows scattered. He could barely move, and when he got back to the bunkhouse he was frozen into the saddle and had to be pried off the horse by two men. He heard cloth rip.

Sink thought the kid had plenty of sand and, muttering that he wasn't no wet nurse, pulled off the icy boots, unbuttoned coat and shirt, half hauled him stumbling to his bunk, and brought two hot rocks from under the stove to warm him up. John Tank, a Texas drifter, said he had an extra pair of overalls Archie could have—old and mended but still with some wear in them.

"Hell, better'n ridin around bare-ass in January."

But the next morning when Archie tried to get up he was overcome by dizziness. Boiling heat surged through him, his cheeks flamed red, his hands burned, and he had a dry, constant cough. The bunkhouse slopped back and forth as if on rockers.

Sink looked at him and thought, Pneumonia. "You look pretty bad. I'll go see what Karok says."

When he came back half an hour later, Archie was on fire.

"Karok says to git you out a here, but the bastard won't let me take the wagon. He says he's got a cancer in his leg and he needs that wagon for hisself to have the doc at the fort cut it out. Lon's fixin up a kind a travois. His ma had some Indan kin so he knows how to fix it. Sometimes he ain't so bad. We'll git you down to Cheyenne and you can ride the train a where your mother is, your folks, Rawlins, whatever. Karok says. And he says you are fired. I had a tell him you was married so he would let you loose. He was all set a have you die in the bunkhouse. We'll get a doc, beat this down. It's only pneumony. I had it twice."

Archie tried to say his mother was long gone and that he needed to get to Rose down on the Little Weed, tried to say that it was sixty-odd miles from Rawlins to their cabin, but he couldn't get out a word because of the wheezing, breath-sucking cough. Sink shook his head, and got some biscuits and bacon from the cook.

Alonzo Lago had trimmed out two long poles and laced a steer hide to them. Sink wrapped the legs of a horse named Preacher in burlap to keep the crust from cutting them and lashed the travois poles to his saddle, a tricky business to get the balance right. The small ends projected beyond the horse's ears, but the foreman said that was to accommodate wear on the drag ends. They rolled Archie and his bedroll in a buffalo robe, and Sink began to drag him to Cheyenne, a hundred miles south. With the wagon it would have been easy. Sink thought the travois was not as good a contraption as Indians claimed. The wind, which had dropped a little overnight, came up again, pushing a lofty bank of cloud. After four hours they had covered nine miles. The snow began, increasing in intensity until they were traveling blind.

"Kid, I can't see nothin," Sink called. He stopped and dismounted, went to Archie. The earlier snow had melted as fast as it touched that red, feverish face, but gradually, just a fraction of an inch above the surface of the hot flesh, a mask of ice now formed a gray glaze.

"Better hole up. There's a line shack somewheres around here could we find it. I was there all summer couple years back. Down a little from the top of a hogback."

The horse had also spent that summer at the line camp and he went straight to it now. It was on the lee side of the hogback, a little below the crest. The wind had dumped an immense amount of snow on the tiny cabin, but Sink found the door to the lean-to entryway, and that would do to shelter Preacher. A shovel with a broken handle leaned against the side of the stall. Inside the cabin there was a table and a backless chair and a plank bunk about twenty inches wide. The stove was heaped with snow and the stovepipe lay on the floor. Sink recognized the chipped enamel plate and cup on the table.

He wrestled Archie inside and got him and the buffalo robe onto the plank bunk, then put the stovepipe together and jammed it up through the roof hole. Neither inside nor in the entryway could he see any chunk wood, but he remembered where the old chip pile had been and, using the broken shovel, scraped up enough snow-welded chips to get the fire going. While the chips were steaming and sizzling in the stove he unsaddled Preacher, removed the gunnysacks from his legs, and rubbed him down. He checked the lean-to's shallow loft, hoping for hay, but there was nothing.

"God damn," he said, and tore some of the loft floorboards loose to burn in the stove. Back outside, he dug through the snow with the broken shovel until he hit ground, got out his knife, and sawed off the sun-cured grass until he had two or three hatfuls.

"Best I can do, Preacher," he said, tossing it down for the horse.

It was almost warm inside the shack. From his saddlebag he took a small handful of the coffee beans he always carried. The old coffee grinder was still on the wall, but a mouse had built a nest in it, and unwilling to drink boiled mouse shit he crushed the beans on the table with the flat of his knife. He looked around for the coffeepot that belonged to the cabin but did not see it. There was a five-gallon coal-oil tin near the bunk. He sniffed at it, but could detect no noisome odors. It was while he was outside scraping up snow to melt on the stove that the edge of the coal-oil can hit the coffeepot, which, for some unfathomable reason, had been tossed into the front yard. That, too, he packed with snow. It looked to him as though the last occupant of the shack had been someone with a grudge, showing his hatred of Karok by throwing coffeepots and burning all the wood. Maybe a Wing-Cross rider.

The coffee was hot and black but when he brought the cup to Archie the kid swallowed one mouthful, then coughed, and finally puked it up. Sink drank the rest himself and ate one of the biscuits.

It was a bad night. The bunk was too narrow and the kid so hot and twitchy that Sink, swooning in and out of forty-wink snaps of sleep, finally got up and slept in the chair with his head on the table. A serious blizzard and fatal cold began to slide down from the Canadian plains that night, and when it broke twelve days later the herds were decimated, cows packed ten deep against barbwire fences, pronghorn congealed into statues, trains stalled for three weeks by forty-foot drifts, and two cowpunchers in a line shack frozen together in a buffalo robe.

## THE STAGE STATION

It was May before Tom Ackler rode up from Taos, where he had spent the fall and winter. Despite the beating sunshine, the snow was still deep around his cabin. Patches of bare ground showed bright green with a host of thrusting thistles. He wondered if Gold Dust had made it through. He could see no cat tracks. He lit a fire using an old newspaper on the table, and, just before the flame swallowed it, glimpsed a few penciled words and the signature "Archie."

"Lost whatever it was. I'll go down tomorrow and see how they are doin." And he unpacked his saddlebags and pulled his blankets out of the sack hanging from a rafter where they were safe from mice.

In the morning, Gold Dust pranced out of the trees, her coat thick. Tom let her in, threw her a choice piece of bacon.

"Look like you kept pretty good," Tom said. But the cat sniffed at the bacon, went to the door, and, when Tom opened it, returned to the woods. "Probly shacked up with a bobcat," he said. "Got the taste for wild meat." Around noon he saddled the horse and headed for the McLaverty cabin.

No smoke rose from the chimney. A slope of snow lay against the woodpile. He noticed that very little wood had been burned. The weasel's tracks were everywhere, right up into the eaves. Clear enough the weasel had gotten inside. "Damn sight more comfortable than a woodpile." As Tom squinted at the tracks, the weasel suddenly squirted out of a hole in the eaves and looked at him. It was whiter than the rotting snow, and its black-tipped tail twitched. It was the largest, handsomest weasel he had ever seen, with shining eyes and a lustrous coat. He thought of his cat and it came to him that wild creatures managed well through the winter. He wondered if Gold Dust could breed with a bobcat, and recalled then that Rose had been expecting. "Must be they went to the station." But he opened the door and looked inside, calling, "Rose? Archie?" What he found sent him galloping for the stage station.

At the station everything was in an uproar, all of them standing in the dusty road in front of the Dorgans' house, Mrs. Dorgan crying, Queeda with her mouth agape, and Robert F. Dorgan shouting at his wife, accusing her of betraying him with a human wreck. They paid little attention to Tom Ackler when he slid in on his lathered horse calling that Rose McLaverty was raped and murdered and mutilated by Utes, sometime in the winter, God knew when. Only Mrs. Buck Roy, the new freighter's wife, who was terrified of Indians, paid him much attention. The Dorgans continued to scream at each other. The more urgent event to them was the suicide that morning of the old bachelor telegraph operator, who had swallowed lye after weeks of scribbling a four-hundred-page letter addressed to Robert Dorgan and outlining his hopeless adoration of Mrs. Dorgan, the wadded pages fulsomely riddled with references to "ivory thighs," "the Adam and Eve dance," "her secret slit," and the like. What Tom Ackler had thought was an old saddle and a pile of grain sacks on the station porch was the corpse.

"Where there's smoke there's fire!" bellowed Robert F. Dorgan. "I took you out a that Omaha cathouse and made you a decent woman, give you everthing, and here's how you reward me, you drippin bitch! How many times you snuck over there? How many times you took his warty old cock?"

"I never! I didn't! That filthy old brute," sobbed Mrs. Dorgan, suffused with rage that the vile man had fastened his attentions on her, had dared to write down his lascivious thoughts as real events, putting in the details of her pink-threaded camisole, the red mole on her left buttock, and, finally, vomiting black blood all over the telegraph shack and the front porch of the Dorgans' house, where he had dragged himself to die, the bundle of lies stuffed in his shirt. For years she had struggled to make herself into a genteel specimen of womanhood, grateful that Robert F. Dorgan had saved her from economic sexuality and determined to erase that past. Now, if Dorgan forced her away, she would have to go back on the game, for she could think of no other way to make a living. And maybe Queeda, too, whom she'd brought up as a lady! Her sense of personal worth faltered, then flared up as if doused with kerosene.

"Why, you dirty old rum-neck," she said in a hoarse voice, "what gives you the idea that you got a right to a beautiful wife and daugh-

ter? What gives you the idea we would stay with you? Look at you—
you want a be the territory surveyor, but without me and Queeda to
talk up the important political men you couldn't catch a cold."

Dorgan knew it was true and gnawed at his untrimmed mustache.
He turned and melodramatically strode into his house, slamming the
door so hard the report killed mice. Mrs. Dorgan had won, and she
followed him in for a reconciliation.

Tom Ackler looked at Queeda, who was tracing an arc in the dirt
with the toe of her kid-leather boot. They heard the rattle of a stove
lid inside the house—Mrs. Dorgan making up a fire to warm the
bedroom.

"Rose McLaverty—" he said, but Queeda shrugged. A tongue of
wind lapped the dust, creating a miniature whirl that caught up
straws, horsehairs, minute mica fragments, and a feather. Queeda
walked away around the shaded back of the Dorgan house. Tom Ackler stood holding the reins, then remounted and started back.

On the way, he thought of the whiskey in his cupboard, then of
Rose, and decided he would get drunk that night and bury her the
next day. It was the best he could do for her. He thought, too, that
perhaps it hadn't been Utes who killed her but her young husband,
berserk and raving, and now fled to distant ports. He remembered
the burned newspaper with Archie's message consumed before it
could be read and thought it unlikely that if Archie had killed his
young wife in a frenzy he would stop by a neighbor's place and leave
a signed note. Unless maybe it was a confession. There was no way to
know what had happened. The more he thought about Archie, the
more he remembered his clear, hard voice and his singing. He
thought about Gold Dust's rampant vigor and rich fur, about the
sleek weasel at the McLaverty cabin. Some lived and some died, and
that's how it was.

He buried Rose in front of the cabin and for a tombstone wrestled
the sandstone doorstep upright. He wanted to chisel her name on it
but put it off until the snows started. By then it was too late, time for
him to head back to Taos.

The following spring, as he rode past the cabin, he saw that frost heaves had tipped the stone over and that the ridgepole of the roof had broken under a heavy weight of snow. He rode on, singing, "When the green grass comes, and the wild rose blooms," one of Archie's songs, and wondering if Gold Dust had made it through again.

Kirstin Allio

# Clothed, Female Figure

I T WASN'T MY first family, and I don't have "favorites," but the
apartment where they lived was closer to my old apartment than
any other I'd worked in, and so I felt loosened, as if my whole body
were the tongue of a sentimental drunk, susceptible to love and forgiveness. The mother, Ivy, was a civil rights lawyer, and the father,
Wendell, was an artist. He was ten years younger than she was—why
should it matter? Because she wore the yoke of someone abused
rather than amused by youth's indulgences. Oddly enough she had a
boyish build in contrast to her heavy harness, and from my position
(I admit there is some dignity in distance), here was a mismatch with
which mischievous fairies entertained each other.

New Yorkers do not like to venture too far west or too far east,
their compasses set to the moral equilibrium of Fifth Avenue. Ivy and
Wendell's building, a narrow brownstone washed down like a bar of
soap, was far to the west, between Tenth and Eleventh avenues.
Chelsea, Wendell insisted, which even I knew was an affect, used to
both mock and elevate his circumstances. From the roof, accessed
by a hatch Pollocked in pigeon droppings, you could see the Hudson River. I had been able to see it from the roof of my own first

apartment. A sense of hope never failed me, walking west, into the sunset . . . although when I arrived for work it was always cinder gray morning.

Ivy and Wendell slept on a Murphy bed in the living room. It hinged precariously off the wall, reminding me of Russia, where the walls really do fall in protest of their cheap construction. Leah, age six, occupied the bedroom, with a ceiling of antique china. She wore frocks that twisted around her pencil body and her ears pushed through her hair like snouts.

She read to herself, poetry. By our Russian giantess, Anna Akhmatova, Leah had read "Evening"; she had also read Tsvetayeva, and Emily Dickinson.

"She read at three," said Ivy, more dutifully than proudly, I noticed.

"Should I tell you the first words my parents discovered me reading?" Leah quizzed me. She had an unmodulated voice, as high as a sopranino recorder. I would have, in my previous life in the Soviet Union, characterized such a voice as antisocial.

"Sorbitol," she enunciated. "Hydrated silica."

I suppose I raised my eyebrows.

"Toothpaste," declared Leah.

By that same, first evening, I had read aloud half of the collected Grimm's fairy tales, cross-legged on the floor of the living room. When she was sure I'd finished Leah rolled over and her belly flashed: hard, green, like a slice of raw potato. "Natasha!" she cried. "I love to listen to your accent!"

Wendell did not like the modern children's books, the ones that came with lunch boxes. Fine with Leah. Besides poetry and Grimm's, she loved lists of ingredients. She had something of a phobia—I use the term as a former professional—regarding compounds. She yearned for the simple.

"Bread and water sounds like a good diet," she said, mournfully. "But do you know how many things they put in *water*?"

There were no doors on the cabinets in the kitchen, due to a campaign against the bourgeois in that house, and Wendell's trumpeted belief in the art of the everyday object. Mismatched student pottery was dustily webbed to dog-eared cereal boxes.

The window in Leah's room was on an air shaft with the diameter of a corpse. I considered all of this close to depravity . . . although in an unsettling way I wondered if I had brought it with me, imposed a film of sorrow and poverty with my very gaze upon Leah's circumstances.

It was true, she was my first only child. My research, in the Soviet Union, had for a time argued in favor of single-child families. In terms of allocation of resources, at our stage of civilization, a single focused beam of light, rather than the messy breadth of competition among siblings, and favorites. Well, according to the posters that slickered my home city, there were no Soviet shortages—of heart or of health—whatsoever.

Leah and I had walked down into the West Village, where she was to meet a friend in a slice of park between two angled, intersecting avenues. We both drew to a stop in front of the window of a florist. My English was excellent, but a bald spot in my vocabulary was botany. That spring Leah had found me out: I hadn't known that ivy, her mother's namesake, was that dark diamond creeper with tough stitches into cement and mortar.

"Natasha!" cried Leah happily. "I'll tell you everything!"

"Leah Halloran," I said. "Private tutor."

I saw her smiling down into her sweater, which was a habit she had, and sometimes she'd come back up sucking the collar.

I stood at attention. We let a couple of young women bob past us.

"Lilac." Leah pointed. "And hyacinth." Smugly, "I call them poodle flowers, Natasha."

Oh, no, Leah Halloran was not a giggler. Her laugh was a serious matter, and as she pushed it out, now, I knew to remain silent.

The window glass through which we looked was as shiny and cold as chrome. Or, of course, a mirror. There we were. A small woman with short dyed hair beneath a boxy white hat, a triangle of wool coat, and a string of girl coming just to the breast of the woman.

Once Ivy said, testing the waters, "Did your mother work, Natasha?"

I didn't immediately answer, and so she added, needlessly, "Growing up in Russia?"

No, Ivy was not curious about my personal childhood. I understood immediately that she was taking the measure of my judgment of her as a working mother.

And, I suspected, she wanted to know what I knew about her daughter that she didn't.

But I simply winked. "Do I have any choice but to be a feminist in this apartment?"

"Feminist!" She laughed. "It sounds so—the way you say it—May Day! Sputnik!" She hit the air with her fists for our relics.

To wink, in those days, was my constant habit, if not directly, then atmospherically, or at an imaginary bystander, my alter ego, off in a corner.

I winked again. Ivy looked around to see if Leah was in the doorway. No, Leah was fast asleep, the tape recorder resting on her pillow, tape like flypaper catching flecks of sound-dust, so that if she talked in her sleep she could listen to it in the morning.

Before my employment, Wendell had stayed home with Leah, sacrificing his art, but leaving plenty of time to meet the dropoff mothers at Leah's school in the West Village who had just rolled out of bed and into those American blue jeans, pulpy and white at the knees and buttocks.

It was five flights up to Leah's apartment at the top of the brownstone, and the stairs were made of solid black rubber. The walls were tiled, with a black border, and the lights were so dim I supposed they cost the landlord a negative number. Leah never touched the railing, descending or ascending, but pedaled in the air, or rather like a drum majorette marching to her own, hectic heartbeat. I had no difficulty imagining what she had been like as a baby: a root face, an early, succinct talker, a body like a tail, too thin, too expressive.

Just as I don't have "favorites," I would say that I never become "close" to a child or a family. I have always suspected it's a work ethic left over from my previous profession; also, I prefer families who refrain from using intimacy as a means to wheedle extra hours. I prefer families who wish—and are cognizant of this wish themselves—to remain a rather closed unit, penetrated only by the specific terms of my contract.

And yet I would not characterize my particular style as "distant." In fact I have been accused, in one mother's fumbling manner, of "apocalyptic thinking," and by another, giggly with reprobation, "your weather eye, Natasha." Clearly, I've been, at times, overly concerned for the safety and well-being of my charges.

I stayed three years, until Leah's parents separated. I had begun to notice that Ivy seemed not so sad as tired, and I admired that, I thought to myself, a mother refusing sadness. I knew that money was tight, in fact Leah had told me, with a child's candor, and I suggested they didn't need me. Ivy said I was very intuitive, and gracious. With Ivy's excellent letter of reference, I was able to find employment almost immediately with a family in Nyack.

It is true that over the years I thought of Leah. At first, it was practical: How would Ivy manage to take her to the museum class she loved so much on Wednesday evenings? Those lovely little leather sneakers—would they last through the season? Would she succeed in making friends with that tall black girl at school she so admired? And once I even heard her voice, a rather comic announcement, "Whoever's in charge of me pours my soy milk." But then, of course, I had new sets of children to think about . . . and in my imagination the apartment between Tenth and Eleventh avenues and my old, first apartment began to swirl together so that I had to think of both, or neither.

I certainly never keep records: in some cases I can't even remember all of the names of the family members. If there were previous marriages, children in college who visited their little half siblings over long autumnal weekends . . . In one case, well, I can picture his two-seater sports car, and the wrinkles on the seat of his suit jacket, but I simply cannot remember the name of the father. Why spend so much time on him? Why not his children? The boy, Harrison, wore a fireman's hat for a year, even, and I suppose especially, in the bathtub; the girl, Morgan, collected pandas.

In any case I don't take solace looking back. I don't take solace at all, and I take my coffee black, which is unusual for a nanny. Nannies are notorious for their sweet tooth, and while every Russian dreams of drinking coffee when he gets to America, he's without fail stricken homesick and tea-addled upon arrival. I am the exception, in both groups I claim membership, to such material and sentimental happiness.

It was last Saturday when I heard my employer's appraising step along the attic hallway that leads to the little room that comes with my paycheck. I have calculated how much is subtracted in "rent," but in this suburban neighborhood it is difficult to compete with the stream of au pairs from Thailand who accept a salary that assumes caring for children is as breezy as summer camp. They are accustomed to summer camp—back home twelve little siblings are waiting.

I rose to greet her. My defense, as always, is formality. My current employer is a female doctor. She is tall, and forced to bow her neck beneath the attic roof, the suggestion being that her own house oppresses her. As a hobby, she figure skates, and I believe figure skating is her true nature. That it fails to bring her recognition . . .

"Oh, Natasha!" said my employer, feigning surprise at finding me in my own private corner. "Here's this . . ." She held out a rather bulky letter, laden with small stamps, as if someone had a tedious math assignment. I had the impulse to snatch it up, but it seemed essential that I measure my response: that it be equal, exactly, to my employer's.

"Thank you, Virginia." There was a pool of quiet around us.

"It's so quiet up here," said Virginia, taking a breath of air distilled by the attic. I remained expressionless. The envelope passed between us.

"Is Colin napping?" I inquired.

"A miracle," said Virginia. I nodded as if to excuse her.

"Oh, Natasha. Would dinner at six be possible?" said my employer.

My day off was always cut short. If I pressed, I could get an evening to make up for it during the week, but I rarely bothered.

"Or shortly before . . ." added Virginia. She looked at me curiously. I was aware that it would have seemed more . . . normal . . . if I told her from whom I had received a letter. It was true: at this address, I had never before had mail.

Very calmly I walked over to my desk with the letter. Of course I had scanned the return address. A woman in my position can't afford not to. I placed it on my desk and turned back to my employer.

She said, "Five-forty-five-ish?" I nodded once, curtly.

Dear Natasha,

I'm writing you from college. Taking it for granted that you remember me, Leah Halloran? I would have written before but did you know that you are the invisible woman? I actually had to get a boy here to help me find you. He is the original computer geek, very sweet, will do anything because he is from Ohio.

My college is one of those Vermont enclaves that used to be all women, with a name that sounds like high tea in Britain, so that now it's not so much coed as college for the *sensitive*. I've given myself away—sensitive. An artist like my dad. My mom is still the only one who makes an honest buck in the family. I rent a room off campus, in the town, perched over a man-made waterfall. I look across the dam at the abandoned mill buildings from the 1800s. Sometimes I take pictures of townies from my windows. You know, girls with Laundromat hair who walk like fat babies? Kind of voyeuristic, but what am I supposed to do, snap shots of trees and historic cottages? I impressed my photography professor, anyway, who is British. Gavin. He gets a lot of washings out of that accent.

You can see my photos for yourself, anyway. I'm sticking a few in the envelope.

I can only describe the sensation on reading Leah's letter as a welling up—was it self-satisfaction? I had done nothing to deserve it, and it certainly wasn't a feeling of completion. No. If anything, such a welling up (never would I have been so sloppy in my descriptions as a psychologist!) was a sensation of business *un*finished.

I do like my work, although I have been harsh, perhaps, in my description of Virginia. But I find it so demanding in its requirement of vigilance, that it would be unusual for me to . . . to allow a moment to feel "self-satisfaction."

What I felt was more like hope—already—that Leah would keep writing.

I finished the letter, and read it all over. I've received Christmas cards from a few of my families, Happy Holidays, the Xs, no more, and I've never expected it. But now I was absurdly, uncontainably excited. How could I rush through time and space to reach Leah?

All capital letters, slanting strongly toward the right-hand margin. Now I was almost sure I'd had a dream—Monday?—about Leah. Could I even have predicted, or willed the letter? How many dreams, I wondered, go unremembered if they are not *fulfilled,* somehow? How reliant are we on the world—I wondered, wildly, euphorically—to supply a coincidence to trigger our memory?

I searched my dream and it seemed, perhaps obviously, that the dream Leah was not the child I remembered (whose dreams are pho-tographic?), nor was she a sort of projection, one of those artist's ren-derings of a kidnapped child, now grown-up, and likely still tied up in a psychopath's basement, of what I would, in a lucid state, think an eighteen-year-old Leah would look like. . . .

Perhaps I'm expressing myself clumsily.

It's one of the Russian poets who said this: Dreams ensoul lost love, for the fleeting life span of a flower.

> You know, Natasha. I was just thinking—this may sound strange—but you were my mother's conscience. I don't mean my mother felt guilty about you—that you were an immigrant, or underpaid (right?), or the whole women-riding-on-other-women's-backs theory. I mean that she couldn't do two things at once, so she split the one thing off for you (me), and along with it, her conscience.
>
> Well, no, she didn't turn evil or something when you left us. She was bereaved. I guess you should know that.
>
> She's more or less famous now, as in people recognize her in restaurants. She still won't take my old bedroom.
>
> Apropos of nothing, I'm going to Italy with one of my pro-fessors and her family for the summer. My mother is really upset about it. She wanted us to hang out on the scenic Hud-son for August. I almost couldn't decide between Tuscany and Eleventh Avenue. My professor—sculpture—has two little boys, Roman and Felix. So I'm their nanny. Any advice for me, Natasha?

How I wished she'd sent a picture. Although her black-and-white photographs of local Vermonters seemed to me perfectly proficient, I wanted to see Leah. Regardless of my dream, at eighteen she must be tall and skinny like her mother, veering around somewhat absent-mindedly, peaked skull, marrow-colored hair, an adolescent crone with arms all wrist, legs all ankle. I admit, I can't imagine her beautiful. I always thought she was rather too shy to be a body. She used to have to hike up her saggy underpants. It galled me, the way it was constant, and that Ivy wouldn't go out and buy her fresh white ones, with new elastic. Was that what Leah meant by her mother's conscience?

All afternoon I anticipated writing, and my little boys, Jack and Colin, were revivified by my anticipation. They sat at their little red table clubbing their pale chunks of dinner and I was overcome with tenderness. Colin, the little one, called me Nata. His father joked, *Nada?* I even laughed along with them.

And suddenly it seemed to me that all my past successes as a nanny were thrown into relief, even exaggerated in the light of my new status. Leah had found me, and my good fortune seemed to radiate out so that any number of other human beings in the world were now also assured their reunions.

I was so eager to write that I skipped drying the pans after dinner (wondering how I ever have the patience to do it) and went straight to the attic.

It so happens that I am also taking care of two boys, I started. What are the ages of Roman and Felix? Mine are one and three, too young to travel to Italy!

I stopped. I looked around my attic room as if I hoped to describe it. For Leah's sake, was it a Grimm's fairy-tale garret? The view over the street trees . . . I suddenly remembered the ring of lamplight on Leah's squirrel-gray pate, the crown of a gentle princess.

The single bed was too soft, a Goldilocks hammock. The walls were steep, and ran right into the ceiling.

The little boys here are very good, I began again, although now it was some time later.

In the Soviet Union I might have become a prominent psychologist.

I wrote, My present family is very demanding.

Then I stopped for such a long time that I lost my train of thought, my intent, entirely.

Several days passed, although I was composing all the while. I almost felt like my own biographer. I wasn't so foolish as to flatter myself it was for my sake Leah found me, but even more, then, I felt a considerable pressure.

Once, I started: The little boys here have plenty of spirit!

In fact, these are my first children who receive medication.

Or better this way?: The little boys I take care of now can be very difficult.

No. She'll think I have allegiances, favorites, and she'll wonder how she stacks up against them.

Are you planning to major in sculpture?

All the children I've ever cared for are good children, Leah.

I laughed at myself harshly. Sometimes I dream they've been snatched—from the park, from the market, it's like a parallel life, really, the fear of it—and then I realize, in the dream, that it is I myself who have vanished.

Dear Natasha,

If you sent me a letter at school, I missed it, so now you'll have to spring for the stamps to Italy. My mother gave me a pack of condoms as a farewell present. Watch out for those *Italians*. Disturbing? Uh-huh. *You* know my mother. She's all about fairness to the point of being blind to human nature!

Emmie, my professor, says time zones are cathartic. We hope for rebirth when we travel. My God, we run ourselves straight into the knives of jet lag, whispers Emmie at takeoff.

It's probably obvious I have a crush on her. Ah! Not just her art but her whole *life* is talented. Her husband. And her children. Roman is three and Felix is one. Any tricks of the trade for me?

I have never allowed the maudlin aspect, but suddenly I remembered Leah's little sack of bones on my lap, her cinder hair beneath my nose, the Murphy bed latched high up on the wall above us.

Emmie hasn't bought a seat for Felix, so he's tethered to me by an orange seat belt looped to my seat belt. Roman effortlessly unclicks his life or death and stands up to regard the folks in the row in back of us. I peek through the seat crack to see if the trio of passengers is receptive. A nine-year-old boy (I'm guessing) encased in electronics is flashing and flinching on some other planet. His mother has newly plucked eyebrows. She might have done it with unsterilized tweezers. She clings to her paperback like it's one of the seat cushions that doubles as a life raft. She does a tiny wave at Roman and then closes her eyes against a death's-head. The third passenger is a business droid with newspaper-colored complexion and goggly eyes like a housefly under a microscope. He says, Do you like flying? Roman falls down as if he's been shot. Are these flying types really ubiquitous or is it my own perception that lacks variety? Sometimes I really just hate growing up. Not just, oh, things used to be so simple, but things used to be so original. Now, everything, absolutely everything, is a repeat.

Which is why I find myself in Italy, and not on the banks of the Hudson River.

Rolls of gold straw, stubbly fields, combed and tufted pine trees line dirt roads off the highway. I look over and Emmie is closing her eyes at the wheel of the car we rented. The boys are bobbleheads in their car seats. For a long moment I think we will just lift off into the shiny sky which I've already decided is the essence of Italy. Then I realize that we are slowing down rather quickly and veering off the road rather dangerously.

I am too shy to wake up my professor! I put my hands on the wheel where they won't touch her hands. I don't even know how to drive in America, let alone *Italy*. I let the car swerve off the highway and roll into a ditch gently. Then I don't know what to do so I turn the keys out of the ignition. I tell myself the car can't spring forward with the keys severed.

How's that for my first adventure?

Oh, that's very fine for an adventure, Leah. I don't know how to drive, either. Perhaps you remember the way I scuttled you across the streets in a state of clinical panic. I don't trust drivers. I close my eyes against them, my breathing choked, irregular, not trusting death, either.

When we get to the compound (Emmie wakes up in the ditch and looks at me strangely. My mouth corkscrews instead of smiles), we are delirious. Felix begins vomiting. I stand back— surely this is Emmie's department. Indeed, Emmie grabs my arm and says, Oh, my God, I throw up when I see throw-up. She turns away and hurls.

Did I mention that we're joining Emmie's two best friends from college? They've each brought their nanny. There's one nanny, hanging out a fan of laundry. The other is a button-nosed eunuch (I decide, cruelly) from Thailand (Emmie's friend Hedwig tells me). She turns the hose on the vomit in the courtyard before she's even said hello to us.

Hedwig, later: You're Emmie's student?

I wilt like a zucchini flower on the end of its phallus.

The laundry-fan nanny is French. Now she's sweeping the patio and when she speaks her voice has the same rasp as the broom on the flagstones. Her name is Eveline. She looks like a black cat—the kind that crosses the street in front of you—black coat shiny from all the baby mice and birds she's been eating.

The first few days we sleep till lunchtime in our slightly dank, tiled apartment with no plastic bags for the dirty diapers. This is my fault, as I am the nanny. My shampoo has exploded in the jet's belly, but so far I am too shy to ask Emmie about hers—she hasn't put it out yet. Natasha, did I ask you if you've ever been to Italy? Do you know what's weird? Is this possible? I had a memory yesterday that I've never had before.

I always used to ask my mother why you didn't have children, Natasha. I think—excuse me if this sounds, I don't know, capitalist—I wanted to know if *I* was doing you a favor by being your child figure, or if *you* were doing me a favor by being my keeper figure. And my mother used to say, Leah! Don't you ever, ever. There could be ghosts of abortions, adoptions in chintzy nightgowns, not to mention drownings in the bathtub.

Of course she didn't say all that, but I got the gist of it. Do you remember this expression, peculiar to my mother? The minute you assume, you get caught out in the rain. Did I tell you that she still won't assume my bedroom?

But here's what I remembered, yesterday. Soon after you left us, I heard my mother telling someone that she felt there was an element of flight to your departure.

Well, is it true? Were you on the lam or something?

Certainly I was glad Virginia didn't choose this moment to quake up the attic stairs with some scheduling conflict. I've always thought laughing was worse than crying because laughing, you have to pretend to be happy.

I made my decision it was not appropriate to write back to Leah. There were a multitude of reasons. I was paid by the hour and I owed it to myself to remain utterly free of children in my unpaid hours. There was never any *joy* for me, with children. Indeed, sleepless nights worrying over Leah left me distracted, even depressed with Jack and Colin.

And yet when I received another letter . . .

You should see the clear-skinned, glinty-eyed women, Natasha. And the dark gangly men with lovers' names; I get why my mother provided me with condoms.

We are invited to a dinner at midnight (I exaggerate the time but not the magic) and climb steep stairs, me carrying Felix, Emmie tugging Roman, to a sprawling red-tiled terrace furnished with monumental potted olives. Two cooks, three courses, faucets of wine in square juice glasses. All candlelight. Then Francesca, the hostess, a tycoon's daughter, spies our children.

The little ones aren't tired?

Emmie swoons into the lovely commotion even as her children are dismissed from the party. Crestfallen, I pull them inside the "apartment."

But the sun is healthy, the Italian language is organic, the cheese tastes like meat, and the milk tastes like flowers! Smooth brown haunches in tiny swimsuits. I look down at my tissue-paper skin, grayish white, tattooed with the soot of NY City. Perhaps having inferior skin consistency makes me try harder at conversation.

Those other trees on the terrace are hazelnuts!

I told myself that Leah's letters were poetic, but not personal. I told myself that I was never more than a stand-in, a warm body, for any of my children, and so was not, categorically, entitled to any sense of guilt I might feel at not writing Leah.

Emmie spends the mornings in a studio she rented. She comes back to the compound for lunch, upsets Roman and Felix with her managing of their diets, and then calculates—as if, every time, it's a special exception—if I could put the boys down while she takes a breather, a.k.a. four hours. After siesta, she runs three miles with Hedwig to a polo field, where they nuzzle the horses like infatuated schoolgirls. Then they walk back, all art and relationships.

Here's how it started. Last semester I had an idea for a life-size sculpture of a woman. The whole point was she would be clothed, suggesting the *opposite* of clothing. Like naked bodies are less sexy, actually, than bodies in bathing suits. Uh-huh, that's my college for you. A clothed sculpture about nakedness, basically. Emmie was the one who drew me out, encouraged me. I told her about you, I admit, and I probably made you out to be some hammer-fisted, kerchiefed Stakhanovite. Emmie said my idea was very precocious. Then I had an idea that the body had to be yours, actually—I mean I became obsessed with likeness and proportion and even your particular wardrobe. I remembered—and it startled me—that you always looked as if you'd just stepped out of the collective closet of the Soviet Union. You looked as if you immigrated every day, to Chelsea.

(Not that my mother's wardrobe was ever up-to-date, but did she ever even offer to walk you down Hudson to the church thrift shop?)

Emmie argued that the power of the work was that it was universal, you know. Woman's lot and all that. I disagreed but didn't know how to express myself. I just felt like it was *mine*. Even though it was yours, in a way, Natasha. Emmie said I didn't understand art and I broke down in tears, knowing girlish capitulation was the only thing that would save the relationship. And here's where the relationship has gotten me.

. . .

I was holding Felix on my hip yesterday—he's the quiet one, with the gourdlike forehead. Roman hurled himself at me, across the lawn—his love is so boisterous. All of a sudden I remembered how I could disarm you by running into your arms—because you were so shy, for a grown-up, and going for a hug was so unlike me.

I found myself wishing she'd return to the nanny on the lam, me, Natasha. I longed to laugh again, imagining myself ducking some black-market thugs, gumshoes wearing masks of Beria and Stalin. Admittedly, there was a hole in the logic of such letters—why did Leah write me? But I couldn't pretend I wasn't exalted. Emotions that would be embarrassingly simple in my psychology days, but now . . . Well, I told myself, there was the possibility that I was a lonely old woman.

I came to New York at twenty-six and married the first man I met, lit-erally and proverbially. He stuck his head around the fire escape. "Hey," he said. "Neighbor."

He had a loopy charming grin and hard eyes the color of lapis. I had just brought home a pot of daisies (*margaritka,* in Russian), and I was setting them out on the little balcony. I wouldn't have called it a fire escape. My English was good, but not specific. He climbed over, still grinning, as if he were shy of my beauty but, like a dog, couldn't help himself. He had long legs in tight jeans and white socks with holes in them. So already we were intimate. We had one son, Arturo, named after my husband's father, the patriarch. The family business was Italian tiles. We were a mismatch from the beginning, although there were never any lighthearted fairies making fun of us.

It didn't take more than ten minutes for me to look through my papers for a picture of Leah. With the way I move around so much I don't have much of anything. No. In those days before digital cam-eras and e-mail snapshots, it seemed more exaggerated, deliberate to take a picture. I wouldn't have wanted Ivy to get the wrong idea. As I said before, there was already some sense, among my previous families, that I could be too vigilant.

Leah's was one of only two families I didn't live with. The other family, in fact, I had started out living with, but the mother, a rubbery-faced woman who had a great deal subtracted from natural beauty, felt that I was "overbearing in the household." I pointed out to her (I had nowhere else to live, but she didn't know that) that most accidents happen in the presence of many adults because each individual adult assumes another is watching the children. Of course, a child can wander to the brink of an unattended swimming pool, I said, mistake the deep for the shallow, but more likely, it is when many mothers in oversize fashionable sunglasses like wasps at the nectar of gossip are present that a drowning actually happens.

The rubbery mother had fallen completely silent.

"Oh, my, Natasha," she said several long seconds after I had finished. All of her lipstick had come off on her coffee cup and she looked both pale and lurid.

It occurred to me she thought I was accusing her of the . . . well, the predeath of one of her children.

"I am sorry, Becky," I said somewhat woodenly.

"It's stressful being with children, Natasha," she managed.

My opinion was that for her, it was, indeed, terribly "stressful."

"I think you should come in the mornings, you know, in the breakfast rush hour . . ." Half smiling, she indicated the war zone of toast and yogurt and mashed banana for the baby. "And then," she continued, "well, *leave* after the baby's dinner."

I bowed my head until she said, "Natasha?"

"Becky, it's as you wish," I said. "Now please allow me . . ." And I moved in on the crumbly carnage, and the baby, who had been watching alarmedly, began banging with her bottle.

I came commuting in to Manhattan every morning by seven o'clock to get Leah to school by nine. Sometimes I volunteered in Leah's classroom, divvying paint or helping at the scissors station. I used to stay there, in "Chelsea," with Leah, until ten or eleven in the evening. A few times Ivy gave me cab fare but—I'm astonished at myself!—I categorically refused it.

Once, only a little bit less than a year after I'd left Leah, I had an opportunity to walk slowly past the front of her school at the dismissal hour. Many of the children who indiscriminately bumped and jostled one another were as tall as I was. I couldn't believe that had been the case when I used to pick up Leah. I felt a terrible clutching and sourness in my stomach: in anticipation of this very moment, I realized, I hadn't eaten anything since I'd left Nyack at six o'clock that morning. Suddenly I knew I was not in the right frame of mind to greet Leah. In any case I had no right to see her, none at all; it would be a compromise of context; like time travel, it was simply not possible.

I almost threw the next letter away as soon as I received it. I had intercepted it in the entrance hallway—Virginia need not creep up to the attic again, justified on her errand—and I stood beneath the chandelier that Jack had many times tried to jump for, holding the letter away from my body. I could see myself from above, too: I was very stilted and ridiculous in this action.

Such a correspondence need not continue, I heard myself whisper, as if I were, indeed, acting. I had a moment to myself—the boys were napping.

But what if I, Natasha, *weren't* just an adolescent idea for a clothed, female figure? What if such a statue . . . took on a life of its own, like a guardian angel? I wouldn't write back, that remained clear to me, but I must remain, somehow, *open*.

Dear Natasha,

Emmie's other college roommate, Lorene, hired a real Italian grandmother to cook ragu that smells like it has a hundred ingredients. The sauce simmers, thickens, reduces, and the grandmother-cook sweeps the patio with one hand and picks herbs in terra cotta with the other. Emmie's all about: Don't come near me; I am a ladysculptor. Molly and Eveline have urged me to let the boys watch TV with their boys. Do you know what? All the children are boys, future kings and princes, and all the grown-ups are women. I'm the only woman with any future to speak of.

Lorene, actually, has just returned from a week of Ashtanga in the center of Italy. Emmie keeps teasing her about being strong and centered—obviously, Emmie wishes she were a svelte yogini. Lorene and Hedwig think it's very cute that I'm the nanny. They tease Emmie that she must really trust Mark, Emmie's husband. They tease Emmie that their nannies have to pick up the slack, like making the kids the lunchtime chopped ham and ketchuppy hot dogs.

A rash and fever called sestina afflicts our Felix. The poetry of it! cries Emmie. Only in Italy!

I guess that's where we are: the space between the verses.

Now it all makes sense. How he threw up upon our arrival, how he's been so clingy, not his usual self, Emmie assures me. Hedwig is a biologist. She calls sestina one of the last remaining childhood illnesses. As if the illness itself were an endangered species! Free to burn, perhaps to purify, intones Hedwig. It occurs to me to ask Hedwig how she feels about death.

Lorene is a fashion designer in Paris. She says, So did we approve of the spaghetti sauce? We did, didn't we. She has a way of pulling her ribs up off her stomach, as if to make more room for spaghetti. Hedwig comes in from wherever she has been with her laptop, wearing a bikini and the gauzy Indian tunic that all the ladies are wearing—really, another kind of housedress. Emmie hands me the sestina.

Mark's arrival. The big personality. Everyone feels loved and it's all worthwhile to be stranded in Italy. Yes, they're already starting to complain about their vacation. Maybe we shouldn't have listened to Francesca, maybe this isn't the best spot. Maybe this is second-tier, maybe we're missing the part where it's going to show up in a glossy mag, stateside. Mark heads down to the beach hours after everyone else has already departed. I know because I must stay in the tiled quarters with maladious Felix.

I'm not really sure if I should talk to him. Only it makes me think of so many things to say when I *don't* talk to him. Last night I was so bottled up that I ended up telling Hedwig about you, Natasha, how you flashed in my mind every day after school, after you left us, and how I'd have to catch myself before running out to meet you.

All right, I'm beginning to recognize something of myself in Leah. I see how she's making friends with those women, her professor and her professor's girlfriends, by confession. She's baring her wounds as a way to be accepted. Sure, she tells them about her daddy, how he left them for another woman; she tells them about her Russian nanny, who left them for a family in Nyack.

Yes, there was a time when my "opening line," as they say, had something to do with losing Arturo. I didn't think I could get a job without it. A mother would show me around her big sunny apartment, and I'd kneel down and greet her children, and then the mother would have to throw in some extra, like a dog who had allergies and had to be fed cooked turkey. Well, then I would make my confession. I thought of it as a special coin. If one side is pain the other must be friendship.

I go around all day worrying about Leah. The other husbands have arrived too, and Leah calls them big shots, and now she calls the women longlegs. She writes,

They've all gone down to the salty still water. They're all parading along the eucalyptus avenue toward the umbrella colony. If

I close my eyes I can hear the sound of scuttling maids coming out from the corners, taking back the house, the loud brusque whisper that can only be the sound of sweeping. Your maid is like your garlic breath. Molly, the Thai nanny, and Eveline share a closet with bunk beds. Molly puts rice in the mouths of seven siblings in Thailand. I don't know this for a fact but I sure can hear my mother say it. All Eveline will tell me about herself is that she hates the food in Italy.

Have you ever been to Italy? I can't believe I forgot to ask you.

One of Francesca's friends (Francesca, sorry: one of Mark's old girlfriends, how we heard about these apartments) arrives from Rome to stay in the apartment upstairs from us. Her name is Giulietta, which is a whole different kettle of fish from Julie, isn't it. Despite her name, she's all bourgeoisie and gristle. She wears a big floppy sun hat and movie-star glasses. She brings her terrible son Brando and an American au pair from Vassar College. Why does the au pair seem more like a house-guest? Because she has some Feminist Theory 101 in her back pocket? Last night we were hanging out on our dark lawn—Roman was waiting to catch a bat or at least hit one with the sand shovel he was waving—when a chair came hurtling through the air from the terrace above us. Brando was having a tantrum.

Mark came out of the tiled quarters. Everyone looked to him to see what was called for.

Vassar slunk down, whining, But why don't they have shower curtains in Italy?

You lost a chair, said Mark, deadpan.

There's a little cutout in the pine trees through which I could see the twinkling lights from boats on the water.

Al-lie? called Giulietta from the terrace above us.

Vassar shivered.

Mark laughed at her and she flickered up for attention. He said, You must be Allie. He reached out his hand for an introduction.

He said, Baths in the sea, Allie.

I happen to know he's forty. He swings his hips when he walks, which might be embarrassing in a younger man but it makes him seem youthful.

My employer, Virginia, asks me, "Who are all the letters from, Natasha?

"I never even asked you." She cocks her head, fleetingly curious. "Do you still have family in Russia?"

I look down at the letter in my hand, with its *Italian* stamp and *Italian* postmark. But my employer is not really a classy person. She works hard, she's a doctor, but she started medical school when she was about fifteen (this is her joke, actually), and hasn't seen the real world since then.

I am no longer in the habit of confessing anything. Oh, I'm friendly, and at once gentle and vigilant with the children. I'm always getting told by the mothers that I'm not like the stereotypical Russian nannies with spare-the-rod-spoil-the-child ideas about discipline. It's funny because that phrase, of course, comes from the Bible, and wouldn't be known to most Soviet Russians of my generation. Also, Russian mamas notoriously spoil their children. As if they had multiples, which they don't, categorically.

I just stand in the hallway not knowing what to say to her. Which is the lesser of two evils? That I'm corresponding with one of my old children (like an affair, almost!), or that I do have family in Russia, with whom I have never, since I emigrated, exchanged so much as a sentence?

Of course, I am not, technically, corresponding.

Luckily my employer doesn't have the time to pursue it. She is already explaining to me some glitch in her schedule, some scheduling conflict, that is a favorite term with her, that overlaps with my afternoon off. . . . All I can think as she's talking is something from her boys' swim lessons, to which I accompany them, which strikes me as very funny indeed, "bubble bubble breath," which is Virginia talking.

> It's all about the women, here, Natasha. The men are spoiled and paunchy, spreading out in the vacated cities, sleeping late, earning money to pay the nannies. There was one flashbulb of awareness when they were teenagers, and the rest of their lives they try to get back to it. Their bodies were strong, a sheer drop. Their hair was black, they drank black coffee and liquor indiscriminately. The only consolation now is to make mad money. Yes, Mark has gone back to New York for a week in the middle of his vacation to make money.
>
> And no, Mark isn't paunchy. He's spoiled; but he's the only one who really pays me any notice. He watches me with Roman and Felix. I figure he'd say something if he didn't like the way I was treating his heirs. They really look like him rather than Emmie. Mark says that one way to travel is to love everything, revere it. I tell him I think the sunbathers on the rocks look like browning dumplings. I tell him I love to watch the family picnics beneath the pine trees. He smiles as if I've just said something very esoteric and he alone understands it.

I don't think she can see it coming. I don't think she's old enough, or pretty enough, to see it coming.

And if I wrote her?

I laugh at myself harshly. I'd disappoint her with my old woman's voice, I'd hurt her with my lack of belief in her beauty.

This Mark, her professor's husband, will come back from his business having justified it to himself—every man can justify it—and

Leah will be a bird in the hand before she's even sighted properly in the binoculars.

I take my afternoon off in Central Park. The commuter rail is empty at one o'clock on a Wednesday, and so I have the sense of swooping silently upon the city. I take a little picnic, and Leah's most recent letter. After I finish eating, I wander around for a bit until I find a nice shady rock to sit on—private but not too private—and listen to the xylophone of bird voices. When I close my eyes for a moment, they seem to be elongated, like raindrops, and when a gust of wind comes up, there is a sudden discordance as if the notes are all struck together.

Dear Natasha,

I'm on the lawn again, looking through the keyhole of hedges to the marine blue (today) Mediterranean. Felix is sleeping. Roman is watching the idiot box with Lorene's kids; Hedwig's husband has actually taken his boys out fishing. So that he won't have to do another thing with them all of August. Everyone else (if I say "the others" it will really sound like a novel, won't it) is out on the count's sailboat. Breezing along the Mediterranean in their sexy skins beneath their sexy sail. Molly and Eveline went into the town—I offered to watch Eveline's charges. I could have taken Felix in his carriage. To town. But I thought I might get points from Emmie for reaching out to Eveline. Ah! I feel like the Christian fundamentalist in an apron and a bonnet making quilts past the year 2000. Life is a sacrifice of the soul; children are the refining fire. Mark said that, with a half smile.

I really can't say you *shouldn't* have left, Natasha, because that's worse than underpaying, or paying for a single doctor's visit instead of Health Insurance—you can be sure my mother's all over labor violations. I can't say you shouldn't have left, because it sounds controlling. But when is love not controlling?

Here comes Mark. Ah! It seems like he's smiling in spite of himself, you know? Like he genuinely likes me.

Yes, I've been to Italy. My husband took me, and Arturo, when Arturo was a ten-month-old baby. There was a great hassle about my passport. I had been planning never, ever to leave America. That was my thinking. But with the problems at the consulate, my husband began to suspect me of a covert Russianness.

"One thing," he said. "If you're my wife, you don't draw this kind of attention."

We fought all the way to John F. Kennedy Airport. Arturo wailed in the backseat and I twisted around to look in his wobbly eyes. I reached my hand back to his soft knee and he hiccuped. I looked in his wet light eyes and thought to myself that there was no reason under the sun, as they say, why he should stop crying. I knew that things were never going to be good between me and his father. Indeed, Arturo began to wail with renewed passion.

"Oh, you're a good mother!" my husband shouted.

I was always the crazy one, as if it had to be one of us. My husband said he should have seen it. He claimed that I mumbled certain things in my sleep.

Indeed, whenever we fought, my English failed me, as did the entire body of my psychologist's training. This fight was something to do with the way I'd left the apartment. I hadn't tidied up sufficiently. I hadn't put away the clean dishes from the previous night's dinner, for example. My husband was suspicious of everyone and everything, and he somehow thought the likelihood of our apartment being broken into—by the police, that is—was greater because I'd left it in shambles. I knew a little bit about the drugs, but I never said anything.

.   .   .

Arturo was just beginning to walk at the time of the trip to Italy. My husband was very proud of him. My husband wanted to take him out and show him on the streets, in the bars and restaurants, as a son of Italy. We visited various cousins of my husband, and my husband always pulled Arturo away from me and presented him as if he belonged solely to my husband.

The last three days of our vacation we spent on the Mediterranean. It reminded me of the Black Sea, where I'd been as a child: so calm, like a bathtub, families like porpoises picnicking on the rocks, riding bicycles down piney paths, eating late and lavishly. We went to the shale beach in the afternoons, and my husband would swim out to the boats while Arturo clapped and paddled in the shallow water.

Our last afternoon there was a terrific thunderstorm. As I remember, there was an ominous warning rustle through the pines and in a matter of seconds the sky was cracking like ice on a river in springtime and the air was throwing off shards of electricity. I could see my husband's slick black head dipping way out in the water and I began waving frantically. Then the sky dumped out its buckets.

What should I do? I tried to shield Arturo, but I had nothing on but a bathing suit. I'd left our clothes and towels at the hotel, in the midst of another fight with my husband. The rain was surprisingly cold, and hard, like one of those "massaging" showerheads. Arturo began to whimper.

Just then, a teenage boy appeared at my elbow. How can I describe it? He was like a courtier in a castle; he had that air of grave attendance. His hair was jet and he had a low forehead and fluted nostrils. His gaze was intent, as if *I* were the sole reason for this moment. His tanned body in a swimsuit was strangely flat, almost one-dimensional. He held out his big towel. I nodded gratefully and wrapped up Arturo. My baby's slightly droopy eyes, one was what they call "lazy," his copper hair like mine in a delicate ridge over the crest of his head (now darkened with water), his soft bare body . . .

"I am Seryozha." The teenage boy bowed to Arturo. Arturo smiled from beneath the towel.

"Come on!" He gestured for us to follow. He pointed to a big pine on the beach of which one half was charcoaled, branded by lightning. "That was last summer," said Seryozha, by way of a warning.

He herded us along the path. Lucky it was wide, because you could hardly see past the curtain of rain in front of you, and I was sure I would have stumbled with Arturo. When we got to the little hotel where we were staying, I held Arturo away from me to unwrap the towel and return it. Seryozha shook his head vigorously. "Tomorrow."

This seemed at the time the kindest thing that anyone had ever offered. He bowed again, and disappeared into the rainstorm.

I'm sorry, Natasha. This has nothing to do with you, really, I mean, you shouldn't be concerned for me like my mother.

Maybe you're *my* conscience, actually. Did you get the letter where I said you were my mother's? I admit I was kind of proud of myself for figuring out that little piece of psychology.

I admit it's kind of funny to keep writing to someone who doesn't write back to you, but in a way it reminds me of some art project sanctioned at my college. Anyway, feel free to destroy these letters. I certainly never want to see them.

Last night we went to a medieval town about an hour's drive from here for a late dinner. Francesca had recommended the restaurant, with outdoor, torchlit tables in a cobblestone chasm walled by stone churches. Emmie and Mark had a bad "row," as Hedwig calls it, beforehand, so Emmie stayed behind with Felix. Mark wanted to take Roman. Hedwig and Lorene urged me to come along in order to help Mark with Roman. I would have stayed home out of loyalty to Emmie, I know I would have. Ah! Could you see this coming? Please tell me you couldn't. Have you ever felt like all that was surreal in the night is a curse in the morning?

It was in the car on the way home. We took a different car from Lorene and Hedwig & Co. because of Roman's car seat. It was with our clothes on. I kept thinking of that diamond-shaped view of the ocean through the hedges, and our keyhole of nakedness. I said, Please don't tell Emmie. And Mark laughed. Emmie and I tell each other everything! The kind of slippery teasing that writes a reprieve for everything. That covers all its bases. Do you know what I mean? I know my mother would say that's not teasing, Leah, that's an abuse of power. Can you just hear her?

My husband roared at me, "You left me in a thunderstorm!" Oh, I needed to laugh. What a baby my husband sounded like. What a stupid baby. It came to me that I would not tell him about Seryozha—whose name couldn't, I realized, possibly have been Russian.

I suppose it was in that moment that I knew I was leaving.

Here is the truth, Leah. I would be the crazy one if crazy was what it took to get free.

I told myself that I did not want to "go down" with my husband; certainly that was his slang, and again I needed to laugh at the evocation. For example I had not the least intention of being at home when the police arrived heaving with petty resentment at having to climb four stories. Ours was a walk-up, just like yours, Leah. I would not pretend I wasn't terrified of those black-nosed German shepherds, police dogs with thick muscular tails used, like kangaroos, for superior balance.

"Where was I supposed to have thought you'd gone, Natalie, Moscow?" my husband shouted.

Yes, I called myself Natalie then. Assimilation. I thought it sounded odd, harsh, nonsense, but that's what I thought a professional immigrant would do. Not a housecleaner or a nanny.

When I take too many painkillers now there's a side effect of my uterus contracting, and I think, mincing down the stairs to Virginia's children from my attic, that children are truly our penance for being, once, ourselves, children. But then I think, Why should you, Leah, have to pay for being Leah?

The storm cleared and my husband said he would take Arturo to the town center where there was an arcade with many small shops, cafés, and a fruit market. They would spend the afternoon making friends with the shopkeepers. Fine, I said. Good-bye, Arturo. I had to kiss him in my husband's arms although I did not want to go near my husband.

I allowed one moment of silence in our little hotel room.

When I think about my son now, it's not the way I knew him, held him, and held on to him when he was a baby. I try to imagine him as a grown man, that he's tall and kind and handsome, that he's been a good son to his father and his stepmother, that he's gone into the tile business or gone to college, that he says with curious pride he's half Russian. Even if he doesn't, that maybe he thinks it's his secret.

I must add that as far as I know he has never tried to find me.

No, I never allow myself to think of him like that—in my arms, on the beach of the Mediterranean, in a wild thunderstorm. Because in that moment, I was sure Seryozha (and I know I didn't hear Sergio) was our guardian angel. I was sure he was a sign. That this was the beginning. The cleansing rain, the hotel room with its welcome, stuffy warmth, Arturo's eyes gleaming with excitement from our rescue.

Chimamanda Ngozi Adichie

# The Headstrong Historian

M ANY YEARS AFTER her husband had died, Nwamgba still closed
her eyes from time to time to relive his nightly visits to her
hut, and the mornings after, when she would walk to the stream
humming a song, thinking of the smoky scent of him and the firm-
ness of his weight, and feeling as if she were surrounded by light.
Other memories of Obierika also remained clear—his stubby fingers
curled around his flute when he played in the evenings, his delight
when she set down his bowls of food, his sweaty back when he
brought baskets filled with fresh clay for her pottery. From the
moment she had first seen him, at a wrestling match, both of them
staring and staring, both of them too young, her waist not yet wearing the menstruation cloth, she had believed with a quiet stubbornness that her chi and his chi had destined their marriage, and so when
he and his relatives came to her father a few years later with pots of
palm wine she told her mother that this was the man she would
marry. Her mother was aghast. Did Nwamgba not know that
Obierika was an only child, that his late father had been an only child
whose wives had lost pregnancies and buried babies? Perhaps some-

body in their family had committed the taboo of selling a girl into slavery and the earth god Ani was visiting misfortune on them. Nwamgba ignored her mother. She went into her father's *obi* and told him she would run away from any other man's house if she was not allowed to marry Obierika. Her father found her exhausting, this sharp-tongued, headstrong daughter who had once wrestled her brother to the ground. (Her father had had to warn those who saw this not to let anyone outside the compound know that a girl had thrown a boy.) He, too, was concerned about the infertility in Obierika's family, but it was not a bad family: Obierika's late father had taken the Ozo title; Obierika was already giving out his seed yams to sharecroppers. Nwamgba would not starve if she married him. Besides, it was better that he let his daughter go with the man she chose than to endure years of trouble in which she would keep returning home after confrontations with her in-laws; and so he gave his blessing, and she smiled and called him by his praise name.

To pay her bride price, Obierika came with two maternal cousins, Okafo and Okoye, who were like brothers to him. Nwamgba loathed them at first sight. She saw a grasping envy in their eyes that afternoon, as they drank palm wine in her father's *obi;* and in the following years—years in which Obierika took titles and widened his compound and sold his yams to strangers from afar—she saw their envy blacken. But she tolerated them, because they mattered to Obierika, because he pretended not to notice that they didn't work but came to him for yams and chickens, because he wanted to imagine that he had brothers. It was they who urged him, after her third miscarriage, to marry another wife. Obierika told them that he would give it some thought, but when they were alone in her hut at night he assured her that they would have a home full of children, and that he would not marry another wife until they were old, so that they would have somebody to care for them. She thought this strange of him, a prosperous man with only one wife, and she worried more than he did about their childlessness, about the songs that people sang, the melodious mean-spirited words: She has sold her womb. She has eaten his penis. He plays his flute and hands over his wealth to her.

Once, at a moonlight gathering, the square full of women telling stories and learning new dances, a group of girls saw Nwamgba and began to sing, their aggressive breasts pointing at her. She asked if they would mind singing a little louder, so that she could hear the words and then show them who was the greater of two tortoises. They stopped singing. She enjoyed their fear, the way they backed away from her, but it was then that she decided to find a wife for Obierika herself.

Nwamgba liked going to the Oyi stream, untying her wrapper from her waist, and walking down the slope to the silvery rush of water that burst out from a rock. The waters of Oyi seemed fresher than those of the other stream, Ogalanya, or perhaps it was simply that Nwamgba felt comforted by the shrine of the Oyi goddess, tucked away in a corner; as a child she had learned that Oyi was the protector of women, the reason it was taboo to sell women into slavery. Nwamgba's closest friend, Ayaju, was already at the stream, and as Nwamgba helped Ayaju raise her pot to her head she asked her who might be a good second wife for Obierika.

She and Ayaju had grown up together and had married men from the same clan. The difference between them, though, was that Ayaju was of slave descent. Ayaju did not care for her husband, Okenwa, who she said resembled and smelled like a rat, but her marriage prospects had been limited; no man from a freeborn family would have come for her hand. Ayaju was a trader, and her rangy, quick-moving body spoke of her many journeys; she had even traveled beyond Onicha. It was she who had first brought back tales of the strange customs of the Igala and Edo traders, she who had first told stories of the white-skinned men who had arrived in Onicha with mirrors and fabrics and the biggest guns the people of those parts had ever seen. This cosmopolitanism earned her respect, and she was the only person of slave descent who talked loudly at the Women's Council, the only person who had answers for everything. She promptly suggested, for Obierika's second wife, a young girl from the Okonkwo family, who had beautiful wide hips and who was respect-ful, nothing like the other young girls of today, with their heads full of nonsense.

As they walked home from the stream, Ayaju said that perhaps Nwamgba should do what other women in her situation did—take a lover and get pregnant in order to continue Obierika's lineage. Nwamgba's retort was sharp, because she did not like Ayaju's tone, which suggested that Obierika was impotent, and, as if in response to her thoughts, she felt a furious stabbing sensation in her back and knew that she was pregnant again, but she said nothing, because she knew, too, that she would lose it again.

Her miscarriage happened a few weeks later, lumpy blood running down her legs. Obierika comforted her and suggested that they go to the famous oracle, Kisa, as soon as she was well enough for the half day's journey. After the *dibia* had consulted the oracle, Nwamgba cringed at the thought of sacrificing a whole cow; Obierika certainly had greedy ancestors. But they performed the ritual cleansings and the sacrifices as required, and when she suggested that he go and see the Okonkwo family about their daughter he delayed and delayed until another sharp pain spliced her back, and, months later, she was lying on a pile of freshly washed banana leaves behind her hut, strain-ing and pushing until the baby slipped out.

They named him Anikwenwa: the earth god Ani had finally granted a child. He was dark and solidly built, and had Obierika's happy curiosity. Obierika took him to pick medicinal herbs, to collect clay for Nwamgba's pottery, to twist yam vines at the farm. Obierika's cousins Okafo and Okoye visited often. They marveled at how well Anikwenwa played the flute, how quickly he was learning poetry and wrestling moves from his father, but Nwamgba saw the glowing malevolence that their smiles could not hide. She feared for her child and for her husband, and when Obierika died—a man who had been hearty and laughing and drinking palm wine moments before he slumped—she knew that they had killed him with medicine. She clung to his corpse until a neighbor slapped her to make her let go; she lay in the cold ash for days, tore at the patterns shaved into her hair. Obierika's death left her with an unending despair. She thought often of a woman who, after losing a tenth child, had gone to her backyard and hanged herself on a kola-nut tree. But she would not do it, because of Anikwenwa.

Later, she wished she had made Obierika's cousins drink his *mmili ozu* before the oracle. She had witnessed this once, when a wealthy man died and his family forced his rival to drink his *mmili ozu*. Nwamgba had watched an unmarried woman take a cupped leaf full of water, touch it to the dead man's body, all the time speaking solemnly, and give the leaf-cup to the accused man. He drank. Everyone looked to make sure that he swallowed, a grave silence in the air, because they knew that if he was guilty he would die. He died days later, and his family lowered their heads in shame. Nwamgba felt strangely shaken by it all. She should have insisted on this with Obierika's cousins, but she had been blinded by grief and now Obierika was buried and it was too late.

His cousins, during the funeral, took his ivory tusk, claiming that the trappings of titles went to brothers and not to sons. It was when they emptied his barn of yams and led away the adult goats in his pen that she confronted them, shouting, and when they brushed her aside she waited until evening, then walked around the clan singing about their wickedness, the abominations they were heaping on the land by cheating a widow, until the elders asked them to leave her alone. She complained to the Women's Council, and twenty women went at night to Okafo's and Okoye's homes, brandishing pestles, warning them to leave Nwamgba alone. But Nwamgba knew that those grasping cousins would never really stop. She dreamed of killing them. She certainly could, those weaklings who had spent their lives scrounging off Obierika instead of working, but, of course, she would be banished then, and there would be no one to care for her son. Instead, she took Anikwenwa on long walks, telling him that the land from that palm tree to that avocado tree was theirs, that his grandfather had passed it on to his father. She told him the same things over and over, even though he looked bored and bewildered, and she did not let him go and play at moonlight unless she was watching.

Ayaju came back from a trading journey with another story: the women in Onicha were complaining about the white men. They had welcomed the white men's trading station, but now the white men wanted to tell them how to trade, and when the elders of Agueke refused to place their thumbs on a paper the white men came at night with their normal-men helpers and razed the village. There was nothing left. Nwamgba did not understand. What sort of guns did these white men have? Ayaju laughed and said that their guns were nothing like the rusty thing her own husband owned; she spoke with pride, as though she herself were responsible for the superiority of the white men's guns. Some white men were visiting different clans, asking parents to send their children to school, she added, and she had decided to send her son Azuka, who was the laziest on the farm, because although she was respected and wealthy, she was still of slave descent, her sons were still barred from taking titles, and she wanted Azuka to learn the ways of these foreigners. People ruled over others not because they were better people, she said, but because they had better guns; after all, her father would not have been enslaved if his clan had been as well armed as Nwamgba's. As Nwamgba listened to her friend, she dreamed of killing Obierika's cousins with the white men's guns.

The day the white men visited her clan, Nwamgba left the pot she was about to put in her oven, took Anikwenwa and her girl apprentices, and hurried to the square. She was at first disappointed by the ordinariness of the two white men; they were harmless-looking, the color of albinos, with frail and slender limbs. Their companions were normal men, but there was something foreign about them, too: only one spoke Igbo, and with a strange accent. He said that he was from Elele, the other normal men were from Sierra Leone, and the white men from France, far across the sea. They were all of the Holy Ghost Congregation, had arrived in Onicha in 1885, and were building their school and church there. Nwamgba was the first to ask a question: Had they brought their guns, by any chance, the ones used to destroy the people of Agueke, and could she see one? The man said unhappily that it was the soldiers of the British government and the merchants of the Royal Niger Company who destroyed villages; they, instead, brought good news. He spoke about their god, who had come to the world to die, and who had a son but no wife, and who was three but also one. Many of the people around Nwamgba laughed loudly. Some walked away, because they had imagined that the white man was full of wisdom. Others stayed and offered cool bowls of water.

Weeks later, Ayaju brought another story: the white men had set up a courthouse in Onicha where they judged disputes. They had indeed come to stay. For the first time, Nwamgba doubted her friend. Surely the people of Onicha had their own courts. The clan next to Nwamgba's, for example, held its courts only during the new yam festival, so that people's rancor grew while they awaited justice. A stupid system, Nwamgba thought, but surely everyone had one. Ayaju laughed and told Nwamgba again that people ruled others when they had better guns. Her son was already learning about these foreign ways, and perhaps Anikwenwa should, too. Nwamgba refused. It was unthinkable that her only son, her single eye, should be given to the white men, never mind the superiority of their guns.

Three events, in the following years, caused Nwamgba to change her mind. The first was that Obierika's cousins took over a large piece of land and told the elders that they were farming it for her, a woman who had emasculated their dead brother and now refused to remarry, even though suitors came and her breasts were still round. The elders sided with them. The second was that Ayaju told a story of two people who had taken a land case to the white men's court; the first man was lying but could speak the white men's language, while the second man, the rightful owner of the land, could not, and so he lost his case, was beaten and locked up, and ordered to give up his land. The third was the story of the boy Iroegbunam, who had gone missing many years ago and then suddenly reappeared, a grown man, his widowed mother mute with shock at his story: a neighbor, whom his father had often shouted down at Age Grade meetings, had abducted him when his mother was at the market and taken him to the Aro slave dealers, who looked him over and complained that the wound on his leg would reduce his price. He was tied to others by the hands, forming a long human column, and he was hit with a stick and told to walk faster. There was one woman in the group. She shouted herself hoarse, telling the abductors that they were heartless, that her spirit would torment them and their children, that she knew she was to be sold to the white man and did they not know that the white man's slavery was very different, that people were treated like goats, taken on large ships a long way away, and were eventually eaten? Iroegbunam walked and walked and walked, his feet bloodied, his body numb, until all he remembered was the smell of dust. Finally, they stopped at a coastal clan, where a man spoke a nearly incomprehensible Igbo, but Iroegbunam made out enough to understand that another man who was to sell them to the white people on the ship had gone up to bargain with them but had himself been kidnapped. There were loud arguments, scuffling; some of the abductees yanked at the ropes and Iroegbunam passed out. He awoke to find a white man rubbing his feet with oil and at first he was terrified, certain that he was being prepared for the white man's meal, but this was a different kind of white man, who bought slaves only to free them, and he took Iroegbunam to live with him and trained him to be a Christian missionary.

Iroegbunam's story haunted Nwamgba, because this, she was sure, was the way Obierika's cousins were likely to get rid of her son.

Killing him would be too dangerous, the risk of misfortunes from the oracle too high, but they would be able to sell him as long as they had strong medicine to protect themselves. She was struck, too, by how Iroegbunam lapsed into the white man's language from time to time. It sounded nasal and disgusting. Nwamgba had no desire to speak such a thing herself, but she was suddenly determined that Anikwenwa would speak enough of it to go to the white men's court with Obierika's cousins and defeat them and take control of what was his. And so, shortly after Iroegbunam's return, she told Ayaju that she wanted to take her son to school.

They went first to the Anglican mission. The classroom had more girls than boys, sitting with slates on their laps while the teacher stood in front of them, holding a big cane, telling them a story about a man who transformed a bowl of water into wine. The teacher's spectacles impressed Nwamgba, and she thought that the man in the story must have had powerful medicine to be able to transform water into wine, but when the girls were separated and a woman teacher came to teach them how to sew Nwamgba found this silly. In her clan, men sewed cloth and girls learned pottery. What dissuaded her completely from sending Anikwenwa to the school, however, was that the instruction was done in Igbo. Nwamgba asked why. The teacher said that, of course, the students were taught English—he held up an English primer—but children learned best in their own language and the children in the white men's land were taught in their own language, too. Nwamgba turned to leave. The teacher stood in her way and told her that the Catholic missionaries were harsh and did not look out for the best interests of the natives. Nwamgba was amused by these foreigners, who did not seem to know that one must, in front of strangers, pretend to have unity. But she had come in search of English, and so she walked past him and went to the Catholic mission.

Father Shanahan told her that Anikwenwa would have to take an English name, because it was not possible to be baptized with a heathen name. She agreed easily. His name was Anikwenwa as far as she was concerned; if they wanted to name him something she could not pronounce before teaching him their language, she did not mind at all. All that mattered was that he learn enough of the language to fight his father's cousins.

Father Shanahan looked at Anikwenwa, a dark-skinned, well-muscled child, and guessed that he was about twelve, although he found it difficult to estimate the ages of these people; sometimes what looked like a man would turn out to be a mere boy. It was nothing like in Eastern Africa, where he had previously worked, where the natives tended to be slender, less confusingly muscular. As he poured some water on the boy's head, he said, "Michael, I baptize you in the name of the Father and of the Son and of the Holy Spirit."

He gave the boy a singlet and a pair of shorts, because the people of the living God did not walk around naked, and he tried to preach to the boy's mother, but she looked at him as if he were a child who did not know any better. There was something troublingly assertive about her, something he had seen in many women here; there was much potential to be harnessed if their wildness were tamed. This Nwamgba would make a marvelous missionary among the women. He watched her leave. There was a grace in her straight back, and she, unlike others, had not spent too much time going round and round in her speech. It infuriated him, their overlong talk and circuitous proverbs, their never getting to the point, but he was determined to excel here; it was the reason he had joined the Holy Ghost Congregation, whose special vocation was the redemption of black heathens.

Nwamgba was alarmed by how indiscriminately the missionaries flogged students: for being late, for being lazy, for being slow, for being idle, and, once, as Anikwenwa told her, Father Lutz put metal cuffs around a girl's hands to teach her a lesson about lying, all the time saying in Igbo—for Father Lutz spoke a broken brand of Igbo—that native parents pampered their children too much, that teaching the Gospel also meant teaching proper discipline. The first weekend Anikwenwa came home, Nwamgba saw welts on his back, and she tightened her wrapper around her waist and went to the school and told the teacher that she would gouge out the eyes of everyone at the mission if they ever did that to him again. She knew that Anikwenwa did not want to go to school and she told him that it was only for a year or two, so that he could learn English, and although the mission people told her not to come so often, she insistently came every weekend to take him home. Anikwenwa always took off his clothes even before they had left the mission compound. He disliked the shorts and shirt that made him sweat, the fabric that was itchy around his armpits. He disliked, too, being in the same class as old men, missing out on wrestling contests.

But Anikwenwa's attitude toward school slowly changed. Nwamgba first noticed this when some of the other boys with whom he swept the village square complained that he no longer did his share because he was at school, and Anikwenwa said something in English, something sharp-sounding, which shut them up and filled Nwamgba with an indulgent pride. Her pride turned to vague worry when she noticed that the curiosity in his eyes had diminished. There was a new ponderousness in him, as if he had suddenly found himself bearing the weight of a heavy world. He stared at things for too long. He stopped eating her food, because, he said, it was sacrificed to idols. He told her to tie her wrapper around her chest instead of her waist, because her nakedness was sinful. She looked at him, amused by his earnestness, but worried nonetheless, and asked why he had only just begun to notice her nakedness.

When it was time for his initiation ceremony, he said he would not participate, because it was a heathen custom to be initiated into the world of spirits, a custom that Father Shanahan had said would have to stop. Nwamgba roughly yanked his ear and told him that a foreign albino could not determine when their customs would change, and that he would participate or else he would tell her whether he was her son or the white man's son. Anikwenwa reluctantly agreed, but as he was taken away with a group of other boys she noticed that he lacked their excitement. His sadness saddened her. She felt her son slipping away from her, and yet she was proud that he was learning so much, that he could be a court interpreter or a letter writer, that with Father Lutz's help he had brought home some papers that showed that their land belonged to them. Her proudest moment was when he went to his father's cousins Okafo and Okoye and asked for his father's ivory tusk back. And they gave it to him.

Nwamgba knew that her son now inhabited a mental space that she was unable to recognize. He told her that he was going to Lagos to learn how to be a teacher, and even as she screamed—How can you leave me? Who will bury me when I die?—she knew that he would go. She did not see him for many years, years during which his father's cousin Okafo died. She often consulted the oracle to ask whether Anikwenwa was still alive, and the *dibia* admonished her and sent her away, because of course he was alive. Finally, he returned, in the year that the clan banned all dogs after a dog killed a member of the Mmangala Age Grade, the age group to which Anikwenwa would have belonged if he did not believe that such things were devilish.

Nwamgba said nothing when Anikwenwa announced that he had been appointed catechist at the new mission. She was sharpening her *aguba* on the palm of her hand, about to shave patterns into the hair of a little girl, and she continued to do so—*flick-flick-flick*—while Anikwenwa talked about winning the souls of the members of their clan. The plate of breadfruit seeds she had offered him was untouched—he no longer ate anything at all of hers—and she looked at him, this man wearing trousers and a rosary around his neck, and wondered whether she had meddled with his destiny. Was this what his chi had ordained for him, this life in which he was like a person diligently acting a bizarre pantomime?

The day that he told her about the woman he would marry, she was not surprised. He did not do it as it was done, did not consult people about the bride's family, but simply said that somebody at the mission had seen a suitable young woman from Ifite Ukpo, and the suitable young woman would be taken to the Sisters of the Holy Rosary in Onicha to learn how to be a good Christian wife. Nwamgba was sick with malaria that day, lying on her mud bed, rubbing her aching joints, and she asked Anikwenwa the young woman's name. Anikwenwa said it was Agnes. Nwamgba asked for the young woman's real name. Anikwenwa cleared his throat and said she had been called Mgbeke before she became a Christian, and Nwamgba asked whether Mgbeke would at least do the confession ceremony even if Anikwenwa would not follow the other marriage rites of their clan. He shook his head furiously and told her that the confession made by women before marriage, in which, surrounded by female relatives, they swore that no man had touched them since their husband declared his interest, was sinful, because Christian wives should not have been touched *at all*.

The marriage ceremony in the church was laughably strange, but Nwamgba bore it silently and told herself that she would die soon and join Obierika and be free of a world that increasingly made no sense. She was determined to dislike her son's wife, but Mgbeke was difficult to dislike, clear-skinned and gentle, eager to please the man to whom she was married, eager to please everyone, quick to cry, apologetic about things over which she had no control. And so, instead, Nwamgba pitied her. Mgbeke often visited Nwamgba in tears, saying that Anikwenwa had refused to eat dinner because he was upset with her, that Anikwenwa had banned her from going to a friend's Anglican wedding because Anglicans did not preach the truth, and Nwamgba would silently carve designs on her pottery while Mgbeke cried, uncertain of how to handle a woman crying about things that did not deserve tears.

Mgbeke was called "missus" by everyone, even the non-Christians, all of whom respected the catechist's wife, but on the day she went to the

Oyi stream and refused to remove her clothes because she was a Christian the women of the clan, outraged that she had dared to disrespect the goddess, beat her and dumped her at the grove. The news spread quickly. Missus had been harassed. Anikwenwa threatened to lock up all the elders if his wife was treated that way again, but Father O'Donnell, on his next trek from his station in Onicha, visited the elders and apologized on Mgbeke's behalf, and asked whether perhaps Christian women could be allowed to fetch water fully clothed. The elders refused—if a woman wanted Oyi's waters, then she had to follow Oyi's rules—but they were courteous to Father O'Donnell, who listened to them and did not behave like their own son Anikwenwa.

Nwamgba was ashamed of her son, irritated with his wife, upset by their rarefied life in which they treated non-Christians as if they had smallpox, but she held out hope for a grandchild; she prayed and sacrificed for Mgbeke to have a boy, because she knew that the child would be Obierika come back and would bring a semblance of sense again into her world. She did not know of Mgbeke's first or second miscarriage; it was only after the third that Mgbeke, sniffling and blowing her nose, told her. They had to consult the oracle, as this was a family misfortune, Nwamgba said, but Mgbeke's eyes widened with fear. Michael would be very angry if he ever heard of this oracle suggestion. Nwamgba, who still found it difficult to remember that Michael was Anikwenwa, went to the oracle herself, and afterward thought it ludicrous how even the gods had changed and no longer asked for palm wine but for gin. Had they converted, too?

A few months later, Mgbeke visited, smiling, bringing a covered bowl of one of those concoctions that Nwamgba found inedible, and Nwamgba knew that her chi was still wide awake and that her daughter-in-law was pregnant. Anikwenwa had decreed that Mgbeke would have the baby at the mission in Onicha, but the gods had different plans, and she went into early labor on a rainy afternoon; somebody ran in the drenching rain to Nwamgba's hut to call her. It was a boy. Father O'Donnell baptized him Peter, but Nwamgba called him Nnamdi, because he would be Obierika come back. She sang to him, and when he cried she pushed her dried-up nipple into his mouth, but, try as she might, she did not feel the spirit of her magnificent husband, Obierika. Mgbeke had three more miscarriages, and Nwamgba went to the oracle many times until a pregnancy stayed, and the second baby was born at the mission in Onicha. A girl. From the moment Nwamgba held her, the baby's bright eyes delightfully focused on her, she knew that the spirit of Obierika had finally returned; odd, to have come back in a girl, but who could predict the ways of the ancestors? Father O'Donnell baptized the baby Grace, but Nwamgba called her Afamefuna—"my name will not be lost"—and was thrilled by the child's solemn interest in her poetry and her stories, by the teenager's keen watchfulness as Nwamgba struggled to make pottery with newly shaky hands. Nwamgba was not thrilled that Afamefuna was sent away to secondary school in Onicha. (Peter was already living with the priests there.) She feared that, at boarding school, the new ways would dissolve her granddaughter's fighting spirit and replace it with either an incurious rigidity, like her son's, or a limp helplessness, like Mgbeke's.

The year that Afamefuna left for secondary school, Nwamgba felt as if a lamp had been blown out in a dim room. It was a strange year, the year that darkness suddenly descended on the land in the middle of the afternoon, and when Nwamgba felt the deep-seated ache in her joints she knew that her end was near. She lay on her bed gasping for breath, while Anikwenwa pleaded with her to be baptized and anointed so that he could hold a Christian funeral for her, as he could not participate in a heathen ceremony. Nwamgba told him that if he dared to bring anybody to rub some filthy oil on her she would slap them with her last strength. All she wanted before she joined the ancestors was to see Afamefuna, but Anikwenwa said that Grace was taking exams at school and could not come home.

But she came. Nwamgba heard the squeaky swing of her door, and there was Afamefuna, her granddaughter, who had come on her own from Onicha because she had been unable to sleep for days, her restless spirit urging her home. Grace put down her schoolbag, inside of which was her textbook, with a chapter called "The Pacification of the Primitive Tribes of Southern Nigeria," by an administrator from Bristol who had lived among them for seven years.

It was Grace who would eventually read about these savages, titillated by their curious and meaningless customs, not connecting them to herself until her teacher Sister Maureen told her that she could not refer to the call-and-response her grandmother had taught her as poetry, because primitive tribes did not have poetry. It was Grace who would laugh and laugh until Sister Maureen took her to detention and then summoned her father, who slapped Grace in front of the other teachers to show them how well he disciplined his children. It was Grace who would nurse a deep scorn for her father for years, spending holidays working as a maid in Onicha so as to avoid the sanctimonies, the dour certainties, of her parents and her brother. It was Grace who, after graduating from secondary school, would teach elementary school in Agueke, where people told stories of the destruction of their village by the white men with guns, stories she was not sure she believed, because they also told stories of mermaids appearing from the River Niger holding wads of crisp cash. It was Grace who, as one of a dozen or so women at the University College in Ibadan in 1953, would change her degree from chemistry to history after she heard, while drinking tea at the home of a friend, the story of Mr. Gboyega. The eminent Mr. Gboyega, a chocolate-skinned Nigerian, educated in London, distinguished expert on the history of the British Empire, had resigned in disgust when the West African Examinations Council began talking of adding African history to the curriculum, because he was appalled that African history would even be considered a subject. It was Grace who would ponder this story for a long time, with great sadness, and it would cause her to make a clear link between education and dignity, between the hard, obvious things that are printed in books and the soft, subtle things that lodge themselves in the soul. It was Grace who would begin to rethink her own schooling: How lustily she had sung on Empire Day, "God save our gracious king. Send him victorious, happy and glorious. Long to reign over us." How she had puzzled over words like "wallpaper" and "dandelions" in her textbooks, unable to picture them. How she had struggled with arithmetic problems that had to do with mixtures, because what was "coffee" and what was "chicory," and why did they have to be mixed? It was Grace who would begin to rethink her father's schooling and then hurry home to see him, his eyes watery with age, telling him she had not received all the letters she had ignored, saying amen when he prayed, and pressing her lips against his forehead. It was Grace who, driving past Agueke on her way to the university one day, would become haunted by the image of a destroyed village and would go to London and to Paris and to Onicha, sifting through moldy files in archives, reimagining the lives and smells of her grandmother's world, for the book she would write called *Pacifying with Bullets: A Reclaimed History of Southern Nigeria*. It was Grace who, in a conversation about the book with her fiancé, George Chikadibia—stylish graduate of King's College, Lagos, engineer-to-be, wearer of three-piece suits, expert ballroom dancer, who often said that a grammar school without Latin was like a cup of tea without sugar—understood that the marriage would not last when George told her that it was misguided of her to write about primitive culture instead of a worthwhile topic like African Alliances in the American-Soviet Tension. They would divorce in 1972, not because of the four miscarriages Grace had suffered but because she woke up sweating one night and realized that she would strangle George to death if she had to listen to one more rapturous monologue about his Cambridge days. It was Grace who, as she received faculty prizes, as she spoke to solemn-faced people at conferences about the Ijaw and Ibibio and Igbo and Efik peoples of Southern Nigeria, as she wrote commonsense reports for international organizations, for which she nevertheless received generous pay, would imagine her grandmother looking on with great amusement. It was Grace who, feeling an odd rootlessness in the later years of her life, surrounded by her awards, her friends, her garden of peer-less roses, would go to the courthouse in Lagos and officially change her first name from Grace to Afamefuna.

But on that day, as she sat at her grandmother's bedside in the fading evening light, Grace was not contemplating her future. She simply held her grandmother's hand, the palm thickened from years of making pottery.

Wendell Berry

# *Stand by Me*

WHEN JARRAT MARRIED Lettie in 1921 and bought the little place across the draw from our home place and started to pay for it, in that time that was already hard, years before the Depression, he had a life ahead of him, it seemed like, that was a lot different from the life he in fact was going to live. Jarrat was my brother, four years older than me, and I reckon I knew him as well as anybody did, which is not to say that what I knew was equal to what I didn't know.

But as long as Lettie lived, Jarrat was a happy man. As far as I could see, not that I was trying to see or in those days cared much, he and Lettie made a good couple. They were a pretty couple, I'll say that, before this world and its trouble had marked them. And they laid into the work together, going early and late, scraping and saving, and paying on their debt.

Tom was born the year after they married, Nathan two years later. And it seemed that Tom hadn't hardly begun to walk about on his own until Nathan was coming along in his tracks, just a step or two behind. They had pretty much the run of the world, Lettie and Jarrat being too busy for much in the way of parental supervision, at least between meals.

The hollow between the two places, that most people call Coulter Branch, before long was crisscrossed with boy-paths that went back and forth like shoestrings between the boys' house on one ridge and the old house on the other, where I lived with Mam and Pap. The boys lived at both houses, you might as well say. They'd drop down through the pasture and into the woods on one side, and down through the woods to the branch, and then up through the woods and the pasture on the other side, and they'd be in another place with a different house and kitchen and something different to eat. They had maybe half a dozen paths they'd worn across there, and all of them had names: the Dead Tree Path, I remember, and the Spring Path, and the Rock Fence Path.

And then, right in the midst of things going on the way they ought to have gone on forever, Lettie got sick and began to waste away. It was as serious as it could be, we could see that. And then, instead of belonging just to Jarrat to pay attention to, she began to belong to all of us. Dr. Markman was doing all he could for her, and then Mam and the other women around were cooking things to take to her and helping with her housework, and us others were hoping or praying or whatever we did, trying to help her to live, really just by wishing for her to. And then, without waiting for us to get ready, she died, and the boys all of a sudden, instead of belonging just to her and Jarrat, belonged to us all. Nathan was five years old, and Tom was seven.

And I was one of the ones that they belonged to. They belonged to me because I belonged to them. They thought so, and that made it so. The morning of their mother's funeral, to get them moved and out of the house before more sadness could take place, I put a team to the wagon and drove around the head of the hollow to get them. Mam had packed up their clothes and everything that was theirs. We loaded it all and them too onto the wagon, and I brought them home to the old house.

Jarrat wasn't going to be able to take care of them and farm too, and they didn't need to be over there in that loneliness with him. But Pap and Mam were getting on in years then. Pap, just by the nature of him, wasn't going to be a lot of help. And Mam, I could see, had her doubts.

Finally she just out with it. "Burley, I can be a grandmother, but I don't know if I can be a mother again or not. You're just going to have to help me."

She had her doubts about that, too. But it didn't prove too hard to bring about. I belonged to them because they needed me. From the time I brought them home with me, they stuck to me like burrs. A lot of the time we were a regular procession—me in front, and then Tom in my tracks just as close as he could get, and then Nathan in Tom's the same way. The year Lettie died I was thirty-four years old, still a young man in my thoughts and all, and I had places I needed to go by myself. But for a long time, getting away from those boys was a job. I'd have to hide and slip away or bribe them to let me go or wait till they were asleep. When I wanted to hunt or fish, the best way to be free of them was just to take them with me. By the time they got big enough to go on their own, we had traveled a many a mile together, day and night, after the hounds, and had spent a many an hour on the river.

The grass and weeds overgrew the paths across the hollow. The boys somehow knew better than to go over there where their mother was gone and their daddy was living by himself. It took them a while to go back there, even with me.

Jarrat did a fair job of batching. He kept the house clean, and he didn't change anything. He sort of religiously kept everything the way Lettie had fixed it. But as time went on, things changed in spite of him. He got busy and forgot to water the potted plants, and they died. And then gradually the other little things that had made it a woman's house wore out, or got lost, or broke. Finally it took on the bare, accidental look of the house of a man who would rather be outdoors, and then only Jarrat's thoughts and memories were there to remind him of Lettie.

Or so I guess. As I say, there was a lot about Jarrat that nobody in this world was ever going to know. I was worrying about him, which I hadn't ever done before, and I was going to worry about him for the rest of his life. I began to feel a little guilty about him, too. I had a lady friend, and by and by we began to come to an understanding. When I wanted company, I had friends. When I didn't want company, I had the woods and the creeks and the river. I had a good john-boat for fishing, and always a good hound or two or three.

Jarrat didn't have any of those things, not that he wanted them. In his dealings with other people he was strictly honest, I was always proud of him for that, and he was friendly enough. But he didn't deal with other people except when he had to. He was freer than you might have thought with acts of kindness when he knew somebody needed help. But he didn't want kindness for himself, though of course he needed it. He didn't want to be caught needing it.

After Lettie died, he wasn't the man he was before. He got like an old terrapin. He might come out of his shell now and again to say something beyond what the day's work required: "Hello," maybe, or he would compliment the weather. But if you got too close, he'd draw in again. Only sometimes, when he thought he was by himself, you'd catch him standing still, gazing nowhere.

What I know for sure he had in his life were sorrow, stubbornness, silence, and work. Work was his consolation, surely, just because it was always there to do and because he was so good at it. He had, I reckon, a gift for it. He loved the problems and the difficulties. He never hesitated about what to do. He never mislaid a lick. And half of his gift, if that was what it was, was endurance. He was swift and tough. When you tied in with him for a day's work, you had better have your ass in gear. Work was a fever with him. Anybody who loved it as much as he did didn't need to fish.

So when Tom and Nathan needed him the most, their daddy

didn't have much to offer. He wanted them around, he would watch over them when they were with us at work, he would correct and caution them when they needed it, but how could he console them when he couldn't console himself?

They were just little old boys. They needed their mother, was who they needed. But they didn't have her, and so they needed me. Sometimes I'd find one or the other of them off somewhere by himself, all sorrowful and little and lost, and there'd be nothing to do but try to *mother* him, just pick him up and hold him tight and carry him around awhile. Their daddy couldn't do it, and it was up to me.

I would make them laugh. It usually wasn't too hard. Nathan thought I was the funniest thing on record anyhow, and sometimes he would laugh at me even when I was serious. But I would sing,

*Turkey in the straw settin' on a log*
*All pooched out like a big bullfrog.*
*Poked him in the ass with a number nine wire*
*And down he went like an old flat tire.*

I would sing,

*Stuck my toe in a woodpecker hole,*
*In a woodpecker hole, in a woodpecker hole.*
*Woodpecker, he said, "Damn your soul,*
*Take it out, take it out, take it out!"*

I would sing one of them or some other one, and dance a few steps, raising a dust, and Nathan would get so tickled he couldn't stand up. Tom would try to hold his dignity, like an older brother, but he would be ready to bust; all you had to do was poke him in the short ribs, and down he would go, too. What raising they got, they got mainly from their grandma and me. It was ours to do if anybody was going to do it, and somehow we got them raised.

·   ·   ·

To spare Grandma, and when they were out of school, we kept the boys at work with us. That way they learned to work. They played at it, and while they were playing at it they were doing it. And they were helping, too. We generally had a use for them, and so from that time on they knew we needed them, and they were proud to be helping us make a living.

Jarrat nor Pap wouldn't have paid them anything. Jarrat said they were working for themselves, if they worked. And Pap, poking them in the ribs to see if they would argue, and they did, said they ate more than they were worth. But I paid them ten cents a day, adjusted to the time they actually worked. Sometimes they'd get three cents, sometimes seven. I'd figure up and pay off every Saturday. One time when I paid him all in pennies, Nathan said, "Haven't you got any of them big white ones?"

They worked us, too. They didn't have minds for nothing. Sometimes, if the notion hit them, they'd fartle around and pick at each other and get in the way until their daddy or grandpa would run them off. "*Get* the hell out of here! Go to the house!"

But they wouldn't go to the house. They'd slip away into the woods, or go to Port William, or down to the river. And since they were careful to get back to the house by dinnertime or suppertime, nobody would ask where they'd been. Unless they got in trouble, which they sometimes did.

I worried about them. I'd say, "Boys, go to the river if you have to, but don't go *in* it." Or I'd say, "Stay *out* of that damned river, now. We ain't got time to go to your funeral."

But of course they did go in the river. They were swimming, I think, from frost to frost, just like I would have at their age. Just like I in fact *did* at their age.

When they were little, you could always see right through Nathan. He didn't have any more false faces than a glass of water. Tom you couldn't always tell about. Maybe because Nathan was coming along so close behind him, Tom needed to keep some things to himself. It did him good to think he knew some things you didn't know. He wanted to call his life his own. He wasn't dishonest. If you could get him to look straight at you, then you had him.

As long as they were little, there would be times when they would be needing their mother, and who would be in the gap but only me? One or the other or both of them would be sitting close to me in the evening while it was getting dark, snuggled up like a chicken to the old hen, and I would be doing all I could, and falling short. They changed me. Before, I was often just on the loose, carefree as a dog fox, head as empty as a gourd. Afterwards, it seemed like my heart was bigger inside than outside.

We got them grown up to where they weren't needy little boys anymore. They were still boys. They were going to be boys awhile yet, but they were feeling their strength. They were beginning to find in their selves what before they had needed from us. Tom was maybe a little slower at it than he might have been, Nathan a little faster; Nathan was coming behind and was in a hurry.

It was a wonderful thing to watch that Tom grow up. For a while there, after he was getting to be really useful, he was still an awkward, kind of weedy, mind-wandery boy who still needed some watching. To him, young as he was, it must have seemed he stayed that way a long time. But before long, as it seemed to me, he had gathered his forces together, body and mind. He got to be some account on his own. He could see what needed to be done and go ahead and do it. He got graceful, and he was a good-looking boy, too.

And then, the year he was sixteen, a little edge crept up between him and his daddy. It wasn't very much in the open at first, wasn't admitted really, but there it was. I thought, *Uh-oh,* for I hated to see it, and I knew there wasn't much to be done about it. Tom was feeling his strength, he was coming into his own, and Jarrat that year was forty-seven years old. When he looked at Tom he got the message— from where he was, the only way was down—and he didn't like it.

Well, one afternoon when we were well along in the tobacco cutting, Tom took it in his head he was going to try the old man. Jarrat was cutting in the lead, as he was used to doing, and Tom got into the next row and lit out after him. He stayed with him, too, for a while. He put the pressure on. He made his dad quiet down and lay into his work.

But Tom had misestimated. The job was still above his breakfast. Jarrat wasn't young anymore, but he was hard and long-practiced. He kept his head and rattled Tom, and he beat him clean. And then he couldn't stop himself from drawing the fact to Tom's attention.

Tom went for him then, making fight. They were off a little way from the rest of us, and both of them were thoroughly mad. Before we could get there and get them apart, Jarrat had just purely whipped the hell out of Tom. He ought to've quit before he did, but once he was mad he didn't have it in him to give an inch. It was awful. Ten minutes after it was over, even Jarrat knew it was awful, but then it was too late.

It was a day, one of several, I'm glad I won't have to live again. Tom was too much a boy yet to get in front where he wanted to be but too much a man to stay and be licked. He had to get out from under his daddy's feet and onto his own. And so he made a bundle of his clothes and went away. Afterwards, because the old ones were so grieved, me too, Nathan too, the house was like a house where somebody had died.

Because he didn't need much and asked little, Tom found a place right away with an old couple by the name of Whitlow over on the other side of the county, far enough away to make him separate from us. I knew he would do all right, and he did. He knew how to work; and the use of his head, that was already coming to him, came fast once he got out on his own. He began to make a name for himself: a good boy, a good hand.

When we had found out where he was, Nathan and I would catch a ride on a rainy day or a Sunday and go over to see him, or we'd see him occasionally in town. After he got his feet under him and was feeling sure of himself, he would come over on a Sunday afternoon now and again to see his grandma and grandpa. In all our minds, he had come into a life of his own that wasn't any longer part of ours. To the old ones, who had given up their ownership of him by then, and their right to expect things from him, every one of those visits was a lovely gift, and they made over him and honored him as a guest.

He stayed at the Whitlows' through the crop year of 1940. Mr. Whitlow died that summer. After the place was sold and Mrs. Whitlow settled in town, Tom struck a deal with Ernest Russet from up about Sycamore. Ernest and Naomi Russet were good people, we had known them a long time, and they had a good farm. Going there was a step up in the world for Tom. He soon found favor with the Russets, which not everybody could have done, and before long, having no children of their own, they'd made practically a son of him.

After Tom had been with them awhile, the Russets invited us to come for Sunday dinner. Jarrat wouldn't go, of course, but Nathan and I did. The Russets' preacher, Brother Milby, and his wife were there too, a spunky couple. I took a great liking to Mrs. Milby. It was a good dinner and we had a good time. Ernest Russet was the right man for Tom, no mistake about that. He was a fine farmer. The right young man could learn plenty from him.

By the time he went to the Russets, Tom was probably as near to the right young man as the country had in it. He had got his growth and filled out, and confidence had come into his eyes. He was a joy to look at.

One Sunday afternoon after the weather was warm and the spring work well started, he paid us a visit. Grandpa had died the summer before, so now it was just Grandma and Nathan and me still at home, and it was a sadder place. But we were glad to see Tom and to be together; we sat out on the porch and talked a long time.

Tom got up finally as if to start his hitchhike back to the Russets, and so I wasn't quite ready when he said he thought he'd go over to see his dad.

That fell into me with sort of a jolt. I hadn't been invited, but I said, "Well, I'll go with you."

So we went. We crossed the hollow, and clattered up onto the back porch, and Tom knocked on the kitchen door. Jarrat must have been in the kitchen, for it wasn't but seconds until there he was, his left hand still on the doorknob, and with a surprised look on his face. Myself, I wasn't surprised yet, but I was expecting to be. I could feel my hair trying to rise up under my hat. I took a glance at Tom's face, and he was grinning at Jarrat. My hair relaxed and laid down peacefully again when Tom stuck out his hand. It was a big hand he stuck out, bigger than mine, bigger than Jarrat's. Jarrat looked down at that hand like it was an unusual thing to see on the end of a man's arm. He looked up at Tom again and grinned back. And then he reached out and took Tom's hand and shook it.

So they made it all right. And so when the war broke out and Tom was called to the army and had to go, he could come and say freely a proper good-bye to his dad.

It wasn't long after Tom got drafted until Nathan turned eighteen, and damned if he didn't go volunteer. I was surprised, but I ought not to've been. Nathan probably could have got deferred, since his brother was already gone and farmers were needed at home, and I reckon I was counting on that. But he had reasons to go, too, that were plain enough.

Nathan and Jarrat never came to an actual fight. Nathan, I think, had Tom's example in mind, and he didn't want to follow it. He was quieter turned than Tom, less apt to give offense. But Jarrat was hard for his boys to get along with. He just naturally took up too much of the room they needed to grow in. He was the man in the lead, the man going away while everybody else was still coming. His way was the right way, which in fact it pret' near always was, but he didn't have the patience of a yearling mule.

"Let's go!" he'd say. If you were at it with him and you hesitated a minute: "Let's go! Let's go!"

When we were young and he would say that, I'd say back to him,

*Les Go's dead and his wife's a widder.*
*You be right good and you might get her.*

But nobody was going to say that back to him anymore, not me, much less Nathan.

After Jarrat's fight with Tom, I would now and again try to put in a word for Nathan. "Why don't you let him alone? Give him a little headroom. Give him time to be ready."

And Jarrat would say, "Be ready, hell! Let him be started."

It didn't take much of that, I knew, to be a plenty. When Nathan came back from the war his own man, Jarrat did get out of his way, and they could work together, but for the time being, Nathan needed to be gone. Of course, he got a bellyful of bossing in the army, but it at least didn't come from his dad. He also had a brotherly feeling that he ought to go where Tom had gone. Grandma was dead by then. There was nothing holding him. I reckon he went because he thought he had to, but I didn't want him to. For one thing, we'd be left shorthanded. For another, I would miss him. For another, I was afraid.

As it turned out, Nathan never saw Tom again. They kept Nathan on this side till nearly the end of the war, but they gave Tom some training and taught him to drive a bulldozer and shipped him straight on across the waters into the fight. He was killed the next year. I know a few little details of how it happened, but they don't matter.

It came about, anyhow, that in just a couple of years the old house was emptied of everybody but me. It took me a while to get used to being there by myself. When I would go in to fix my dinner, or at night, there wouldn't be a sound. I could *hear* the quiet. And however quiet I tried to be, it seemed to me I rattled. I didn't like the quiet, for it made me sad, and so did the little noises I made in it. For a while I couldn't bring myself to trap the mice, I so needed to have something living there besides me. All my life I've hunted and fished alone, even worked alone. I never minded being by myself outdoors. But to be alone in the house, a place you might say is used to talk and the sounds of somebody stirring about in it all day, that was lonesome. As I reckon Jarrat must have found out a long time ago and, like himself, just left himself alone to get used to it. I've been, all in all, a lucky man, for the time would be again when the old house would be full of people, but that was long a-coming. For a while there it was just Jarrat and me living alone together, it seemed to me, he in his house on one side of the hollow, me in mine on the other. I could see his house from my house, and he could see mine from his. But we didn't meet in either house, his or mine. We met in a barn or in a field wherever the day's work was going to start. When quitting time came we went our ways separately home. Of course, by living apart we were keeping two houses more or less alive, and maybe there was some good in that.

The difference between us was that I wasn't at home all the time. When the work would let up, or on Saturday evenings and Sundays, for I just flat refused to work late on Saturday or much at all on Sunday, I'd be off to what passed with me for social life, or to the woods or the river. But Jarrat was at home every day. *Every* day. He never went as far as Port William except to buy something he needed.

If you work about every day with somebody you've worked with all your life, you'd be surprised how little you need to talk. Oh, we swapped work with various ones—Big Ellis, the Rowanberrys, and others—and that made for some sociable times along, and there would be good talk then. But when it was just Jarrat and me, we would sometimes work without talking a whole day, or maybe two. And so when he got the government's letter about Tom, he didn't say but two words. We were working here at my place. After dinner, when he walked into the barn, carrying the letter in his hand, he said, "Sit down."

I sat down. He handed me the letter, and it felt heavy in my hands as a stone. After I read it—"killed in action"—and handed it back, the whole damned English language just flew away in the air like a flock of blackbirds.

For a long time neither one of us moved. The daily sounds of the world went on, sparrows in the barn lot, somebody's bull way off, the wind in the eaves, but around us was this awful, awful silence that didn't have one word in it.

I looked at Jarrat finally. He was standing there blind as a statue. He had Tom's life all inside him now, as once it had been all inside Lettie. Now it was complete. Now it was finished.

And then, for the first and last time, I said to Jarrat, "Let's go." The day's work was only half finished. Having nothing else we could do, we finished it.

What gets you is the knowledge, that sometimes can fall on you in a clap, that the dead are gone absolutely from this world. As has been said around here over and over again, you are not going to see them here anymore, ever. Whatever was done or said before is done or said for good. Any questions you think you ought to've asked while you had a chance are never going to be answered. The dead know, and you don't.

And yet their absence puts them with you in a way they never were before. You even maybe know them better than you did before. They stay with you, and in a way you go with them. They don't live on *in* your heart, but your heart knows them. As your heart gets bigger on the inside, the world gets bigger on the outside. If the dead were alive only in this world, you would forget them, looks like, as soon as they die. But you remember them, because they always were living in the other, bigger world while they lived in this little one, and this one and the other one are the same. You can't see this with your eyes looking straight ahead. It's with your side vision, so to speak, that you see it. The longer I live, and the better acquainted I am among the dead, the better I see it. I am telling what I know.

It's our separatedness and our grief that break the world in two. Back when Tom got killed, and the word came, I had never thought of such things. That time would have been hard enough, even if I had thought of them. Because I hadn't, it was harder.

That night after supper I lit the lantern and walked over to Jarrat's and sat with him in the kitchen until bedtime. I wasn't invited. I was a volunteer, I reckon, like Nathan. If it had been just me and I needed company, which I did, I could have walked to town and sat with the talkers in the poolroom or the barbershop. But except that I would go to sit with him, Jarrat would have sat there in his sorrow entirely by himself and stared at the wall or the floor. I anyhow denied him that.

I went back every night for a long time. There was nothing else to do. There wasn't a body to be spoken over and buried to bring people together, and to give Tom's life a proper conclusion in Port William. His body was never going to be in Port William again. It was buried in some passed-over battlefield in Italy, somewhere none of us had ever been and would never go. The word was passed around, of course. People were sorry, and they told us. The neighbor women brought food, as they do. But mainly there was just the grieving, and mainly nobody here to do it but Jarrat and me.

There was a woman lived here, just out the road, a good many years ago. She married a man quite a bit older—well, he was an old man, you just as well say—and things went along and they had a little boy. In four or five years the old man died. After that, you can imagine, the little boy was all in all to his mother. He was her little man of the house, as she called him, and in fact he was the world to her. And then, when he wasn't but nine or ten years old, the boy took awfully sick one winter, and he died, and we buried him out there on the hill at Port William beside his old daddy.

We knew that the woman was grieved to death, as we say, and everybody did for her as they could. What we didn't know was that she really was grieving herself to death. It's maybe a little hard to believe that people can die of grief, but they do.

After she died, the place had to be sold. I went out there with Big Ellis and several others to set the place to rights and get the tools and the household stuff set out for the auction. When we got to the room that had been the little boy's, it was like opening a grave. It had been kept just the way it was when he died, except she had gathered up and put there everything she'd found that reminded her of him: all his play pretties, every broom handle he'd ridden for a stick horse, every rock or feather or string she knew he had played with. I still remember the dread we felt just going into that room, let alone moving the things, or throwing them away. Some of them we had to throw away.

I understood her then. I understood her better after Tom was dead. When a young man your heart knows and loves is all of a sudden gone, never to come back, the whole place reminds you of him everywhere you look. You dread to touch anything for fear of changing it. You fear the time you know is bound to come, when the look of the place will be changed entirely, and if the dead came back they would hardly know it, or not recognize it at all.

Even so, this place is not a keepsake just to look at and remember. You can't stop just because you're carrying a load of grief and would like to stop, or don't care if you go on or not. Jarrat nor I either didn't stop. This world was still asking things of us that we had to give.

It was maybe the animals most of all that kept us going, the good animals we depended on, that depended on us: our work mules, the cattle, the sheep, the hogs, even the chickens. They were a help to us because they didn't know our grief but just quietly lived on, suffering what they suffered, enjoying what they enjoyed, day by day. We took care of them, we did what had to be done, we went on.

Jess Row

*Sheep May Safely Graze*

I T WAS A tiny leak, no more than a pinprick, and a few eyedroppers' full of gas that killed my youngest daughter, Jolie, at summer camp when she was eight years old. She was in a motorboat on a lake, Lake St. Clair, learning to waterski. The fuel line ruptured; gas leaked into the bilge, and when the driver started the engine the boat exploded. The two other girls next to her on the rear seat, in life-jackets, also died. The driver, who should have checked the fuel tanks, who should have smelled the gas—a nineteen-year-old, named Rick Paradisi—suffered third-degree burns over most of his body and survived for three months in a coma.

The story was in the newspapers all up and down the East Coast that July. In our neighborhood, at the supermarket, at the filling station, we were briefly famous. Nobody would take our money. The front hallway was lined with flowers. Strangers mowed the lawn and picked up our dry cleaning.

Then something else happened. It may have been the McDonald's massacre, or the Democratic convention where Mondale was nominated. It was the summer of 1984: the world was full of unexpected calamities. Mercifully, we were forgotten. The film footage of my life, which records this event in the glare and jagged shadows of midsummer, dims, grows grainy, goes dark.

I can offer only commonplaces.

A certain stony afternoon light in the sky outside my office window. The aftertaste of a thousand watery cups of coffee. My hands and feet were always cold; I wore gloves and wool socks in May. At night I turned on every light in the house: I hated the look of a shadowy corner.

Wherever I was alone, in the car, on the Metro, in my study, I had to have music playing. I went out and bought a Sony Walkman expressly for this purpose. Rossini, Stravinsky, Gounod, Telemann: it didn't matter. At work my secretary slid papers under my elbow with little notes attached: *Sign here. This is due next Monday. Call Evans at the GAO.* It was as if, by degrees, without noticing, I'd become deaf, and everyone around me was too polite to point it out.

In those days—before I took early retirement, did some desultory computer consulting, and finally stopped working for good, in 2002—I ran the small in-house publishing office at the National Security Agency. This was an administrative post, and I was a civilian, not an agent. Nonetheless, for obvious reasons, I had a very high security clearance. All twelve of us did: copy editors, designers, secretaries, technicians. A jammed page pulled out of a Xerox machine in that office might be worth a hundred thousand dollars. I published our most sensitive materials: the reports that went to the Joint Chiefs of Staff. No one else was allowed to see them. I stood in front of the printer myself, and carried them in a plain manila envelope to the rear entrance of the Old Executive Office Building.

On the rare occasions when someone asks about my career, I offer a standard, canned response: I have nothing to add to the historical record. I suppose this makes me look like the proverbial cog in the wheel, the faceless bureaucrat. (I should know: Rachel and I were German majors in college; we read *Der Prozess* in the same seminar.) But I have to accept that silent—almost imperceptible—humiliation, because the more unpleasant truth is that I paid very little attention to the content of the materials we published. I had trouble remembering specifics even from day to day. It wasn't necessary, and it would have been distracting. I was an editor, a proofreader. Innocent people, civilians, can die, *have* died, over a misplaced comma in a sensitive document, let alone a badly chosen word, like *friendly* or *unfortunate.* In intelligence you come to appreciate that behind every word on a sheet of paper is a vulnerable human body. My counterpart at the CIA once showed me a file of examples, with photographs. For years I kept a typed quotation from Wittgenstein on the bulletin board above my desk: *Whereof one cannot speak, thereof one must be silent.*

I had a therapist, of course, assigned by my doctor. At each session he tried to explain to me what stage of the grieving process I was experiencing. I couldn't help myself: I kept insisting that he give me an exact definition of each word he used, what function it served, what could be considered X and not Y. This last point particularly bothered me. If I had a bad day at work, and missed my stop, and then barked at the cabdriver for running a red light and refused to tip him, was that grief? If I found myself unexpectedly tearing up during the final scene of *Un Ballo in Maschera,* having to grope in Rachel's handbag for a tissue, was that, too, grief? And why should I victimize myself by reliving these feelings, by groping to find equivalents for them in words? Wasn't it enough to have had the feelings in the first place?

The advantage of this calamity, I told him, was that it was utterly arbitrary: a clean break, a window opened and closed. There was no way Rachel and I could blame ourselves, no way we could associate ourselves with it at all. Jolie had existed and one day had ceased to exist. We had no interest in lawsuits or safety campaigns or any of the other desiderata of grieving parents. Our mourning, I said, was purely and simply that. A clean wound. One day it would be healed.

He said he found it interesting that I thought the same rules that applied to everyone else wouldn't apply to me.

I lost my temper. I told him I thought it was a sham, these systems, these lists, these processes he kept proposing. An emotion, I said, isn't an abstraction, isn't an object, can't be verified, and therefore can't be categorized. I told him he should stop playing God.

He laughed, and said I should read Wittgenstein. That was the end of therapy for me.

Of Rachel during all that time I have only one memory: perched on the edge of Alex's bed, still in her librarian's brown mules, drying her hands on a towel, and telling a story, whispering it, into the darkened room where both children slept. Whether she made the stories up beforehand or improvised on the spot I have no idea, but she spoke without hesitation, without a text, for half an hour or forty-five minutes at a time. One day it was a romance between two hedgehogs in Scotland and the next a unicorn searching for her mother in the Himalayas. It was her unshakable confidence in the happy outcomes of her stories, I like to think, that saved Alex and Merrill some of the pain of the randomness of this one.

In my own way I too was an undistracted parent. I could wait an hour in the pickup line at school, or sit through a Parents' Association meeting, or spend an entire morning at a swim meet, without once checking my watch, without wishing I had brought the paper. Reagan was reelected. It was hard to summon up the expected outrage.

I should say—by way of disclaimer? of apology?—that I've never held particularly strong political beliefs. In this I take after my father, the postmaster of Sheffield, Connecticut, who sometimes would come out onto the post office floor and collect mail from waiting customers just for the pleasure of canceling it at his desk by hand. I shared with him a special appreciation for the beauty of the impersonal gesture. An old woman in Topeka receives her Social Security check every month not because anyone loves her or even remembers her name. The crossing guard stopping traffic in front of the elementary school need not recognize a single child who scampers past. One's human inadequacies are not the point. Efficiency, permanence, and careful design, I would have said, are the basis of real human charity and kindness.

If it was grief that I was feeling—and I still hate to use the word—it was this sense of the implacable nature of these structures that I wrapped around myself, like a blanket, or a cocoon. The momentary life of sensations, feelings, opinions, went right through me. Just existing, for the time being, was enough. I paid the mortgage, I bought groceries, I balanced the checkbook. I slept deeply and dreamlessly in the arms of a beautiful machine. It was a not entirely unpleasant existence.

In November of 1985, during an early cold snap, a homeless man named Jevon Morris froze to death on a grate downtown, in front of the National Archives. He stayed there, frozen, through the morning rush hour, with hundreds passing by on their way to work or to the Mall and the museums. They walked past a heap of rags, a motionless form wrapped in an oily blanket, unable to tell whether it—he, she—was alive or dead. Finally, around noon, the smell of putrefaction was so strong that a passing policeman noticed it.

I read the story in the newspaper sitting at our kitchen table after work, drinking tea, listening to WGMS. It was Rachel's day to pick up the children. When I finished I found I couldn't lift my arms from the table. I sat paralyzed, my elbows resting on the outspread paper, my eyes locked on the windowsill, where, I noticed, someone or something had knocked a knuckle-sized crater in the wood. The sill jutted out a few inches from the wall; it had an old-fashioned fleur-de-lis carved molding underneath, and had been painted over probably twenty times in the sixty years of the house's life, so that the original edges and fine detail had long since disappeared. I myself had applied the most recent coat, seven years before. Whatever it was had been sharp enough to dig through that quarter-inch skin of paint and gouge into the bare wood, leaving a few tiny splinters sticking out. It was, in all likelihood, Alex's fault. He sat nearest the windowsill at dinnertime, and he was the kind of careless child who wasn't above putting his soccer cleats on in the front hall, or idly swinging something hard and heavy—a pair of scissors, say—enough to chip paint, or break glass.

The radio, at that moment, was playing the third movement of Charles Ives's first string quartet, *adagio cantabile,* with its odd, stately movement between simple major triads and dissonant flatted fifths. Its inability to stay on one track seemed to mock me. As I stared at it, that little divot of raw wood grew larger and larger; I felt that I could look into it and through it, that I might be swallowed up inside it, and that in there, from the other side, came screams of ceaseless pain. Without seeing it, precisely, I knew what was there: a human face, a black man's face, pressed up against the other side of the wall, not three feet away from my own. And behind him were other faces, other bodies, packed in tight. In the space between the interior latex paint of that wall and the cedar shingles outside, I felt certain, were countless bodies, unable to move.

I know it sounds absurd. In my entire life, my thoroughly ordinary existence in a leafy, mostly peaceful, sheltered corner of the planet, I've never again experienced anything like it. If I were given to hyperbole I might say that I had looked through a window into the world's wounded soul.

I came out of the daydream, went to the sink, poured out my tea, and quickly took a swig of Rachel's double-strength coffee, cold, straight from the carafe. The sudden shock of the caffeine would do it, I thought, would wake me up, finally, from the months of stupor, from my collapsing will, now turning into midday hallucinations, bizarre narcissistic fantasies. Either this, I thought, or a doctor for real, a psychiatrist, someone with a prescription pad and admitting privileges.

That didn't happen. Instead, almost unwillingly, I began to think about procedures, systems, chains of command. Whose job it was, for example, to write the rules that dictated to the Capitol Police when they should and should not patrol the streets for the sleeping homeless. I never doubted that there was such a policy. We are extremely good at writing policies in this city. And we are also good at understanding the difference between an empty rule and an enforceable one.

The radio announcer that day had a strange sense of humor. Immediately after the Ives came the Eugene Ormandy recording of Bach's "Sheep May Safely Graze," its treacly melody like a jingle from an old commercial. Ordinarily I would have risen and turned it off. But the chiming chords had the strangest, most inexplicable effect on me. I began to think of his childhood, of Jevon Morris's childhood. I saw him in his kindergarten class, on a threadbare carpet, kneeling, separate from the others. The teacher, I knew, had just shouted at him, had humiliated him, for something he hadn't done. Someone had wadded up a little ball of white bread and thrown it at him, and it was still there, stuck to his collar. He was blushing fiercely, even to the tips of his ears, and throttling back a sob.

As the music shifted into minor chords I found my eyes pooling with tears.

Someone is responsible, I thought. Someone knows why this has happened, and I will punish him.

On Wednesday of the week before Thanksgiving I took our office's box of donated canned goods to a shelter inside an abandoned school on P Street. It was all very organized; a girl not much older than Merrill took the box and started systematically unpacking it, putting each can and box into a different marked bin, one for each food group. I stared at her for a moment, at the extraordinary quickness of her slim, pale arms, and the way she methodically brushed her sandy hair out of her eyes every time she bent down. Her expressionless competence. Someone had told her that the world could be saved this way. I turned and walked up the stairs, past the sign marked *Paid Shelter Staff Only*, and knocked on the director's door.

Her name was Jenny Parker; she was about thirty-five, in jeans and a hooded sweatshirt and ripped sneakers. The ashtray on her desk was full. It wasn't an office, of course, but an old classroom, with chairs piled up against one wall. One of the windows had a pane missing; someone had tried to cover it with a piece of cardboard and Scotch tape, which had, of course, flapped away. It would be polite to say that she looked like she hadn't slept for a number of days. The circles under her eyes were as dark as bruises.

Listen, I said, I'm not here to take up your time. But I'm just wondering, as a citizen, if there's anything we can do on a bigger level. On a national level. I mean, this is an emergency. People are dying in the streets.

I could tell, in the moment that it took her to respond, that she was trying hard to stop herself from saying something derisive, that it took an effort for her to control the muscles that wanted to twist her lips into a bleak and skeletal grin.

Well, she said, we appreciate whatever you can give us here. We need all the grassroots support we can get. Right now we can only keep the heat on in the building for twelve hours of the day. Six at night to six in the morning. I haven't been paid in a month and a half.

I can write you a check right now.

Well, fine, she said. We appreciate that. But there is a bill, actually, if you're interested. It's in the Senate right now, in committee. To introduce a line item for homeless services into the HUD budget for the first time. It's a lost cause, but you're welcome to write a letter if you like. You work for the government, don't you?

Why is it a lost cause?

Oh, she said, the secretary doesn't support it. Frank Murphy. He's your typical Republican troglodyte from Idaho. He doesn't understand why a Vietnam vet in a wheelchair, on disability for twenty years, missing all but three teeth, can't get a job. Sorry if I'm offending you.

No, I said, I'm not an appointee. Civil service for fifteen years.

Yeah. She looked at her watch and began checking things off on a clipboard. I'd bet you work out at Langley, she said. That would be my first guess.

Why do you say that?

Because of your eyes, she said, without looking up. I grew up here. I should know.

I did my research. I read the reports in *Congressional Quarterly* and the *National Journal* and the Hill newsletters. What she had said was true, broadly speaking. Murphy had used his allies in the House to cut off discussion of the line item in committee before the Democrats had had a chance to pounce on it. He'd been unsuccessful. There had been three days of hearings, a whole stream of activists and homeless people and lobbyists of all shapes and sizes. Hardly any of it made the news, of course, because it was all doomed in advance: an item never makes it into a department's budget without the secretary's support. Humiliation, in this case, hadn't done a bit of good. The final vote on the bill had been delayed until January, a last-ditch attempt by the Democrats to put pressure on the White House over the Christmas holiday. Politically speaking, that year, it was one lost cause among many.

Next to one article—"Homeless Abandoned a Second Time"—I found a small, grainy photograph: a middle-aged, fair-haired man, with a long jaw and a pronounced V-shaped wrinkle in his forehead—a perpetually pained look, a man who hated to have his picture taken. He had made a small fortune consolidating stockyards; he'd chaired the Idaho Chamber of Commerce and the state GOP. There was more, but I brought out my nail scissors and cut out the picture, leaving the rest in the wastebasket. Fearing the newsprint would rub off, I slid it carefully into a nylon holder in my wallet, next to my library card, just opposite a family picture, taken in our backyard the week after Jolie was born.

The gun came from Tim's Hunting Supply, far out on Rockville Pike, near Gaithersburg. It was a .38 Police Special, and it cost $150, including the Maryland registration and license. I used a false address in Bethesda I'd gotten out of the phone book. When I told the man behind the counter I'd never fired a pistol before, hoping he would at least show me how to load it, he shook his head and handed me a gun-safety pamphlet.

On my way back into the District I pulled off Georgia Avenue into a disused parking lot behind a dry cleaner's and took the pistol out of its box. In the store, on a flannel mat on the counter beside three other guns, it had seemed small, thin-barreled, pedestrian. A sensible starter gun, the man had said, you can get the ammo anywhere, it's foolproof, never jams. He looked like he wished he had somewhere else to be.

In my hand, now, it felt heavy enough to pull my hand to the floor.

Am I capable of this, I wondered, am I capable of murder? A month had elapsed, now, since Jevon Morris's death. It was early December; the children had two weeks left until winter vacation. The next weekend we would caravan out to Turkey Run Farm with two other families to pick our own Christmas trees, an old tradition by now. And I had grown used to the memory of that afternoon, that strange vision, a gnawing stomachache of an obligation unmet. It wouldn't let me rest. I was afflicted with compassion, I thought. I was carrying it around me like tuberculosis.

I wrapped my left hand around my right, holding the pistol in a position of prayer. The longer I held it, the heavier it became, until I felt—I swear—that it could carry my whole body with it, that it would lead me wherever it wanted.

Frank Murphy's house was a small white-brick Cape Cod on Ellicott Street, near New Mexico Avenue and the Russian embassy, on the boundary of Rock Creek Park. The houses on Ellicott are built high on the slope, high enough to look out over the treetops across the park and see the Washington Monument and the Capitol dome. Many of them have garages built into the hill at street level, but Murphy's, as it happened, did not. He would park his car—or walk the long downhill slope from the Metro—and approach the stone steps up to his house on foot.

In December in Washington the light begins to fail at quarter of four; by four-thirty it is completely dark. I knew his face only from photographs. In order to make sure it was him I would have to be no more than ten feet away.

I left work as soon as I could, and parked in front of the house next door at five after five. Rachel had promised the children macaroni and cheese with cut-up hot dogs for dinner, and I had promised I would bring home ice cream after the meeting, by eight at the latest. Neapolitan ice cream, Merrill was particular about that, a brick of it, from the High's dairy store at Connecticut and Woodley Road.

When he approached, I thought, I would get out of the car, walk as close as possible, shoot once, at his chest, get back into the car, and drive away. At the corner I would pause, momentarily, roll down the passenger-side window, and throw the gun over the rail into the woods. That was all. If I was followed, if I was caught, I would not resist, I would not plead innocence. That was all I knew. As soon as I switched off the car an extraordinary calm descended over me; I could feel, or imagined I could feel, not just my heartbeat, but the tidal push-pull of blood traveling from my heart to the tiniest capillaries of my fingers and toes, and receding back again.

The car I drove in those years was a 1982 Toyota Tercel station wagon, dark blue, with vinyl upholstery. It was the first new car Rachel and I had owned. I can describe it in intimate detail: the four-speed automatic transmission that lasted ten years, the parking brake that tended to stick on cold winter nights, the oil light blinking at random. By that December it had accumulated the dents and stains of three years' hard use in a family with young children. There was, for example, a tear in the ceiling fabric where someone had jammed a loose tent pole on a camping trip two summers back. I was in the habit of carrying coffee to work in a thermos that once had leaked on the passenger seat, and that particular odor always lingered, no matter how many times we used shampoo and hung air fresheners off the dashboard.

It had no cassette player, of course, and I didn't trust the radio at that hour, didn't want to hear traffic reports and news bulletins, the bustle of a city tidying up its day. So I had brought with me my Walkman, that delightful invention, and looped its headphones around my neck, so that the music would play sotto voce, underneath the sound of cars swishing by, doors slamming, leather soles clacking on the sidewalk. The cassette I had selected—need I even say this? should I have to explain everything?—was the Eroica Symphony, Leonard Bernstein conducting.

At quarter of seven I heard the unmistakable chugging of a car downshifting, and the white glare of headlights came up over my shoulders and raked across the dashboard. A tan Mercury sedan slowed three car lengths ahead of me, and backed, at a creep, into an open spot. The driver had to correct his turn twice; even so, he left the rear of the car sticking out six inches too far from the curb, at an almost insouciant angle.

I disentangled the headphones from my neck and opened the door as quietly as I could. The gun was in my right hand. I had on a pair of thin green cotton gloves, and as I moved out into the cold I realized sweat had soaked through the palms and fingers. It was as if I'd dipped my hands in ice water. Instinctively I shoved the gun into the waistband of my pants and dug my hands into the pockets of my jacket, balling them into fists. I was afraid they might become numb.

It shouldn't have surprised me that the man who stood up out of his car looked quite different from his photograph. He had gained weight, recently; his jacket flapped open on either side of his belly, too tight to button, and his pants looked as if they had been cinched at the waist. As he came up the sidewalk he transferred his briefcase from one hand to the other and ran his fingers through his hair, which was badly, unmistakably dyed, several shades darker than his natural color.

I've spent my life surrounded by federal bureaucrats and the unlucky outsiders, the appointees, who oversee them. I've seen the former executives dashing around with charts and graphs, with turquoise bracelets and onyx pinkie rings; the buzz-cut ex-marines who want to take you out for barbecue and Jack and Cokes, the holy-eyed Mormons with the crates of Pepsi and the LDS Christmas cards. Over time—if they last long enough—all of them are defeated by Washington. They exchange their monogrammed briefcases for navy blue duffel bags; they enroll in wine-tasting classes and buy subscriptions to the Kennedy Center. They learn the unhurried pace of their secretaries, and the names of all the security guards and the janitors. Their faces take on a certain placid softness that is easy to confuse with mere slack disappointment.

Never have I seen one as undone as Frank Murphy. Whatever pallid and insubstantial comforts he took from the world in his former life were now gone. He walked with a slight rolling motion, from side to side, as if buffeted by winds only he could feel. Everything about him seemed to express a certain muted panic, a wild grasping for reassurance.

I wouldn't call it pity, this feeling I had. Pity is far too weak a word. I was gripped with a terrible feeling that this stranger, this contemptible specimen, was someone I had known all my life. I was enmeshed; I was caught. But I had already stood up out of the car, and he could see me; it was too late to drive away. I had to complete the plan. I walked toward him, crossing the sidewalk at a slight angle, keeping my hands in my pockets, out of sight.

I lost my dog, I said. He ran off with his leash. It's never happened before.

He stopped walking and stared at me, holding his briefcase with both hands, protectively, at crotch level. His eyes seemed to rotate in their sockets, as if straining to establish parallax, to see me from the proper angle. His nose twitched. He gave a little ghostly cough, a whispery expulsion of breath.

Haven't seen him, he said. Sure he came up this way? He'll be in the park by now. That's what they all do. Run toward the park.

His breath stank of the kind of cheap red wine served with Triscuits and blocks of white cheese. He had been at a retirement party. I knew it immediately. It was what they served at a secretary's retirement party, alongside candied almonds and white layer cake.

You ought to yell for him, he said. Shouldn't you? What's his name?

Her name, I said. Trixie.

*Trixie,* he shouted, in a high, reedy, strangling voice. He clasped his briefcase between his knees and cupped his hands around his mouth. I had to join in. *Trixie,* we both shouted, and listened to the reverberations dying away, and the faint hiss of traffic on the Parkway, invisible in the dark below.

Well, keep walking, then, he said. It's the only thing to do.

He stuck out his hand. I recognized it; an instinctive gesture, a habit you pick up around politicians. Shake hands at the least opportunity. I loosened my right fist from the pocket of my jacket, where the edge of the glove had gotten stuck on something, a loose stitch, a hidden zipper. And in my clumsiness I butted the heel of my hand against the butt of the pistol, and it fell out of my waistband and clattered onto the sidewalk.

He looked down at it, slowly, and even more slowly raised his head and stared at me. His eyes had turned blood-black, like obsidian beads.

Where I come from, he said, his head weaving slightly, we don't carry one of those around unless we intend to use it.

I remembered a line of poetry, unable to place the author: *intimate as a dog's imploring glance, and yet again, forever, turned away.*

His mouth was a crumpled tissue of misery. Kill me, he was saying, and I won't tell, and no one will suspect you. Another random murder on a dark Washington street, a botched robbery, a man bleeding to death on the sidewalk steps outside his house.

I must have looked at him with something like horror, because his eyes widened, and he took a step back. Easy now, he said. No offense.

Go on, pick it up. Get it out of here. They're illegal in this town, you know. You must not be from Washington.

As I stooped down I noticed one of his shoelaces was untied. I had a strange protective urge to reach out and tie it for him. Instead, saying nothing, I covered the pistol with my palm and scooped it up and into my pocket in one smooth motion, as if I'd been doing this kind of thing for years.

Go on, he said. Go find your dog. As if he'd just remembered why I was there.

I walked away from him; I turned, to be precise, and walked back to my car, in full view of my formerly intended victim. Without so much as looking back to see if his eyes followed me or if he was lurching up the steps as if I had never existed. It was eight-fifteen, I saw, as soon as I turned over the engine. I drove away feeling, for the first time, defeated, and relieved, by the world's sheer unrelenting ugliness.

It's possible, when you've been married for twenty-five or thirty years, when your children have grown up and moved away, to keep coming across the tail ends of conversations you started in a different decade, and to realize that whole areas of existence have lain dormant all that time, like seeds in an envelope. There's nothing unusual in that.

Or, to put it another way: when one becomes a parent, when you are charged with the care of tiny, shivering, vulnerable creatures—I picture them, all three of them, just out of the swimming pool, wrapped in towels, shuddering, their fatless bodies unable to protect them from the faintest breeze—you lose the capacity to see beyond the immediate visible world. Losing a child, of course, only makes this worse. Abstractions, including the abstraction which is romantic love, lose their luster. You and your spouse become more like partners in a business enterprise. I'm trafficking here in pure clichés, of course. But one can't avoid them. I accepted that long ago. We are who we are.

Rachel's career and mine have had opposite trajectories. When I was at the NSA she toiled away for years as an art librarian in the city system; once Alex and Merrill went to college she returned to school and finished her PhD on Klimt and Schiele at Johns Hopkins; and now she's much in demand as a museum consultant, a specialist in securing government funding for immense and unpopular projects. A few years ago we tore down the wall between Alex's and Merrill's old bedrooms and replaced the windows with a glass curtain wall, and now half the second floor is her office: a beautiful room, if I may say so, a sunlit gallery with floor-to-ceiling white bookshelves, antique barnwood flooring, and a replica George Nakashima desk. I think I enjoy it more than she does. I go in there to dust and vacuum and stare through the window through the branches of the enormous white oak that dominates our backyard.

Last Wednesday—the fourteenth of October, 2004—she called me from a hotel in Berlin. They have her there for three weeks, helping to prepare plans for the Unification Museum. It was midnight in Central Europe, five o'clock in the evening on the East Coast.

I was walking through the Alexanderplatz, she said, after the meeting, full of coffee and pastry, and I was headed back to the hotel, wrapped up in my gray wool cape, you know the one I mean, and I felt very *European*. Jürgen and Peter and the rest of them were so quiet and respectful, they complimented me on my German, they wanted to know if I was being properly cared for, if I had a ride to the airport. I was floating on a cloud of gentleness and propriety. I was halfway across the square, and then, apropos of nothing, I thought, *Sobibor.* And I burst into tears. There were people all around me, but they were too polite to notice. Maybe it happens all the time here. Maybe Berliners are used to seeing strangers sobbing on street corners.

And then I got back to the hotel, she said, and I cleaned myself up. I was brave about it. Peter picked me up at seven and took me to an Indian restaurant, somewhere out in the suburbs. It was quite a drive. He didn't say much while we were in the car. Maybe he sensed that something had happened.

Well? *Had* something happened?

I don't know, she said. Yes. I mean, I began thinking, I'm too old for this shit. I wondered whether I took too many of those new blood-pressure pills. But it's not that. I just felt that . . . I just didn't understand how they do it, how they can look around and not feel everything just *steeped* in blood. I know, I know. It's melodramatic. And hypocritical.

Don't be so hard on yourself, I said. Things like that happen when you're traveling.

Well, she said, I was an idiot, I was feeling fragile, I don't know, but I brought it up at the restaurant. Talk about tactless and crude. I've never seen such a long silence, I think, at a dinner table. Everybody got very interested in their food.

And then finally Jürgen said to me: Let me tell you a little story.

She was quiet for long enough that I noticed a faint fizzing over the phone line, like a can of soda just opened: the only indication that she was not next door, but five thousand miles away. My heart quaked.

And? What was the story?

Give me a minute, she said. I have to stretch out my legs. I don't want to paraphrase. All right. You ready? This is what he said.

When I was young, he said, I would go to visit my grandparents in Koblenz, in the Rhine Gorge. They lived a little way outside of town on a large property that originally belonged to my great-grandfather. On one side of the property was the main house, where they stayed, and around the other side, there was a large pond, and then a little stucco house on the opposite side of that. In that stucco house lived my uncle Willem. He was blind in one eye, and he was very fat, and he lived alone, never leaving the grounds. He mowed the lawns and collected apples from the apple trees and so on. And he loved to see me whenever I would come. He loved chocolate bars, and I always brought him a whole box of them. My parents gave me the money. I was the only person in the family he would talk to.

She let out a long sigh, cracked the seal on a bottle of water, and took a swig; I heard, or imagined I could hear, the plastic knocking against her teeth. It was then, strangely, with that sound, that I understood what she was doing: relaxing into the role, into the extemporaneous pleasures of the story. She had never needed notes, only an audience. An occasion.

I don't remember when I realized that he had been in the Waffen SS, that he had been a *Lagerkommandant* at Treblinka. He certainly didn't keep it a secret. He had his uniform hanging up in a closet in his house, covered with medals. But I remember very clearly that there was a year when I fully came to realize what that meant. I watched a program, in English class, as it happens, a documentary on the Nuremberg trials. And then I had to go back to my grandparents' house the next summer and decide what I was going to do about Uncle Willem.

Would I still talk to him? Would I visit him, as I had before, and drink the very sweet cider that he made himself, in barrels, in the back of his house? Should I punish him by having nothing to do with him, like the rest of the family? I thought for a time that I should push him into the pond and make it look like an accident.

And what happened? I asked her. What did he say?

He died. He had a heart attack, that same year, in the springtime. And this is what Jürgen said: I've never in my life felt more relieved. For once in my life I was spared having to stand in judgment over what no single human being can judge. I sometimes wonder, he said, what it would be like to have no one in my own family whose crimes I could point to. I imagine it must be like being in a balloon with no ballast, nothing tethering me to the earth. My own children, of course, are in that position. Their grandparents are all long dead. It's a terrible thing, to think of yourself always as innocent. Because you see the world, as it were, from the air. You can't help it. There are the innocent like you, and then there are the others, the terribly, terribly guilty.

It's late, I said. You ought to get some rest. It's another long day for you tomorrow, and then you have to catch an early flight the next morning. Christ, you're not thirty-five anymore, Rachel. Get to bed. He's a stranger. And a self-righteous jerk, if I may say so. He doesn't know anything about our lives.

Well, I started it, she said. I opened my stupid mouth. And he was polite enough not to mention any more *recent* events. Abu Ghraib. Guantánamo. I would say he showed remarkable restraint. And of course I never told him what *you* used to do for a living.

I had just opened the freezer, holding the phone in my left hand, wondering what I would eat for dinner that night. I stayed there, staring at a stack of Lean Cuisine entrees, in a cloud of cold mist. It isn't like me to get angry at her over the phone. When we argue, it's face-to-face, over some minor irritant: Who lost the water bill? Who threw away the grapefruit spoons? But lately, I've noticed, when she's tired, sleepy, or drunk, Rachel has a glib and reckless way of running down our lives. I don't know what it's about. I ought to be more solicitous, more concerned; instead I grow annoyed and dismissive. It's as if I've decided the era of discussions in our marriage is over. Wittgenstein, I thought, Wittgenstein, you have cursed me, with the crutch of principled silence.

Oh, come on, she said. You were up to your ears in it. El Salvador, Nicaragua, Angola. Just because we never really discussed it, does that make me an idiot? Listen, I'm not excusing myself. We all lived off that salary. I could have taken the kids and left. I enjoyed it a little. It was like being married to a secret agent without the risk.

You're still drunk, I said. Go to sleep, Rachel. Before you say something really stupid.

Innocent people commit the most terrible crimes, she said. Sometimes without even lifting a finger. Don't say you don't know what I mean. You know exactly what I mean.

Not for the first time it occurred to me, remembering Frank Murphy's swollen face, the desperate thrust of his outstretched hand, that if one more streetlight had been broken on Ellicott Street I might still be in prison. But given the right circumstances, I thought, in those same months, I could have done almost anything. Set off a car bomb.

Worn a dynamite belt. I had been, in my own small way, a fanatic. Listening to her, I observed this about myself with a certain perverse satisfaction. It was the one aspect of my life that had evaded all suspicion.

Oh, Rachel, I said, with a half-pantomimed sigh, as if gathering up breath for some unspecified future purpose. You have no idea. It could have been much worse.

You mean it *is* much worse, she said. She had gotten into bed; I could see her, kicking off her shoes, lying back with the receiver tilted up in the air. Worse than the Age of Reagan, I mean. Who would have thought that was only the beginning? But eventually you would have resigned. I know you would have. Like Stu Rushfield and Parker and Bill Thorndike at the State Department. You would have made me proud.

Maybe I would have, in one way or another, I said. But I didn't, is that right? Isn't that what matters? I disappointed you.

No, she said. That's the worst of it. You're a good man. You stayed. You took care of us. At the time I don't think I would have minded if you were Eichmann. It breaks my heart, thinking back on it. I would have overlooked almost anything. I hope you don't mind my saying this. You can't argue with the truth, I suppose.

It occurred to me that this would be the moment to test her theory. A confession, if ever, was in order right then. But there was no way I was prepared to make one. It was too late in the day; I had already stuck a frozen pizza in the toaster oven and poured a half measure of Dewar's over ice. I wasn't in the mood for a marathon phone call, as if we were two teenagers. This was the converse of history, I thought, the secret unwritten history, of men yawning late at night, too ashamed to tell their wives who said what about the nuclear test or the planned assassination of the prime minister, and dying of a stroke the next day.

And yet otherwise I didn't deserve her forgiveness, or her love.

What I had been arguing for, silently, hoping for, working for, was to become a ghost, to disappear, like the others, into the walls of my own house. I didn't want to be replicated. I never wanted there to be another story like this one. If I could, I thought, I would stop this story, too. If it were a tape recorder, I would go back to the beginning and erase it, erase the sound of my own voice. The weight of years on these sagging vocal cords, the gravelly burr, the pretend wisdom. No one should be allowed to speak this way, I thought, even into the unknown, even to you. But I drank the drug of inertia long ago. I can't spit it out.

No, I said. You can't argue with the truth.

In our living room we have a framed photograph I took of Jolie at six, playing in the sprinkler in the backyard. She looks over her shoulder at the camera, her face crinkled up with pleasure, the water striking between her shoulder blades and spraying everywhere, dotting the lens with droplets.

She had enormous bottle-green eyes and very dark, very straight brown hair. And a dimpled chin, and fair skin, much paler than any of the rest of us. My mother was descended from an Anglo-Irish family, and I suppose a few of those genes made their way to her. She sunburned easily and freckled everywhere. A little slip of a girl, my God. Even by that summer she was just four feet tall.

Schafe können sicher weiden,
*Sheep can safely graze*
Wo ein guter Hirte wacht.
*where a good shepherd watches over them.*
Wo Regenten wohl regieren,
*Where rulers are ruling well,*
Kann man Ruh und Friede spüren
*we may feel peace and rest*
Und was Länder glücklich macht
*and what makes countries happy.*

At the kitchen table, I cut the brown paper backing with a razor blade, remove the paperboard and the photograph and the mat, and carefully lift out the square pane of glass, so no one will be injured; the glass goes into the recycling bin, and the rest of it into a garbage bag, which I wrap around again and again, like a precious parcel, to carry out to the sidewalk for tomorrow's pickup. I cut the brown paper backing with a razor blade; I expect it to hurt; I expect it to bleed. I expect the razor blade to stray across the palm of my outstretched hand. But that is never the way it is with me. In my life I have been the shepherd watching from the air, praying, don't look up, don't let me see your faces, for who knows what I'll do to the world if I lose you.

Preeta Samarasan

# *Birch Memorial*

LAST WEEKEND SUGU went back to Ipoh town. Twenty years we never gone back, since we came to Kuala Lumpur for Sugu to get the office job, and then just like that one day he says he wants to go.

Sightseeing, he said. Like a tourist like that, like he never lived there for nineteen years. Wanted to show his wife, it seems.

Show what? I asked him. Ipoh town got nothing to see also.

Got, what, he insisted. I'll take her to the cave temples and D. R. Seenivasagam Park. We'll eat all that famous Ipoh hawker food. Char kuay teow, taugeh chicken, chee cheong fun.

Inside my head I knew where he was going to go first. I didn't say one word, but sure enough when he came back to Kuala Lumpur it burst from his mouth like a sick man's cough: Akka, you won't believe it! The Birch statue is gone, the whole thing missing, just like that! Like somebody could just pick it up and walk off with that thing on their head!

If you ask me, I said, the Government itself carted the thing off and sold it as scrap metal to a bothakadai for a few dollars. They'll melt it down and make forks and spoons and dog chains.

And you know what else, Akka? my brother went on. On the

plaque itself they carved one nice message to tell people it's missing. Carved it! That means they'll never put a new statue of Birch, isn't it?

A new statue? I said. How you think they can make a new statue? Nobody can remember how the man looked also. Nobody wants to remember.

Then for a long time my brother and I didn't say anything, because it was as if I said his name for the first time after twenty years. Took us right back to that time we never talk about. When I think about it that time seems like someone else's life, like a picture flim full of funny-funny upside-down too-big too-loud fairy-tale characters you can't even believe. Those were his words, you see, not mine. That was what Sebastian Mills told us, exactly like that: Nobody wants to remember J. W. W. Birch.

Aha, now you know who I am, isn't it? No need to bluff. I know you heard all the stories at that time. Yah, I was that girl. Innocently selling my appam opposite the clock tower. Hot-hot, sweet-sweet, the men used to say when they ordered their appam, and I used to say, Okay, sir, I make your appam hot-hot sweet-sweet, and pretend I couldn't see them winking and showing dirty-dirty things with their hands. I just wanted to do my work and send my brother for his operation and save money for a house. You want to buy appam means buy, I used to say to them inside my head. Otherwise go away and leave me alone.

The only one who was different from all the rest was Millionaire Komalam. Oh, you remember him, all right. He was about as far from a millionaire as anyone could get. Poor old crackpot with knees as big as his head, that thin he was. No wonder he was always cold. Wrapped himself in that gunnysack until it got stolen, remember? What kind of heartless no-shame bastard wants to steal a homeless old man's gunnysack, I also don't know. But from that time onwards Millionaire Komalam was always digging, digging in the dustbin to find any cloth to cover his backside. Not that he was shy, I tell you. Only in the mornings or when the weather was coming cold he wanted to cover himself; in the hot sun he would at once throw off whatever he was wearing and walk around like that, ding-dong dan-gling, I didn't even know where to look sometimes. But embarrassed also, I was never scared of him. Something about him, you know, like a little boy only? Like a lost goat baby, the mouth always open, the eyes looking here looking there, but in such a thing where got dan-ger? The hardest part was not to laugh. Like that one time he found a small girl's dress in the dustbin, so damn tight that thing was, some more made of one kind of lace so got big-big holes everywhere. Somehow the man managed to struggle into it, I think so it must have torn a bit but still he put it on and what do you think? Of course the thing only came down to his waist, I tell you for me it was worse than looking at a naked man. Seeing those jewels under that frilly pink hem, who won't feel geli? And then wearing that dress somehow he started to feel like a flimstar I think. Up and down, up and down he was walking like the road divider was a catwalk, shaking his back-side, putting one hand on his hip and the other hand on the head to pose, singing loudly with a microphone only he could see, wah, all the moves he had, Sudirman himself would've lost to him, I tell you! For a man who never even saw a TV program let alone a real picture flim it was damn impressive. He even went and plucked one flower from in front of the railway station to put behind his ear. And he put on that whole flimshow for me only, you know or not? Other people stopping and pointing also he couldn't even see. The whole time he was singing for me only, looking at me every two seconds, trying to see from all the way over there if I was enjoying it.

"Eh, Kalyani!" he used to call to me from across the road. All of you, when you were rushing past on your lunch breaks and tea breaks and don't-know-what-what important business, when you were bouncing down the road in the bus or zooming through in your air-con cars, all of you used to turn your heads this way that way to pre-tend you couldn't hear, like you were looking for birds in the sky, but you remember it just fine, yes or not? Anyway Millionaire Komalam didn't care where all you looked. "One of these days," he would go on, and his eyes would be so sharp and bright, like a superhero's eyes shooting magic beams into my head like that, "one of these days I'm going to marry you, don't laugh!" And then he would shout to Sugu also: "Eh, Sugu thambi! Tell your akka I'm going to marry her! As soon as I get my money back! I'm a millionaire, you know or not? Don't play the fool!"

Millionaire Komalam had a long story about his lost money. Sometimes when you people had nothing better to do while smoking your cigarettes or stretching your legs or squeezing out the last few minutes of your tea break, you used to simply-simply ask him about it to make fun of him. Oh, yes, no use to deny it now. So who knows what you remember. Probably you never even listened to half of it, because of course he would start from the beginning and tell you the whole thing in detail, how he was born to a poor rubber-tapper but studied hard in school and then worked worked worked like a donkey until he was a millionaire with a gigantic mansion in Tambun. He would tell you how at one time he had twenty-thirty businesses all over Malaysia, and how even sultans and datuks were eating out of his hand. To come and talk to me, he would say, they had to make appointments one year in advance.

And what happened to all that, you remember or not?

What happened was that his loins made a fool of him, just like what happens to plenty of not-so-rich men. Fell madly in love with some beautiful woman and showered her with jewels and got her to marry him, and then of course she emptied all his bank accounts and ran off with another feller, cheated him without even blinking. To track down that bitch of a woman he sold all his houses and his cars and whatnot and traveled all over the world for years, to Singapore, to India, to Australia, even further places also. I didn't find her, he would say, but you know what? I'm still looking, man! The day I catch her and that baddava rascal of a porukki, I'll pull even the clothes from their backs and leave them like that!

That's the part his audiences used to wait for: that threat was your cue, isn't it? How you looking for them, Millionaire Komalam? you'd tease him. Every day we see you sitting here and scratching your balls, but you say you looking?

That all you don't worry, he would retort. I got my people everywhere. I got my people to look for those two.

Ohohoho! you would say every time. And then—oh, I remember everything, you no need to pretend to be angels now—you would whack each other on the back and laugh like owls until cannot laugh anymore also. Ohohoho, you got people all over the world, is it? London New York Paris?

But still, you know, to sit and listen to the way he told his story, sometimes—admit it!—even you would start to think, What if? And who knows? Because whatever question you could think of to try to ask him, he would come back with an answer without even stopping to think, and tomorrow if you asked him the same question to try to catch him the answer would be the same. His wife's name was always Indira; the other feller's name was Vasu; the two of them met in 1960 at a big Deepavali open house Millionaire Komalam threw at his mansion (address: 65 Hala Zamrud).

So who knew?

Millionaire Komalam's real name was not even Komalam. He said his name was Nagarajan, but the boys who played hockey on the padang in the evenings gave him a new name because he liked to shout at people as they passed: Ni oru komali! You're a clown!

Komali, komali, those boys turned that into Komalam so that one shot they could make fun of the old man and of Chief Minister Komalam.

And so fast everyone else picked it up too: Shaddup, Millionaire Komalam! You're the one who's a clown! And on top of that, a pariah dog and a whore's son! you all used to shout back at him whenever you had enough of his carrying-on. Even I got fed up sometimes, what you think, standing there at my appam stall the whole morning every day hearing his nonsense? But however angry I got also I couldn't bring myself to shout back at him, I just couldn't. Sometimes at the end of the morning I would call him across the road to me, and quietly-quietly when nobody was looking I would give him two-three leftover appams.

I felt so sorry for him, you know?

And the other thing is, not once did he call me a komali. Not once.

Always he would take the appams from me with both hands and stuff as much as he could inside his mouth until he could not chew also, until all the wet parts like kanji will be coming out from the corners of his mouth. Eee, so disgusting, my brother used to say sometimes, but for that I would wallop him nicely. You want to make fun means find a bigger man to make fun of, I would tell him. No need to pick on this humble spirit.

Because once in a while, especially when he was sitting on the ground and eating with both his hands in front of me, that was how I felt about Millionaire Komalam. That he was almost like—I don't think I can make any of you understand it, you will laugh only, just like you always laughed at him—but to me he was almost like God. Like some religious story old people tell to teach young people, you know what I mean, where God disguises himself to be the most humble of the humble? A monk, a beggar, a monkey? Then—in that type of story—everyone always kicks Him and spits at Him, isn't it? That is why I would call him to me, and say, Here, take these appams, otherwise all going to be thrown out only. And with both hands he would take them, and after eating he would always, always without fail, say:

One day I'm going to come and marry you, Kalyani; you see if I don't. I put my hand on my mother's head and swear: one day I'll come and marry you and give you the best of everything you deserve. Kanchipuram silk sarees, gold chains and bangles, an air-con house. I'll pay for your thambi's operation. I'll send him to university in England.

That part all I didn't believe, of course. But what I believed was this: Millionaire Komalam felt for me something nobody else knew how to feel. I don't know what to call it also. So thankful he was for those two-three half-stale appams, so thankful you could see it in his eyes like a prayer. But not just that. He had a kind of respect for me, like when he looked at me he saw his dead mother, or some older sister or cousin he used to love as a child—no, it was even bigger than that. As if when he looked at me he saw a goddess, just like I saw God in disguise when I looked at him. He saw the Mother of the whole world. He looked at me like he could almost fall at my feet like that. It was different from anything else. All those things he promised me on his mother's head, he really wanted to give me. So what if he was an old man and I was twenty years old? So what if he was as ugly as a tree lizard and I was beautiful? Still he made me feel special. Nobody else talked to me like that, you know? All the lawyers and clerks from the courthouse, even the young peons fresh out of school, and the lorry drivers and ditchdiggers, they all thought they could try to be funny with me because I was just a poor appam seller, no father, no mother, no one to protect me in this world but my poor lame brother with his legs so crooked he couldn't even walk properly, let alone fight.

*Hot-hot, sweet-sweet.* That's all they knew. Lawyer Sivalingam whose fat wife lay dying—that time we all didn't know, but now we do, yah?—in her private-hospital bed while he winked and drooled at me. Lawyer Srirangam whose bald head sparkled like a satellite dish in the sun, just put your TV underneath his backside sure can catch signal one. Lawyer Kanaparan trying to distract everyone from his luscious-mango daughter's own antics (in which KL hotel did they find her half-naked and drunk with some minister's son? Shangri-La, Bangri-la, who knows) by treating me like a cheap call girl. And then Bala, Ariffin, Chee, Indian Malay Chinese in a row like one bloody muhibbah poster, nicely learning from their bosses: Hey, miss, hot-hot, sweet-sweet! Ha ha hee hee! First behind their hands, and then when the bosses buzzed off, openly, shamelessly. For us also hot-hot sweet-sweet, okay? Don't think only the big bosses can get your special-special bargain! Damn great they thought they were, like their stupid joke was so funny. Of course, if Millionaire Komalam shouted at them for showing dirty signs with their hands they only laughed louder and made even dirtier signs. Nobody was scared of him.

In the end you know who made them shut up?

Sebastian Mills himself.

First time he came out of the train station with that huge bag on his back like they all have—why is that however rich also they must carry everything by themselves like a tortoise?—I thought, Oh, no, don't tell me. I saw him looking straight at my stall, and I knew he was coming. Another one of them, I thought. Feller won't even know what I'm selling; he'll just point and do sign language like as if I can't understand English, and when I say anything he'll look at me like I'm talking Chinese. Just because we don't talk like them, like got twenty-five marbles in the mouth, they pretend they can't understand one word.

But Sebastian was not like that. Can you believe he talked almost like one of us? Hot-hot, he said. Of course he didn't say sweet-sweet or wink or nudge the other fellers. Only our Indian doonggus will act like that with a woman they don't even know, isn't it? But when I asked him if he wanted my brother to fetch him tea from the tea stall, he answered without staring at my lips to see what I said, Can also. *Can also!*

I must've given him one kind of look, because he smiled and said, What's the matter? Never heard a vellakaran talk Manglish?

I didn't want him to think he could impress me so easily, so I said, Manglish-Nanglish all fine, but you still have to pay the same as everyone else, mister.

Apparently he liked that even more than if I said please thank you saar hee-hee-ha-ha like all the other people did when they saw a white man. He leaned back and laughed without taking his eyes off me, like we were two men lepaking at the mamak joint and I just told the funniest joke of all. Like he didn't mind me being the winner, I was that good.

He folded his appam in half and then half again and ate it like it was a sandwich.

From across the road Millionaire Komalam was watching us like a hawk. That day he had found a big cardboard box in one of the dustbins, and he had unfolded that and wrapped it around himself. When he saw Sebastian Mills stop talking to eat his appam he threw off the cardboard box like a Tamil-flim hero breaking his chains, stood up, and yelled: Eh, Kalyani! Someday I'm going to marry you, my kannu, my chellam!

Sebastian Mills didn't even seem to hear him. What do you know about that statue over there? he asked me.

What statue? I said.

What statue, what statue, like got five-six statues there or what? he said. The statue of James Birch lah, how many other statues you see?

I said, James Birch? What for I care about him?

*What for you care?* You know who he was or not?

Some useless British bastard, what do I know? I said.

Yah, a useless bastard, all right. You don't mind that they put up a nice big statue of him right in the middle of your town?

Why, he's alive, ah? I said. What is he going to do to me? Statue or no statue, as long as I can sell my appam what do I care? Is he a ghost to be scaring off my customers?

Not exactly, no, said Sebastian Mills, and when he said that one line, Not exactly, no, he sounded just like an Englishman you hear on TV, just like the rest of them.

Tell me what you know about J. W. W. Birch, he said then.

Eh, macchan, what the hell is your problem? I asked him. You think I got no work that I can stand here and talk to you about a statue all day?

I'm doing a project, he said. I'll belanja you, I'm not asking you to talk to me for free. Lunch, dinner, whatever you want. Your thambi also can come.

Are you joking? For telling you what I know about James Birch?

Yes, that's all. It's for my project.

You no need to have a job like everybody else, is it? I asked him. You live on fresh air and sunshine?

I'm getting paid to do this project. That's how I can afford to belanja you.

You're getting paid for this half-past-six project? Which poor fool is paying you to ask me what I know about that statue?

A university, he said. It's not just you I'm asking. And not just about James Birch. I'm asking different-different people all over Malaysia what they think about these statues and these road names. And what they remember about the men themselves—James Birch and Francis Light and Frank Swettenham and all the rest of them— now that it's been twenty-five years since the British left. Can you remember what you studied in history class?

I didn't study anything about any of those great heroes, I said. I didn't have any history-mistory class all. I only went to school up to Standard Three, mister, I'm not so lucky like you to find someone to pay me to do nothing. I had to feed myself and my brother.

Doesn't matter, he said. Even those who went to school don't remember anything. Nobody wants to remember J. W. W. Birch. And it serves him right. I tell you, if I were you I'd be pissing on that statue every day.

Kalyani, Kalyani! Millionaire Komalam howled. Don't be fooled by that vellakaran bastard! Don't be taken in by his sweet talk! Sugu thambi, tell your akka! Tell her to wait for me! Any day now I'll be getting my money back!

This time Sebastian Mills heard him. He turned and put a hand over his eyes, as though he was looking far away across an ocean to see where the noise was coming from. Who's that? he asked me.

We call him Millionaire Komalam, I said. He's harmless.

Does he live there under the statue?

More or less, I said. He lives here there everywhere. He comes and goes.

That first day I never expected Sebastian to wait for me all morning until I finished my business, especially after I told him, Look here, mister, what I know about your J. W. W. Birch is this: Zero. Jeelo. Kosong. One big duck egg. Understand? I held up one hand in a kosong shape to make my point clear.

That's okay, he said. I'm going to go into that coffee shop over there, see? After you close your stall, come and find me and I'll take you and your brother to lunch. You can tell me about other things.

At first I thought, Why should I go? Millionaire Komalam is probably right. This man is just some crook who thinks I'm a stupid Indian girl he can sweet-talk.

But then I said to myself, Why not? It's a free lunch. And he said I can bring Sugu. How much mischief can he get up to in front of my fourteen-year-old brother?

At most he'll take us to Rama Vilas, I thought. But that's better than nothing. That's better than the rice and pickle Sugu and I eat every day.

But you remember the type of places Sebastian Mills took us to. Oh, you heard about all that, don't pretend now. No Rama Vilas Bhavani Vilas, right? He took us to the FMS Bar and Restaurant, the French Hotel, the Eastern Hotel, all these posh-posh places I never entered before that. Even to touch their forks and spoons, I whispered to Sugu the first time he took us to one of those places, they'll charge us one hundred dollars. Even to breathe their air.

Though I whispered it in Tamil, Sebastian Mills must have got the gist of it from my face, or from the frightened way Sugu was sitting, like he felt he was dirtying the chair, or something.

Don't worry, Sebastian said. Order what you want. Consider it a present from James Birch to make up for all the havoc he caused when he was alive.

The first time, I didn't even know how to order. You order for us lah, I said to Sebastian.

But one thing about me: I learn fast. Within a few days I knew how to style-style order all these things I never even heard of before. French onion soup. Omelet. Toasted Cheese Sandwich. Chef's Salad.

Twenty-five years since I ate that type of thing, but still I remember the names. Sugu is a senior clerk now, his wife answers the phone for the same company, and even my pay at Loga's Curry House is not bad compared to what I used to make in Ipoh. We eat okay, chicken two-three times a week, prawns or cuttlefish on our birthdays, but where we want to waste money on the type of hi-funda food Sebastian taught me to eat?

You want to know what kind of Other Things Sebastian asked me about while we ate our soup and our sandwiches? Nothing so special. Not what you all thought. How much money I made in one year, what I thought of the Government, what was Sugu's sickness. What happened to my Appa and Amma, where I learned to make appam, what I would be if I had a choice.

I told you, no big secrets. But all the same, once I started to talk I almost couldn't stop, even if it was just for someone doing a project. I knew he was getting paid for everything, I even saw him busily writing-writing sometimes while talking to me, but still sometimes I forgot all that, you know? Sitting there talking to him it was like he was my friend and I was telling him all the things I never had a chance to tell anyone because nobody else asked. Nobody else asked me about my Appa and Amma and about me, about who I was and who I wanted to be.

I think he himself forgot that I was only part of his project, because after two-three days he started to hold my hand. That you yourselves saw. Even if I want to also I can't lie. And then once in Café Rendezvous he put his arm around my shoulder in front of everyone, like I was his girlfriend. Sugu just stared at his shoes like as if Sebastian Mills took off all my clothes in front of him, poor boy. And all the high-class people sitting around us—the Chinese towkays, the businessmen all coated-and-suited so that they could sweat nicely all day, the ladies in dresses so small you felt like telling them, no need to wear also, what for you bother?—all those people were looking up and down and to the side so that they didn't have to see us, but I knew for them we were as big as an elephant in front of their eyes. They couldn't think about anything else. They couldn't talk. They couldn't even breathe.

A straight-from-the-rubber-estate girl, sitting there with an Englishman!

A girl in a dress she bought at the night market, sipping through a straw at the Café Rendezvous!

Isn't that the girl who owns the appam stall in front of the railway station?

Eat my shit, you bastards, I thought to myself. No joke, your eyes are not bluffing you, I'm the appam girl, all right. Why, you think I alone must fill out some special form to sit here?

In the mornings the lawyers' peons and the louts had even more fun than they used to. Each day their tongues grew cruder. Hot-hot, sweet-sweet, they said. It seems you make it even hotter and sweeter for the vellakaran? Someone told us he gets the hottest, sweetest appam of all. With extra egg, extra coconut milk, and extra something else also. Is it true? What about us? Just because we're humble office boys bus drivers road workers means we can't get the same treatment, ah?

You no-work idiots, I told them. Just because I sit with one gentleman in a restaurant you think what, I'm going to spread my legs for the lot of you, is it? You think I'm like your mothers and your sisters?

But whatever I said also they just laughed. Right there in front of my stall they started to behave like drunkards coming out of a massage parlor. Hooting and braying, thrusting their loins at me and making kissing noises with their lips.

And then one day Sebastian Mills rushed all the way across the road from the coffee shop where he used to sit and talk to other people, and grabbed one of the bus drivers by the collar. *Pattaaaa!* He slapped the side of the man's head with the back of his hand, so smooth and easy like he was just stretching or waving to a friend.

All you maddayans, he said, is that the way to talk to a woman? How much all of you can sit and grumble to each other about the life of Indians in this country, yes or not? In grumbling alone you'll win first prize. The Government won't give us this, the Government won't give us that. You want to know why you Indians are in this condition? Left behind in the dust while the Malays get all the power and the Chinese fill their coffers? It's because you treat your women like this. It's because you got nothing better to do with your time than to stand here and harass a girl trying to make an honest living. It's because you got no respect for anything under the sun.

To this day I don't know how much of that speech those goondas understood. But the feller Sebastian slapped was still rubbing his ear like a small boy, and all the other fellers' faces changed. I tell you if they could have pulled black cloths over their heads like some of those Malay women you see nowadays, then and there they would've done it. Sorry, sorry, akka, they muttered. And would you believe it, they queued up like schoolboys in front of my stall? Two appams, each one said quietly. Please give me two appams as usual. And one by one they paid and went off.

The only one who wasn't scared of Sebastian Mills was Millionaire Komalam. From that first day onwards I think he hated the sight of Sebastian's face. Was he just jealous or was there some other reason, I don't know. But every time he saw Sebastian near my stall he would shout to me to remember his promise, and slowly-slowly his shouting became more like threatening like that.

"Kalyani!" he would warn me. "You tell that bastard I'm watching him! I've got my eye on him! If he tries anything with you, I'll go into a trance like he's never seen! Then he'll know!"

And another time he started to chant like a temple priest: "Oh, those vellakaran, can You see them, God? You whose eyes see everything, can You see what-what they come and do? They spoil our women just like they spoiled our country! They take what they want just like they always did! And nobody can do anything because they are white, they are powerful, the whole world is blind it seems, but You, God, You see, don't You? Give me the strength to show them, God! Give me the strength to protect our women!"

I tell you, that was the one time Millionaire Komalam gave me a real funny feeling. I don't think he ever hated anybody like he hated Sebastian Mills, except maybe his wife and that other man.

That's why one day when Sebastian Mills said he wanted to go and ask him about James Birch I said, No need, no need, don't be silly. What is that poor old coconut-head going to tell you, anyway?

Maybe nothing, Sebastian said. But I just want to see if he even knows whose statue he's standing under.

He won't know anything, I said, but Sebastian was already crossing the street and walking towards Millionaire Komalam. And sure enough, what did I tell him!

Dai! Millionaire Komalam screamed, and nobody ever heard him scream like that before, like somebody was attacking him with a parang, like a crow was plucking his eyes out. He screamed till his voice ripped into shreds like an old saree: Dai! You take one more step towards me and I'll kill you, you thendi you dog you whore's son, I'll kill you!

Sebastian turned around and came back. I don't think he'll kill me, he said, but he's definitely not going to talk to me about J. W. W. Birch. Well, never mind that.

We laughed and shook our heads. I told you, I said.

You're a clever girl, Kalyani, he said.

I never expected Sebastian Mills to marry me and take me to England, okay? Not even for one minute I expected that. Why would I think he would want to bring back a girl like me, a girl he had to teach how to order from a menu? As if he would want to speak Manglish for the rest of his life in London! And neither did I think he would drop his whole life and stay with me, leave behind his rich university who could pay him to ronda-ronda around the world and sit in coffee shops. Me and Sebastian Mills and Sugu in a nice semi-detached house in Canning Gardens, yah, happily ever after?

What you all thought, I was crazy or what?

I know half of you were ashamed of me and the other half pitied me for falling for a feller who was going to jump on the train and leave whenever it suited him. But for me it was just a few weeks of fun. What was the harm in it?

Six weeks of clean fun. Walking around town like a grand lady. Sitting in air-con restaurants. That's all I expected. Believe or don't believe, it's the truth. I was wise for my age. At ten years old already I was an old lady, why would I have believed in fairy tales at twenty? Hanh? Sooner or later, Sebastian would get on the train and go to Penang, Alor Setar, Langkawi, wherever he was going, and then back to Kuala Lumpur, and then London, England, and even if he wrote letters to me I wouldn't be able to read half of it, isn't it?

They say if you expect nothing you'll always get more than you expect, and that's what happened. I thought one fine day Sebastian would shake my hand and say thank you very much and buy two appams for the train journey and leave, but I got more than that.

The day before he left he asked me to close my stall early, and he gave Sugu ten ringgit to go and watch a double feature at the Grand Cinema. Then he and I went to D. R. Seenivasagam Park. We fed the fish and rode on the Ferris wheel, like we were two Standard Four children. He bought me kacang puteh and candy floss and I couldn't even finish half of it, I tell you, it was so sweet. Then he asked me to take him to our house.

It's not a house, I said. I told you isn't it, we just rent a room in someone else's house.

That's all right, he said. I have to see where you live before I go. So I can remember it.

You all want to hear what you want to hear, I know. That we slept together like husband and wife, that I was spoiled all right just like Millionaire Komalam feared, even that I got pregnant and had to find a way to get rid of the child. I know you and your greed for those ugly stories. But the truth is, Sebastian Mills really just wanted to see our room. He took a picture of me standing near the window. And then he gave me a kiss. Just one kiss, and not on the lips or the cheek. On the forehead. Like I belonged to him. He didn't promise to write letters or come back. He didn't promise anything he couldn't give. All he said was, I'll always remember you, Kalyani.

And suddenly all I wanted was to believe that one small thing, because I couldn't have the white-dress wedding or the plane trip to London or the semidetached house in Canning Gardens.

After Sebastian turned around and left I could still smell his white-man smell in my room, and I could still see the small-small bits of brown in his blue eyes when he leaned towards me to kiss my forehead. All that was real. But when I closed my eyes to remember, I kept imagining tears in his eyes, not falling but just collecting there in the corners, like somebody had pinched him hard like that. What-what tricks a lonely mind can play on you, yah?

I won't lie to you: of course I cried and cried, because that fairy-tale time was over, and now, I thought, it was time to go back to my old life, all the days exactly the same as each other, working until my feet pained so much I wanted to chop them off with a Chinaman's cleaver, fending off the goondas who were going to start disturbing me again now that my protector was gone, eating plain rice and pickle for dinner, scrimping and saving for Sugu's operation. Poor Sugu, seeing me like that, he also hid his face and cried.

But that crying was nothing compared to the crying I did when I found the money.

Five thousand ringgit, under my pillow. I don't know when he put it there. How he put it there and I didn't see, I still can't understand. There was a note: *For Sugu's Operation.*

Even after all these years, I myself can't explain properly why it made me cry like that.

I suppose one reason was, I suddenly realized that whole time Sebastian Mills was pitying me. But what was so bad about that? And how could he not pity me, knowing what little money we lived on, seeing my brother limping to the tea stall fifty times a morning to fetch people's tea so that maybe, one day, we could get his legs fixed?

I also don't know. I just knew I didn't want that pity. I wanted to be the girl who made Sebastian Mills laugh better than anyone else could. The one who was different because I nicely gave it to him that first day instead of kowtowing like everyone else. I wanted to think of him showing my picture to his friends in England and boasting about how he sat in the Café Rendezvous and ate Chef's Salad with this girl all the other men wanted.

So did he stay six weeks instead of two weeks like he said in the beginning just because he felt guilty about leaving me, and not for the joy of walking around town with a beautiful girl? Supposing, just supposing those tears were real, did he cry just because he was sorry about what a sad life I was going to have without him? What would he say when he showed his friends my picture, if he showed it to them at all? This poor orphan girl had a lame brother. I gave her five thousand ringgit for his operation.

I just couldn't believe it. So easy it was for him to disguise the pity in his smile, and there I was all the time thinking—thinking so many things. I didn't want to ask myself any questions anymore; remembering any of it made my eyes narrow like I ate something sour. I just wanted to erase all that, Sebastian Mills, that whole week, the FMS Bar and Restaurant, the French Hotel, the Eastern Hotel, all of it, like it never happened.

I was still sitting up on my mattress and crying in the dark that night when I heard the noise at the window. A cat, I thought at first. A rat running down the pipe outside.

But my stomach turned inside out when a hand smashed the window open with a brick, and I saw it was Millionaire Komalam. He had found a big straw hat somewhere, one of those Chinese hats the farmers and people like that wear. His eyes were shining like a rat's, all right, but he was no rat running down the pipe. He was shaking, shaking as he broke all the window glass, and we had so much time to scream, but we didn't. Mrs. Ganesan would have rushed up at once, but Sugu and I both stood there like as if someone put a charm on us like that. Millionaire Komalam's hat was so big, even after he broke all the glass he had to struggle to climb in. The sight of him, climbing in completely naked except for that hat, turning his head this way that way to free it from the window frame, my God, I tell you. Sugu started to laugh, even though Millionaire Komalam had that brick in one hand, and in his teeth he had some kind of knife. Where he found it, I don't know.

I was so sad and so frightened, I also started to laugh. I wasn't frightened for us, no. I told you, I was never frightened of Millionaire Komalam, and I wasn't frightened now, knife or no knife. I was frightened for him. Frightened for what would happen to him if anyone saw him, what would happen if Sugu panicked and screamed, what would happen. What would happen to that peaceful life he lived under the Birch statue, digging through the dustbins, singing as if there was nobody else in the world but him and me?

As soon as he managed to get his head through the window, Millionaire Komalam dropped the brick, closed his eyes, and slid right down onto his backside on the floor.

Akka! Sugu whispered.

Shh, I said. Don't worry.

Millionaire Komalam picked himself up and came towards me, slowly, slowly, his eyes big and his arms curved wide, as if he was expecting me to bolt. Kalyani! he said. I know you brought that bastard here.

I kept quiet.

After everything I told you, he said. After what I promised you. You think I make those kinds of promises to every woman?

He was shaking like a man with fits: his voice, his legs, his hands, everything shaking.

Where is he? he said. I'll kill him. I'm going to kill him with this knife.

He's not here, I said. He's gone.

Don't lie to me, Kalyani. Don't protect your dirty vellakaran porukki. You, of all people, you—

He started to cry, choking on his tears like a woman in a Tamil flim.

Don't cry, I said.

Then suddenly he fell towards me, like someone pushed him from behind, and he grabbed my wrists, so tightly, as if he was going to break them just by squeezing.

Akka, Sugu whimpered.

Go away, Sugu, I said. Go back to your bed.

Why did you do this to me? Millionaire Komalam said. You know what I've been through, how I've suffered. How could you turn around and do the same thing?

He was still squeezing my wrists, but somehow I moved my hands to his face and put my palms on his wet cheeks.

Shh, I said. I didn't do anything.

And he started to let go, just like I knew he would, his fingers curling, his shoulders slouching. At once I slipped my wrists out of his grasp and took his hands in mine. I held him like that for a long time before I said anything, just looking at him, feeling his dry old fingers.

Then finally I said, You're a good person. You're an old soul. I know what you've been through.

If you know, he said. If you know. Everything, all that. One day I'll get my money back, Kalyani. One day it'll come.

Look, I said. Isn't this your money? I picked up Sebastian Mills's money from my mattress and pushed it into his right hand. Your money, I said again.

My money? But . . . You . . . He looked at the money in his hand, at my face, at the money again. His thin, full-of-tears spit was leaking from his open mouth onto his chin. In the dark the white parts of his eyes were as white as the light of street lamps. My money, he whispered. Kalyani, you brought back my money. With his free hand he wiped his tears from both cheeks.

I didn't want to let him go then. I wanted him to stay with us, in our room. I wanted to put him in my bed and sleep on the floor at his feet, because he was all I had. Everything else was just tricks, illusion, fakery. After everything else disappeared, this old man would still be there, skinny and naked, loud and proud, promising me the world. But I couldn't keep him here tonight. If Mrs. Ganesan found out, if anyone found out—

Sugu, I called. Sugu! Come and take Millionaire Komalam to the door.

Sugu came, his eyes as big as bullock-cart wheels, and stood there like a tree.

Stop acting like an idiot, I said. What's wrong with you? Take Millionaire Komalam downstairs and open the door for him.

That was the last we saw of Millionaire Komalam. The next day he wasn't under the Birch statue, or the next day or the next.

Even you all never cared anything for him also, you noticed when he disappeared, isn't it? That you remember. You knew what-what to ask me. Where's your friend? The only one who means it when he promises to marry you? Even he also got away from you, ah?

How should I know? I said. I made like I didn't hear their other questions, even when they waited like water buffaloes for my answers. What was I supposed to say? *Everyone gets away from me, you bastards, now you happy? I've lost everything. Clap your hands and dance if you want.* The money didn't matter, and even Sebastian Mills—well, I always knew the day would come when he would turn around and buzz off to England, isn't it? But Millionaire Komalam was different. I never used to imagine a future without him. He was just there, every day, across the street, and now he was gone. My head was like a block of ice. I didn't know whether I was sick or frightened or sad.

After four days I went to the police, but they just laughed at me.

Sure sure, they said. We'll drop everything and go and look for your crazy naked man right now.

It could have been anything, isn't it? At first I thought, Someone must have seen him with all that money, oh, God, I should never have let him out into the night with that money in his hand.

If that's what you fear, I don't blame you.

But it's not what I believe anymore.

Because one week after Millionaire Komalam came to our room in the night, a new customer came to my stall one morning. A rich man, sitting at the back of a big black car. Tinted windows, all that. The Malay driver came out and ordered two appam for his boss, and then went straight back to the car to sit. Oo wah the feller, I thought, just a driver but wants to act like a king, man! Thinks he's ten steps higher than me or what, that I have to hand-deliver his appam to the car window? But I didn't have time to pick a fight so I made the appam and then I sent Sugu out to the car with the bundle.

Next thing you know, the big boss is getting out and walking towards me. Saw him only my heart went patapatapata like that, I don't know why, maybe his dark glasses or his mustache, maybe the way he was walking, like a gangster in a Tamil flim only. What did I do wrong? I wondered. What trouble did I get myself into? At once I thought of Millionaire Komalam and the money, I mean it made no sense of course but I thought, Maybe he did something bad with the money, or who knows where Sebastian got that money, or—you know lah a person's thoughts when they get frightened. Got no logic to it.

But this man was not a gangster or a police big shot. When he took off his dark glasses and looked at me his eyes were tired and kind.

Is the boy your brother? he said in Tamil.

Yes, I said, my thambi Sugu.

How long has he been like this?

Can't say exactly, saar, I said. Sugu never walked like normal. His whole life his legs have been like rubber, every day bending more and more.

Next thing I know the man is style-style taking one business card out of his pocket like in a flim only. Doctor M. S. Sudhananthan, he said, and I was waiting for music and white horses and one dsh-dsh fighting scene coming from nowhere. But there was nothing like that. He and some other famous doctors were leading some study, he said, on Sugu's type of illness.

If your parents will agree—

We got no parents, I said. Just me and Sugu. What you see here, that's the whole family.

Well, in that case, you. If you will agree to let Sugu be one of our patients, the treatment will be free. We'll even pay you a small fee on top of that. If you are interested you can come to the hospital and I will give you all the details. Address telephone number all on the card. Think about it.

He put his dark glasses back and disappeared into his boat-size car.

For days I thought about it. I asked Sugu if he was scared, hoping he would say yes and we wouldn't have to do it.

What for scared? Sugu said. What's the worst thing that could happen? If it doesn't work, so what? Is a wheelchair so much worse than what I have now?

That's how Sugu was. Maybe because of his sickness, or maybe because we lost our Amma-Appa so young, but he never hid the truth from himself.

I asked our friend Aminah, maybe you remember her, the lady who sold nasi lemak on the other side of the railway station. You know anything about this kind of experiments? I said. What if my brother—

Pray to God for an answer, she said. He will help you, even though you're not Muslim.

But where I believe in that type of magic answer? What, it'll be like one voice in my head, is it? I wanted to ask her. If God is so cekap to be giving answers left and right then how come he didn't tell my Appa and Amma not to go on the motorcycle that day, or to turn off the main road before the lorry got them?

So I didn't ask God. I just thought for myself. And somehow, thinking thinking, Millionaire Komalam's face came into my head, just like that. Just like Aminah said. Millionaire Komalam said to me: How much worse can your thambi get? Like one big O his legs are when he tries to stand up straight. Be brave. Have a bit of faith. After arranging everything this far, will I abandon you now?

I admit I doubted him till the end. If it doesn't work, I told myself—if Sugu ends up in a wheelchair—it'll serve me right for believing voices inside my head.

But sure enough, after the first operation, already we could see the difference in Sugu's legs. Like two plants that somebody had tied to sticks they were stretching themselves out. I let him rest nicely, just like they told me. I knew a bit of extra running around for two-three months would pay off in the end if Sugu could be cured, even if every night I was so tired I came home and fell down on the floor like a dead body—no bathing no washing face nothing—and slept with my mouth wide open, aaaah like that until morning. With the money Dr. Jeganathan was paying us, I bought proper milk from the bhayyi, mutton, haruan fish to heal Sugu faster. Two more operations and even you all who used to see him all the time almost couldn't recognize him anymore. Like Rajnikanth he was, like a superhero. Now when the goondas looked at my brother they had no balls to sing their old hot-hot-sweet-sweet song.

Akka, one of them dared to ask me one day, must be your brother went for special treatment, is it?

Yah, I said. Why you care?

Oh, nothing, simply asking only. That Englishman gave you money for operation or what?

You think you who? I said. My father or my grandfather, that you can come here and ask me where I got money for this and for that? What else you want to know? What size panties I'm wearing? How many times a day I shit? Don't worry, I'm not selling my backside to pay my brother's hospital bills, so it's nobody's business except mine.

I could have just as easily told him straight, No, the Englishman didn't pay for the operation, so you no need to talk behind my back. But they were going to talk anyway, isn't it? Let them say what they like, I thought. Let them make up stories to pass their time. Only I know the truth.

And I looked under the Birch statue, where Millionaire Komalam used to sit, and thought how lucky I had been to see through his disguise.

Brad Watson

*Visitation*

L OOMIS HAD NEVER believed that line about the quality of despair being that it was unaware of being despair. He'd been painfully aware of his own despair for most of his life. Most of his troubles had come from attempts to deny the essential hopelessness in his nature. To believe in the viability of nothing, finally, was socially unacceptable, and he had tried to adapt, to pass as a believer, a hoper. He had taken prescription medicine, engaged in periods of vigorous, cleansing exercise, declared his satisfaction with any number of fatuous jobs and foolish relationships. Then one day he'd decided that he should marry, have a child, and he told himself that if one was open-minded these things could lead to a kind of contentment, if not to exuberant happiness. That's why Loomis was in the fix he was in now.

Ever since he and his wife had separated and she had moved with their son to Southern California, he'd flown out every three weeks to visit the boy. He was living the very nightmare he'd tried not to imagine when deciding to marry and have a child: that it wouldn't work out, they would split up, and he would be forced to spend long weekends in a motel, taking his son to faux-upscale chain restaurants, cineplexes, and amusement parks.

He usually visited for three to five days and stayed at the same motel, an old motor court that had been bought and remodeled by one of the big franchises. At first the place wasn't so bad. The Continental breakfast included fresh fruit and little boxes of name-brand cereals and batter with which you could make your own waffles on a double waffle iron right there in the lobby. The syrup came in small plastic containers from which you pulled back a foil lid and voilà, it was a pretty good waffle. There was juice and decent coffee. Still, of course, it was depressing, a bleak place in which to do one's part in raising a child. With its courtyard surrounded by two stories of identical rooms, and excepting the lack of guard towers and the presence of a swimming pool, it followed the same architectural model as a prison.

But Loomis's son liked it, so they continued to stay there, even though Loomis would rather have moved on to a better place.

He arrived in San Diego for his April visit, picked up the rental car, and drove north on I-5. Traffic wasn't bad except where it always was, between Del Mar and Carlsbad. Of course, it was never "good." Their motel sat right next to the 5, and the roar and rush of it never stopped. You could step out onto the balcony at three in the morning and it'd be just as roaring and rushing with traffic as it had been six hours before.

This was to be one of his briefer visits. He'd been to a job interview the day before, Thursday, and had another one on Tuesday. He wanted to make the most of the weekend, which meant doing very little besides just being with his son. Although he wasn't very good at doing that. Generally, he sought distractions from his ineptitude as a father. He stopped at a liquor store and bought a bottle of bourbon, and tucked it into his travel bag before driving up the hill to the house where his wife and son lived. The house was owned by a retired marine friend of his wife's family. His wife and son lived rent-free in the basement apartment.

When Loomis arrived, the ex-marine was on his hands and knees in the flower bed, pulling weeds. He glared sideways at Loomis for a moment and muttered something, his face a mask of disgust. He was a widower who clearly hated Loomis and refused to speak to him. Loomis was unsettled that someone he'd never even been introduced to could hate him so much.

His son came to the door of the apartment by himself, as usual. Loomis peered past the boy into the little apartment, which was bright and sunny for a basement (only in California, he thought). But there was no sign of his estranged wife. She had conspired with some part of her nature to become invisible. Loomis hadn't laid eyes on her in nearly a year. She called out from somewhere in another room, "Bye! I love you! See you on Monday!"

"Okay, love you, too," the boy said, and trudged after Loomis, dragging his backpack of homework and a change of clothes. "Bye, Uncle Bob," the boy said to the ex-marine. Uncle Bob! The ex-marine stood up, gave the boy a small salute, then he and the boy exchanged high fives.

After Loomis checked in at the motel, they went straight to their room and watched television for a while. Lately, his son had been watching cartoons made in the Japanese anime style. Loomis thought the animation was wooden and amateurish. He didn't get it at all. The characters were drawn as angularly as origami, which he supposed was appropriate and maybe even intentional, if the influence was Japanese. But it seemed irredeemably foreign. His son sat propped against several pillows, harboring such a shy but mischievous grin that Loomis had to indulge him.

He made a drink and stepped out onto the balcony to smoke a cigarette. Down by the pool, a woman with long, thick black hair— it was stiffly unkempt, like a madwoman's in a movie—sat in a deck chair with her back to Loomis, watching two children play in the water. The little girl was nine or ten, and the boy was older, maybe fourteen. The boy teased the girl by splashing her face with water, and when she protested in a shrill voice he leaped over and dunked her head. She came up gasping and began to cry. Loomis was aston-ished that the woman, who he assumed was the children's mother, displayed no reaction. Was she asleep?

The motel had declined steadily in the few months that Loomis had been staying there, like a moderately stable person drifting and sinking into the lassitude of depression. Loomis wanted to help, find some way to speak to the managers and the other employees, to say, "Buck up, don't just let things go all to hell," but he felt powerless against his own inclinations.

He lit a second cigarette to go with the rest of his drink. A few other people walked up and positioned themselves around the pool's apron, but none got into the water with the two quarreling children. There was something feral about them, anyone could see. The woman with the wild black hair continued to sit in her pool chair as if asleep or drugged. The boy's teasing of the girl had become steadily rougher, and the girl was sobbing now. Still, the presumptive mother did nothing. Someone went in to complain. One of the managers came out and spoke to the woman, who immediately, but without getting up from her deck chair, shouted to the boy, "All right, God damn it!" The boy, smirking, climbed from the pool, leaving the girl standing in waist-deep water, sobbing and rubbing her eyes with her fists. The woman stood up then and walked toward the boy. There was something off about her clothes, burnt-orange Bermuda shorts and a men's lavender oxford shirt. And they didn't seem to fit right. The boy, like a wary stray dog, watched her approach. She snatched a lock of his wet black hair, pulled his face to hers, and said something, gave his head a shake and let him go. The boy went over to the pool and spoke to the girl. "Come on," he said. "No," the girl said, still crying. "You let him help you!" the woman shouted, startling the girl into letting the boy take her hand. Loomis was fascinated, a little bit horrified.

Turning back toward her chair, the woman looked up to where he stood on the balcony. She had an astonishing face, broad and long, divided by a great, curved nose, dominated by a pair of large, dark, sunken eyes that seemed blackened by blows or some terrible history. Such a face, along with her immense, thick mane of black hair, made her look like a troll. Except that she was not ugly. She looked more like a witch, the cruel mockery of beauty and seduction. The oxford shirt was mostly unbuttoned, nearly spilling out a pair of full, loose, mottled-brown breasts.

"What are you looking at!" she shouted, very loudly from deep in her chest. Loomis stepped back from the balcony railing. The woman's angry glare changed to something like shrewd assessment, and then dismissal. She shooed her two children into one of the downstairs rooms.

After taking another minute to finish his drink and smoke a third cigarette, to calm down, Loomis went back inside and closed the sliding glass door behind him.

His son was on the bed, grinning, watching something on television called *Code Lyoko*. Loomis tried to watch it with him for a while, but got restless. He wanted a second, and maybe stronger, drink.

"Hey," he said. "How about I just get some burgers and bring them back to the room?"

The boy glanced at him and said, "That'd be okay."

Loomis got a sack of hamburgers from McDonald's, some fries, a Coke. He made a second drink, then a third, while his son ate and watched television. They went to bed early.

The next afternoon, Saturday, they drove to the long, wide beach at Carlsbad. Carlsbad was far too cool, but what could you do? Also, the hip little surf shop where the boy's mother worked during the week was in Carlsbad. He'd forgotten that for a moment. He was having a hard time keeping her in his mind. Her invisibility strategy was beginning to work on him. He wasn't sure at all anymore just who she was or ever had been. When they'd met, she wore business attire, like everyone else he knew. What did she wear now? Did she get up and go around in a bikini all day? She didn't really have the body for that at age thirty-nine, did she?

"What does your mom wear to work?" he asked.

The boy gave him a look that would have been ironic if he'd been a less compassionate child.

"Clothes?" the boy said.

"Okay," Loomis said. "Like a swimsuit? Does she go to work in a swimsuit?"

"Are you okay?" the boy said.

Loomis was taken aback by the question.

"Me?" he said.

They walked along the beach, neither going into the water. Loomis enjoyed collecting rocks. The stones on the beach here were astounding. He marveled at one that resembled an ancient war club. The handle fit perfectly into his palm. From somewhere over the water, a few miles south, they could hear the stuttering thud of a large helicopter's blades. Most likely a military craft from the marine base farther north.

Maybe he wasn't okay. Loomis had been to five therapists since separating from his wife: one psychiatrist, one psychologist, three counselors. The psychiatrist had tried him on Paxil, Zoloft, and Well-butrin for depression, and lorazepam for anxiety. Only the lorazepam had helped, but with that he'd overslept too often and lost his job. The psychologist, once she learned that Loomis was drinking almost half a bottle of booze every night, became fixated on getting him to join A.A. and seemed to forget altogether that he was there to figure out whether he indeed no longer loved his wife. And why he had cheated on her. Why he had left her for another woman when the truth was that he had no faith that the new relationship would work out any better than the old one. The first counselor seemed sensible, but Loomis made the mistake of visiting her together with his wife, and when she suggested that maybe their marriage was kaput his wife had walked out. The second counselor was actually his wife's coun-selor, and Loomis thought she was an idiot. Loomis suspected that his wife liked the second counselor because she did nothing but nod and sympathize and give them brochures. He suspected that his wife simply didn't want to move out of their house, which she liked far more than Loomis did, and which possibly she liked more than she liked Loomis. When she realized that divorce was inevitable, she shifted gears, remembered that she wanted to surf, and sold the house before Loomis was even aware it was on the market, so he had to sign. Then it was Loomis who mourned the loss of the house. He visited the third counselor with his girlfriend, who seemed constantly angry that his divorce hadn't yet come through. He and the girlfriend both gave up on that counselor because he seemed terrified of them for some reason they couldn't fathom. Loomis was coming to the conclusion that he couldn't fathom anything; the word seemed appropriate to him, because most of the time he felt as if he were drowning and couldn't find the bottom or the surface of this murky body of water he had fallen, or dived, into.

He wondered if this was why he didn't want to dive into the crashing waves of the Pacific, as he certainly would have when he was younger. His son didn't want to because, he said, he'd rather surf.

"But you don't know how to surf," Loomis said.

"Mom's going to teach me as soon as she's good enough at it," the boy said.

"But don't you need to be a better swimmer before you try to surf?" Loomis had a vague memory of the boy's swimming lessons, which maybe hadn't gone so well.

"No," the boy said.

"I really think," Loomis said, and then he stopped speaking, because the helicopter he'd been hearing, one of those large twin-engine birds that carry troops in and out of combat—a Chinook—had come abreast of them, a quarter mile or so off the beach. Just as Loomis looked up to see it, something coughed or exploded in one of its engines. The helicopter slowed, then swerved, with the slow grace of an airborne leviathan, toward the beach where they stood. In a moment it was directly over them. One of the men in it leaned out of a small opening on its side, frantically waving, but the people on the beach, including Loomis and his son, beaten by the blast from the

blades and stung by sand driven up by it, were too shocked and confused to run. The helicopter lurched back out over the water with a
tremendous roar and a deafening, rattling whine from the engines.
There was another loud pop, and black smoke streamed from the forward engine as the Chinook made its way north again, seeming hob-
bled. Then it was gone, lost in the glare over the water. A bittersweet
burnt-fuel smell hung in the air. Loomis and his son stood there
among the others on the beach, speechless. One of two very brown
young surfers in board shorts and crew cuts grinned and nodded at
the clublike rock in Loomis's hand.

"Dude, we're safe," he said. "You can put down the weapon." He
and the other surfer laughed.

Loomis's son, looking embarrassed, moved off as if he were with
someone else in the crowd, not Loomis.

They stayed in Carlsbad for an early dinner at Pizza Port. The place
was crowded with people who'd been at the beach all day, although
Loomis recognized no one they'd seen when the helicopter had nearly
crashed and killed them all. He'd expected everyone in there to know
about it, to be buzzing about it over beer and pizza, amazed, exhila-
rated. But it was as if it hadn't happened.

The long rows of picnic tables and booths were filled with young
parents and their hyperkinetic children, who kept jumping up to get
extra napkins or forks or to climb into the seats of the motorcycle
video games. Their parents flung arms after them like inadequate las-
sos or pursued them and herded them back. The stools along the bar
were occupied by young men and women who apparently had no
children and who were attentive only to one another and to choosing
which of the restaurant's many microbrews to order. In the corner by
the restrooms, the old surfers, regulars here, gathered to talk shop
and knock back the stronger beers, the double-hopped and the barley
wines. Their graying hair frizzled and tied in ponytails or dreads or
chopped in stiff clumps dried by salt and sun. Their faces leather

brown. Gnarled toes jutting from their flip-flops and worn sandals like assortments of dry-roasted cashews, Brazil nuts, gingerroot.

Loomis felt no affinity for any of them. There wasn't a single person in the entire place with whom he felt a thing in common—other than being, somehow, human. Toward the parents he felt a bitter disdain. On the large TV screens fastened to the restaurant's brick walls surfers skimmed down giant waves off Hawaii, Tahiti, Australia.

He gazed at the boy, his son. The boy looked just like his mother. Thick bright-orange hair, untamable. They were tall, stemlike people with long limbs and that thick hair blossom on top. Loomis had called them his rosebuds. "Roses are red," his son would respond, delightedly indignant, when he was smaller. "There are orange roses," Loomis would reply. "Where?" "Well, in Indonesia, I think. Or possibly Brazil." "No!" his son would shout, breaking down into giggles on the floor. He bought them orange roses on the boy's birthday that year.

The boy wasn't so easily amused anymore. He waited glumly for their pizza order to be called out. They'd secured a booth vacated by a smallish family.

"You want a Coke?" Loomis said. The boy nodded absently. "I'll get you a Coke," Loomis said.

He got the boy a Coke from the fountain, and ordered a pint of strong pale ale from the bar for himself.

By the time their pizza came, Loomis was on his second ale. He felt much better about all the domestic chaos around them in the restaurant. It was getting on the boy's nerves, though. As soon as they finished their pizza, he asked Loomis if he could go stand outside and wait for him there.

"I'm almost done," Loomis said.

"I'd really rather wait outside," the boy said. He shoved his hands in his pockets and looked away.

"Okay," Loomis said. "Don't wander off. Stay where I can see you."

"I will."

Loomis sipped his beer and watched as the boy weaved his way through the crowd and out of the restaurant, then began to pace back and forth on the sidewalk. Having to be a parent in this fashion was awful. He felt indicted by all the other people in this teeming place: by the parents and their smug happiness, by the old surfer dudes, who had the courage of their lack of conviction, and by the young lovers, who were convinced that they would never be part of either of these groups, not the obnoxious parents, not the grizzled losers clinging to youth like tough, crusty barnacles. Certainly they would not be Loomis.

And what did it mean, in any case, that he couldn't even carry on a conversation with his son? How hard could that be? To hear him try, you'd think they didn't know each other at all, that he was a friend of the boy's father, watching him for the afternoon or something. He got up to leave, but hesitated, then gulped down the rest of his second beer.

His son stood with hunched shoulders, waiting.

"Ready to go back to the motel?" Loomis said. There was plenty of light left in the day for another walk on the beach, but he wasn't up to it.

The boy nodded. They walked back to the car in silence.

"Did you like your pizza?" Loomis said when they were in the car.

"Sure. It was okay."

Loomis looked at him for a moment. The boy glanced back with the facial equivalent of a shrug, an impressively diplomatic expression that managed to say both, "I'm sorry," and, "What do you want?" Loomis sighed. He could think of nothing else to say that wasn't even more inane.

"All right," he finally said, and drove them back to the motel.

When they arrived, Loomis heard a commotion in the courtyard, and they paused near the gate.

The woman who'd been watching the two awful children was there at the pool again, and the two children themselves had returned to the water. But now the group seemed to be accompanied by an older heavyset man, bald on top, graying hair slicked against the sides of his head. He was arguing with a manager while the other guests around the pool pretended to ignore the altercation. The boy and girl paddled about in the water until the man threw up his hands and told them to get out and go to their room. The girl glanced at the boy, but the boy continued to ignore the man until he strode to the edge of the pool and shouted, "Get out! Let them have their filthy pool. Did you piss in it? I hope you pissed in it. Now get out! Go to the room!" The boy removed himself from the pool with a kind of languorous choreography, and walked toward the sliding glass door of one of the downstairs rooms, the little girl following. Just before reaching the door the boy paused, turned his head in the direction of the pool and the other guests there, and hawked and spat onto the concrete pool apron. Loomis said to his son, "Let's get on up to the room."

Another guest, a lanky young woman whom Loomis had seen beside the pool earlier, walked past them on her way to the parking lot. "Watch out for them Gypsies," she muttered.

"Gypsies?" the boy said.

The woman laughed as she rounded the corner. "Don't let 'em get you," she said.

"I don't know," Loomis said when she'd gone. "I guess they do seem a little like Gypsies."

"What the hell is a Gypsy, anyway?"

Loomis stopped and stared at his son. "Does 'Uncle Bob' teach you to talk that way?"

The boy shrugged and looked away, annoyed.

In the room, his son pressed him about the Gypsies, and he told him that they were originally from some part of India, he wasn't sure which, and that they were ostracized, nobody wanted them. They became nomads, wandering around Europe. They were poor. People accused them of stealing. "They had a reputation for stealing people's children, I think."

He'd meant this to be a kind of joke, or at least lighthearted, but when he saw the expression on the boy's face he regretted it and quickly added, "They didn't, really."

It didn't work. For the next hour, the boy asked him questions about Gypsies and kidnapping. Every few minutes or so, he hopped from the bed to the sliding glass door and pulled the curtain aside to peek down across the courtyard at the Gypsies' room. Loomis had decided to concede that they were Gypsies, whether they really were or not. He made himself a stiff nightcap and stepped out onto the balcony to smoke, although he also peeked through the curtains before going out, to make sure the coast was clear.

The next morning, Sunday, Loomis rose before his son and went down to the lobby for coffee. He stepped out into the empty courtyard to drink it in the morning air, and when he looked into the pool he saw a large dead rat on its side at the bottom. The rat looked peacefully dead, with its eyes closed and its front paws curled at its chest as if it were begging. Loomis took another sip of his coffee and went back into the lobby. The night clerk was still on duty, studying something on the computer monitor behind the desk. She only cut her eyes at Loomis, and when she saw he was going to approach her she met his gaze steadily in that same way, without turning her head.

"I believe you have an unregistered guest at the bottom of your pool," Loomis said.

He got a second cup of coffee, a plastic cup of juice, and a couple of refrigerator-cold bagels (the waffle iron and fresh fruit had disappeared a couple of visits earlier) and took them back to the room. He and his son ate there, then Loomis decided that they should get away from the motel for the day. The boy could always be counted on to want a day trip to San Diego. He loved to ride the red trolleys there, and tolerated Loomis's interest in the museums, sometimes.

They took the commuter train down, rode the trolley to the Mexican border, turned around, and came back. They ate lunch in a famous old diner near downtown, then took a bus to Balboa Park and spent the afternoon in the air-and-space museum and the natural-history museum, and at a small, disappointing model-railroad exhibit. Then they took the train back up the coast.

As they got out of the car at the motel, an old brown van, plain and blocky as a loaf of bread, careened around the far corner of the lot, pulled up next to Loomis, and stopped. The driver was the older man who'd been at the pool. He leaned toward Loomis and said through the open passenger window, "Can you give me twenty dollars? They're going to kick us out of this stinking motel."

Loomis felt a surge of hostile indignation. What, did he have a big sign on his chest telling everyone what a loser he was?

"I don't have it," he said.

"Come on!" the man shouted. "Just twenty bucks!"

Loomis saw his son standing beside the passenger door of the car, frightened.

"No," he said. He was ready to punch the old man now.

"Son of a bitch!" the man shouted, and gunned the van away, swerving onto the street toward downtown and the beach.

The boy gestured for Loomis to hurry over and unlock the car door, and as soon as he did the boy got back into the passenger seat. When Loomis sat down behind the wheel, the boy hit the lock button.

"Was he trying to rob us?" he said.

"No. He wanted me to give him twenty dollars."

The boy was breathing hard and looking straight out the windshield, close to tears.

"It's okay," Loomis said. "He's gone."

"Pop, no offense"—and the boy actually reached over and patted

Loomis on the forearm, as if to comfort him—"but I think I want to sleep at home tonight."

Loomis was so astonished by the way his son had touched him on the arm that he was close to tears himself.

"It'll be okay," he said. "Really. We're safe here, and I'll protect you."

"I know, Pop, but I really think I want to go home."

Loomis tried to keep the obvious pleading note from his voice. If this happened, if he couldn't even keep his son around and reasonably satisfied to be with him for a weekend, what was he at all anymore? And (he couldn't help but think) what would the boy's mother make of it, how much worse would he look in her eyes?

"Please," he said to the boy. "Just come on up to the room for a while, and we'll talk about it again, and if you still want to go home later on I'll take you, I promise."

The boy thought about it and agreed, and began to calm down a little. They went up to the room, past the courtyard, which was blessedly clear of ridiculous Gypsies and other guests. Loomis got a bucket of ice for his bourbon, ordered Chinese, and they lay together on Loomis's bed, eating and watching television, and didn't talk about the Gypsies, and after a while, exhausted, they both fell asleep.

When the alcohol woke him at three a.m., he was awash in a sense of gloom and dread. He found the remote, turned down the sound on the TV. His son was sleeping, mouth open, a lock of his bright-orange hair across his face.

Loomis eased himself off the bed, sat on the other one, and watched him breathe. He recalled the days when his life with the boy's mother had seemed happy, and the boy had been small, and they would put him to bed in his room, where they had built shelves for his toy trains and stuffed animals and the books from which Loomis would read to him at bedtime. He remembered the constant battle in his heart those days. How he was drawn into this construction of conventional happiness, how he felt that he loved this child more than he had ever loved anyone in his entire life, how all of this was possible, this life, how he might actually be able to do it. And yet whenever he had felt this he was also aware of the other, more deeply seated part of his nature that wanted to run away in fear. That believed it was not possible after all, that it could only end in catastrophe, that anything this sweet and heartbreaking must indeed one day collapse into shattered pieces. How he had struggled to free himself, one way or another, from what seemed a horrible limbo of anticipation. He had run away, in his fashion. And yet nothing had ever caused him to feel anything more like despair than what he felt just now, in this moment, looking at his beautiful child asleep on the motel bed in the light of the cheap lamp, with the incessant dull roar of cars on I-5 just the other side of the hedge, a slashing river of what seemed nothing but desperate travel from point A to point B, from which one mad dasher or another would simply disappear, blink out in a flicker of light, at ragged but regular intervals, with no more ceremony or consideration than that.

He checked that his son was still sleeping deeply, then poured himself a plastic cup of neat bourbon and went down to the pool to smoke and sit alone for a while in the dark. He walked toward a group of pool chairs in the shadows beside a stunted palm, but stopped when he realized that he wasn't alone, that someone was sitting in one of the chairs. The Gypsy woman sat very still, watching him.

"Come, sit," she said. "Don't be afraid."

He was afraid. But the woman was so still, and the expression on her face he could now make out in the shadows was one of calm appraisal. Something about this kept him from retreating. She slowly raised a hand and patted the pool chair next to her, and Loomis sat.

For a moment, the woman just looked at him, and, unable not to, he looked at her. She was unexpectedly, oddly attractive. Her eyes were indeed very dark, set far apart on her broad face. In this light, her fierce nose was strange and alarming, almost erotic.

"Are you Gypsy?" Loomis blurted, without thinking.

She stared at him a second before smiling and chuckling deep in her throat.

"No, I'm not Gypsy," she said, her eyes moving quickly from side to side in little shiftings, looking into his. "We are American. My people come from France."

Loomis said nothing.

"But I can tell you your future," she said, leaning her head back slightly to look at him down her harrowing nose. "Let me see your hand." She took Loomis's wrist and pulled his palm toward her. He didn't resist. "Have you ever had someone read your palm?"

Loomis shook his head. "I don't really want to know my future," he said. "I'm not a very optimistic person."

"I understand," the woman said. "You're unsettled."

"It's too dark here to even see my palm," Loomis said.

"No, there's enough light," the woman said. And finally she took her eyes from Loomis's and looked down at his palm. He felt relieved enough to be released from that gaze to let her continue. And something in him was relieved, too, to have someone else consider his future, someone aside from himself. It couldn't be worse, after all, than his own predictions.

She hung her head over his palm and traced the lines with a long fingernail, pressed into the fleshy parts. Her thick hair tickled the edges of his hand and wrist. After a moment, much sooner than Loomis would have expected, she spoke.

"It's not the future you see in a palm," she said, still studying his. "It's a person's nature. From this, of course, one can tell much about a person's tendencies." She looked up, still gripping his wrist. "This tells us much about where a life may have been, and where it may go."

She bent over his palm again, traced one of the lines with the fingernail. "There are many breaks in the heart line here. You are a creature of disappointment. I suspect others in your life disappoint you." She traced a different line. "You're a dreamer. You're an idealist, possibly. Always disappointed by ordinary life, which of course is boring and ugly." She laughed that soft, deep chuckle again and looked up, startling Loomis anew with the directness of her gaze. "People are so fucking disappointing, eh?" She uttered a seductive grunt that loosened something in his groin.

It was true. No one had ever been good enough for him. Not even the members of his immediate family. And especially himself.

"Anger, disappointment," the woman said. "So common. But it may be they've worn you down. The drinking, smoking. No real energy, no passion." Loomis pulled against her grip just slightly, but she held on with strong fingers around his wrist. Then she lowered Loomis's palm to her broad lap and leaned in closer, speaking more quietly.

"I see you with the little boy—he's your child?"

Loomis nodded. He felt suddenly alarmed, fearful. He glanced up, and his heart raced when he thought he saw the boy standing on the balcony, looking out. It was only the potted plant there. He wanted to dash back to the room, but he was rooted to the chair, to the Gypsy with her thin, hard fingers about his wrist.

"This is no vacation, I suspect. It's terrible, to see your child in this way, in a motel."

Loomis nodded.

"You're angry with this child's mother for forcing you to be here."

Loomis nodded and tried to swallow. His throat was dry.

"Yet I would venture it was you who left her. For another woman, a beautiful woman, eh, *mon frère?*" She ran the tip of a nail down one of the lines in his palm. There was a cruel smile on her impossible face. "A woman who once again you believed to be something she was not." Loomis felt himself drop his chin in some kind of involuntary acquiescence. "She was a dream," the woman said. "And she has disappeared, poof, like any dream." He felt suddenly, embarrassingly, close to tears. A tight lump swelled in his throat. "And now you have left her, too, or she has left you, because"—and here the woman paused, shook Loomis's wrist gently, as if to revive his attention, and indeed he had been drifting in his grief—"because you are a ghost.

Walking between two worlds, you know?" She shook his wrist again, harder, and Loomis looked up at her, his vision of her there in the shadows blurred by his tears.

She released his wrist and sat back in her chair, exhaled as if she had been holding her breath, and closed her eyes. As if this excoriation of Loomis's character had been an obligation, had exhausted her.

They sat there for a minute or two while Loomis waited for the emotion that had surged up in him to recede.

"Twenty dollars," the woman said, her eyes still closed. When Loomis said nothing, she opened her eyes. Now her gaze was flat, no longer intense, but she held it on him. "Twenty dollars," she said. "For the reading. This is my fee."

Loomis, feeling as if he'd just been through something physical instead of emotional, his muscles tingling, reached for his wallet, found a twenty-dollar bill, and handed it to her. She took it and rested her hands in her lap.

"Now you should go back up to your room," she said.

He got up to make his way from the courtyard, and was startled by someone standing in the shadow of the Gypsies' doorway. Her evil man-child, the boy from the pool, watching him like a forest animal pausing in its night prowling to let him pass. Loomis hurried on up to the room, tried to let himself in with a key card that wouldn't cooperate. The lock kept flashing red instead of green. Finally the card worked, the green light flickered. He entered and shut the door behind him.

But he'd gone into the wrong room, maybe even some other motel. The beds were made, the television off. His son wasn't there. The sliding glass door to the balcony stood open. Loomis felt his heart seize up and he rushed to the railing. The courtyard was dark and empty. Over in the lobby, the lights were dimmed, no one on duty. It was all shut down. There was no breeze. No roar of rushing vehicles from the 5, the roar in Loomis's mind canceling it out. By the time he heard the sound behind him and turned to see his son come out of the bathroom yawning, it was too late. It might as well have been someone else's child, Loomis the stranger come to steal him away. He stood on the balcony and watched his son crawl back onto the bed, pull himself into a fetal position, close his eyes for a moment, then open them. Meeting his gaze, Loomis felt something break inside him. The boy had the same dazed, disoriented expression he'd had on his face just after his long, difficult birth, when the nurses had put him into an incubator to rush him to intensive care. Loomis had knelt, then, his face up close to the incubator's glass wall, and he'd known that the baby could see him, and that was enough. The obstetrician said, "This baby is very sick," and nurses wheeled the incubator out. He'd gone over to his wife and held her hand. The resident, tears in her eyes, patted his shoulder and said, for some reason, "You're good people," and left them alone. Now he and the child were in this motel, the life that had been their family somehow dissipated into air. Loomis couldn't gather into his mind how they'd gotten here. He couldn't imagine what would come next.

William Trevor

# The Woman of the House

W ELL, THERE'S THAT if you'd want it," the crippled man said. "It's a long time waiting for attention. You'd need tend the mortar."

The two men who had come to the farmhouse consulted one another, not saying anything, only nodding and gesturing. Then they gave a price for painting the outside walls of the house and the crippled man said it was too much. He quoted a lesser figure, saying that had been the cost the last time. The men who had come looking for work said nothing. The tall one hitched up his trousers.

"We'll split the difference if that's the way of it," the crippled man said.

Still not speaking, the two men shook their heads.

"Be off with you in that case," the crippled man said.

They didn't go, as if they hadn't understood. It was a ploy of theirs to pretend not to understand, to frown and simulate confusion because, in any conversation, it was convenient sometimes to appear to be at a loss.

"Two coats we're talking about?" the crippled man inquired.

The tall man said they were. He was older than his companion, gray coming into his hair, but that was premature: both were still young, in their twenties.

"Will we split the difference?" the crippled man suggested again. "Two coats and we'll split it?"

The younger of the men, who had a round, moon face and wire-rimmed glasses, offered another figure. He stared down at the gray, badly cracked flags of the kitchen floor, waiting for a response. The tall man, whose arms hung loosely and were lanky, like his body, sucked at his teeth, which was a way he had. If it was nineteen years since the house had been painted, he said, the price would have been less than would be worthwhile for them now. Nineteen years was what they had been told.

"Are ye Polish?" the crippled man asked.

They said they were. Sometimes they said that, sometimes they didn't, depending on what they had previously ascertained about the presence of other Polish people in a locality. They were brothers, although they didn't look like brothers. They were not Polish.

A black cat crept about the kitchen, looking for insects or mice. Occasionally it would pounce on a piece of bark that had fallen off the firewood, or a shadow. Fourteen days the painting would take, the young man said, and they'd work on a Sunday; then the cost of the work surfaced again. A price was agreed.

"Notes," the tall man said, rubbing a thumb and forefinger together. "Cash."

And that was agreed also.

Martina drove slowly, as she always did driving back from Carragh. More than once on this journey, the old Dodge had stopped and she had had to walk to Kirpatrick's Garage to get assistance. Each time the same mechanic told her the car belonged to the antique brigade and should have been off the road for the last thirty years at the very least. But the ancient Dodge was part of Martina's circumstances, to be tolerated because it was necessary. And, driven slowly, more often than not it got you there.

Costigan had slipped in a couple of streaky instead of back rashers, making up the half pound, he'd said, although he'd charged for back. She hadn't said anything; she never did with Costigan. "Come out to the shed till we'll see," he used to say, and she'd go with him to pick out a frozen pork steak or drumsticks she liked the look of in the shed where the deep freeze was, his hands all over her. He no longer invited her to accompany him to the deep freeze, but the days when he used to were always there between them and she never ate pork steak or chicken legs without being reminded of how afterward he used to push the money back to her when she paid and how in the farmhouse she hid it in the Gold Flake tin.

She drove past the tinkers at the Cross, the children in their rags running about, feet bare, heads cropped. The woman whom the noise of the Dodge always brought out stared stonily, continuing to stand there when the car went on, a still image in the rearview mirror. "We'd do it for four and a half," the man in Finnally's had offered when she'd asked the price of the electric cooker that was still in the window. Not a chance, she'd thought.

About to be fifty and putting on more weight than pleased her, Martina had once known what she wanted, but she wasn't so sure about that anymore. Earlier in her life, a careless marriage had fallen apart, leaving her homeless. There had been no children, although she had wanted them, and often since had thought that in spite of having to support them she might have done better if children had been there to make a center for her life.

She drove through the turf bogs, a Bord na Móna machine drawn up at the cuttings, an uncoupled trailer clamped so that it would stay where it was. Nothing was going on, nothing had changed at the cuttings for maybe as long as nine months. The lack of activity was lowering, she considered every time she saw, yet again, the place as it had been the last time.

She turned at Laughil, the road darkened by the trees that overhung it. She couldn't remember when it was that she'd last met another car on this journey. She didn't try to. It didn't matter.

. . .

The two men drove away, pleased that they'd found work, talking about the man who'd called out and said come in when they'd knocked on the door. All the time they were there he had remained in his chair by the fire of the range, and when the price was agreed he'd said go to the scullery and get the whiskey bottle. He had gestured impatiently when they didn't understand, lifting his fist to his mouth, tossing back his head, the fist going with it, until they knew he meant drinking. He was convivial then; and they were quick, he said, to see the glasses on the dresser and put three on the table. They were uncertain only for a moment, then unscrewed the cap on the bottle.

"We know about Poland," he'd said. "A Catholic people, like ourselves. We'll drink to the work, will we?"

They poured more whiskey for him when he held out the glass. They had more themselves before they left.

"Who was here?"

She put the groceries on the table as she spoke. The whiskey bottle was there, out of his reach, two empty glasses beside it, his own, empty now also, in his hand. He held it out, his way of asking her to pour him more. He wouldn't stop now, she thought; he'd go on until that bottle was empty and then he'd ask if there was one unopened, and she'd say no, although there was.

"A blue van," she said, giving him more drink, since there was no point in not.

"I wouldn't know what color it was."

"A blue van was in the boreen."

"Did you get the listful?"

"I did."

He'd had visitors, he said as if this subject were a new one. "Good boys, Martina."

"Who?" she asked again.

He wanted the list back, and the receipt. With his stub of a pencil, kept specially for the purpose, he crossed off the items she took from the bags they were in. In the days when Costigan was more lively she had enjoyed these moments of deception, the exact change put down on the table, what she had saved still secreted in her clothes until she could get upstairs to the Gold Flake tin.

"Polish lads," he said. "They'll paint the outside for us." Two coats, he said, a fortnight it would take.

"Are you mad?"

"Good Catholic boys. We had a drink."

She asked where the money was coming from and he asked, in turn, what money was she talking about. That was a way he had, and a way of hers to question the money's source, although she knew there was enough; the subject, once raised, had a tendency to linger.

"What'd they take off you?"

With feigned patience, he explained he'd paid for the materials only. If the work was satisfactory he would pay what was owing when the job was finished. Martina didn't comment on that. Angrily, she pulled open one of the dresser's two drawers, felt at the back of it, and brought out a bundle of euro notes, fives and tens in separate rubber bands, twenties, fifties, a single hundred. She knew at once how much he had paid. She knew he would have had to ask the painters to reach in for the money, since he couldn't himself. She knew they would have seen the amount that was left there.

"Why would they paint a house when all they have to do is walk in and help themselves?"

He shook his head. He said again the painters were fine Catholic boys. With patience still emphatic in his tone, he repeated that the work would be completed within a fortnight. It was the talk of the country, he said, the skills young Polish boys brought to Ireland. An act of God, he said. She wouldn't notice them about the place.

They bought the paint in Carragh, asking what would be best for the walls of a house.

"Masonry," the man said, pointing at the word on a tin. "Outside work, go for the Masonry."

They understood. They explained that they'd been given money in advance for materials and they paid the sum that was written down for them.

"Polish, are you?" the man asked.

Their history was unusual. Born into a community of stateless survivors in the mountains of what had once been Carinthia, their natural language a dialect enlivened by words from a dozen others, they were regarded often now as Gypsies. They remembered a wandering childhood of nameless places, an existence in tents and silent nighttime crossing of borders, the unceasing search for somewhere better. They had separated from their family without regret when they were, they thought, thirteen and fourteen. Since then their lives were what they had become: knowing what to do, how best to do it, acquiring what had to be acquired, managing. Wherever they were, they circumvented what they did not call the system, for it was not a word they knew; but they knew what it meant and knew that straying into it, or their acceptance of it, however temporarily, would deprive them of their freedom. Survival as they were was their immediate purpose, their hope that there might somewhere be a life that was more than they yet knew.

They bought brushes as well as the paint, and white spirit because the man said they'd need it, and a filler because they'd been told the mortar required attention: they had never painted a house before, they didn't know what mortar was.

Their van was battered, the blue patched up a bit with a darker shade, without tax or insurance, although there was the usual evidence of both on the windscreen. They slept in it, among contents that they kept tidy, knowing that they must: tools of one kind or another they had come by, their mugs, their plates, a basin, saucepan, frying pan, food.

In the dialect that was their language the older brother asked if they would spare the petrol to go to the ruins where they were engaged in making themselves a dwelling. The younger brother, driving, nodded and they went there.

. . .

In her bedroom Martina closed the lid of the Gold Flake tin and secured it with its rubber band. She stood back from the wardrobe looking glass and critically surveyed herself, ashamed of how she'd let herself go, her bulk not quite obese but almost now, her pale-blue eyes—once her most telling feature—half lost in folds of flesh. She had been still in her thirties when she'd come to the farmhouse, still particular about how she looked and dressed. She wiped away the lipstick that had been smudged by Costigan's rough embracing when for a few minutes they had been alone in the shop. She settled her underclothes where he had disturbed them. The smell of the shop—a medley of rashers and fly spray and the chickens Costigan roasted on a spit—had passed from his clothes to hers, as it always did. "Oh, just the shop," she used to say when she was asked about it in the kitchen, but she wasn't anymore.

They were distantly related, had been together in the farmhouse since his mother died, twelve years ago, and his father the following winter. Another distant relative had suggested the union, since Martina was on her own and only occasionally employed. Her cousin—for they had agreed that they were cousins of a kind—would have otherwise had to be taken into a home; and she herself had little to lose by coming to the farm. The grazing was parceled out, rent received annually, and now and again another field sold. Her crippled cousin, who since birth had been confined as he was now, had for Martina the attraction of a legal stipulation: in time she would inherit what was left.

Often people assumed that he had died, never saying a word, but you could tell. In Carragh they did, and people from round about who never came to the farmhouse did; talking to them, you could feel it. She didn't mention him herself except when the subject was brought up: there was nothing to say because there was nothing that was different, nothing she could remark on.

He was asleep after the whiskey when she went downstairs and he slept until he was roused by the clatter of dishes and the frying of their six-o'clock meal. She liked to keep to time, to do what it told her to do. She kept the alarm clock on the dresser wound, and accurate to the minute by the wireless morning and evening. She collected, first thing every morning, what eggs had been laid in the night. She got him to the kitchen from the back room as soon as she'd set the breakfast table. She made the two beds when he had his breakfast in him and she had washed up the dishes. On a day she went to Carragh she left the house at a quarter past two; she'd got into the way of that. Usually he was asleep by the range then, as most of the time he was unless he'd begun to argue. If he had, that could go on all day.

"They'll be a nuisance about the place." She had to raise her voice because the liver on the pan was spitting. The slightest sound— of dishes or cooking, the lid of the kettle rattling—and he said he couldn't hear her when she spoke. But she knew he could.

He said he couldn't now and she ignored him. He said he'd have another drink and she ignored that, too.

"They're never a nuisance," he said. "Lads like that."

He said they were clean, you'd look at them and know. He said they'd be company for her.

"One month to the next you hardly see another face, Martina. Sure, I'm aware of that, girl. Don't I know it the whole time."

She cracked the first egg into the pool of fat she made by tilting the pan. She could crack open an egg and empty it with one hand. Two each they had.

"It needs the paint," he said.

She didn't comment on that. She didn't say he couldn't know; how could he, since she didn't manage to get him out to the yard anymore? She hadn't managed to for years.

"It does me good," he said. "The old drop of whiskey."

She turned the wireless on and there was old-time music playing.

"That's terrible stuff," he said.

Martina didn't comment on that, either. When the slices of liver were black she scooped them off the pan and put them on their plates with the eggs. She got him to the table. He'd had whiskey enough, she said when he asked for more, and nothing further was said in the kitchen.

When they had eaten she got him to his bed, but an hour later he was shouting and she went to him. She thought it was a dream, but he said it was his legs. She gave him aspirins, and whiskey, because when he had both the pains would go. "Come in and keep me warm," he whispered, and she said no. She often wondered if the pains had maddened him, if his brain had been attacked, as so much else in his body was.

"Why'd they call you Martina?" he asked, still whispering. A man's name, he said; why would they?

"I told you."

"You'd tell me many a thing."

"Go to sleep now."

"Are the grass rents in?"

"Go back to sleep."

The painting commenced on a Tuesday because on the Monday there was ceaseless rain. The Tuesday was fine, full of sunshine, with a soft, drying breeze. The painters hired two ladders in Carragh and spent that day filling in the stucco surface where it had broken away.

The woman of the house, whom they assumed to be the crippled man's wife, brought out soda scones and tea in the middle of the morning, and when she asked them what time was best for this—morning and afternoon—they pointed at eleven o'clock and half past three on the older brother's watch. She brought them biscuits with the tea at exactly half past three. She stayed talking to them, telling them where they could buy what they wanted in Carragh, asking them about themselves. Her smile was tired but she was patient with them when they didn't understand. She watched them while they worked and when they asked her what she thought she said they were as good as anyone. By the evening the repairs to the stucco had been completed.

Heavy rain was forecast for the Wednesday, and it came in the middle of the afternoon, blown in from the west by an intimidating storm. The work could not be continued, and the painters sat in their van, hoping for an improvement. Earlier, while they were working, there had been raised voices in the house, an altercation that occasionally gave way to silence before beginning again. The older painter, whose English was better than his brother's, reported that it had to do with money and the condition of the land. "The pension is what I'm good for," the crippled man repeatedly insisted. "Amn't I here for the few bob I bring in?" The pension became the heart of what was so crossly talked about, how it was spent in ways it shouldn't be, how the crippled man didn't have it for himself. The painters lost interest, but the voices went on and could still be heard when one or other of them left the van to look at the sky.

Late in the afternoon they gave up waiting and drove into Carragh. They asked in the paint shop how long the bad weather would last and were advised that the outlook for several days was not good. They returned the ladders, reluctant to pay for their hire while they were unable to make use of them. It was a setback, but they were used to setbacks and, inquiring again in the paint shop, they learned that a builder who'd been let down was taking on replacement labor at the conversion of a disused mill—an indoor site a few miles away. He agreed to employ them on a day-to-day basis.

The rain affected him. When it rained he wouldn't stop, since she was confined herself, and when they had worn out the subject of the pension he would begin again about the saint she was named after. "Tell me," he would repeat his most regular request and if it was the evening and he was fuddled with drink she wouldn't answer, but in the daytime he would wheedle and every minute would drag more sluggishly than minutes had before.

He did so on the morning the painters took down their ladders and went away. She was shaking the clinker out of the range so that the fire would glow. She was kneeling down in front of him and she could feel him examining her the way he often did. You'd be the better for it, he said, when she'd tell about her saint, you'd feel the consolation of a holiness. "Tell me," he said.

She took the ash pan out to the yard, not saying anything before she went. The rain soaked her shoulders and dribbled over her face and neck, drenched the gray-black material of her dress, her arms, ran down between her breasts. When she returned to the kitchen she did as he wished, telling him what he knew: that holy milk, not blood, had flowed in the body of Saint Martina of Rome, that Pope Urban had built a church in her honor and had composed the hymns used in her office in the Roman Breviary, that she perished by the sword.

He complimented her when she finished speaking, while she still stood behind him, not wanting to look at him. The rain she had brought in with her dripped through her clothes onto the broken flags of the floor.

The painters worked at the mill conversion for longer than they might have, even though the finer weather had come. The money was better and there was talk of more employment in the future: in all, nine days passed before they returned to the farmhouse.

They arrived early, keeping their voices down and working quickly to make up for lost time, nervous in case there was a complaint about their not returning sooner. By eight o'clock the undercoat was on most of the front wall.

The place was quiet and remained so, but wisps of smoke were coming from one of the chimneys, which the painters remembered from the day and a half they'd spent here before. The car was there, its length too much for the shed it was in, its rear protruding, and they remembered that, too. Still working at the front of the house, they listened for footsteps in the yard, expecting the tea that had come before in the morning, but no tea came. In the afternoon, when the older brother went to the van for a change of brushes, the tea tray was on the bonnet and he carried it to where the ladders were.

In the days that followed this became a pattern. The stillness the place had acquired was not broken by the sound of a radio playing or voices. The tea came without additions and at varying times, as if the arrangement about eleven o'clock and half past three had been forgotten. When the ladders were moved into the yard the tray was left on the step of a door at the side of the house.

Sometimes, not often, glancing into the house, the painters caught a glimpse of the woman whom they assumed to be the wife of the crippled man they had drunk whiskey with, who had shaken hands with both of them when the agreement about the painting was made. At first they wondered if the woman they saw was someone else, even though she was similarly dressed. They talked about that, bewildered by the strangeness they had returned to, wondering if in this country so abrupt a transformation was ordinary and usual and was often to be found.

Once, through the grimy panes of an upstairs window, the younger brother, from his ladder, saw the woman crouched over a dressing table, her head on her arms as if she slept, or wept. She looked up while he still watched, his curiosity beyond restraint, and her eyes stared back at him, but she did not avert her gaze.

That same day, just before the painters finished for the day, while they were scraping the last of the old paint from the kitchen window frames, they saw that the crippled man was not in his chair by the range and realized that since they had returned after the rain they had not heard his voice.

She washed up their two cups and saucers, teaspoons with a residue of sugar on them because they'd been dipped into the bowl when they were wet with tea. She wiped the tray and dried it, and hung the damp tea towel on the line in the scullery. She didn't want to think, even to know that they were there, that they had come. She didn't want to see them, as all day yesterday she had managed not to. She hung the cups up and put the saucers with the others, the sugar bowl in the cupboard under the sink.

The ladders clattered in the yard, pulled out of sight for the night in case they'd be a temptation for the tinkers. She couldn't hear talking and doubted that there was any. A few evenings ago when they were leaving they had knocked on the back door and she hadn't answered.

She listened for footsteps coming to the door again but none came. She heard the van being driven off. She heard the geese flying over, coming from the water at Dole: this was their time. Once the van had returned when something had been left behind, and she'd been collecting the evening eggs and had gone into the fields until it was driven off again. In the kitchen she waited for another quarter of an hour, watching the hands of the dresser clock. Then she let the air into the house, the front door and the back door open, the kitchen windows.

The dwelling they had made for themselves at the ruins was complete. They had used the fallen stones and the few timber beams that were in good condition, a door frame that had survived. They'd bought sheets of old galvanized iron for the roof, and found girders on a tip. It wasn't bad, they said to one another; in other places they'd known worse.

In the dark of the evening they talked about the crippled man, concerned—and worried as their conversation advanced—since the understanding about payment for the painting had been made with him and it could easily be that when the work was finished the woman would say she knew nothing about what had been agreed, that the sum they claimed as due to them was excessive. They wondered if the crippled man had been taken from the house, if he was in a home. They wondered why the woman still wasn't as she'd been at first.

She backed the Dodge into the middle of the yard, opened the right-hand back door, and left the engine running while she carried out the egg trays from the house and settled them one on top of another on the floor, all this as it always was on a Thursday. Hurrying because she wanted to leave before the men came, she locked the house and banged the car door she'd left open. But the engine, idling nicely, stopped before she got into the driver's seat. And then the blue van was there.

They came toward her at once, the one with glasses making gestures she didn't understand at first and then saw what he was on about. A rear tire had lost some air; he appeared to be saying he would pump it up for her. She knew, she said; it would be all right. She dreaded what would happen now: the Dodge would let her down. But when she turned off the ignition and turned it on again, and tried the starter with the choke out, the engine fired at once.

"Good morning." The older man had to bend at the car window, being so tall. "Good morning," he said again when she wound the window down although she hadn't wanted to. She could hear the ladders going up. "Excuse me," the man who was delaying her said, and she let the car creep on, even though he was leaning on it.

"He's in another room," she said. "A room that's better for him."

She didn't say she had eggs to deliver because they wouldn't understand. She didn't say when you got this old car going you didn't take chances with it because they wouldn't understand that, either.

"He's quiet there," she said.

She drove slowly out of the yard and stalled the engine again.

The painters waited until they could no longer hear the car. Then they moved the ladders, from one upstairs window to the next, until they'd gone all the way round the house. They didn't speak, only glancing at one another now and again, conversing in that way. When they had finished they lit cigarettes. Almost three-quarters of the work was done: they talked about that, and calculated how much paint was left unused and how much they would receive back on it. They did no work yet.

The younger brother left the yard, passing through a gateway in which a gate was propped open by its own weight where a hinge had given way. The older man remained, looking about, opening shed doors and closing them again, listening in case the Dodge returned. He leaned against one of the ladders, finishing his cigarette.

Cloudy to begin with, the sky had cleared. Bright sunlight caught the younger brother's spectacles as he came round the side of the house, causing him to take them off and wipe them clean as he passed back through the gateway. His reconnoitre had led him, through a vegetable patch given up to weeds, into what had been a garden, its single remaining flower bed marked with seed packets that told what its several rows contained. Returning to the yard, he had kept as close to the walls of the house as he could, pressing himself against the stucco surface each time he came to a window, more cautious than he guessed he had to be. The downstairs rooms revealed no more than those above them had and when he listened he heard nothing. No dogs were kept. Cats watched him without interest.

In the yard he shook his head, dismissing his fruitless efforts. There was a paddock with sun on it, he said, and they sat there munching their stale sandwiches and drinking a tin of Pepsi-Cola each.

"The crippled man is dead." The older brother spoke softly and in English, nodding an affirmation of each word, as if to make his meaning clear in case it was not.

"The woman is frightened." He nodded that into place also.

These conjectures were neither contradicted nor commented upon. In silence the two remained in the sun and then they walked through the fields that neglect had impoverished, and in the garden. They looked down at the solitary flower bed, at the bright-colored seed packets marking the empty rows, each packet pierced with a stick. They did not say this was a grave, or remark on how the rank grass, in a wide straight path from the gate, had been crushed and had recovered. They did not draw a finger through the earth in search of seeds where seeds should be, where flowers were promised.

"She wears no ring." The older brother shrugged away that detail, depriving it of any interest it might have had, irrelevant now.

Again they listened for the chug of the car's unreliable engine but it did not come. Since the painting had made it necessary for the windows to be eased in their sashes, the house could now be entered. But when the woman returned she would see it had been in safe hands while she'd been away, its rooms as she had left them, the money untouched. The painting began again and, undisturbed, the men worked until the light went. "She will be here tomorrow," the older brother said. "She will have found the courage, and know we are no threat."

In the van on the way back to their dwelling they talked again about the woman who was not as she had been, and the man who was not there. They guessed and wondered, supposed, surmised. They cooked their food and ate it in uncomfortable confinement, the shreds and crumbs of unreality giving the evening shape. At last impatient, anger had not allowed a woman who had waited too long to wait, again, until she was alone: they sensed enough of truth in that. They smoked slow cigarettes, instinct directing thought. The woman's history was not theirs to know, even though they now were part of it themselves. Their circumstances made them that, as hers made her what she'd become. She would see to it that still the pension came. No one would miss the crippled man, no one went to a lonely place. Tomorrow she would pay for the painting of the house. Tomorrow they would travel on.

Daniel Alarcón

# *The Bridge*

TWO DAYS AGO, at approximately three-forty-five Thursday morning, a truck driver named Gregorio Rabassa misjudged the clearance beneath the pedestrian overpass on the thirty-second block of Avenida Cahuide. His truck, packed with washing machines and destined for a warehouse not far from there, hit the bottom of the bridge, shearing the top off his trailer and bringing part of the overpass down onto the avenue below. The back of the trailer opened on impact, spilling the appliances into the street. Fortunately, at the time of the accident there were no other cars on that stretch of road, and Mr. Rabassa was not seriously injured. Emergency crews arrived within the hour, flooding Cahuide with light, and set about clearing the road of debris. Scraps of metal, pieces of concrete, the exploded insides of a few washing machines, all of it was loaded and carted away. Except for the ruined bridge, little evidence remained of the accident by the morning rush, and many people who lived nearby didn't even hear what had happened while they slept.

The neighborhood to the east of Cahuide does not have one name but many, depending on whom you ask. It is known most commonly as the Thousands, though many locals call it Venice, because of its tendency to flood. I've heard it referred to in news reports as Santa Maria, and indeed it does border that populous district, but the name is not exactly correct. A few summers ago, after a wave of kidnappings, police dotted the area with checkpoints and roadblocks, and the neighborhood became known as Gaza, an odd, rather inexact reference to troubles on the other side of the world, only briefly and occasionally noted in the local press. How this nickname stuck is a mystery. The Thousands is an ordinary neighborhood of working poor, crammed with modest brick houses lining narrow streets. It is set in the foggy basin between two hills, and the only people who know it well are those who call it home. A turbid, slow-moving creek runs roughly parallel to Cahuide and is partially canalized, a project intended to alleviate the annual flooding but which has had, I am told, the opposite effect. The main road entering the neighborhood is paved, as are most others, but some are not. My uncle Ramón, who was blind, lived there with his wife, Matilde, who was also blind, and their road, for instance, was not paved.

On Thursday morning, my uncle and his wife left their house early, as they always did, drank tea, and chatted briefly with Señora Carlotta, who sells hot drinks and pastries from a cart at the corner of José Olaya and Avenida Unidad. She tells me they were in good spirits and that they held hands as they left, though she can't recall what it was they spoke about. "Nothing really," she said to me this afternoon when I went to visit. Her broad face and graying hair give the impression of someone who has seen a great deal from her perch at the corner of these two rather quiet neighborhood streets. Her cheeks were wet and glistening as she spoke. "We never talked about anything in particular," she said, "but I always looked forward to their visit. They seemed to be very much in love."

Each working day, after drinking their tea and chatting with Carlotta, my blind uncle and his blind wife boarded the 73 bus to the city center, a long, meandering route that took over an hour, but which left them within a few steps of their work. They were both employed as translators by a company whose offices are not far from the judicial building where I work: Ramón specialized in English to Spanish; Matilde, Italian to Spanish. All sorts of people are willing to pay for the service and the work could be, from time to time, quite interesting. They would spend their days on the phone, transparent participants in bilingual conversations, translating back and forth between businessmen, government officials, or old couples in one country speaking to their grandchildren in another. Those cases are the most taxing, as the misunderstandings between two generations are far more complex than a simple matter of language.

I went to visit the offices yesterday in my lunch hour, to clean out their desks and talk to their colleagues. I have been named executor of their estate and these sorts of tasks are my responsibility now. Everyone had heard about the accident, of course, and seemed stunned by the news. I received condolences in eight languages from an array of disheveled, poorly dressed men and women, who collectively gave the impression of hovering just slightly above what is commonly known as reality. Each translator wore an earpiece and a microphone, and seemed to have acquired, over the course of a career, or a lifetime, a greenish tint like that of the computer screen that sat before him. All around, the chatter was steady and oddly calming, like the sea, or an orchestra tuning up. One after another, the translators approached and shared a few hushed, accented words, all in a strange patois that seemed both related to and completely divorced from the local dialect. I had to strain to make out their words, and everything would end with an embrace, after which they would shuffle back to their desks, still lilting under their breath in a barely identifiable foreign language. Eventually, an elderly gentleman whose surname was Del Piero, who had worked in the Italian section with Matilde, pulled me aside and led me to a bank of ashy windows that looked out over a crowded side street. He was bent, had a thin, airy voice, and his breath smelled strongly of coffee. His sweater was old and worn, and looked as if you could pull a loose strand of yarn and unravel the entire garment. Mercifully, he spoke a clear, only slightly accented Spanish. They had worked together for years. He thought of Matilde as his daughter, Del Piero told me, and he would miss her most of all. "More than any of these other people," he said, indicating the open floor of the translation offices with a disappointed nod. Did I hear him? He wanted to know if I could hear him.

"Yes," I said. "I hear you."

"She was a saint, a miracle of a woman."

I squeezed his arm and thanked him for his kind words. "My uncle?" I asked.

"I knew him too." Del Piero shrugged me off and straightened his sweater. "We never got along," he said. "I don't speak English."

I let this rather puzzling remark go by with barely a nod. We stared out the window for a moment, not speaking. A slow-moving line had formed along the wall on the street below, mostly elderly people, each clutching a piece of paper. Del Piero explained that on the last Friday of each month, one of the local newspapers held a raffle. Their offices were around the corner. You only had to turn in a completed crossword puzzle to enter. The man in a baseball cap leaning against the wall was, according to Del Piero, a dealer in completed crosswords. By his very stance, by the slouch of his shoulders, you might have guessed he was involved in something much more illicit—the trade in stolen copper, the trafficking of narcotics, the buying and selling of orphans. I had barely noticed him, but now it was clear: one after another the buyers approached, furtively slipped the man in the cap a coin or two, and took the paper he handed them. The old people rushed off with their answer key, to join the line and fill in the squares of their still incomplete puzzles.

"What are they giving away this month?"

"How should I know?" Del Piero said. "Alarm clocks. Blenders. Washing machines like the ones that killed my Matilde." His face went pallid. "Your uncle wasn't blind. I know you won't believe me. But he murdered her, I just know he did."

Del Piero muttered a few words to himself in Italian and then walked back to his desk. I followed him. "Explain yourself," I said, but he shook his head sadly and slumped in his chair. He looked as if he might cry.

No one else seemed to notice our miniature drama and I wondered if translators in this office often fell to weeping in the course of their labors. I grabbed a chair and sat in front of his desk, staring at Del Piero as I do in court sometimes when I want a witness to know I will not relent. "Say it again. Explain it to me."

Del Piero raised a hand for a moment, then seemed to reconsider, letting it drop slowly to the desk. There were beads of sweat gathering at his temples. The man was wilting before me. "What is there to explain? He could *see.* Your uncle moved around the office like a ballerina. I don't do anything all day, you know. No one speaks Italian anymore. Two calls a day. Three at most. All from young men who want visas, boys whose great-grandfathers were born in Tuscany, or Palermo, or wherever. And I negotiate with a court clerk to get a copy of an ancient birth certificate. Do you realize that Italy barely existed as a nation then? All this fiction, all these elegant half-truths, just so yet another one of ours can flee! I know the score. They're all flying to Milan to get sex changes. Cheap balloon tits, like the girls in the magazines. Collagen implants. I can hear it in their voices. They're not cut out for life here. And so, what do I do? All day, I wait for the phone to ring, and while I wait, I watch them. The Chinese, the Arabs, the Hindus. I listen. I watch."

"What are you talking about?"

"He could *see,* damn it. I know this. Matilde and I would sit by that window, waiting for the phone to ring, drinking coffee, and I would describe for her what was happening on the street below. That swarthy guy in the baseball cap—we talked about him every Friday! And she loved it. She said your uncle described things just as well. That he had a magical sense of direction, so perfect that at times she doubted he was blind."

"He wasn't born like that, you know. What she said sounds like a compliment to me."

"If you say so." Del Piero looked unimpressed. "They're going to fire me now."

I didn't want to feel pity for him, but I couldn't help it.

He went on: "Matilde would have quit in protest. She loved me that much. And if she quit, your uncle would have too. He was their best worker—they never would've let him walk. His English was better than the Queen's!"

The Queen? I stood to go. "I appreciate your time," I said, though his phone had been silent since I'd arrived.

Del Piero caught me looking. "I got a call earlier. I might get another this afternoon." Then he shrugged; he didn't believe it himself. He walked me out, his sad, heavy eyes trained at the floor. At the staircase, he stopped. "*Coloro che amiamo non ci abbandonano mai, essi vivono nei nostri ricordi,*" he said.

"Is that so?"

Del Piero nodded gravely. "Indeed. It's not much, but it'll have to do."

I thanked him. Whatever it meant, it did sound nice.

Ramón lost his sight in a fireworks mishap at age seven, when I was only three. I have no memories of him before the accident, and to me he has always been my blind uncle. He was my father's youngest brother, half brother actually, separated by more than twenty years, and you could say we grew up, if not together, then in parallel. By the time Ramón was born, my grandfather's politics had softened quite a bit, so the child was spared a Russian name. My grandfather lived with us, but I never heard him and my father exchange more than a few words. I spent my childhood ferrying messages between the two men—*Tell your father this, tell your grandfather that.* . . . They'd had a falling-out when I was very young, a political disagreement that morphed into a personal one, the details of which no one ever bothered to explain. Ramón's mother, my grandfather's last mistress, was a thin, delicate woman who never smiled, and when I was in elementary and middle school, she would bring her boy over every week or so to see my grandfather. I was an only child in a funereal house and I liked the company. Ramón made a point of addressing me as *nephew,* and my father as *brother,* with such rigor that I understood his mother had taught him to do so. I didn't mind. He always had a new dirty joke to share, something beautifully vulgar he had learned from his classmates at the Normal School for Boys in the old city center. He was a serious student of English even then, would record the BBC evening news on the shortwave, and play it back, over and over, until he understood and could repeat every word. By then, the news might be two weeks old or more, but even so his dedication to the exercise always impressed me.

To my ear, the house got even quieter whenever Ramón and his mother arrived, but he liked our place for precisely the opposite reason: with its creaky wooden floors, he could hear himself coming and going, he said, and the space made sense to him. It was large and the high ceilings gave the human voice a sonority that reminded him of church. Sometimes he would ask me to lead him on a tour of the place, just to test his own impressions of the house, and we would shuttle up and down the steps, or tiptoe along the walls of the living room so he could trace its dimensions. He had memories of the house from before the accident, but they were dimmer each day, and he was aware that his brain had changed. It was changing still, he'd tell me ominously, even now, even at this very moment. I thought he was crazy, but I liked to hear him talk. My mother had lined the stairwell with framed photographs, and Ramón would have me describe what seemed to be quite ordinary family scenes of birthday parties and vacations, my school pictures, or my father with a client celebrating some legal victory.

"Am I in any of them?" Ramón asked me once, and the question caught me so off guard that I said nothing. I remember a ball of pain in the hollow of my stomach and panic spreading slowly up to my chest, my arms. I held my breath until Ramón began laughing.

He would have been forty-four this year.

The centerpiece of each visit was a closed-door sit-down with my grandfather. They spoke about Ramón's studies, his plans, my ailing grandfather dispensing stern bits of wisdom gathered from his forty years as a municipal judge. I was always a bit jealous of these; the undivided attention my grandfather gave Ramón was something my father never gave me. But by the time I was ten, the old man was barely there, his moments of lucidity increasingly brief, until everything was a jumble of names and dates, and he could barely recognize any of us. In the twenty-odd years since my grandfather passed away, my father's mind has collapsed in a similar, if slightly more erratic pattern, as perhaps mine will too, eventually. My inheritance, such as it is.

One day, after Ramón's conversation with my grandfather, he and I went on a walk through the neighborhood. I must have been twelve or thirteen. We were only a few blocks from my house when Ramón announced that he wouldn't be coming to visit anymore. "There's no point," he said. He was finishing school and would soon be attending the university on a scholarship. We were walking in the sun, along the wide, tree-lined median that ran down the main avenue of my district. Ramón, with a hand in his pocket, had insisted on going barefoot so he could feel the texture of the grass between his toes. He had tied the laces of his sneakers and wore them slung around his neck.

"What about me?" I said.

He smiled at the question. "You're a lucky boy. You live with your dad."

I had nothing to say to that.

"Do you want to see something?" Ramón took his hand from his pocket, opening it to reveal a small spool of copper wire, bent and coiled into an impossible knot. I asked him what it was.

"It's a map," he said.

I took it when he passed it to me, careful not to disturb its shape.

"Every time we turn, I bend it," he explained. "And so I never get lost."

"Never?"

"I'm very careful with it."

"It's nice," I said, because that was all I could think to say.

Ramón nodded. "My father isn't coming back. Your grandfather. His mind has . . ." He cupped his hands together, then opened them with a small sound, as if he'd been holding a tiny bomb that had just gone off.

"The old guy's not going to miss me."

The sun was bright and Ramón turned toward it, so that his face glowed. I couldn't deny that he looked very happy.

When we got back to the house, my grandfather was in the living room, asleep in front of the television, taking shallow breaths through his open mouth. He'd been watching opera and now Ramón's mother sat by his side, combing his hair. She stood when she saw her son, nodding at me without a hint of warmth, and then gathered her things. She left the comb balanced on my grandfather's knee.

"It's time to go," she said. "Careful. Don't wake your father. Now say good-bye to your nephew."

He shook my hand very formally, and I saw little of him after that.

My grandfather died two years later.

Last night, I couldn't sleep. For hours, I lay on my back, the bedside lamp on, admiring the ceiling and its eerie yellow tint. My wife slept with the blanket pulled over her head, so still it was possible to imagine I was all alone. I thought of the truck, out of control and speeding, tearing the bridge down as it raced south. Or Ramón, walking Matilde steadily, lovingly, to her death. In their haste, the local emergency crews neglected to block off the bridge's stairs on either side of the avenue. Four hours later, my uncle and aunt climbed these same stairs on their way to the bus stop, but they never made it, of course, tumbling onto the avenue instead, where they were killed by oncoming traffic. It had been in all the afternoon papers on Thursday, along with photos of the truck driver, Rabassa, an unshaven young man with a sheepish smile, who wore his light brown hair in a ponytail. In interviews, he offered his heartfelt condolences to the families, but, on the advice of counsel, had little else to say about the accident. I would have given him the same advice. In the classic understated style common to our local journalists, the ruined bridge was now being called the Bridge of Death, or alternatively the Bridge to Death. At home, my wife and I instructed the maid to let the phone ring, and at the office, I asked my secretary to screen all the calls and hang up on radio, television, or print reporters. It was only a matter of time, and by yesterday morning, when it was discovered that Ramón was related to my father, the scrutiny intensified. There were now two scandals in play. In the afternoon, when I went to pick my daughters up from school, a young reporter, a boy of no more than twenty, followed me to my car, asking for a comment, for anything, a phrase, a string of expletives, a word, a cry of pain. He had hungry eyes and the sort of untrustworthy smile common to youth here: he could commit neither to smiling nor to frowning, the thin edges of his lips suspended somewhere in between. "Do you plan to sue?" he shouted, as my daughters and I hurried toward the car.

Last night I read the afternoon editions very carefully, with something approximating terror: what if someone had managed to get through to my father, to prize a comment from him? It would be difficult, given his situation, but not unthinkable, and surely he would oblige with something outrageous, something terrible. I bought a dozen papers and read every page—testimonials from neighbors, interviews with civil engineers and trucking experts, comments from the outraged president of a community advocacy group and the reticent spokesman of the transport workers' union, along with photos of the site—a hundred opinions through which to filter this ordinary tragedy, but thankfully nothing from my father, and not on the television either.

This morning, Saturday, I went to see my old man to tell him the news myself and make certain the asylum's authorities were aware that soon the press would be calling. Apparently there had been attempts already, but I was relieved to discover my father had lost more of his privileges, including just last week the right to receive incoming calls. He'd long ago been barred from making them. Of course, there were some cell phones floating among the population of the asylum, so the secretary couldn't offer me any guarantees. She didn't know all the details, but his nurse, she assured me, would explain everything.

My old man has been in the asylum for three years now. He is only sixty-eight, young to be in the shape he's in. Every time I go, he's different, as if he's trying on various pathologies to see how they suit him. It happened so slowly I hardly noticed, until the day three and a half years ago that he attacked a man in court—his own client—stabbing him multiple times in the neck and chest with a letter opener, nearly killing him. It came as a great surprise to us, and the press loved the story. It went on for months, and no aspect of the scandal went unreported. For example, it was noted with evident delight that my father's client, the victim—on trial for money laundering—might serve time with his former lawyer if convicted. One columnist used the matter to discuss the possibility of prison reform, while a rather mean-spirited political cartoonist presented the pair as lovers, holding hands and playing house in a well-appointed prison cell. My mother stopped answering the phone or reading the papers; in fact, she rarely left home. But none of this chatter was relevant in the end: the money launderer was acquitted; my father was not.

His trial was mercifully brief. My old man, charged with assault and attempted murder, facing a prison sentence that would take him deep into his eighties, wisely opted for an insanity plea. Out of respect for his class and professional history, room was made for him at the asylum, and though it was jarring at first, over time he has become essentially indistinguishable from the other guests.

I was shown to the visitors' room by a pale, tired-looking nurse who told me my old man had been in a bad mood recently. "He's been acting out."

I'd never seen her before. "Are you new?" I asked.

She walked briskly and I struggled to keep up. She told me she'd been transferred from the women's pavilion. I tried to make small talk, about how things were over there, if she was adjusting to the inevitable differences between the genders, but she wasn't interested and only wanted to tell me about my father. "He's a real sweetheart," she said, and she was worried about him. He wasn't eating and some days he refused to take his medication. The previous week, he had tossed his plate at a man who happened to bump him in the lunch line. "It was spaghetti day. You can imagine the mess."

In case I couldn't, she went on to describe it: how my old man walked calmly from his victim, sat in front of a television in a corner of the cafeteria watching a nature show with the sound off, waiting for the nurses to arrive; how when they did, he crossed his wrists and held his arms out in front of him, as if expecting handcuffs, which, she assured me, "we rarely use with men like your father." Meanwhile, a few terrified patients had begun to cry: they thought the victim was bleeding to death before their very eyes, that those were his organs spilling from his wounded body. The nurse sighed heavily. All sorts of ideas held sway among the residents of the asylum. Some believed in thieves who stole men's kidneys, their livers, and their lungs, and it was impossible to convince them otherwise.

We had come to a locked door. I thanked her for telling me.

"You should visit him more often," she said.

A fluorescent light shone above us, cold, clinical. I kept my gaze fixed on her, until I could see the color gathering in her cheeks. I straightened my tie.

"Should I?" I said. "Is that what you think?"

The nurse looked down at her feet, suddenly fidgety and nervous. "I'm sorry." She pulled a key ring from her jacket pocket and, as she did, her silver cigarette case fell with a crash, a dozen long, thin smokes fanning out across the cement floor like the confused outline of a corpse.

I bent to help her gather them. Her face was very red now.

"My name is Yvette," she said. "If you need anything."

I didn't answer.

Then we were through the door and into a large, rather desolate common room. There were a few ragged couches and a pressboard bookcase along a white wall, its shelves picked almost clean, save for a thin volume on canoe repair, a yellowing cold-war spy novel, and some fashion magazines with half the pages missing. There were a dozen men, not more, and the room was quiet.

Where was everyone?

Yvette explained that many of the patients—she had used this word all along, not inmates, or prisoners, as some others did—were still in the cafeteria and some had retired to their rooms.

"Cells?" I asked.

Yvette pursed her lips. "If you prefer." She continued: many were outside, in the gardens. The morning had dawned clear in this part of the city and I imagined a careless game of volleyball, a couple of men standing flat-footed on either side of a sagging net, and quickly realized these were images culled from movies, that in fact I had no idea how those confined against their will to a hospital for the criminally insane might make use of a rare day of bright, limpid sun. They might lie in the grass and nap, or pick flowers, listen for birds or the not-so-distant sounds of city traffic. Or perhaps glide across the open yard, its yellow grass ceding territory each day to the bare, dark earth, these so-called gardens, each inmate just one man within a ballet much larger, much lonelier than himself. My father preferred to stay indoors. Early on he wasn't permitted outside and so had become, like a house cat, accustomed to watching from the windows, too proud to admit any interest in going out himself. In the three years I've been visiting him, we'd walked the gardens only once: one gray morning beneath a solemn sky, on his birthday, his first after the divorce. He'd walked with his head down the entire time. I mentioned this and Yvette nodded.

"Well, they're not exactly gardens, you know."

Just as Yvette was not exactly a nurse, this prison was not exactly a hospital. Of course I knew. I watched a woman read to a group of inmates, what amounted to a children's story, and she could hardly get through a sentence without being interrupted. My father sat in his usual spot, by the high window in the far corner, overlooking a few little-used footpaths that wended between the trees surrounding the main building. He was alone, which upset me, until I noticed that all the patients in this group were essentially alone; even the ones who were, nominally at least, together. A dozen solitary men scattered about, lost in thought or drugged into somnolence, in a room in which eye contact, the very bedrock of human interaction, seemed to be frowned upon.

Yvette brushed my arm and excused herself wordlessly.

I made my way toward my father, past a small table along a salmon-colored wall, stacked with games and pamphlets, and a bulletin board just above it, announcing the week's program—POETRY NIGHT, SPORTS NIGHT, CEVICHE NIGHT. Hardly an evening passed, as far as I could tell, without a planned activity of some kind; it was no wonder these men seemed so tired. They all wore their own clothes, ranging from the shabby to the somewhat elegant, and this lack of uniform dress operated as a kind of shorthand, revealing at first glance which of these men had been abandoned and which still maintained, however tenuously, some connection to the world outside. There were disheveled men in threadbare, faded T-shirts and others who looked as if they might have a business meeting later, who still took the trouble to keep their leather shoes oiled and polished. A man in denim overalls sat at one of the two long tables writing a letter. An unplugged television was placed at an angle to the small couch, its gray, bulbous eye reflecting the light pouring in through the windows. The curtains were pulled, but the windows themselves did not open, and the room was quite warm.

I sat on the windowsill.

"Hi, Papa," I said.

He didn't respond, only closed his eyes, gripping the arms of his chair as if to steady himself. He looked like my grandfather had so many years ago, shrunken, with long, narrow fingers, the bones of his hands visible beneath the skin. I hadn't seen him in six weeks or so. I asked him how he was, and he looked up and all around me, gazing above me and beyond me, with a theatrical expression of utter confusion, as if he were hearing a voice and couldn't figure where it was coming from.

"Me?" he asked. "Little old me?"

I waited.

"I'm fine," my father said. "A robust specimen of old age in the twilight of Western civilization. It's not me you should worry about. Someone snuck a newspaper in here two weeks ago. You can't imagine the scandal it caused. Is it true the oceans are rising?"

"I suppose so," I said.

He sighed. "When will the Americans learn? I can picture it—can you picture it? The seas on a slow boil, turning yellow, turning red. The fish rise to the surface. They feel pain, you know. Those people who say they don't are liars."

"Who says that?"

"Water heightens sensitivity, boy. When I was a child, I loved to sit in the bathtub. I liked watching my cock float in the bathwater and then shrivel and shrink as the water got cold."

"Papa."

"Sometimes it's so loud in here, I can't breathe. I will break that television if anyone attempts to turn it on. I will pick it up and break it over the head of anyone who goes near it. Just keep your eye on it. Just tell me if someone plugs it in. Will you do that, boy?"

I nodded, if only to keep him calm, and tried to imagine the act. My father versus the television: his back would crumble, his fingers crack, what remained of his body would collapse into a thimbleful of dust. The television would emerge unscathed; my father most certainly would not. When he spoke he waved his arms, fidgeted and shook, and even these small gestures seemed to be wearing him out. He was breathing heavily, his bird chest rising and falling.

"The nurse says you haven't been eating."

"The menu is not interesting," my old man said. He bit his bottom lip.

"And your meds? Are they interesting?"

He glared at me for a second. "Honestly, no. There is a gentleman here with whom I have made a small wager. He says there is a women's pavilion, not far from this building, loose women, crazier than hell. They tear your clothes off with their teeth. I say that's impossible. What do you know of it?"

"It's a beautiful day, Papa. We could go out and see for ourselves."

"No need for that."

"What does the winner of this wager get?"

My father smiled. "Money, boy—what else?"

"I don't know anything about it, Papa," I said, "but I have some news."

At the sound of these words, after all the talk and movement, he fixed his stare on me, nodding, then closed his eyes to indicate he was listening.

"Ramón. Your brother Ramón. He's dead."

My father squinted at me. "The young one?"

I nodded. "Has anyone called you about this?"

He looked surprised. "Called me? Why would anyone call me?"

"The press, I mean. Have you talked to anyone?"

He dismissed the very idea with a wave of his hand. "Of course not," he said. "Am I in the papers?"

"The usual."

He smiled with a melancholy pride. "They don't get tired of me."

"I'm executor of the estate," I said.

"What estate? Ramón doesn't have an estate!" My old man laughed. "Let me guess . . . You're *honored*."

I could have hit him then. It happens every time I visit, and each time I breathe, I wait for it to pass. And I think of my daughters, who will never see their grandfather again, and specifically of my youngest, who has no memories of him at all.

"How did it happen?" my old man asked.

And so I told him the story, what I knew of it—Rabassa's truck and the washing machines, the pedestrian bridge and the bus—as my father listened with eyes closed, letting his chin drop to his chest. As I recounted the events, the order of them, their inevitable conclusion, it sounded so asinine I felt he might not believe me at all. They had not been close. They had spoken little since my grandfather died, after the unpleasant work of dividing up the inheritance had been rendered to our advantage with the help of a small platoon of lawyers and consultants. Ramón used his share to support his mother and, when she passed away, to buy the house where he and Matilde lived. There was little left over for anything else. My father's sister, my aunt Natalya, and his full brother, my uncle Yuri, pooled their shares and bought a condo in Miami overlooking Biscayne Bay. My father got the bulk of the estate, of course, enough to live comfortably for many years, and eventually to cover his defense, the divorce settlement, his upkeep at the asylum. He even set aside a portion for me, his only child, which my wife and I used as a down payment on a house in a part of the city with only one name and no pedestrian bridges. We have lived there since we were married eight years ago.

When I finished, he was quiet for a long moment and seemed to be processing what I had told him. He could have just as easily been trying to recall who this brother was, and why it should bother him that Ramón was dead.

"She wasn't blind," my father said finally. "That bitch had cataracts, it's true, but she could see. She killed him."

For a moment, I couldn't say anything; I just stared at my father, wondering why I'd bothered. "Jesus," I said. "She sure seemed blind at the wedding."

My father looked at me. "How do you *seem* blind?"

"I was joking."

"Jokes," he said, disgusted. "I don't like your jokes." He stood abruptly. His shirt hung off him like a robe and his belt had been pulled tight to the last hole, cinching his pants high above his waist, the fabric ballooning about his midsection. I reached to help him, but he shook me off.

"Papa, you have to eat," I said.

He ignored me, covered his eyes with one hand, and began walking slowly, with heavy, plodding steps, staggering toward the center of the room, a shaky arm raised before him. He stumbled toward the lesser of the two couches, where a nicely dressed gentleman sat thumbing through a pornographic comic book. As my father approached, the man cried out and fled. I called out to my father, but he paid no attention, only changed direction, moving toward one of the tables now. There, the man writing the letter abandoned his work and shuffled off to the corner of the room. The nurse who had been reading saw what was happening, tucked her black hair behind her ears, and hurried over to find out what was the matter, but I got to my father first, this blind, wobbling zombie; I put an arm around him, holding him gently, his thin frame, his hollow chest.

It took almost no effort to restrain him.

"I'm blind, I'm blind," he murmured.

I listened to the cadence of his breath. The other inmates had spread out to the pink corners of the room, as far as they could manage from my old man. They eyed one another tensely and no one spoke. Just then, the black-haired nurse appeared before us. She wanted to know if everything was all right.

"Yes," I said, but my father shook his head. He cleared his throat, and it was only then that he dropped his hand from over his eyes, blinking as he adjusted to the light.

"Alma," he said, "my brother has died and I am bereft. I must be released for the funeral. He has been murdered. It is a tragedy."

The nurse looked at my old man, then at me. I shook my head very slightly, hoping he wouldn't notice.

"Mr. Cano, I'm very sorry for your loss." Alma sounded as if she were reading from a script.

Still my father thanked her. "You're very kind, but I must leave at once. There are details to be taken care of."

"I'm afraid that's not possible."

"My brother . . ."

"Papa," I said.

"Mr. Cano, you cannot leave without a judge's approval."

I held my father and felt the strength gather within him at the very sound of these words. He puffed up; his shoulders straightened. This was likely the least effective pretext one could give my father, the son of a judge, a man who had spent first his childhood and then his entire adult life wandering the corridors of judicial power, a man who had passed on to his own son, if little affection, at least much of this same access. He smiled triumphantly and turned to me. "Your cell phone, please, boy. I know a few judges."

I pretended to search my pockets for my phone, as my old man watched me hopefully. By then Yvette had joined us, somehow gentler than I had noticed her to be at first, and she met his gaze, then touched his shoulder, and just like that he slipped from my hold and into her orbit entirely.

"They've murdered my brother . . ." I heard my old man say, his voice mournful and low. Yvette nodded, leading him to the blue-green couch, and he went without a fight, collapsing into it heavily. She knelt next to him. Alma went off to soothe the other patients, who had been watching us with great anxiety, and suddenly I was alone. I could hear Yvette and my father murmuring conspiratorially, fraternally, now laughing tenderly, a voice breaking, now humming in unison what sounded like a nursery rhyme. With Alma's encouragement, the other inmates were gradually spreading about the room again, in slow, tentative steps, as if trying to move without being seen. Yvette walked over to me.

"I'm sorry about your uncle," she said.

She glanced back at my father and then left us alone. I took her spot beside him and together we watched the men drifting back to their former places. The days here, I realized, were punctuated by these outbursts, these small crises that helped break up the hours. These men had been socialized to expect discrete moments of tension, to defer to the impulse, whether theirs or someone else's, to fashion a disturbance from thin air. And they were experts, too, at forgetting it all, at recovering, at turning back into themselves and whatever private despair kept them company. Except one of them: a slight, well-dressed man pacing back and forth in front of me and my father, occasionally pausing to flash us a confused glare. It took me a moment to realize what had happened: he carried a comic book in his right hand. We'd taken his seat.

I pointed him out to my father and he shrugged. "I've never seen him before in my life."

"He was sitting right here."

"Of course. They were all sitting right here. And they can all sit right here again as soon as I get up."

"Papa, don't get upset."

"I'm not upset," he said, then corrected himself. "That's not true. I *am* upset. I would prefer he stop staring. It's rude. Tonight I will take his belt and hang him with it."

I sighed. "Why would you do that, Papa?"

"I don't know," he said, his voice suddenly weak.

It was honest, at least: he *didn't* know. My father remained, all these years later, the person most mystified by his predicament, by the actions and impulses that had brought him here. "It's okay, Papa." I tried to put an arm around him, but he shook me off.

"It's not okay. I'm going to die here. Not tomorrow, not next week, but eventually. The oceans are rising and my blind brother has been murdered. My ungrateful son never visits and my whore-wife has forgotten me."

"Ex-wife," I said. I didn't mean to.

My father scowled, his gaze narrowing. "Whore-ex-wife," he said. "Go. No one wants you here. Leave."

The last time I saw Ramón was at a family party, about three years ago. It was my father's sixty-fifth birthday, his first since the arrest. This was before the divorce got under way and my mother was still hanging in there. We decided to get my old man out for the party, just for the evening—not an easy task, but certainly not unheard-of for a family of our connections and our means. I was optimistic in the weeks before the party, and saw to it that my mother was as well. I thought it would be good for them both to see each other, and especially good for him to be reminded of the life he'd once had. I paid courtesy visits to bureaucrats all over town, spoke elliptically about my father's situation and looked for the right opening, the right moment, to place money discreetly in the hands of those men who might be able to help us. But nothing happened: my calls went unreturned, the openings were never provided. In the end, I had to tell my mother, only hours before the party, that the director of the asylum, whom I had spoken to directly and pressured through various surrogates, wouldn't take the bribe, just as no judge would sign the order and no prison official would allow themselves to be bent. My father wouldn't be joining us.

She had spent a lifetime with him and become accustomed to getting her way. It was clear she didn't believe me. "How much did you offer?"

"More than enough," I told her. "No one wants to help him anymore."

My mother sat before her mirror, delicately applying makeup, her reddish brown hair still pulled back. She had outlined her lips and examined them now, getting so close to the glass I thought she might kiss herself. "It's not that. It's not that at all," she said. "You just didn't try hard enough."

That night Ramón arrived by himself, dressed as if for a funeral in a sober black suit and starched white shirt. His hair was cut so short that he looked like an enlisted man, or a police officer, and he had chosen to come without the dark glasses he sometimes wore. I'd never seen him this way. I was surprised to find him there, as was my mother, and for a moment much of the whispered conversation at the party had to do with his presence: Who had invited Ramón? How did he know? Why had he come? I led him through the thin crowd of friends and well-wishers, introducing him to everyone. *Oh, you're Vladimiro's younger brother,* some colleague of my father's might say, though for most of them, this was the first they'd ever heard of Ramón. If he noticed the chatter, he didn't let on. There were many fewer guests than we had imagined—even my uncle Yuri had called with an excuse—and the brightly decorated room seemed rather dismal with only a handful of people milling around. It was early yet, I told myself. Ramón moved easily through the party, falling gracefully in and out of various conversations. He let go of my arm every time we stopped before a new group of people, holding his hand out and waiting for someone to shake it. Eventually, someone would. He held Natalya in a long embrace, whispering, *Dear sister, dear dear sister.* I left him chatting with my wife while I went for drinks, and our daughters, three and four years old at the time, climbed into his arms without hesitation. He beamed for a quick photo, and then released them, and measured their height against his waist. My wife told me later that he had remembered not only their names, but also their birthdays and their ages, though he hadn't seen them since my youngest was born.

My mother had positioned herself at the landing of the staircase, at one end of the large room, where she could survey the entire affair, and eventually we made our way over to her. Ramón asked me to leave them alone. They huddled together for a few moments, whispering, and when my mother raised her head again, her eyes were glassy with tears. She gathered herself and called for everyone's attention. Ramón stood by her side. She began by thanking everyone for coming to celebrate this difficult birthday, how much it meant to all of us, to my father and his family. "We did what we could to have him here with us this evening, but it just wasn't possible," she said. She looked at me. "My husband has sent his youngest brother, Ramón, in his place and I want to thank him for coming to be with us."

After acknowledging the polite applause, Ramón scanned the crowd, or seemed to, his lifeless gray eyes flitting left and right. There couldn't have been more than fifteen people altogether, everyone standing, waiting for something to happen. Someone coughed. Ramón asked that the music be turned down, cleared his throat, then went on to describe a version of my father I didn't recognize. A generous man, always available with a loving hand for his younger brother, a man who had helped guide and encourage him. Who had sat with him "after the accident that left me blind, the accident that made me who I am." My mother was sobbing softly now. "Vladimiro helped pay for my studies. He paid for my tutor and helped me land the job where, by the grace of God, I was to meet my wife, Matilde." Then he raised a hand and began singing "Happy Birthday," his voice clear and unwavering.

He sang the first line entirely alone before anyone thought to join in.

I found him, not long after, sitting in what had been my grandfather's favorite chair. He smiled when he heard my voice; he called me *nephew.* I asked him about life. It had been so long since we'd really talked. Matilde was well, he told me, they'd bought a house in the Thousands—*Where?* I thought to myself—and were talking about having a baby. He congratulated me on my family and said, with a playful smile, that he could tell by the timbre of my wife's voice that she was still quite beautiful. I laughed at the compliment.

"Your instincts are, as ever, unfailing," I said.

We were—my wife and I—very happy in those days.

Ramón talked briefly about his work, which in spite of the feeble economy remained steady: Italian was an increasingly irrelevant language, of course, but as long as America remained powerful, he and Matilde would never go hungry. Each day he took calls from the embassy, the DEA, or the Mormons. They trusted him. They asked for him by name.

We fell silent. The party hummed around us and, looking at our uncomfortable guests, I wondered why anyone would want to be part of our family.

"How did my father sound," I asked, "when you talked to him?"

Ramón ran his fingernails along the fabric of the armrest. "I didn't actually speak to him, you know. He had someone call me." He paused and let out a small, sharp laugh. "I haven't spoken to him in years, to be honest. Not since Matilde and I were married. I guess he couldn't get to a phone. I assume they're very strict about those things."

"I guess so."

"But then, I've heard you can get anything in prison," he said. "Is that true?"

"It's not exactly a prison, where he is."

"But he could've called me himself if he'd wanted to?"

I looked over my shoulder at the thinning party. "He's never called me, if that's what you want to know."

Ramón tapped his fingers to the slow rhythm of the music that was playing, an old bolero, something my father would've liked.

"That was quite a performance," I said. "Your speech, I mean."

"It was for your mother."

"Then I suppose I should thank you."

"If you like." He sighed. "My father loved Vladimiro very much. He was so proud of your dad; he talked about him all the time. He was heartbroken that they'd stopped speaking."

"Is that true?"

"Why do you ask if you won't believe my answer?" Ramón shook his head. "Do you visit him?"

"As much as I can."

"What's that mean?"

"As much as I can stand to."

Ramón nodded. "He's not an easy man. Matilde didn't want me to come. She has a sense about these things. And she's never wrong."

I thought he might explain this comment, but he didn't. It just lingered. "So why are you here?" I asked.

"Family is family." He smiled. "That's what I told her. She had quite a laugh with that one."

. . .

And then, this afternoon, I went to Gaza. I took the bus, because I wanted to ride the 73 and sit, as Ramón and Matilde so often had, in the uncomfortable metal seats, beside the scratched and dirty windows, closing my eyes and listening to the breathing city as it passed. The air thickened as we rode south, so that it felt almost like rain, heavy, gray, and damp. The farther we went on Cahuide, the slower the traffic became, and when I got off at the thirty-second block, beneath the remains of the bridge, I saw why: a stream of people filtered across the avenue in a nearly unbroken line, women carrying babies, stocky young men bent beneath the loads teetering on their backs, and children who appeared to be scampering across just for the sport of it. The median fence was no match for this human wave: already it had been knocked over, trampled, and appeared in places to be in danger of disappearing entirely. The harsh sounds of a dozen horns filled the street with an endless noise that most people seemed not to notice, but which shook my skull from the inside. I stopped for a moment to admire the bridge, its crumbling green exterior and shorn middle, its steel rods poking through the concrete and bending down toward the avenue. A couple of kids sat at the scarred edge, their legs dangling just over the lip. They laughed and floated paper airplanes into the sky, arcing them elegantly above the rushing crowd.

I walked up from the avenue along an unnamed street no wider than an alley, blocked off at one end with stacks of bricks and two rusting oil drums filled with sand. A rope hung limply between the drums and I slipped under it, careful not to let it touch my suit. A boy on a bicycle rolled by, smacking his chewing gum loudly as he passed. He did a loop around me, staring, sizing me up, then pedaled off, unimpressed. I kept walking to where the road sloped up just slightly, widening into a small outdoor market, where a few people milled about the stalls stocked with plastics and off-brand clothes and flowers and grains.

I came to the corner of José Olaya and Avenida Unidad, and there I found Carlotta. The lawyer who'd called me yesterday with the news had advised me to look for a woman at a tea cart. *She can show you the house,* he said over the phone. *Your house.* That afternoon, as promised, a courier came by with Ramón's keys, along with a hand-written note from the lawyer once again reiterating this small piece of advice: *Look for Carlotta,* the note read, though there was no description of her. *You'll never find the house without help.*

In fact, it did all look the same, each street indistinguishable from the last, each house a version of the one next to it. Carlotta was sitting on a small wooden stool reading a newspaper when I walked up. I introduced myself and explained that I needed to take a look at my uncle's house. She stood very slowly and wrapped me in a tight embrace.

"They were so wonderful," she said. She kept her hand on mine and didn't let go, just stood there, shaking her head and murmuring what sounded like a prayer. I waited for her to finish. Finally she excused herself, went inside the unpainted brick house just behind her, and emerged a few moments later dragging a boy along. He was eighteen or so, skinny, and looked as if he'd just been sleeping. He wore unlaced white high-top sneakers with no socks and his thin, almost girlish ankles emerged from these clownish shoes with a comic poignancy. Her son, Carlotta explained, would watch the stand while we went to Ramón and Matilde's house. It wasn't far. The boy glanced in my direction through red, swollen eyes, then nodded, though he seemed displeased with the arrangement.

As Carlotta and I walked up the street, she pointed out a few neighborhood landmarks: the first pharmacy in the area, the first Internet kiosk, an adobe wall pockmarked with bullet holes, site of a murder that had made the news a few years ago. A police checkpoint, from the days when the name Gaza came into use, had stood right at the intersection we strolled through now. These were peaceful times, she said. She showed me the footbridge that crossed over the canal, and the open field just beyond it, where the turbid floodwaters gathered once a year or so. It was where the teenagers organized soccer tournaments, where the Christians held their monthly revivals, and where a few local deejays threw parties that lasted until first light. Awful music, she said, like a blast furnace, just noise. Her son had been at one of those, she told me, just last night. He was her youngest boy. "He's not a bad kid. I don't want you thinking he's trouble. Do you have children?"

"Two daughters."

She sighed. "But girls are different."

We turned left just before the footbridge and walked a way along the canal, then turned left again to the middle of the block, stopping in front of a saffron yellow house. It was the only one painted on the entire street.

"It's yellow," I said to Carlotta, disbelieving. "Why is it yellow?"

She shrugged. "He did translations, favors. People paid him however they could."

"By painting a blind man's house?"

Carlotta didn't seem to find it that funny, or remarkable at all. "We called your uncle *Doctor*," she said, and gave me a stern look. "Out of respect."

I said nothing. There was a metal gate over the door, two dead bolts, and it took a moment to find the right keys. I'd never been to their house before and I felt suddenly guilty visiting for the first time under these circumstances. Just inside the door there were a jacket and hat hanging from a nail, and below it, a small, two-tiered shoe rack containing rubber mud boots, beige men's and women's slippers, and two pairs of matching Velcro sneakers. There were a couple of empty spaces on the rack. For their work shoes, I supposed, the ones they had died in. Without saying a word, Carlotta and I left our shoes behind and walked on into the house, wearing only our socks. We didn't take the slippers.

The space was neatly laid out, as I had assumed it would be, and dark, with no lightbulbs anywhere and no photos, not of family, not of each other. Because the long, damp winters are even longer and damper in this part of the city, heavy translucent plastic sheeting hung from every doorjamb in wide strips, so that moving from one room to another required a motion not unlike swimming the butterfly stroke. The idea was to trap heat in each room, but the effect, along with the hazy light, was to give the house the look and feel of an aquarium. I parted the plastic curtains and found myself in a sparsely furnished kitchen, kept in meticulous order. The refrigerator was nearly empty and there were no extra utensils in the drawers, just a pair of everything—two forks, two spoons, two steak knives. I opened the tap and a thin line of water dribbled into a single dirty bowl. There was another one, a clean bowl already dry, sitting by the sink.

I walked to the bedroom, as spare and clean as the kitchen, where a small wooden cross hung just above the neatly made bed. I opened and closed a few drawers, looked into the closet, and found two pairs of glasses in a box on top of the dresser, one with plastic yellow lenses, one with blue. I tried on the yellow pair, charmed by this small evidence of my uncle's vanity, and even found myself looking for a mirror. Of course, there wasn't one. This is all mine, I thought, to dispose of as I see fit. To sell, or rent, or burn, or give away. There was nothing of my family in this house and maybe that was the only attractive thing about it. My father kept everything of any value and Ramón got everything else, all this nothing—these clothes, this cheap furniture, this undecorated room and nondescript house, this parcel of land in a neighborhood whose name no one could agree on. It was all paid for, the lawyer told me, they owned it outright, and my uncle had no debts to speak of. Unfortunately, he also had no heirs besides his wife, and she had none besides him. I was the nearest living relative.

After a long pause, the lawyer added: "Well, except for your father."

"What do I do with it?"

"See if there's anything you want to keep. You can sell the rest. It's up to you."

And now I was here, hidden in the Thousands. At home, my phone was ringing, the city's frantic journalists demanding a statement. Soon they would be camping out in front of the asylum, tossing handwritten notes over the walls and into the gardens, or crowding before the door to my house, harassing my children, my wife. Say something, entertain us with your worries, your fears, your discontent, blame your father, the men who built the bridge, or the pony-tailed truck driver. Blame your blind uncle, his blind wife, the fireworks vendors, or yourself. My head hurt. I miss Ramón, I thought, and just as quickly the very idea seemed selfish. I hadn't seen him in years.

Carlotta had stayed in the living room and from the hallway I watched her blurred outline through the plastic. I swam through the house to see her.

"Are you all right?" I asked. "I'm sorry to make you wait."

She had nested into the soft cushions of my uncle and aunt's white sofa. There was a throw rug on the floor, somewhere near the middle of the room, and the soles of her feet hung just above, not touching it. Her hands lay in her lap. She seemed much younger in the subdued light of my uncle's home, her skin glowing, and her hair, graying in the daylight, appeared, in this shadowed room, to be almost black.

"What are you looking for?" she asked.

It was a fair question for which I had no answer.

"Nothing," I said. "Maybe I could live here."

Carlotta smiled generously. "You're not feeling well," she said.

My wife would be surprised this evening when I told her about my day. She listened patiently as we prepared the meal, our daughters clamoring for our attention, and told me only that I must be careful. That places like that weren't safe. She'd never been to the Thousands or Venice or Gaza but, like all of us, believed many things about our city without needing them confirmed. Hadn't there been a famous murder there a few years ago? And didn't this latest accident only prove again that our world had nothing to do with that one? And I agreed quietly, *Yes, dear, you're right, he was my uncle, my brother, but I barely knew him*—and I stopped my story there. I walked around the counter, gave her a kiss on the neck, picked up my eldest daughter, and laughed: Ramón's yellow glasses, can you believe it? His blue ones? His yellow house? And we put the girls to sleep, my wife went to bed, and me, I stayed in the living room, watching television, flipping channels, thinking.

"What will you do with it all?" my wife asked before she left. She leaned in the doorway, already in her nightclothes, and I could see the graceful outline of her body beneath the fabric. She was barefoot, her toes curling into the thick carpet.

"I was thinking we should move there," I said, just to hear her horrified laughter.

She disappeared into the bedroom without saying good night.

"Did you know them well?" I asked Carlotta.

She thought about this for a second. "They were my neighbors."

"But did you know them?"

"I saw them every day," she said.

And this means a good deal; I know it does. There was a time when I saw him every week, and we were closer then, maybe even something like brothers. "Ramón and I grew up together. And then we lost touch."

"You look tired," Carlotta said. "Why don't you sit? It might make you feel better."

But I didn't want to, not yet. I went to the record player, lifting the dull plastic dustcover. A few dozen old LPs leaned against the wall and I thumbed through them: they were my grandfather's opera records. I put one on, a woman's elegant voice warbled through the room, and, just like that, this melody I hadn't heard in so long—decades—dropped my temperature and made the ceiling seem very far above me, at an unnatural height. Carlotta tapped her toe to the music, though it seemed utterly rhythmless to me. It was true: I didn't feel well.

"What did people think of them in the neighborhood?" I asked.

"Everyone loved them."

"But no one knew them?"

"We didn't have to know them."

And I thought about that, as the singing went on in Italian, a lustrous female voice, and I was struck by the image of the two of them—Ramón and Matilde—sitting on this very same couch, my aunt whispering translations directly in his ear. Love songs, songs about desperate passion, about lovers who died together. I could almost see it: his smile lighting up this drab room, Matilde's lips pressed against him. They had died that way, best friends, strolling hand in hand off the edge of a bridge, until they sank. I sat down on the throw rug, leaning back against the sofa, staring ahead at an unadorned wall. My feet were very cold. My eyes had adjusted to the light now and the house seemed almost antiseptic. Clean. Preposterously dustless for this part of the city. We sat listening to the aria, Carlotta and I, a melody spiraling out into the infinite. The singer had such energy, and the more she drew upon it, the weaker I felt. I could stay here; I might never leave. I could inherit this life my uncle had left behind, walk away, I thought, from my old man and his venom.

"My father did everything he could to ruin my uncle," I said. "He cheated him out of his inheritance. He's in prison now, where he belongs."

"I know. I read about him today in the paper. They talked to him."

For a moment I thought I had misheard. "What? Which paper?"

I turned to see Carlotta smiling proudly. Perhaps she hadn't heard the terror in my voice. Already I'd begun imagining all the horrible things my father might say, the conspiracy theories, the racist remarks, the angry insults with which he might have desecrated the memory of his dead brother.

"I don't remember the name of it," Carlotta said. "The same one I was in."

"What did my father say?"

"There were journalists all over the neighborhood yesterday. My son was on television. Did you see him?"

I raised my voice, suddenly impatient: "But what did he say?"

"Mr. Cano," Carlotta whispered.

Her shoulders were hunched and she had leaned back into the couch, as if to protect herself, as if I might attack her. I realized, with horror, that I had frightened her. She knew who my father was. I stammered an apology.

She took a deep breath now. "He said he didn't have a brother. That he didn't know anyone named Ramón."

"That's all?" I asked, and Carlotta nodded.

"No one named Ramón," I said to myself, "no brother."

She stared at me like I was crazy. How could I explain that it didn't sound like him, that it was too sober, too calm?

"Why would he say that?" Carlotta asked.

I shook my head. I felt my eyes getting heavier. Was it cruel or just right?

"We should go," I said. "I'm very sorry, there's nothing here I need." But it wasn't true and I couldn't leave. We sat, not speaking, not moving, only breathing, until I became aware that Carlotta was patting my head with a maternal affection, that my shoulders were sinking further toward the floor, and I gave in to it: loosened my tie, wiggling my toes in my socks, my feet frozen, the chill having spread through my body now. This record will not end, I thought, I hoped, but then it did: a long, fierce note held without the orchestra, culminating in a shout of joy from the singer, the audience chastened, stunned by the beauty of it. A long silence and then, slowly, applause, soft at first, then waves of it, which on this old recording came across like a pounding rain. I was shivering. There was no question we were underwater.

Daniyal Mueenuddin

# *A Spoiled Man*

THERE HE STOOD at the stone gateway of the Harounis' weekend home above Islamabad, a small bowlegged man with a lopsided, battered face. When the American wife's car drove up, turning off the Murree road, Rezak saluted, eyes straight ahead, not looking at her. She sat in the back and smiled at him from the milky darkness of the car's interior. What a funny little man! Once, he had happened to be walking past as she was driven through the gate, and she had waved. In the few weeks since, he had waited hours to receive this recognition from her, Friday when the family came, Sunday when they left. He had plenty of time.

The car continued up the winding flagstone drive and disappeared among the rows of jacaranda trees, blooming purple now in late April. Below lay the roadside town of Kalapani, the bazaar pierced by the horns of buses collecting passengers; above stood these walls, which enclosed ten acres of steep land, planted with apples, pine, jasmine, roses, and lilies that the wife had brought from America. The wind blew with a rushing sound through the pine branches and combed the fresh green grass sprouting all over the hillside after the winter rains.

He made himself useful. In May, pickup trucks full of summer flowers were brought from the nurseries that surrounded the city on the plains below. When the first truck arrived, he stood at the gate, watching the gardeners unload the pots, handing them down to each other and then carrying them up to the house—the loaded vehicle couldn't climb the steep drive. Without asking, he passed through the gate, which he had never done before, took one of the clay pots in his arms, and walked up to the house with it, rolling slightly on his down-at-heel shoes.

"Hey, old man, you better leave that before you hurt yourself," called a gardener standing in the bed of the pickup.

"I'm from the mountains, brother," Rezak said. "I can carry you up on my back, and one of these in each hand."

The pickup driver, who stood to one side smoking a cigarette, grinned.

The old majordomo, Ghulam Rasool, had strolled down to watch the show, a potbellied figure with a tall lambskin hat resting at a slight angle on a fringe of white hair. He sent one of the gardeners up to get his hookah and, comfortably settling himself in the watchman's chair by the gate, looked out over the valley below. At midday, he said to Rezak, "Come on then, and break bread with us."

Rezak looked down at his feet. "I'd need to put stones in my gizzard like a chicken to digest the rich food that you good people eat."

The majordomo tried to convince him, and the gardeners also pressed, but Rezak remained stubborn. "You didn't ask for help—you don't owe me anything."

"Suit yourself then," Ghulam Rasool said finally. The gardeners walked up the drive, talking, and Rezak stood watching them, wishing he had accepted. He was alone now. In the distance, he could see a swimming pool with curving sides, overhung by chinar trees and willows. Melancholy invaded him, and also peace, borne by the whirring of cicadas nestled among the rocks that punctuated the grounds of the estate. He took a bag from his pocket, undid the elastic band, and tucked a quid of tobacco in his cheek, chopped green *naswar*.

. . .

In the Kalapani bazaar, he ate at his usual teahouse, day-old bread soaked in milk, prescribed by a quack homeopath against a fistula that had tormented him for many years. The waiter brought the sopping bread and, when the crowd subsided, came over to have a few words about the flow of tourists up to Murree, more each year, this season begun so early. Lonely as he was, Rezak relied upon his welcome in the teahouse, his connection with it. When the older chickens at the poultry sheds where he worked were culled, Rezak would bring down one of the healthier birds, asking the teahouse to cook it, as a holiday from his bread diet. He shared with whoever was there, insistent, forcing his friend the waiter to eat.

"There, look, I've taken some," the waiter would say, pulling off a wing. Even he, hardened by a diet of stale leftovers from the kitchen, was dubious about eating this time-expired bird.

"No, you have to really eat." Once, Rezak even became angry about it, leaving abruptly, the chicken still on the table.

After finishing his lunch, Rezak walked through a government pine forest to the poultry sheds. The owner had bribed the wardens to allow construction extending into the forest, and each summer his men set fires at the base of pines planted by the British a hundred years earlier, in order to kill the trees and open up more space. Rezak came to his home—not the workers' quarters attached to the sheds but a hut that he had built for himself, a little wooden cubicle, faced with tin and mounted on thick legs. Several decades before, in his early twenties, he had fallen out with his stepbrothers over shared property up in the mountains, a few acres of land on which they grew wheat and potatoes, bordered by apricot trees. Outmaneuvered, dispossessed, he had come down to the plains, vowing never to see his family again. This box had become his home and consolation. Each place he worked, he set it up, and then, when he quarreled with the other workers or the boss, as he invariably did, he would take it apart and cart it away—always he kept a store of money, untouched no matter what, enough to pay for trucking this little house, this nest, to whatever place his heart had set on next. This was his guarantee of independence.

Opening the heavy padlock, he lifted the door hatch and climbed in, tucking his shoes into a wooden box nailed below the cramped hatch. Tiny red lights, run off an electrical connection drawn from the poultry sheds, were strung all over the ceiling and warmed the chamber. He could sit but not stand inside, and had covered the floor with a cotton mattress, which gave off a ripe animal odor, deeply comforting to him. A funnel and pipe served as a handy spittoon, a mirror and shelf allowed him to shave without getting out of bed, an electric fan cooled him. Photographs of actresses plastered the walls and ceiling, giving him company. Fickle and choosy, he shuffled and moved them, discarding one, stripping the photographs from the wall with a cold expression. For several months, he had been favoring a Pathan actress known as the Atomic Bum, who had wagged her way through a string of hit movies in the past year.

A few days later, loitering around the gates of the Harouni estate again, Rezak decided to go in, stepping through a narrow entry set into the wall. The owners would be in Islamabad for the week, and earlier he had seen the watchman down in the bazaar. By climbing the slope of the mountain opposite, he had observed the household routine, marked the servants' quarters, watched the owners sitting on a terrace, brightly clothed. Close up, the house seemed to him ugly, made of large rough-hewn stones, with a vast wall of glass across the front, looking out over the valley and down to Islamabad, forty kilometers below. Nothing to it—no metalwork, no paint, no decorative lights, only size to recommend it. The house blended into the landscape, as if it were one of the boulders littering the mountain slope.

He found Ghulam Rasool sitting in a chair under a tree, reading a newspaper.

"Ah, the volunteer," he said amiably. "Come on then, have a pull on the hookah."

Rezak sat down on the edge of a charpoy, dangling his short legs.

"I'm killing myself with this poison instead." He spat and then dipped coarse green tobacco under his gum.

"You work up in Ayub's sheds, don't you?"

"When Ayub needs me, I work. He pays me in dying chickens and loose change." He tried to make a joke of it.

"That's what I hear—Ayub shaves both sides and then trims out the middle piece."

Rezak laughed mirthlessly. "The way I'm going, soon I'll be eating grass." He paused. "I've been thinking. I can do woodwork. I know about trees. I'll carry things, work in the garden. Feed me and I'll work here and do whatever you want. You don't even have to give me a room. I've got a portable cubicle that I live in—you can stick me in some corner."

The owner of the estate, Sohail Harouni, the son of a man who made a fortune in cement and other industries, had, while he was at university in the United States, married an American woman named Sonya. "No, I really love it here," she would say defensively when asked at a party. "It's strange, it's like a drug. I think I miss the States so much—and I do—and then after a month there I'm completely bored. Pakistan makes everything else seem washed-out. This is my place now. I don't do enough, but I feel as if here I can at least do something for the good." She did fit in more than most foreign women. She studied Urdu, to the point where she could communicate quite effectively, made an effort to meet Pakistanis outside the circuit in Islamabad. Even her husband's catty aunts admitted that she was one of the few foreigners who wore Pakistani clothes without looking like either an Amazon or a Christmas tree.

And yet, though she insisted that she loved Pakistan, sometimes it all became too much. "I hate it, everyone's a crook, nothing works here!" she would sob, fighting with her husband. Then she would storm out to her car and retreat to the Kalapani house, forty minutes away, arriving unannounced, withdrawing darkly into the master bedroom, while the servants scrambled to prepare her meal. In the evening she would wander the large stone house, slowly becoming calm, speaking with her friends on the telephone. Her husband would drive up to spend the night with her, bringing their little son as a pledge of their love, and they would make peace.

It happened that, soon after Rezak made his plea to Ghulam Rasool, Sonya had a huge row with her husband and ran away to Kalapani. The next morning, she sat drinking coffee on the sunny terrace, which had a view out over the government forest, now heavily logged by poachers, and then down to Islamabad and Rawalpindi. The strain of the fight had shaded into a desire for simplicity and order, an almost pleasant teariness.

Ghulam Rasool came up from the garden, coughing so that she would not be startled. Of all the servants, he was the one she most trusted with her son. She herself felt comfortable with him, with his gentle, stoic manner, with his prayers and his superstitions.

Her blond hair held back by a black velvet band, she wore a simple white blouse, white slacks, and lay on a divan, immaculate, reading a slender volume of poetry. She had been an English major, and turned to a handful of familiar books as a restorative—Yeats or Rilke, Keats, to be taken as needed.

"Excuse me, Begum Sahib. I wanted to ask, it's time to think about the roses."

She knew that he wanted to soften her attitude toward her husband. In any case, she liked him to come and talk with her, and they used as a pretext his supervision of the garden, although he had always been a valet and knew almost nothing about flowers or trees.

She put down her book, and they considered the roses and the placement of the annuals.

"Begging your pardon, the local people drive their goats into the Ali Khan orchard, and they're destroying the saplings that you brought from America. There's an old man. He can't do hard labor, but he's a reliable person. His family abandoned him. He even has his own portable hut—he'll take it there and live as a guard. You don't have to give him a salary. Just food and a few rupees for pocket money."

But she wanted to give the old man the same as all the others. It made her happy to think of spoiling him in his old age.

Newly hired, Rezak moved to the Ali Khan lands, a walled parcel of four or five acres just up the road from the main house. Like the other servants and gardeners, he received a salary of nine thousand rupees a month, more than he had ever made in his life. The gardeners from the big house transported his cubicle in pieces, then helped him reassemble it next to a hut that was already standing there, a single stone-walled room, with an open hearth, which Rezak could use as a storeroom and kitchen. The land had no electrical connection, so he bought oil lamps, which glowed soothingly as he went about his evening chores, his routine of dinner and bedtime.

The season turned hot just as Rezak moved to his new home, coloring the green fruit on the apple and peach and pear trees imported from America. He devoted all his grateful heart to the small orchard, watering the trees with a bucket from the stream that ran through the property, working manure into the soil with a spade. Taking a bus to Islamabad, with his own money he bought three grapevines, carried them back wrapped in straw, and trained them up the legs of his tin-clad cubicle. He planted radishes, corn, cauliflower, onions, peas, more than he alone could eat, so that as they ripened he could take baskets of produce to the big house. With his second paycheck he bought a goat for milk—before, in his previous jobs, it would have cost many months' savings.

One day, the master and his wife took some guests to the Ali Khan land for a picnic lunch. In the morning, servants brought carpets and divans, tubs full of ice for the wine, grills for the meat, firewood in case the party lasted into the night. Rezak spent the morning hours ferrying boxes and chairs and rugs down from the main road to the picnic spot, taking the biggest loads, pushing himself forward, claiming precedence on his plot of land.

The guests arrived, Pakistanis and foreigners, a dozen or so of them, and were soon sprawled on the carpets, drinking wine, resolved into several groups. Walking briskly down the steep path, sure-footed, holding a floppy yellow sun hat with a trailing ribbon in her hand, Sonya had said to Rezak as she passed, "Salaam, baba." His heart, his soul melted, as if a queen had spoken to a foot soldier. She had given him charge of the garden, of the trees that she had brought from her homeland, and now she was seeing the results of his husbandry for the first time.

All the other servants knew what to do—Ghulam Rasool poured the wine and passed the hors d'oeuvres, a cook readied the fire and skewered kebabs on metal rods, the gardeners spread out as a kind of picket, to prevent anyone from looking over the walls. Rezak's shyness and diffidence contested with a desire to take part, to show off all the work he had done in the orchard. He squatted under an apple tree, trying not to look at the sahibs, pulling up sprigs of grass, tying them into figures and knots, hoping to be summoned. Restless, he knelt down by the cook and took over the job of tending the fire, pushing aside the weedy boy who acted as the cook's helper.

Sohail Harouni was a handsome, cheerful man with not a care in his life, who enjoyed giving parties more than anything else. After a few glasses of wine, he called a young valet and told him to bring the stereo from the main house and hook it up. A driver raced to Murree, ten kilometers up the mountain, and bought a roll of heavy wire. Glasses in hand, the guests and even the host enthusiastically helped string the wire from a roadside shop down through the trees.

When the party had come far along, when Harouni and the guests were standing in a circle, drinks in hand, gesturing expansively, speaking loudly, Sonya walked away from the group. Looking along the length of the valley, she caught sight of Rezak's cabin, several terraces below the picnic spot. Finding the path, she picked her way toward it, and Rezak, who had been watching her, quickly followed, leaping down a steep bank so that he could receive her at his little hut, saluting.

"It's wonderful!" Sonya exclaimed, circling around the cubicle, Rezak at her heels. "Hey, everyone," she called to her guests, going over to where she could be heard. "Come see."

Short, bowlegged Rezak bustled around, showing off the appliances and the refinements—the pipe that drained the inside spittoon, the cupboards and drawers set into the outside walls for his tools and clothes and kit, windows that could be propped open or removed entirely, a skylight of red glass, thick rush matting on the roof to keep the inside cold or hot, with a rubber bladder fixed to the walls that shot water up through a pipe when he squeezed it, wetting the rushes—evaporative cooling. Sonya poked her head inside the stuffy, lurid chamber, considered the photographs of movie starlets plastered on the walls. The guests peered about, inspecting this nest, its door and windows ajar, like a car on a dealer's lot with hood and trunk propped open.

"If there's electricity, then it's really something," Rezak said, eager, grinning with all his teeth, surrounded by the sahibs and the memsahibs. "I used to have colored lights inside. There's work to be done, that's true. It's all broken from carrying it up and down and all over." In his exuberance, he pulled at a cupboard door that wouldn't open till it tore off in his hand. Even this didn't dampen him. "See, that's one way to take it apart!"

"That's the man's whole life in a nutshell, isn't it?" the Australian ambassador, a tall man with a correspondingly tall forehead and ginger hair, remarked.

As they were returning to the picnic, Sonya said to her husband, "The poor man should have electricity for a radio and for lighting. He lives all alone here—imagine how bored he is."

"Are you kidding?" Harouni said. "These guys don't get bored."

But, after the party, the wire that had been laid temporarily so that there would be music remained in place—for the next party. Rezak strung lights on the outside of the cubicle, like wedding decorations, and hung a lightbulb in the stone hut where he cooked. He bought a radio and, finally, a cheap television, something he had never even thought of wanting. He would lie in his little cocoon, soft red lights glowing, the television volume turned up, and drink cup after cup of tea kept hot in a vacuum thermos, a refinement that made him smack his lips with appreciation.

Sitting in the Kalapani teahouse one morning, Rezak met a young man who lived near his childhood village, high in the mountains.

"The government pushed the road up to Koti," the man told him. "The bus runs from Kowar now. That changed things, you can bet."

Hearing of the places he had known all his life made Rezak restless. He had left home determined never to go back. Now he wondered what his stepbrothers had told the neighbors about his disappearance. He wanted his family to know of his success.

"You and I grew up drinking from the same streams, breathing the same air. You have to accept my hospitality now that we've met. I beg you. Come for a cup of tea, and then I'll walk you back down here." He took the man by the arm and almost dragged him out of the tea stall.

He hurriedly carried a charpoy onto the terrace in front of the stone cooking hut, put a pillow on it, ran inside and lit a fire in the hearth, then brought out a table, wiping it with a rag. Luckily, he had a packet of biscuits and he arranged these on a plate and carried them out with the tea.

The man knew of Rezak's family, but had little news of them. Forgetting his bitterness and the wrong they had done him, Rezak began speaking of his stepbrothers and nephews, of their fertile land, of the well near their fields.

"God has been good to me, more than I deserve. I have only one wish, that he had given me sons of my own, as my brothers have." He ran his hands over his face.

Rezak had not been able to resist boasting of his salary.

The man considered for a moment, his eyes alighting on a locked trunk inside the cooking hut that must be full of clothes and who knew what else. He looked at the neat vegetable patch and at the two goats—Rezak had bought another when fodder ran low in the forest and they were cheap. The man had been shown the weird little cubicle, furnished with a radio, a television even.

"Look, my cousin has a daughter. Something went wrong when she was born, and she's a bit simple. But she can cook and sew and take your goats out to graze. She's quite pretty even. She's young enough to bear you a son. Her father can barely take care of his other children. Why don't you let me arrange a marriage?"

"You're making fun of an old man," Rezak replied. But hope and desire pierced his heart when he thought of it. A woman in his house, even one who was not right in the head! And she could bear him a son, and that would be worth anything at all. Now that Rezak had money, the boy would go to school, he would learn to read and write, become . . . Rezak could not even imagine what. The son of an old servant at the main house had become a doctor and now continually begged his father to retire and come live with him. Rezak would die happy after that.

They spoke back and forth all afternoon. In the end, they agreed not only that the girl would be without a dowry but even that Rezak would pay a quite substantial amount of money for her, which the family would take in installments.

A few days later, the father delivered the feebleminded girl. The girl's family had not come, and the two men did not celebrate the marriage, but brought the *maulvi* quietly to perform the *nikah*. When the father left, the girl followed him and cried, until they were forced to lock her in the hut.

After seeing the father onto the bus, Rezak wandered down through the bazaar, stopping to talk for a minute with the man who sold samosas, saying nothing of his marriage, but saving it for himself. He felt more equal now among these people, the shopkeepers, passersby, families. Someone waited for him also, the house he returned to would not be empty.

The poor girl must be frightened, he thought, and turned homeward, stopping to buy a three-kilo box of sweets, fat yellow ludhoos, ghulab jaman, barfi, shahi tukrah.

He rattled the chain as he opened the lock, so that she wouldn't be startled. She wore makeup, lipstick that had smudged, rouge that made her cheeks almost pink, new clothes made of shiny white cloth—at least that much had been done to celebrate their wedding day. It pleased him that she reached and covered her head with her dupatta—shy before him, her husband.

He sat across from her. She kept her eyes cast down.

He opened the box of sweets, carefully unknotting the string, took a ludhoo, and held it out to her on his palm, whispering, "Take this, it's okay, don't be afraid." He held it there. "Go on." And after a moment, without looking up, she reached out and took it.

Gradually, she became accustomed to living with him. Once he saw that she would not run away, he let her roam as she wanted. The girl, a tiny thing of nineteen or twenty, had an impediment and spoke not in sentences but rather in strings of sound, cooing or repeating words—her condition was really worse than Rezak had expected—but when she settled in he found that she could more or less cook.

He let her sleep in the stone hut, until one night, as he was watching television in his cubicle, she cautiously lifted the door flap, stood absorbing the lit red chamber for a moment, and then nimbly leaped in, eyes fixed on the television. After that, she always slept with him.

As an adolescent boy, Rezak had been married, so long ago that he couldn't remember what his bride looked like. She had died in childbirth, less than a year after the marriage, and the child had died, too. Now, after so many years, Rezak again had a companion in his home. Life and hope, the flames of individuality that had burned out to nothing, to smoke, again flickered within him. Returning at night from the bazaar with a treat of late-season mangoes or a bit of meat, or stopping work in the orchard at noon to have his midday meal, which the girl warmed and served to him with hot chapatis, he looked forward to her chattering. She had a pretty, almost animal way of watching him while he ate, perched beside him, and after he finished she brought him a glass of water from the clay pot. In the evening, before he came in, she made tea, and when he groaned because of the aching in his legs she massaged him. Gradually, he found himself able to communicate with her, and, more important, she communicated with him, showed happiness when he returned at night, cared for him when he felt ill or sad. She did not, however, bear him a child.

Now that his wife cooked for him and pastured the goats, Rezak had less to do, especially after the trees lost their leaves and work in the orchard ceased. His wife sat in the dark smoky hut, cooing to herself. He would often go down to the teahouse in Kalapani bazaar and sit for several hours, watching buses fill and lumber off up the mountain to Murree or to Kashmir, or race, brakes squealing at the curves, down to the cities, honking their horns to call the passengers. He strolled idly through the bazaar, wearing a new woolen vest and carrying a walking stick; or he went to the big house and sat smoking a hookah with Ghulam Rasool.

Returning to his hut at dusk after one of these excursions, he found that the fire had burned out in the hearth and his wife was gone. The goats, too, were missing, although she should have brought them in by this time. Sitting in the cold room, he stared at the calendar nailed up on the wall, which showed an elaborate Chinese pagoda. He rubbed his hands together, trying to control his anger. Twice before, she had disappeared at nightfall, and he'd found her far down in the valley, cowering behind some rocks. When he approached her, she grew frightened and covered her face with her hands.

At dark, she still had not returned. Rezak took the lantern, lit the tiny flame, and went out, the two goats scrambling in, bleating, when he opened the wooden gate that led down into the valley.

One of the neighbors called, "Hey, Rezak, can't it wait till morning?"

"What can I tell you. My poor old lady's disappeared again."

The neighbor sent a little boy to help with the search.

Rezak walked all over and called and called. He went home, hoping that she would be there waiting for him, but he saw no glimmer of light in the cooking hut. As he sat in the cold, the sound of twigs breaking as he laid the fire seemed particularly loud. The fire caught, crackling, slowly warming the room. Mechanically he threw a handful of tea in the kettle, boiled the water, mechanically poured it into the cup. He didn't have it in him to be angry now. Without eating dinner, without turning on the television, as he did every night, he lay alone in the dark cabin, wondering what could have become of her. What if she was lying hurt somewhere in the forest?

In the morning he woke before first light, hurriedly dressed, and went out. He didn't know where to look, which direction to turn. Living alone for years, he had learned not to ask for help. Neighbors would do whatever they could once or twice or five times, but, ultimately, they would grow cold and resentful. He walked along the paths that she might have taken, then deep into the woods to the places where she cut grass. Once, he saw a cloth that he thought might be her shawl, but coming close he saw that it had been rained on and must have been lying there for days.

Finally, he went to ask the Harouni retainers for help. Going into the servants' common room, he found Ghulam Rasool lying peacefully on a charpoy, his unlit hookah beside him. The fireplace chimney had backed up, as it always did, filling the low-ceilinged room with layers of acrid pine smoke.

As Rezak walked into this familiar room, he broke down for the first time. His arms hung loosely as he shuffled up to the bed and stood with his face contorted.

"My wife disappeared," he blurted out, before he had even said salaam. "I can't find her anywhere. She's gone." Flat tears slipped out of his gummy eyes and disappeared into the wrinkles of his face. Remembering himself, he reached down and shook Ghulam Rasool's hand respectfully.

"What do you mean, disappeared?" Ghulam Rasool asked, startled. Squeezing Rezak's arm to make him sit on the charpoy, he called out through the door, "Hey, one of you boys, come here."

Four gardeners answered the summons and, after asking a few questions, ignored Rezak. They huddled together and laid out their plan, eager as a pack of hounds, then headed out, their wooden staffs tapping quickly as they walked off on separate paths.

Late at night, they straggled back, one by one, having found no trace of the woman. In the morning, early, they went out again, determined to find her. They searched the mountains, the farthest terraced fields, went to the nearby villages. The next day, again they searched from dawn to dusk, and then the next, but with less and less determination. One of them asked at every bus stop from Murree down to Rawalpindi. Another went all the way to the girl's family home up in the mountains, almost in Kashmir, but they had seen nothing of her—in any case, she couldn't possibly have made the long journey alone.

Finally, only Rezak kept searching. He forgot where he had already been, returning to the same places, as if this time he might find her there.

One morning, getting ready to go out and continue the search, he sat down again, took off his coat, and lay down on the bed. Imbecile, chattering—but she was gone, dead or stolen, taken to the brothels of Pindi or Karachi. He prepared himself to bear the loneliness again.

Every year at Christmas, the Harounis gave a big party at Kalapani, with roast goose, a twenty-foot tree in the entrance hall of the house, and a hohoing Santa Claus for the children. Trucks brought logs for a bonfire from the Harounis' farm down on the plains, so that late at night the servants could grill spicy, greasy kebabs on the coals for the heavy drinkers and mull cauldrons of spiced punch for the rest. The guests came up from Islamabad singly or in long chains of cars, blowing in through the door with wrapped presents and bottles of wine and champagne, which Ghulam Rasool piled on a long table in the hall.

Before dinner, the mistress came into the kitchen. The cook stood rubbing his hands on his apron, sidelined in his own domain, as she took a big bowl under her arm and poked with a spatula at the mashed potatoes, which the cook had already beaten to a creamy smoothness.

Ghulam Rasool had been following her impassively as she performed her inspection.

"Excuse me, Begum Sahib, may I trouble you with a small request?"

"Of course," she said, touching him lightly on the shoulder. He had become accustomed to this, although at first it had disturbed him.

Briefly, he explained about the disappearance of Rezak's wife.

"But Ghulam Rasool, you should have told me right away. What can I do?"

Ghulam Rasool had an encyclopedic knowledge of his master's friends, their power, their wealth, and he took great pride in these connections. When he saw Omar Bukhari, the son of the Inspector General of Police, arrive at the party, he had sent a gardener to fetch Rezak and told him to wait in the kitchen.

"If Bukhari Sahib would speak to the police in Murree . . ."

She went into the living room and found Bukhari looming over a French girl, who had come with someone else, insisting that she must let him arrange a trip into the tribal areas of the frontier, which were off-limits to foreigners.

"Really, Delphine, you should go—it's amazing, and you'll never have the chance otherwise," the hostess said. "Omar, can I pull you away for a moment?"

Bukhari followed her to the candlelit dining room. "So, Ghulam Rasool Sahib, what's going on?" he asked.

The Harounis' friends all knew Ghulam Rasool and joked that he had more power than many federal ministers.

Ghulam Rasool explained, emphasizing the girl's attractiveness to make it seem like an abduction by one of the gangs who kidnap or buy women for prostitution—a scenario in which the police could help, since these things generally happened under their protection and they received a cut of the take.

"We'll break the bastards' legs when we catch them," Bukhari, who had been drinking quite heavily, said. "Go fetch the husband."

Rezak came in, trembling, and couldn't explain himself, but stood with a grief-stricken face, expectant, as if his wife might there and then materialize through the power of this important sahib.

Bukhari had dealt with many cases of missing women, and knew that the family was almost always involved. He fixed Rezak with a hard gaze. "Who took her? The father? Did the family take her back?"

"Only God above in his mercy knows, sir—I came home one night and she had gone; I couldn't find her, sir. I'm an old man; I'm nothing. . . ."

Recalling the presence of his hostess, Bukhari relented. Flipping open his tiny cell phone, he punched a number.

"Get me the D.S.P. Murree." After a moment, a voice came on the line. "Hello, Qazmi, how are you? This is Omar Bukhari. Yes, everything's fine. I'm in Kalapani, at the house of Mr. Sohail Harouni. The wife of one of his servants has been abducted. I want her back by tomorrow night. . . . Yes . . . No, come to the house in the morning and take down the details. I want you personally to handle this." Without saying good-bye, he snapped shut the phone.

He smiled at Sonya. "Done."

Rezak, who understood none of the conversation, which had been conducted in English, crouched and touched Bukhari's knee with both hands, began to speak, and then fell silent, bowing his head. Ghulam Rasool raised him up by the arm and led him away.

In the morning, the Deputy Superintendent of Police himself showed up at the house, in his official Jeep, flying a police flag, and accompanied by a pickup full of policemen carrying beat-up rifles. Unfortunately, the Harounis and all the guests had already left for Islamabad. The D.S.P. sat on a chair placed in the middle of the hall, with the quivering staff lined up in front of him.

"Where's the husband?"

Ghulam Rasool, the only one not perturbed by this policeman with stars on his shoulders, explained that Rezak lived at another property, down the road.

"Get him."

Rezak came in, breathless, led by a policeman.

"So, old man," the D.S.P. stated, "they tell me your wife has run away." He began asking questions, in a low voice. Though at first he spoke gently, his tone soon became irritated.

"What you're saying is, her parents sold her to you. Where did you get that much money?"

Ghulam Rasool stepped forward. "Sir, she's not well in the head— this man took her out of kindness as much as anything. And then our sahib is very good to us; he gives us everything we need and more."

"Women don't just fly away on their own. Either this man knows something about it or she's in Karachi by now. The best thing is for him to be quiet."

The D.S.P. looked intently at Rezak for a moment, clasping his hands on his stomach, then stood up.

"Please give my regards to Harouni Sahib," he said to Ghulam Rasool, speaking politely and almost formally. "I am always at his service." He begged off taking a cup of tea, claiming that he had an appointment.

Watching the policeman and his escort drive off, Ghulam Rasool said to Rezak, "Better stay away from the bazaar for a couple of days. He seemed like a pretty rude character."

Just after dusk, four policemen in an unmarked car picked up Rezak from his hut and took him to the police post at Tret, twenty kilometers down the road.

"Did you find her?" he had asked, when they came to his cubicle.

The youngest policeman, the only one in uniform, said, "Yes, yes, don't worry."

But he grabbed Rezak by the shoulder, took his arms, and handcuffed him. Rezak said nothing more, and allowed them to do as they liked.

Only when they put him in the back of the car did Rezak ask, "But what have I done? Where are you taking me?"

"Shut up, baba," said the young policeman, who up till then had been quite gentle.

They walked him into a windowless room in the police station and hung him up on a hook by the manacles around his wrists, so that his feet touched the ground only when he stood on his toes.

He hung on the wall all evening, long past the time when it seemed possible that the excruciating pain in his shoulders and back could be borne. In the next room, policemen came and went, but he was no longer aware of them.

At one point, a policeman who had just come in from outside asked, "Who's he?"

"No idea. The D.S.P.'s guys sent him in. Strip, polish, and paint, I suppose."

"Ah," the newcomer said. He went out, singing, "The night is made for lovers. . . ."

After midnight, a large man wearing civilian clothes came into the room. Two uniformed policemen came behind him and shut the door.

"All right, let's see," the big man said. "So, what's your name, old man?"

"Mohammed Rezak, sir." He began weeping and blubbering. "I beg you, I've done nothing, I'm innocent, and now you've hung me up here. I beg you, remember, there's a God above who judges everything. . . ."

The large man became suddenly angry. "I see," he said menacingly, gritting his teeth. "I'm the one who's being judged? It's my fault, is it, I'm the one who's guilty?" He slapped Rezak with all his strength. "Where's your wife, you bastard? I know all about it. Nobody took her—you sold her down the road, you pimp, and now you'll tell me to whom and when and for how much." He walked to the opposite wall and back, then came up and looked closely into Rezak's face. "Or perhaps you killed her? She didn't have children? You bought a lemon? Ready for a new one, moneybags?"

He slapped Rezak again, cutting his lip. "You listen to me, I can make you fuck your own daughter if I want to, you'll hump her all night, like a dog fucking a bitch."

"For God's sake, for God's mercy, I don't have a daughter, sir. . . ."

"You're really trying to piss me off, aren't you?" And then, to one of the men, "Take him down."

The two uniformed policemen lifted Rezak off the hook and threw him to the ground. Rubbing his hands together, the big man looked down at Rezak appraisingly, as if considering his next move.

"Stretch him out and bring me the strap."

They pulled down his shalwar, carried him to a bench, and stretched him on it, one pulling his arms and one pulling his feet. They had removed his kurta when they hung him up on the wall.

The big man brandished what looked like the sole of an enormous shoe, with writing on one side in thick black script. "See what this says? It says, 'Sweetheart, where did you sleep last night?' Understand?"

Without warning, he swung.

Rezak shrieked, a startled high-pitched sound. He never had felt pain like this, which spread flickering all through his body.

Another policeman came into the room when Rezak screamed and stood by the door, watching, with a grin on his face.

"Come here," the big man said. "You do it, since you're so interested. You need the practice, anyway."

Of course, he could tell them nothing. "I don't know," he sobbed. "She's gone; I don't know anything." After a few strokes, he fell into a rhythm, shrieking when they hit him, then, when they stopped, groaning, "Oh my God, Oh my God, Oh my God . . ."

After beating Rezak for five or six minutes, they threw him into a storeroom.

The D.S.P. stopped at the Tret post on his way down to Islamabad from Murree. The big man stood up and casually saluted when the officer walked in. They shook hands.

"What's going on? Anything new?"

"Call from Awaz Khan Sahib. He keeps asking why we haven't picked up those two clowns from Mariani."

They discussed this, something to do with a road contractor, villagers blocking the line of a new road—they needed to be shown the stick.

As he started to leave, the D.S.P. asked, "What about that missing girl?"

"Someone driving by must have seen her and snatched her. The Chandias say they didn't do it."

Only the most powerful of the gangster clans in the area would have presumed to abduct a woman without cutting in the police.

"And we pulled in the husband and worked on him—he's clean."

The D.S.P. made a face. "You didn't! This is some American woman's pet servant. Tell me you didn't do anything severe."

"He's fine, he's fine. Do you want to see him?"

"No. You're positive, right?"

"I'm definitely positive."

"No marks?"

"Well, sir, no visible marks. I have to work somewhere."

The D.S.P. laughed. "I suppose you do."

After thinking for a moment, he said, "I'll have to go see Bukhari Sahib and explain that she's disappeared off the face of the earth. It's a good idea to put in an appearance there anyway."

"What about the old man?"

"Dump him at home and tell him he better keep his mouth shut."

Shortly before dawn, almost tenderly now, they bundled Rezak into the same unmarked car and sneaked him back into his hut.

"You've tasted it once. Don't make us dose you again. Not a word to anyone—do you understand?"

Rezak stared at his feet. Finally, he nodded his head.

He lay all that day without sleeping, into the dusk, then the dark. His buttocks had swollen up, puffy and white like bread dough, so that he had to lie on his stomach. His mind whirled, without touching on any one thing for more than a moment—the wife he married when almost still a boy, who died so many years ago, then his second wife, the little mentally disturbed girl. His stepbrothers, who took his land, the fruit trees in the garden there in Kashmir and the fruit trees here, brought from America. His things, his television, the day he went to the store and bought the bright red plastic television.

"Why should I complain? The policemen did as they always do. The fault is mine, who married in old age, with one foot in the grave. God gave me so much more than I deserved, when I expected nothing at all."

He made sure to be perfectly silent about what had happened.

After he recovered, he was left with one last wish. In Rezak's mind, good fortune and grace were wound together, so that the Harouni family's connections and wealth established not simply the power of the household but also its virtue. Ghulam Rasool had served the Harounis for more than fifty years, some of the other retainers had served almost as long. He could never equal that service. But never-theless the family took him in when otherwise he might have begged in the streets. They gave him the money to live beyond his station, they made him hope—for too much. And when he lost the girl their instruments punished him for having dared to reach so high, for owning something that would excite envy, that placed him in the way of beatings and the police. Now he belonged to the Harounis. This was how he understood justice.

He said to Ghulam Rasool, "I beg you, ask our master to bury me here on this land, in one corner, whichever one he likes."

This became his dream and his consolation. He lived on for another year, then six months more, collecting his salary, never spending a rupee more than was sufficient to keep his body warm. He sold the television, sold the goats. At the end of eighteen months, he went up to Murree, to the stonecutter, and said that he wanted the very best gravestone in the shop, and carved marble to sheathe the rest of the grave.

After his night in the police station, Rezak walked gingerly and made grunting noises under his breath—everyone remarked on how he had changed after his wife disappeared. The stonecutter, seeing his bent, trembling figure, thought, This old bird doesn't know what good marble costs.

But Rezak took out a roll of bills, tied in a greasy handkerchief that he pulled from under his shirt. Blue notes, thousands.

"Well, that's different," the stonecutter said, taking Rezak's hand and leading him into the back room. "Look at this piece, now. Look at the color, the grain. Look at the size of that. I swear to God, I've been saving it for my own mother."

No one had seen the old man for several days, and the gardener sent to inquire rattled and knocked and then found him dead in the little cubicle. Ghulam Rasool had the gardeners dig a grave along the wall of the property, and that evening they buried him, just a few people attending the *janaza*—the servants from the big house, a few men from the bazaar and from houses on the hillside next to the Ali Khan lands. A poor woman from nearby had been paid to wash the body, the *maulvi* from the mosque in the bazaar said the prayer.

The next Friday, Sonya came up from Islamabad at nightfall, bringing just her young son and his ayah. Ghulam Rasool, dropping a pill of sweetener into a cup of tea, which she took in her room in front of a fire, said, "I beg your pardon, Begum Sahib. The old man Rezak, whom you so kindly put in charge at the Ali Khan lands, has passed away."

The electricity had failed, as it often did up on the mountain. At dusk, by candlelight, the tall rooms of the stone-built house were solemn and chilled, like an empty church or a school when the children are gone.

"Poor poor thing. All alone, and his wife disappeared."

At moments, as now, she felt closer to Ghulam Rasool than to anyone else in Pakistan, his large dark compassionate face, heavy body, his shrewd and yet ponderous manner, his orthodox unshakable beliefs.

He was silent for a moment, then continued, "Please forgive me, but I took the liberty of having him buried in the Ali Khan orchard. He had asked me to speak with you."

Still not touching her tea, looking up at him, as he stood with his hands crossed on his belly, she said gently, "I'm so glad you did, Ghulam Rasool. Of course, Mian Sahib and I would want that."

The old servant had come far by knowing the ways of his masters. Saying no more or less than this, he withdrew quietly, leaving Sonya musing by the fire on having done the right thing for a lonely old man, having done a little bit for the good.

The next morning, slipping out of the house, Sonya took Ghulam Rasool and a single gardener and walked up to the Ali Khan lands. The smallness of the grave surprised her, the mound decorated with tinsel in advance of her visit, the marble stones he had bought stacked beside it. Ghulam Rasool and the gardener said the *fatiyah*, holding their upturned palms in front of them and silently reciting a prayer, and Sonya stood also with her hands upturned and eyes closed, thinking first of the old man, a life drawn to a close with so little fanfare, and then of her own dead, her father and mother lying under the snow in a Wisconsin graveyard.

When they had finished, she walked around the garden, looking at the fruit trees, the leaves colored and falling as the autumn advanced.

"What would you have us do with this?" Ghulam Rasool asked, leading her to the cabin, which sprouted a television antenna and bouquets of crude plastic flowers, their petals thick as tongues, bought by Rezak soon after his marriage, nailed up along the roof one day, to please his wife's innocent heart. "The old man didn't want his family to have anything from him."

It seemed to her vividly alive, a motionless hirsute presence, the antenna, the flowers, the four massive legs, the pipe that drained the inside spittoon trailing into the grass as if drawing nourishment.

She told them to bring it to the big estate and park it in a shaded corner somewhere not too visible, as a memorial. Her husband, a raconteur, could show it to his guests and tell them about Rezak, the old man who entered service bringing his own house.

At first, the cabin sat inviolate below the swimming pool, locked, Rezak's things still in the cupboards and drawers. Sonya went once to look at it, then did not return, her attention fading. Gradually, like falling leaves, the locks were broken off, one person taking the thermos, another the wood tools—files and a hammer, a plane, a level. The clothes disappeared, the last cupboard emptied, even the filthy mattress pulled out and put to use, taken by the sweeper who cleaned the toilets in the big house. The door of the little cabin hung open, the wind and blown rain scoured it clean.

James Lasdun

## Oh, Death

THE PARKERS, FATHER and son, came over to introduce themselves when we moved in, five years ago. Dean, the father, was slow to speak, awkward when he did. But Rick was talkative, his eyes roving inquisitively over us and our boxes of possessions. A fuzz of reddish stubble covered his neatly rounded head and pointed chin. His voice was soft, almost velvety, with a sprung quality, each word like a plucked banjo note. He told us he did a variety of odd jobs in land-scaping and construction. Tree work was what he enjoyed most, the more difficult the better. He would climb up in a harness and spiked boots to drop limbs from trees that stood too close to people's houses to fell conventionally, or he'd drive out in his pickup to haul storm-tangled, half-blown-over trees out of each other's branches, then cut them up for firewood. "Any jobs like that you need doing," he told us, "I'm your man."

Some time after that visit my wife and I passed two small children climbing the steep slope of Vanderbeck Hollow. They were both in tears, and we stopped to see if we could help. Their mother had put them out of the car for fighting, they told us, and they were walking home.

Home, it turned out, was Rick's house. Rick had met their mother, Faye, a few weeks earlier, at a Harley-Davidson rally, and she'd moved in, bringing her kids with her. Rick's father had already moved out. Faye herself we met when we dropped off the children. She didn't seem to care about our interference in their punishment. She was a thin, black-haired woman with pitted skin, bright blue eyes, and a dab of hard crimson at the center of her upper lip. She didn't say much.

They had their first baby the next year, a girl. Rick used to tuck her into his hunting jacket while he worked in his front yard, fixing his trucks or sharpening his chain-saw blades. He liked being a father—from the start he'd treated Faye's two elder children as his own—but it was soon apparent that his new responsibilities were a strain for him. After a day operating the stone crusher at the Andersonville quarry or cutting rebar with one of the construction crews in town, he'd come home, eat dinner, then turn on a set of floodlights he'd rigged up to the house and start cutting and splitting firewood to make extra money. He sold it for seventy dollars a cord, which was cheap even then. I often bought a cord or two for our woodstove. Once, he asked how I made my living. "Gaming the system," I replied, intending to sound amusingly cryptic. "You must be good at it" was all he said, pointing to our new Subaru.

He bought a car for Faye, cutting wood later and later into the night to pay for it, renting a mechanical splitter from the hardware store and erecting huge log piles all around his house. A note of exasperation entered his talk; he seemed bewildered by the difficulty of making ends meet. Here he was, a young man in his prime—able to take care of his physical needs, to plow his own driveway, to fix his own roof, to hunt and butcher his own meat—and yet every day was a struggle. If it wasn't money, it was offenses to his pride, which was strung tight, like every other part of him. He was always recounting (reliving, it almost seemed) insults and slights he'd received from various bosses and other representatives of the official world, along with the defiant ripostes he'd made. When Faye got a job on the night shift at Hannaford and was kept past her clocking-out time, he called up the manager at the store: "I told that freakin' weasel to get off her back," he said to me with a satisfied grin. She was fired soon after.

To blow off steam he would barrel up and down the hill in his truck, churning up clouds of dust from the gravel surface. Or he would carry a six-pack up to the woods above the road and sit drinking among the oaks and ashes along the ridge. I would often find a can of Molson by a rock up there in the bracken where he'd dumped it—his gleaming spoor. He was building a little cabin on the other side of the ridge, he told me once. It was state land there, but he figured no one would care. What was it for? I asked him. He shrugged. "Just somewhere to go . . ."

Another time he told me he'd seen a lion up there.

"A mountain lion?"

"Yep. A catamount."

"I didn't know they lived around here." In fact I'd read that despite rumored sightings, there were no mountain lions in this area.

He gave me a glance and I saw he'd registered my disbelief, but also that he didn't hold it against me. "Yep. Came right up to the cabin. Sucker just stood there in the entranceway, big as a freakin' buffalo. I kept one of the paw prints he left in the dirt. Dug it out and let it dry. I'll show you someday."

As a boy, when the Parkers' property had marked the end of the road, he'd had the run of Vanderbeck Hollow, hunting deer and wild turkey, fishing for trout in the rock pools along the stream that wound down the deep crease between Spruce Clove and Donell Mountain. He wasn't exactly a model of ecological awareness, with his beer cans and his oil-leaking ATV that he used for dragging tree carcasses down to his truck, not to mention the roaring, fumy snowmobile he drove along the logging trails all winter, but he knew the woods up here with an intimacy that seemed its own kind of love. I walked with him up to one of the old quarries one spring morning and found myself at the receiving end of a detailed commentary on the local wildlife. To my uninformed eye, the trees and plants were more or less just an undifferentiated mass of brown and green matter, and the effect of his pointing and naming was like having a small galaxy switch itself on star by star around me. "Trout lily," he said, and a patch of yellow flowers lit up under a boulder. "Goat's rue," and a silvery-stemmed plant shone out from a clearing a few yards off. "Mountain laurel," he went on, gesturing at some dark green shrubs, "blossoms real pretty in late spring. Won't be for another month or more yet. They call 'em laurel slicks when it grows in thickets like this. Sometimes heath balds. It's poisonous—even honey made from the flowers is supposed to be poisonous. See here, the burl?" He put his finger on a hard, knotlike growth—"old-timers used to make pipes out of 'em. My dad has one."

In his lifetime he'd seen the road developed a mile and a half beyond the family property, the surrounding land sold off in twenty-acre lots, with timber frames and swimming pools and chain-link fences and NO HUNTING signs going farther and farther up the hill every year, and he hated it all, though his hatred stopped short of the actual human beings responsible for these incursions. One afternoon he was standing on the road with me, complaining about the arrival of backhoes to dig the foundation for a new house on the property of Cora Chastine, the neighbor below him, when Cora herself rode out of her driveway on her chestnut mare. Seeing him, she began thanking him for a favor he'd done her the night before, pulling a dinner guest's car out of the ditch at one in the morning. Smiling gallantly, he assured her it was no problem and that he hadn't minded being woken at that hour. "Nice lady," he said in his purring voice when she rode on, as if there were no important connection in his mind between the person herself and her contribution to the destruction of his haunts.

He and Faye had a second child, another girl. A hurricane—unusual in these parts—struck that year. Torrential rain had fallen for several days before, loosening roots so that the trees came crashing down like sixty-foot bowling pins when the wind hit, turning the woods into scenes of carnage, the trees lying in their sap and foliage and splintered limbs like victims of a massacre, the vast holes left by their roots gaping like bomb craters. Within the hurricane there were localized tornadoes, one of which plowed a trail of devastation through our own woods. Rick offered to do the cleanup for us, pointing out that there were some valuable trees we could sell for timber. He proposed doing all the work himself over the course of a year: to use a cousin's team of horses to drag the timber out so as to avoid the erosion big machines caused, to load it with a hand-winched pulley (a "come-along" was his quaint name for this), to chop up all the crowns for firewood and haul off the stumps to the town dump.

I hesitated, knowing he had no insurance and anticipating problems if he should injure himself. A lawyer friend told us on no account to let him do the work, and we hired a fully insured professional logging crew instead. They brought in a skidder the size of a tugboat, a bulldozer, two tractors, and a grappler with a claw that could grab a trunk a yard thick and hoist it thirty feet into the air. For several weeks these machines tore through our woods, bulldozing rocks, branches, and stumps into huge unsightly piles and ripping a raw red trail across streambeds and fern-filled clearings to the landing stage by the road, where the crew loaded the limbless trunks onto a double-length trailer to sell at the lumberyard. I ran into Rick several times on the road during the operation. He never reproached us for passing him over for the job; in fact he offered good advice on how not to get cheated out of our share of the proceeds. But I felt uncomfortable seeing him walk by, as though I'd denied him work that was his by rights.

He and Faye got married the following summer. We were invited to the celebratory pig roast. It was a big party: beat-up old pickup trucks lining the road halfway down the hill and twenty or thirty motorcycles parked in the driveway. We recognized a few neighbors;

otherwise it was all Faye's and Rick's biker friends in leather jackets and bandannas. At the center of the newly cleaned-up front yard a dance floor had been improvised out of bluestone slabs that Rick must have dragged from one of the old quarries up in the woods. Beside it a band was playing fast, reeling music: two fiddles, a guitar, a banjo, and a mandolin, the players belting out raucous harmonies as they flailed away at their instruments.

I liked this mountain music. I'd started listening to it a few years before and found myself susceptible to its mercurial moods and colors—more so than ever since we'd moved up here to mountains of our own, where it had come to seem conjured directly out of the bristly, unyielding landscape itself, the rapid successions of pain and sweetness, tension and release, frugality and spilling richness, arising straight out of these thickly wooded crags and gloomy gullies with their sun-shot clearings and glittering, wind-riffled creeks. I would listen to it in the car as I drove to work, an hour down the thruway. The lucrative drudgery of my job left me with a depleted sensation, as though I'd spent the days asleep or dead, but driving there and back I would play my Clinch Mountain Boys CDs at full volume, and as their frenzied, propulsive energies surged into me I would bray along at the top of my lungs, harmonizing with unabashed tuneless-ness, and a feeling of joy would arise in me as if a second self, full of fiery, passionate vitality were at the point of awakening inside me.

A van drove into the yard shortly after we arrived. In it was the pig for the pig roast. As a wedding joke, their friends had arranged to have the animal delivered alive instead of dead. Two of them helped the butcher lead it from the van, roping its bucking, scarlet-eyed head and shit-squirting rear end, and dragging it over to Rick. One of them handed him a gleaming knife.

"What's this?"

He stared down at the animal, writhing frantically in its ropes.

Faye had appeared, dressed in a denim skirt and red cowboy boots. She looked on, smoking a cigarette with an air of neutral but attentive interest.

"You gotta do the honors, buddy," one of the bikers said. "Duty of the groom."

There was loud laughter, a shout of, "Go on, cut his goddamn throat."

"I'll cut your goddamn throat," Rick muttered. He went into the house and there was a brief, awkward hiatus. He came back out with a shotgun. Faye turned away.

"Hey, you can't do that, he has to bleed to death, don't he?" a guest said, looking at the butcher, who gave a noncommittal shrug.

Ignoring them both, Rick loaded a cartridge into the gun and fired it straight into the pig's head, splattering himself and several others with blood and brains. This set off guffaws of laughter among the bikers, and Rick himself cracked a smile. "I'll get the come-along," he said. They hoisted the pig up with the device—an archaic-looking assemblage of cords and gears and wooden pulleys—hanging it by its hind legs from a tree branch, and the butcher slit it open, spilling its innards into a bucket. Then they drove a spit through it and set it up over a halved oil drum grill, and the band, which had fallen silent during this episode, struck up again, three high voices in a blasting triad calling out, "Weeee-ill you miss me?" followed by the single morose rumble of their thick-bearded baritone: "miss me when I'm gawwwn . . ."

Rick came up to us with a bottle of applejack that he claimed to have brewed himself with fruit from his grandfather's old prohibition orchard at the back of their lot. He insisted we take a swig from the bottle—it was pure liquid fire—then reeled away, grabbing Faye for a dance on the stone floor.

It was at this moment, watching him cavort around his bride with one hand on his hip and the other brandishing the bottle high in the air, while she stared out across the valley at the dusty emerald flank of Donell Mountain, that I registered, for the first time, the tinge of sadness in Faye's expression, underlying the more visible cold severity.

I was away much of the following year and aside from a few fleeting glimpses didn't see them again until the fall, when I ran into them at a neighbor's party. Arshin and Leanne, the hosts, were therapists, Buddhists, members of the local "healing community": Leanne shaven-headed like a Tibetan monk, Arshin gaunt and dark, a set of prayer beads forever clicking in his fingers. Their friends were mostly either acupuncturists or qigong practitioners. Rick and Faye were standing in a corner, drinking beers with a tall man in a scuffed leather jacket and a pair of muddy work boots. The three of them looked out of place among these shoeless, tea-drinking wraiths. I went over to say hello. Rick introduced their friend as his "buddy" Schuyler. I noticed a string of numbers tattooed across the back of his neck, like a serial number. He gave a nod, then faded swiftly back into what appeared to be some immensely pleasurable private reverie. Purely to make conversation I asked Rick if he was planning to sell firewood again this fall.

"Maybe."

"I'd like a cord if you are."

"Okay."

He didn't seem all that interested in talking. I moved away, wondering if I'd offended him by talking business at a social gathering. Schuyler and Faye left the party but Rick stayed on, drinking steadily. At one point he started asking women to dance, even though it wasn't that kind of party. One or two of them did, just to humor him.

The next night, at two in the morning, he started firing off his gun. The same thing happened for the next several nights. I called to ask what was going on. He answered the phone with the words, "Hello, you've reached the Vanderbeck Hollow Cat-House and Abortion Clinic," then hung up. A few days later I came home from the train station to find a pile of logs dumped over the lawn. It was true that I'd asked for wood, but normally we would discuss the price and the time of delivery before Rick brought it over, and he would help me stack it. I called him that evening. Without apologizing for dumping the wood, he said he wanted a hundred and twenty dollars for it.

"That's quite a bit more than you usually charge."

"That's the price."

I stacked the wood. It seemed less than a full cord, and I said so when I took the check down to Rick the next day. He was outside, talking with Faye by the stone oven he'd built in their front yard. He barely looked at me as I spoke.

"That was a full cord," was all he said, taking the check. "I measured it."

It was only when I spoke to Arshin a few days later that I began to understand Rick's behavior, and it is only since I've spoken with a cousin of Rick's who works at the post office that I've been able to piece together the sequence of events in the month that followed.

Schuyler, their companion at Arshin's party, was not a friend of Rick's at all, let alone his "buddy," but an old acquaintance of Faye's. The exact nature of their relationship was not made apparent to any of us at this time: all we knew was that he had turned up at Rick's house, having just come out of jail, where he'd spent eighteen months for selling methamphetamine. Faye ran off with him the day after that party, leaving the four kids behind. She was gone for five nights. Those were the nights Rick fired off his gun. She came back, they had a fight, a reconciliation, then she took off again. The sequence repeated itself a third time, after which Rick told her to stay out of the house for good. She could take the children or leave them, he told her, but she had to go. At this point Faye became violently angry, throwing furniture and dishes at the walls till one of the older kids called the cops. Before they arrived Rick chamber-locked his gun and set it outside the house. "That was so the cops would see there wasn't no gun violence in the house," his cousin told me. Faye had cooled down by the time they showed up. Very calmly she told them that Rick had threatened to kill her and the children and then himself. The police, obliged to take such threats seriously, carted Rick off to the Andersonville Hospital psychiatric wing for a week's enforced observation. By the time he came out of the hospital, Faye had obtained a protection order, barring him from coming within a mile of the house.

The next few days are a mystery, obscured by conflicting reports and gaps in the record. What was known for sure was that Rick spent them at the home of a relative, a woman named Esther whom he referred to as his "second mother," his first having disappeared when he was small. He was distraught, drinking heavily, but also looking for work: intent on supporting his family even though he wasn't allowed to see them. The Saturday after Thanksgiving he took a job with a landscaper who'd been hired to do tree work on a property in town. We first heard about the accident when Arshin called on Sunday to ask if we knew whether it was true that Rick had been killed the day before: hanged, up a tree. An hour later he called back to confirm the report. A heavy branch, roped to the ground to make it fall in a particular direction, had been caught by a gust and blown the wrong way, slashing the rope across Rick's neck and chest, asphyxiating him. He was seventy feet up in the air and the fire department couldn't reach him with their cherry picker. They put out a call for a bucket ladder. A local contractor brought one and grappled him down. He was blue. The emergency helicopter on its way from Albany was sent back.

The funeral service was in town, at the Pinewood Memorial Home. It was already crowded when we arrived: young, old, suits, overalls, biker jackets, everyone in a state of raw grief. We signed the register and made our way inside. Loud, agitated whisperings rose and fell around us, anger glittering along with tears. Already there was a sense of different versions of Rick's last days forming and hardening, of details being exchanged and collected, variants disputed. The two older children sat on the front bench on one side of the chapel, fearful-looking as they had been when we first saw them, walking alone up the twilit slope of Vanderbeck Hollow. On the other side were Rick's relatives, his father sitting rigid, hands on his knees, broad back motionless.

Faye appeared from a side room with the two little girls and slid next to the older two, glancing briefly over her shoulder at the congregation, her face stricken, though whether with grief, guilt, or terror was hard to say. Even among her four children she seemed a solitary, unconnected figure.

A minister came in and told us to rise. After he read from the Bible and we sang a hymn, people went up to the front to speak. High school anecdotes were recounted, fishing stories, the time Rick was chased out of his front yard by a bear. A tall, silver-haired woman stood up. As she began speaking, I realized she was Esther, Rick's second mother. She said she'd had a long conversation with Rick a few days before his death, when he was staying with her.

"In hindsight," she continued, "*unbelievably,* I see that I have to take this conversation as the expression of Rick's last wishes."

With a firm look around the crowded chapel, she announced that he'd said he still loved Faye.

"He told me he still hoped to have another child with her, a son."

She paused a moment, then concluded:

"Therefore, Faye, I honor you as his widow, and I love you."

An unexpected brightening sensation passed through me at these words. I, like everyone else no doubt, had arrived at the funeral believing Rick had been up in that tree in a state of impaired judgment, if not outright suicidal despair, and that this was a direct result of Faye's behavior. I still did believe this to be the case, but I was caught off guard by the implicit plea for compassion in Esther's speech. I found myself thinking again of the expression I'd glimpsed on Faye's face at the wedding, gazing off into the late-summer greenness of the hollow, and although I still had no more idea what it signified than I had at the time, I wondered if there was perhaps something more in the nature of a torment underlying her behavior than the purely banal selfishness and manipulation by which I had so far accounted for it.

The service ended. Whether by design or some unconscious collective assent, our departure from the chapel was conducted more formally than our arrival: a single, slow line formed, passing out by way of the casket. It was open, and there was no avoiding looking in. Ribboned envelopes were pinned to the white satin lining of the lid.

*Dear Daddy,* they read, in childish handwriting. I mounted the single step, bracing myself for the encounter. There he lay: eyes closed, beard trimmed, cheeks and lips not-so-subtly made up, chalky hands together holding a turkey feather. I stared hard, trying to recognize in this assemblage of features my neighbor of five years. For a moment it seemed to me that I could make out a trace of the old mischievous grin that floated over him even when his luck was down, and it struck me—God knows why—as the look of someone who knows that despite everything having gone wrong with his life, at some other level everything was all right.

That was November. Knowing what I know now—what we all know now—I go back to that ghost of a grin on Rick's face and find I must read into it a note of resignation as well as that appearance of contentment: submission to a state of affairs as implacably out of reach of human exertion as the shift of wind that took his life. And by the same token I go back to the look on Faye's face at their wedding and find in it, beyond the general sadness, the specific expression of a person observing that nothing after all, not even the charm of one's own wedding day, is powerful enough to purge the past or stop its taint from spreading into the future. Whether this disposes of the "banal" in her subsequent actions, I am not sure, the situation being, in a sense, the precise essence of banality. Schuyler had been her foster brother from the time he was fifteen and she eleven. Arshin had the story from an acquaintance who used to work for the Andersonville Social Services. Over the course of several years, in a small house in the section of town known as the Depot Flats, he had—what?— seduced her? Taken advantage of her? Raped her? No word seems likely to fit the case, not in any useful way, which is to say in any way that might account for the disparate, volatile cluster of wants, needs, aversions, and fears the experience appears to have bequeathed her: the apparent determination to put a distance, or at any rate the obstacle of another man, between herself and Schuyler, her equally apparent undiminished susceptibility to him, her cold manner, her strange power to make a man as warm and tender as Rick fall in love with her nevertheless.

She stayed in the house all December and January, though I barely glimpsed her. Arshin claimed Schuyler was living with her, sneaking up there at night and leaving first thing in the morning, but we saw no sign of him. In February we went on vacation. When we got back there was a realtor's board up outside the house. Faye had left abruptly—for Iowa, we heard later, where she had relatives—and Rick's father had decided to sell the place. It sold quickly, to a couple from New York who wanted it for a weekend home.

A few days ago I met Cora Chastine coming down the road on her mare. We stopped to talk and at some point I remarked how quiet Vanderbeck Hollow had become without Rick roaring up and down it in his truck. Cora looked blank for a moment and I wondered if she was growing forgetful in her old age. But then, in that serene, melodious voice of hers, she said:

"Do you know, I realized the other day that Rick is the first person whose life I've observed in its entirety from birth to death within my own lifetime. I was living here when he was born and I'm still living here now that he's no longer alive. Isn't that remarkable?"

I nodded politely. She gave the reins a little flick and glided on.

I'd been planning to take my usual late-afternoon walk to the top of the road and back, but something was making me restless—some faint sense of shame, no doubt, at having failed to protest that Rick's existence might be regarded as something other than merely the index of this genteel horsewoman's powers of survival—and instead of turning back I continued along the logging trail that leads from the end of the road up through the woods to the ridge.

It had been years since I'd been up there. The trail was muddy and puddled from the late thaw but the service blossoms were out, ragged yellow stars, and the budding leaves on the maples and oaks made high domes through which the last of the daylight glowed in differ-ent shades of green. Reaching the top of the ridge I followed the path down the far side, past the rusted swing gate with its STATE LAND sign and on down the uninhabited slope that faces north across Spruce Hollow.

The trees here were different: hemlocks and pines, with some kind of dark-leafed shrub growing between them, its leaf crown held up on thin, bare, twisting gray stems like strange goblets. It took me a moment to recognize this as mountain laurel—deer must have stripped it below shoulder level, creating this eerie appearance—and I was just trying to remember the things Rick had told me about this plant the time we walked up through the woods together when my eye was caught by a straight-edged patch of darkness off in the distance. I realized, peering through the tangled undergrowth, that I was looking at a man-made structure.

Leaving the path, I made my way toward it, and I saw that it was a hut built out of logs. It stood in a small clearing. The walls were about five feet high, the peeled logs neatly notched into each other at the corners. The roof had been draped with wire-bound bundles of brush. A door made of ax-hewn planks hung in the entrance. I pushed it and it swung open onto a twilit space, and by a swift chain reaction of stimulus and remembrance, I became abruptly aware that I was standing in the cabin that Rick had built himself in order to have, as he had put it, somewhere to go.

The top few inches of the rear wall had been left open under the eaves, giving a thin view of Spruce Clove. On the dirt floor below stood a seat carved out of a pine stump, with a plank shelf fitted at waist height into the wall beside it. An unopened can of Molson stood on this, next to what looked like an improvised clay ashtray.

I sat on the stump, struck by the thought that this would make a good refuge from the world if I too should ever feel the need for somewhere to go. And then, as I was sizing up the shelf for possible use as a desk, I saw that what I'd thought was an ashtray was not in fact an ashtray at all. I picked it up: it was a piece of dried clay that had been hollowed by the imprint of an enormous, clawed paw.

A sudden apprehension traveled through me. Despite a strong impulse to swing around, I stopped myself: I dislike giving way to superstition. Even so, as I sat there gazing up at the granite outcrops of Spruce Clove streaked in evening gold, I had an almost overpowering sense of being looked at myself, stared at in uncomprehending astonishment by some wild creature standing in the doorway.

Natalie Bakopoulos

## *Fresco, Byzantine*

**GREECE, 1970–71**

THEY HAD COME of age in such places, those island prisons—
during the Nazi occupation, during the civil war, throughout
the fifties, and now—and now some were growing old there. "We
were wondering about you," many said when Mihalis arrived. "About
how long you'd be spared."

He had evaded detainment during this junta's earlier years, but
then, after an outburst at the ridiculous propaganda reels run at the
movie house, Mihalis was arrested. After twenty-one days of detainment (and beatings, and torture) on Bouboulinas Street, he was sent
to an island prison. "How auspicious," he had said to the officer who
had come to collect him. "I've spent time on several, but the detention center of L—— I haven't yet seen."

Once there he found many artists and writers and the rank-and-
file of the Left and Center, many he had known before and with
whom he was now reunited. That was not surprising. Still, out of all
the possible island detention centers, he had not anticipated to find
his friend Vagelis, a cabdriver and painter from Halandri who had
sometimes seemed more like a personal chauffeur to Mihalis's

teenage nieces. Mihalis remembered when the officers had come to arrest him.

"But we already have here some more-famous poets," Vagelis said when they found one another, and the two men embraced.

Vagelis had been there awhile. But even had Mihalis not known this, the look of him gave it away. Mihalis waited for Vagelis to ask of news from Athens, from Halandri. When he didn't, Mihalis mentioned that he had seen Vagelis's wife just a month before, walking home from the girls' school where she taught. Vagelis scanned the room where they ate, distracted. Finally, his gaze settled on a skinny girl, no older, it seemed, than Mihalis's nieces, now university students. Later, Mihalis would learn her name was Nefeli. She sat alone, sketching, the long drape of her hair, black with hints of red, covering most of her face. If lice were a problem at this camp, she didn't seem to be afflicted.

"She's well, I hope?" Vagelis asked. He drew his spoon to his mouth but didn't take a bite. He glanced again over at the girl.

"Who's that?" Mihalis asked.

Vagelis, distracted, took a bite, moved his soup bowl aside, and lit a cigarette. "What?" he asked.

They slept in barracks left over from the Italians. Some days, they were allowed to swim and walk on the shore; other days they were not. They rarely knew what was allowed because it seemed to change from hour to hour. Sometimes they ate fish, sometimes only broth. Things were inconsistent; how they were fed depended on who was in charge from day to day. They talked about food often. Sometimes, when they lay at night, some in cots, some in double bunks, the room would be quiet, until someone would cry out: "Roast beef!" And another would answer: "Galaktoboureko!" And another "Spanikopita!" and they would continue like that, shouting out favorite foods, until they'd fall asleep. Sometimes, they called out names of women: "Irini!" "Melina!" "Sophia Loren!"

Yet they were better off there, they knew, than on some of the other islands, and surely better off than in previous times of exile: this Mihalis knew firsthand. But this didn't make it unobjectionable, and it certainly didn't make it morally excusable, so many people exiled simply for having a voice. It was still absurd. It was like paying some-one one cent per day for his labors and then arguing that at least he was receiving that lousy cent. Or a man claiming he only beats his wife occasionally, on Sundays and holidays.

When it rained for stretches at a time, everything grew moldy and damp. The drinking water was sometimes brackish. Mihalis, though always a little thirsty, felt he would never be dry. He wrote poems he did not finish, a whole notebook of unrefined work. They'd surely take it from him if and when he was released.

When they were not working, cleaning the camp, doing laundry, or preparing their meals, the detainees busied themselves taking walks or studying the flora of the island. Some read or wrote or sketched. Many, even if they had not arrived as artists, would leave at least as craftsmen: they created things from delicate worry beads to nice sitting chairs to tables they could gather around. Something from nothing, something in nothing.

A few boys from the village sometimes hung around the barbed wire fence that enclosed them, at first to observe, like curious anthro-pologists, and then to provoke. But soon the prisoners had become used to them, and they to the prisoners, and sometimes, for a fee, they'd bring chocolate or cigarettes or just provide amusing conversa-tion. One boy's father was a guard, a less severe one who seemed as unsympathetic to the regime as they were. He had not asked for this, his look seemed to say; he was only doing his job. But that was why, of course, fanatical regimes prevailed. Too many people doing their jobs, not wanting to make a scene.

Though they ate their meals together, the men and women were lodged separately. The women's sleeping quarters were a short walk away, separated by a paltry, unintimidating fence. Near the back of the camp, someone had slashed a hole through it, and they passed through as nonchalantly as if ducking beneath a low copse of shrubs on a path. The guards seemed not to notice, or if they did, not to care. Perhaps they, too, conveniently used this entrance.

During the day, when they were not working, Vagelis and Nefeli were suspiciously absent, a detail that most of their fellow prisoners seemed to take as matter-of-fact. The two seemed to always appear for their mess duties together. Sometimes, at night, Mihalis heard Vagelis rise from his bed when the guard had disappeared for a moment to relieve himself. Once, Mihalis woke uncharacteristically early to find Nefeli sneaking from their barracks, like a child at scout camp, barefoot. On the top of her delicate, tanned feet were splatters of paint: crimson and gold, like the marks of the stigmata. "Hi," she said. And then she shrugged, as if to say, How much more can they do to me? Plenty, Mihalis thought. She was young, this was her first prison, and Mihalis hoped she would not have to learn the things he already knew.

One day, Mihalis and Vagelis sat inside their barracks, beneath blankets. Outside fell a cold, miserable rain. Vagelis said, "When I get out, I'm going to live. I'm going to screw every woman I see. Eighteen-year-olds, fifty-year-olds, it doesn't matter. I'll pick them all up in my cab." Vagelis stretched his arms over his head and wiggled his fingers.

This was all audacity, for show. Vagelis had always been faithful to his marriage, as far as Mihalis knew. But Mihalis didn't mention Vagelis's wife; rather, he asked about Nefeli.

Vagelis dropped his elbows down to the table abruptly. "What about her?" he asked.

"You're very covert, but our quarters are small," said Mihalis.

"Has it been so long since you've been with a woman that you can't recognize the act? It's something else entirely."

"You've got a creature like that sneaking into your tiny cot, and you're telling me you're not having sex?"

Vagelis smirked. But then his face changed; he grew quiet. "You don't think there could be something between a man and a woman besides sex?" he asked.

"Yes, of course there can," Mihalis said. "But in addition to sex."

Vagelis drew his legs to his chest and set his chin on his knees, rocking back and forth, the same way Mihalis knew Nefeli sat when alone, staring out at the water. "I came here with a good marriage, you know."

"And I came with a devastated one," Mihalis said. It was true. His wife, Irini, wrote him countless letters, some of which he actually received. Through these letters, they began to communicate again, like yearning, adventurous teenagers. "These separations are doing wonders for it."

Vagelis managed a smile, though absentminded. "Come on," he said, unfolding himself. "Let's go for a walk. I'll show you something."

Mihalis dressed in the raincoat Irini had sent, and he gave Vagelis a heavy sweater. Along with the letters, Irini sent packages filled with supplies: two wool blankets, soap and toothpaste and cigarettes and tins of fish, sleeves of crackers. Even a set of flannel pajamas, for which the other prisoners mocked him but of which Mihalis knew they were jealous. In this cold, dreary spell, Mihalis was happy to have all of it.

Vagelis held above them an almost-broken umbrella that threatened to snap down, and Mihalis then recalled a day when they were much younger men, ambling around Athens. A downpour had begun, and they ducked onto a parked bus, jumping off just as it was about to leave and darting onto another, all the while maintaining their conversation. Two middle-aged men had glared at them, and Vagelis and Mihalis had laughed.

Now, they themselves were middle-aged, and they walked, their hands held behind their backs, through the wet, fragrant pines, the thick shrubs of eucalyptus, until they came upon an old husk of a church, the outside visibly neglected, overgrown with weeds.

"Don't tell me. You're taking me to church?" Mihalis asked.

Vagelis opened the front door, a large, creaky wooden gate, and motioned to Mihalis to follow him.

There were only a few rows of wooden pews; the rest, Mihalis realized, had been torn out and now served as the seating for their mess hall. Vagelis seemed impatient. "Well?" he asked. He pointed at the frescoes that covered the walls and, so far, some of the barrel-vaulted ceiling. It was a work in progress; Mihalis smelled the dizzying smell of paint.

And it was truly spectacular. One image melted into the next, as if a continuous Byzantine dream: Saint Nicholas, and around him small, crude, brightly rendered scenes of his miracles; the Raising of Lazarus; Saint Peter with his staff and a scroll tied up not with a simple string but with an oversize red ribbon tied into a bow. It brought to mind the bright red bows Mihalis's sister would tie in his nieces' hair when they had been little, and how once they had come home sobbing, saying the teacher had taken them away. A symbol of Communism. He remembered the way his sister had put her hands in the air, calling the accusation ridiculous and the offense completely unintentional. But beneath her incredulity he had detected an insolent smile. The girls, from then on, demanded only white adornments for their hair.

Neither Mihalis nor Vagelis were religious men. But Mihalis found the image in the center, what appeared to be the Dormition of the Theotokos, to be stunningly moving. The Virgin lay atop a bier, and the faces of those who surrounded her, apostles, bishops, angels, were distorted with grief, and the emotion present in each figure's face was far unlike that of more traditional iconography. Some even appeared to be shouting. Where one would expect a Christ at the top of the image, holding the Virgin's spirit, there was only empty, blue space, like a cloudless spring sky. Mihalis could not tell if the omission was a statement or simply a matter of being incomplete.

Then, in the corner, Mihalis noticed a ladder and a scaffold, and above it, Nefeli. She was painting the sky a deep blue, a continuation of the previous image, and up there she seemed even more diminutive. She sat up and brushed her hair back with her forearm. Usually, she looked at Vagelis in a way that made Mihalis sick with envy. But this time her face didn't brighten.

"Why did you bring him?" she asked.

"You hate the rain," said Vagelis. "I assumed you'd be inside, sleeping."

Mihalis looked around. He felt as if he had somehow intruded upon a tender, intimate act. "You did this?" Mihalis asked.

"The two of us, together," said Vagelis. He stepped back toward the door and surveyed the scene. "All of it."

For two days following, a torrent of rain kept them all inside; most huddled in their beds with their thin, worn blankets. Vagelis, who for two nights had not seen Nefeli, was insufferably restless. He cheated at card games, not to win, but so they would be over quickly and he could return to his pacing. He looked out the window to see if she were coming up the path that linked their two quarters. "Why don't you just go find her?" Aleko, a young artist, asked. "Maybe she's waiting for you."

Vagelis muttered something and flopped down on his bed, sulking.

Mihalis felt embarrassed at how much he had become fixated with Vagelis and Nefeli, but he couldn't help but wonder if they had fought because Vagelis had brought Mihalis to see the paintings.

Because so many of the prisoners were artists or writers, they often discussed matters of craft and style and substance. They had long stretches of time for such conversations, which seemed to continue and evolve through the days.

"It seems futile," one of them said, a young novelist. "To write. During all this."

"Everything will be censored," Aleko said. And, as an afterthought, he added: "I asked my wife to send nude photographs of herself but then worried they'd Magic Marker out the important places." They had only been married two months before his arrest; he had been here now for ten.

"Idiot," Mihalis said. "The guards would keep them for themselves."

"She wouldn't have sent them anyway," another man said. "She's probably screwing the gardener."

Aleko shrugged. Later that afternoon, he finished a nude painting of his wife in a dense, overgrown garden, with thick black bands covering her privates.

The next day, the rain continued, heavy and unyielding like some sort of biblical plague. Rivulets of water formed throughout the camp, tiny rivers going nowhere. The roof of the barracks began to leak, and the men busied themselves finding containers to catch the rain so the dirt floor would not be muddied. One of the more sympathetic guards arrived with coffee and cigarettes (for a fee, of course), something they hadn't had in days.

That afternoon, they talked of the rumor that had been suspended over them like a dead animal hung up to bleed. There it was: whoever signed papers of allegiance to the regime would be released.

"Never," said Vagelis. "I won't do it." Others agreed with him, though a few looked sheepish.

"Your intentions are less noble," Mihalis said. "Am I wrong?" Mihalis proposed that Vagelis was in no hurry to leave, that his stubbornness was not a matter of political conviction but one of simple emotion instead. That the make-believe life he'd created here suited him, that he liked being able to run around with a beautiful woman and throw paint around and believe in artistic transcendence and the Platonic ideal and not drive his cab around Athens. "Meanwhile," Mihalis continued, "your wife is at home, worried, broke. Alone."

And then Vagelis punched him, square under his eye. Mihalis was knocked out cold.

. . .

When he came to, he saw Vagelis's face hovering over him, closely, checking both his eyes and studying his cheek. Vagelis then put on his shoes and walked out into the downpour with his broken umbrella. Mihalis drew his hand to his throbbing face. He noticed Vagelis was wearing his raincoat. "Bastard."

When Vagelis returned, not long after, Mihalis was ready to punch him back. But Vagelis was sopping wet, visibly distressed: to hit him now would be like socking a child. "The women are gone," Vagelis said. "They've moved their camp." He was panting, as if he had been running.

"To where?" Aleko asked.

"The guard said he didn't know. More men are arriving today, and they needed the room."

"Maybe they've been released," Mihalis said.

"Or the guards want the women to themselves," Aleko added.

"No," Vagelis said. Mihalis wasn't sure to whose comment, his or Aleko's, Vagelis had been responding.

"Maybe they've all signed loyalty oaths," another man said.

No one responded to this, all of them lost in their own verdicts. In quieter tones, one-to-one conversations, they talked of the women, how there had been rumors of their planning an intricate, mass escape, or some sort of insurrection. Perhaps, they thought, this was why they were isolated, and if so another testament to the powers'- that-be bizarre ways of reasoning. It was like throwing a match at a gas tank. Everyone knew that men left alone destroy themselves, and women alone flourish.

"Maybe their escape plan simply involved the loyalty oaths," Mihalis said, though he didn't believe it.

They were introspective awhile, thinking about women. Some of them dozed off. In the corner of the room, near the stove that blazed to seemingly no effect, Vagelis slowly peeled off his wet clothes, care- fully hanging Mihalis's coat to dry. In his underwear, he crawled beneath his blanket.

Mihalis woke to Aleko's gravelly voice: "Mihalis had a point, Vagelis. What he said earlier, about Nefeli. What is it, exactly, that you're doing?"

Vagelis said nothing, though he exhaled intently, as if he had been holding his breath. Mihalis knew he was, in spite of himself, thinking of Nefeli, wondering why she hadn't somehow come to tell him what had happened. Mihalis was wondering the same.

"I would sign something," Aleko said. "They're only words on a page."

"Only words on a page?" Mihalis blurted. "That's everything." But what he'd do to be back home with his own wife, to wander through Athens, to drink coffee at Zonar's, to sit on his terrace and look out over the lemon trees. But he knew this was a dangerous way of thinking. I'll get out when I get out, he told himself. This can't last forever.

The next morning, the rain had subsided to a measly drizzle, and Vagelis asked Mihalis to walk to the church with him. This was evidently his apology for the deep blue shiner beneath Mihalis's left eye. Mihalis shrugged and went along. After all, they had been friends for years.

On the way, Vagelis narrated to him the details of the paintings' creation—how they collaborated, the way Nefeli was allowed, with a guard, to go into the village and send for paint; the way another guard, a closeted artist whose father did not approve, had secured the scaffold and the paintbrushes in exchange for being allowed to add a few touches while pretending to keep an eye on them.

Inside, the two men sat in a pew, looking up at the unfinished ceiling. "I'm going to stay here a bit," Vagelis said. A few purple flowers, which grew all over the island, were scattered on the pew ahead. Mihalis recalled having seen one tucked behind Nefeli's ear once, an embellishment both ironic and sincere.

"Don't wait for her too long," Mihalis said as he left, and Vagelis agreed. But when he wasn't back for hours, Mihalis assumed she had shown up, from wherever she was now being held. When Vagelis returned later that day, though, bleary-eyed and glowering, Mihalis knew he hadn't had any luck.

"Send her a message," Mihalis said. "Those young boys by the barbed wire. They'd be happy to deliver a declaration of love."

"Make it dirty, so it's worth their while," Aleko added. He was the youngest, and most in touch with the minds of preadolescent boys.

"We don't know if the women are even on this island," Vagelis said. "For all we know they've been moved to Yiaros, or Syros, or back to Athens. It's nothing to joke about."

"Those boys will know. And of course they know Nefeli. She's the loveliest of the women," Mihalis said. He paused, grinned, and looked right at Vagelis. "And much closer to their age."

Vagelis lunged at Mihalis again, but this time Aleko stopped him.

The boys knew nothing of the women's whereabouts, but they liked the challenge of a puzzle. Two smaller boys were anxious to deliver the message, but the oldest one, too pale for the Dodecanese islands, even for winter, wanted payment for their services. He must have spent most of his time indoors, scheming.

Vagelis asked Aleko to draw some naked pictures, no black bands over the privates. Later, when the boys returned, he presented them. "We can give you nude ladies."

The younger boys examined the first picture with intense concentration. "These are drawings!" the oldest boy said. "We want real pictures."

Aleko, insulted, told the boys his drawings were more accurate than what their imaginations could ever conjure, and this seemed to appease them.

"Check by the old church in the evening," said Vagelis.

"We haven't seen her there," the oldest boy said, knowingly. Of course the boys would have known about the paintings, Mihalis thought, but the admission had still surprised him. Vagelis didn't seem fazed.

The boys set off.

A new rule came after the transfer of the women: they were not allowed to leave the immediate confines of the camp. They could not walk through the dense path to the church, not even with an accompanying guard. Many of the guards they had come to trust, those guards who seemed just as unsympathetic to the regime as they were, were being replaced. A new batch of freshly cut, surly ones was now arriving.

The boys didn't return that night, but they did come back the next, excited and energetic. The oldest boy's eyes were wild, like an enraged horse.

Vagelis ran to the fence. "Talk to me."

"The frescoes in the church," the oldest said, out of breath. "They've transformed!"

"It's God!" said another. Mihalis noticed the large cross that hung around his neck, too big for his small body.

"It's magic!" said the youngest. His name was Niko, and his father was the one guard left whom they liked. "And one of them has your face," he said to Vagelis. "I'll be back with my father. He'll take you there." He turned and ran off.

As promised, Niko and his father returned an hour later. "I can accompany you," his father said. "I've obtained permission."

The boys were right. The frescoes had been transformed, some subtly, others in huge and glaring ways, and the tone had gone from mostly pious sobriety to unbridled drunkenness. Some of the faces looked more ecstatic than grief stricken. But the Virgin was now faceless, her features painted over to a blank slate, and instead of a blue robe covering her head, her hair fell down to the ground in thick, dark ropes.

The figure above her indeed had the face of Vagelis, the eyes exaggeratedly wide-set, the thick hair, an impish smirk. Another image bore the hairline, the large nose, and the unruly eyebrows of Mihalis.

Some of the men in the painting were now women, modern-looking Greek women, many of them fellow prisoners. Some drank from large wine jugs; others threw their heads back, laughing. It was almost bacchanalian.

"Nefeli," Vagelis said.

Aleko, the most talented artist among them, was impressed. "Or divine intervention, like the boys say?"

"You're an atheist," said Mihalis.

"What's that got to do with it?" he asked.

"If it's indeed Nefeli," Aleko asked, "how is she still allowed here? She must have some relationship with a guard."

Both Aleko and Mihalis could see this thought alone was maddening to Vagelis, the idea of her and a young guard coming here, to their—hers and Vagelis's—space, in the night.

"She's communicating with me," Vagelis said. "About the loyalty oaths. Whether to sign one."

"Well?" Mihalis asked. "Does she want you to?"

"That I haven't figured out." He climbed atop the ladder, grabbed a brush, and to the image of Mihalis painted beneath the left eye a sizable bruise.

That night, Mihalis watched Vagelis rise from his bed and peer out the small window, looking for the guard. The old one, who got up frequently to use the bathroom and did not seem to care about Vagelis's moonlit couplings, had been relieved of night duties, and two younger, more fanatical ones took his place. There was never a moment without close watch, and although daytimes they were able to convince some guards to bend the rules, during the night they were draconian. Nights, after all, were the time of escapes.

But the next morning the sun was shining and the air was drenched with warm and wet. Spring was coming, and everyone's spirits lifted slightly. The guards allowed them to walk back and forth on the shore, a meager fifty-meter distance, but it was something. Niko's father and another guard accompanied them back to the church. "One last time," they said. On the way, Mihalis tried to coax from them the women's whereabouts, but they claimed ignorance.

Inside the church, the frescoes had begun to resemble modernist painting more than intricate, Byzantine icons. The image of Mihalis now wore dark sunglasses, the blue of his bruise only a hint. The Virgin's face had been recast as that of Nefeli: the large forehead, sharp cheekbones, and golden eyes were unmistakable.

And this: every one of the figures had one limb covered in a glaring white plaster cast. And in the top corner, Nefeli had painted herself up on a scaffold, her arms stretched above her head and her hands pressed firmly down, as if she were hanging the entire fresco, or holding up the sky.

Now, Vagelis suddenly wanted out. He wanted to sign a loyalty oath, and he wanted to somehow communicate to Nefeli that she should, too. In fact, he was convinced that the plaster casts on the figures meant just this: I surrender.

And then what? Mihalis wanted to know. "Then you'll go back to Athens and live happily ever after? Is that what will happen?" He did not know why he felt so angry.

For the next two weeks, the guards received strict orders not to let the prisoners leave the camp for any circumstances: no walks on the shore, no walks to the village, no walks to look at the frescoes. The whereabouts of the women were still unknown, and the village boys were kept far away from the barbed wire fence. They were, once again, cut off from everything.

One warm evening, Aleko and Vagelis played chess outdoors, in what they sardonically called their courtyard, a little area beside the barracks where they had some tables and chairs and rocks to sit on. Mihalis lay on the ground nearby, feeling the late-day sun on his face, dozing. He was startled by the crack of the loudspeaker.

A guard, in a typical self-important tone, announced that a batch of new prisoners was arriving from another island, and that some of the current residents would be released. The boat was already waiting at the port, he said, and when their names were called, they should immediately assemble their things. Over the shoddy intercom, papers crackled and shuffled, and the men immediately stood up and began to scramble around.

Vagelis stood up from the table so quickly he jostled the chessboard. The small wooden pawns scattered.

The first two whose names were called disappeared into the barracks immediately to pack their bags.

Another prisoner threw some pebbles in their direction. "Cunts," he called out after them.

"They've signed something?" Mihalis asked.

"They haven't said anything," said Vagelis.

The names were called slowly and erratically; sometimes two in a row; other times one, a three-minute pause, and then another. They were listed in no particular order. In itself it was a kind of torture, such lack of rhythm.

Then, they heard Vagelis's name, loud and clear.

"I knew it!" Mihalis said. "What are you scheming now?"

"I haven't signed a thing," he said. He, in fact, looked distraught. Mihalis saw him as the man that he was: forlorn, emotionally devastated, and utterly exhausted.

And then Mihalis was called. The two men regarded each other but said nothing.

The same man who had thrown the stones called out to Mihalis: "You've barely been here six months!"

Mihalis thought about his wife, his bed, the clean sheets, he thought about what he would eat, the things he would drink, the poems he would finish. Vagelis sat back down and put his head in his hands. Aleko stood up and touched both men's shoulders. "Good luck," he told them. Mihalis watched him walk across the yard.

Aleko joined some of the younger prisoners who, still full of the bravado of young men, sat at the other end of the yard, sharing one cigarette. The young, they stayed close together—because their spirits had not yet been broken, they were treated the most brutally. From the looks on their faces, they knew they would not be among the lucky.

Inside, Mihalis gathered his things, spread them on his cot, and began to pack. Some whose names had not been called looked on in envy. To these men it did not matter who had or hadn't signed anything—they were traitors just by their fortune. The one of course who rattled Mihalis most was Aleko, who even imparted good wishes, his face so open and sincere. He himself would not have been so generous. He too would have thrown stones.

Vagelis came inside and opened his small duffel bag.

"She might be on the boat, too," Mihalis said. He removed a sweater, a blanket, and a few cigarettes from his bag and placed them on Aleko's bunk.

Vagelis sat down on his bed and put his head between his hands. "This is a good thing," he said, his voice muffled. "Of course it is."

As they boarded, their bodies massed up against one another and spilled onto the narrow staircases and up to the ship's various decks. There were already other prisoners from other islands aboard, strewn like garbage on the benches and floor. Vagelis strained to find Nefeli.

"I wonder if the women are here," said another man, giving voice to Vagelis's thoughts.

Some women did mill around, though whether they had come from other islands or were from their camp was unclear. As they ascended one stairway, though, Vagelis exclaimed. He recognized one of the women from their camp. He tried to get her attention, but she didn't see him. Still, for the first time that day, his face relaxed a bit.

Mihalis followed Vagelis around the ship: the middle deck, back to the top, the middle again.

"Let's try the top one more time," Vagelis said. "We'll get the warmth of the sun."

"Maybe she's not here," Mihalis said. The boat was getting crowded, and Mihalis wanted to make sure he'd have a decent place to sit.

Vagelis said he was certain she was.

Mihalis snapped. "When, exactly, do you plan on resuming your real life?"

Vagelis listened but said nothing.

Mihalis continued. "When we get off the boat? The first time you sleep with your wife?"

"Who are you to say what's real?" Vagelis asked. His face twisted in anger. "You've lived your entire life in some sort of ideological bubble."

"I'm the idealist?"

"Who communicates with his wife only through the romance of letters? And your false sense of importance—you were actually upset you hadn't been arrested sooner. It was a blow to your ego."

"That's preposterous."

Vagelis dropped his bag to the ground, as if he had forgotten he was carrying it. He kicked it along the floor to an open bench, and he used his jacket sleeve to wipe away the grimy water before he laid his head on his small, dirty rucksack. Mihalis lay on the other side, feet to feet with Vagelis. They had taken these boats coming and going from places of detainment; they had taken them to the islands for holiday. But the former had long ago tainted the latter, and lying on those long, white benches would never be anything but gloomy and disquieting. If they used discrete boats to transport prisoners, he couldn't tell the difference. A boat ride to or from an island would always feel a certain way.

Then, Vagelis sat back up. He brushed himself off, stood up, and walked away. He left his bag on the bench.

"Don't blame me if someone takes your seat," Mihalis said.

"Fuck you," said Vagelis.

And as Vagelis turned around, there stood Nefeli. Though they barely touched one another, their reunion was both tender and bittersweet. There had been a great intimacy in their separation. From his bench Mihalis was able to watch them. They sometimes seemed to be talking, but mostly they were quiet. Later, when the wind picked up and the waters grew turbulent, Mihalis watched as Vagelis kept his hand on Nefeli's back while she vomited over the edge.

The trip was long; they stopped at other islands, sometimes for minutes, other times for hours, and more tired and mangy-looking men and women boarded, looking hopeful and exhausted and proud. Mihalis fell asleep, and when he woke, he didn't see Nefeli, though Vagelis stood nearby, staring out at the horizon. How bizarre that the outline of a mass of land, a rocky island, a narrow shore, could fill one with both dread and hope.

When night came, the weather calmed. They lay across benches, or on the ground.

Mihalis, unable to sleep, looked out at the blue-black of the night sea, the frothy white of waves, illuminated by the ship's light. If we could film the workings of our minds, he thought, they would look like this.

They arrived at the port at dawn, the same port where tourists set sail for islands for holidays of drinking and screwing, and the brow-beaten, skinny, and sickly prisoners materialized back into their own lives. Families milled about anxiously, craning their necks to see.

Mihalis noticed the way Vagelis and Nefeli deboarded, temporar-ily united, looking out together at everything else. Vagelis leaned in and whispered something into her ear, and Nefeli's long face lifted, just for a moment.

If someone had seen the two of them then, Vagelis and Nefeli, they would have been given away. But then they moved farther apart from one another so as to not cause suspicion. Only minutes later, Vagelis greeted his wife. Mihalis hoped that someone, a husband, a boyfriend, a sister, her father, had come for Nefeli.

Nefeli brushed past Mihalis. Up close like this, the closest he had ever stood to her, he noticed she was older than she had appeared; he could tell by the crinkles around her eyes. Her eyes were light, amber colored, and almost disarming, unexpected against the black of her hair, as if they had been taken from another's face and planted there by mistake, or afterthought.

She clutched her sketchbook close to her body and dragged her bag behind her, the curtain of dark hair covering her face. He watched her disappear into the crowd. What had Vagelis said to her, in her ear? What quick, swift words? It drove Mihalis mad to think of it.

He recalled that first day he had seen her, that day in the mess hall. She had left her drawings on the table, and he had sifted through them when no one was looking. They were of long-faced, limp-haired women, almost featureless—cartoony, sad caricatures of herself. And this: they were without hands, or feet, or mouths.

Mihalis saw his own wife approaching, lovely in a beige trench coat and red blouse, her hair tied back in a patterned scarf. His niece and sister followed closely behind her, the confusion of early morning still on their faces. Everyone looked so clean and Technicolored. Irini kissed his lips, and Mihalis was taken aback by the taste of her lipstick, so soapy, perfumed. Mihalis's hair had grown unruly, and when she tried to run her fingers through it, they became ensnarled.

Mihalis turned back to Vagelis, whose wife was glued to his side. He lifted his hands and shoulders slightly, a gesture of defeat he didn't want anyone else to see.

Once, back in Athens, on a warm April day three weeks after their release, Mihalis and Vagelis were walking together when they saw Nefeli leaving the police station. They had to report weekly and were headed to do just that. Nefeli stepped out the door hesitantly, blinking into the blazing noon. Vagelis hid behind a kiosk and watched her, pretending to look at newspaper headlines. Mihalis bought some tobacco, and when Nefeli was out of sight, they continued to the station. Mihalis went to mention something, but then he thought better of it. There was nothing, really, to say.

Like he did each week, Mihalis signed in first and then recorded the time. He handed Vagelis the pen, but Vagelis was too preoccupied by the sign-in book. There was Nefeli's name and the time, 12:05, signed in only ten minutes before. He took the pen, he set it down, he ran his hands through his hair. He thought he had evaded her, but here she was again. Mihalis waited patiently. Was he looking, there, for some sort of signal? Some articulation of affection in her small, neat script?

The police officer on duty, bored and disaffected, sat behind the desk, his feet propped atop it. He sighed loudly. Vagelis picked the pen back up and painstakingly wrote his name in large, uncharacteristically legible letters. He stopped before he recorded the time, looking again at her name. Mihalis looked at his friend and thought of the church and all those broken images, their emptiness pealing to no one, like the clamor of wooden bells.

Peter Cameron

# The End of My Life in New York

WHEN I COME home from Paula's dinner party, Phillip is still awake, sitting up in bed, contemplating a book. I know from experience that he is not reading.

He doesn't look at me, but furrows his brow and stares intently at the splayed pages, as if reading is very hard work. After enjoying this charade for a moment, he makes a display of turning back the corner of a page—something, of course, a real reader would never do—and closes the book. He watches me undress and says, "How was it?"

I can feel his gaze upon me, assessing my girth. I turn sideways. "Oh, fairly dismal," I say.

"Fairly dismal" is one of our descriptive catchphrases. The others are "adequate" (lifted from a time we dined with Phillip's parents, and his father, after tasting the wine, declared it "adequate") and "sick-making."

"Was Paula drunk?" he asks.

"Of course," I say. "Everyone was."

"Everyone?"

"Except for me. How was your evening?"

"Quiet," he says.

Since Phillip and I started dating—well, sleeping with—other men, many of our friends, including Paula, refuse to invite us both to their soirees. They think it's hypocritical for us to reap the social benefits of coupledom whilst covertly enjoying romance (and sex) with others. Sour monogamous grapes.

"I sat next to Ramona," I say.

"Oh, how is Ramona?"

"She's fantastic," I say. "Her word. She's just emerged, incandescently, from rehab."

"For what?"

"I'm not sure," I say. "With Ramona, it could be just about anything, and she seemed to assume I knew, so I didn't hazard a guess."

"I'd like to go to rehab," says Phillip.

"For what?"

"Oh, nothing in particular. But it changes you, doesn't it? I'd like to be changed."

I find this remark somewhat unnerving, and I am naked. "Can I turn out the light?" I ask.

Phillip looks up at the light, considering. At the present time in our relationship, any question like this, which involves a decision that affects us both, is fraught. "I suppose you might as well," he says.

I do and get in bed. The bed seems to make more noise than necessary accommodating my weight, and I feel, irrationally, that it is in some ventriloquistic way expressing Phillip's judgment. I am not fat. When the options on online profiles are *slim/swimmers/gym fit/ bodybuilder/average/some extra/fat,* I can still tick the *average* box without perjuring myself. Before my accident, my body was different: I went to the gym. I wasn't exactly *gym fit* but I was better than *average.* In some ways, it's a relief to be done with—to be banished from—all that. Phillip is still a citizen of that world. He ticks the *gym fit* box.

In bed we almost touch but don't. We move so that the sheet moves and touches us. Then I reach out and touch Phillip, his neck. His tendon is mysteriously taut.

"She told me an awful story," I say.

In an uninterested faux-sleepy fashion he asks who.

"Ramona," I say.

"Forgive me, but I don't want to hear Ramona's awful story," he says.

I smell the nape of his neck, and gently part his hair with my nose.

"There is something I should tell you," Phillip says.

I want to say, Forgive me, but I don't want to hear what you have to tell me, but I don't. I don't say anything. I just wait.

"It's about Corsica," says Phillip.

Phillip is renting a house in Corsica for the month of August, although of course he calls it a villa. I'm not going for a lot of reasons, but the official reason is that I can't bear flying that far: sitting in an airplane seat for more than an hour makes my body spasm in agony. Phillip is going with his brother and his brother's partner and his brother's partner's ex-boyfriend.

"What about Corsica?" I ask.

"I'm taking Caleb with me."

Caleb is Phillip's boyfriend.

"He's never been out of the country," Phillip adds.

"That's hardly a reason to take him to Corsica," I say. "Millions of people have never been out of the country."

"You know I would like you to be there with me. But since you can't, why shouldn't Caleb come?"

I realize that if you have to argue with your partner about him taking his boyfriend along on his vacation, it isn't really worth arguing about, so I say nothing.

"And plus," Phillip says, "this would be a good chance for you to get your life in order."

"What do you mean?" I make the mistake of asking him.

"Well," he says, "you seem at loose ends. Maybe you can try to find a job."

Phillip is a partner in the law firm where he has seamlessly worked since graduating from law school. People who have jobs don't understand how impossible it is to get one. Employability, like lovability, is a trait that must remain active; if extinguished, the pack senses your failure and turns its back on you.

"I've been looking for a job," I say. "It isn't easy, you know."

"I know," says Phillip. "But it isn't impossible, either." He guides my hand gently from his taut neck to his solar plexus and holds it there. I can feel his heart beating. He pushes himself back against me, and I think of drivers parallel parking in the street, how they gently make contact with the car behind them, and then pull forward, placed.

The next day I see Caleb at the acupuncturist. Caleb is young—he claims to be twenty-five in his profile—and rather attractive in that messy, organic way that works for certain younger people. Eventually he will look a mess, but it hasn't happened yet. He's wearing an ironic thrift-store shirt and cargo shorts and cowboy boots. He points his pointy feet outward, like a dancer, which he isn't.

We are the only ones in the waiting room. Except for the fish in the aquarium and the bird in the cage. It's that kind of acupuncturist—the waiting room cluttered with flora and fauna, in an effort, no doubt, to suggest that life here is appreciated and successfully sustained. The sign on the entrance door says:

DR. AUGUSTUS YEE, M.D., L.Ac., LMT

HOLLY AMBERGIS, N.C., C.N.C.

HEALTH RENOVATIONS

Yet the fish seem bored and the bird is sullen. The plants could use a good dusting.

"Fancy meeting you here," says Caleb.

"Didn't I tell you about Dr. Yee?" I ask.

"Yes," he says, "you did."

"Well, then, you can hardly fancy meeting me here."

"Of course I can," he says. "I can fancy anything I want." Caleb is one of those people who say everything with the same benignly pleasant intonation. He speaks as if the world is a Romper Room and he is Miss Nancy. "Did Phillip tell you about my new job?" he asks.

"No," I say. "Phillip and I don't discuss our lovers."

"Do you have a lover?" He stands up and bothers the bird, which ignores him.

I lie and say yes. I realize he'll ask Phillip and Phillip will tell him that I don't have a lover, but that will be later and this is now. Or perhaps by then I may have a lover.

Caleb turns away from the bird and gives me an I-know-you-don't-have-a-lover look. It's a look I've been getting often lately, even from strangers on the street. "I'm working at Athos Papadiamantopoulos's new bookstore," Caleb says. "Actually, I'm *managing* Athos Papadiamantopoulos's new bookstore, but that sounds like bragging."

"Who's Athos Papadiamantopoulos?" I ask.

"You don't know who Athos Papadiamantopoulos is?"

"Apparently not," I say.

"You should. He owns the Papadiamantopoulos Gallery on Twenty-fifth Street. And he's just opened this bookstore in Dumbo. It's called One Hundred Books. We only carry one hundred books at a time and only one copy of each book. For one hundred dollars."

"Are they editions of one?"

"Oh, no. I mean some of them might be scarce or rare, but not necessarily. The idea isn't about books as commodity. It's about books as artifacts. As art."

"Interesting," I say. *Sick-making,* is what I think.

"We choose a different person to curate the collection every fortnight," Caleb says.

"Fortnight?"

"Yes. Biweekly. Or is it semiweekly? Every other week. Every two weeks. You're a writer or something, aren't you? Would you be interested in curating a collection? I could suggest you to Athos if you are.

It wouldn't be for a while, though—we're pretty booked up for the next year or two."

"I'm not a writer," I say.

"Oh, I thought you were. Aren't you something with books?"

"I was an editor."

"Oh, right—of a magazine or something, right?"

"Yes," I say. "*Performance Art Today.*"

"It's a daily?"

"No," I say. "It was a quarterly."

"Then shouldn't it be called *Performance Art Quarterly?*"

"You're absolutely right, but it's a moot issue. It folded several years ago."

"What do you do now?" Caleb asks.

"What do I do?"

"Yes," says Caleb. "What do you do? Now?"

"Lots of things," I say. "I talk to you, for instance."

Caleb laughs, as if this is very clever.

"But what about you? I didn't know you were a fellow denizen of the literary world. I thought you were a skateboarder or something like that."

"Ha-ha," says Caleb. "I could actually have turned pro if I'd wanted. Or still could, for that matter. But, no—I was an English major at CCNY."

I happen to know that this is a line that Barbra Streisand sang in her Broadway debut as Miss Marmelstein in *I Can Get It for You Wholesale* but I'm not sure if Caleb is quoting it or not. Could he really have been an English major at CCNY? Does CCNY still exist? More intriguingly, could he be a musical theater queen, and if so, does Phillip, an opera snob, know?

"I heard an awful story last night," I say. I don't know why I want to tell someone Ramona's awful story, but I do. It's like a curse I feel compelled to pass along. A hot potato.

"I love awful stories," said Caleb. "I'm writing a book of awful stories. It's like an anti-Bible. Full of stories that have no redeeming value at all. Stories that corrupt and degrade. Stories about sweet little girls in pinafores who get eaten alive by rats. I once saw a headline: 'Tiny Tot Beauty Queen Attacked by Rabid Rat.'"

"That sounds very jolly," I say, "compared to my awful story."

"You're very competitive, you know," says Caleb. "You should work on that."

Dr. Yee opens the door of his consulting room and looks out at us dolefully. Freeing people from their pain does not appear to make him the least bit happy. Even though I'm fairly certain my appointment is the earlier one, he calls Caleb in first.

I make sure I'm in the bathroom when Caleb emerges from the consulting room, because I don't want to interact with him anymore. It upsets me. Dr. Yee's office is one of the few places of refuge left for me in the increasingly difficult and inhospitable city, and I don't know why I told Caleb about it. I have this awful need to endear myself to everyone, even my partner's new boyfriend. The night I met Caleb, he was complaining about chronic pain in his left shoulder, a result of a recent skateboarding accident, so I immediately told him about Dr. Yee. I practically set up an appointment for him on the spot, so I have no one to blame but myself. I realize that I have no one to blame but myself for most of my problems, but that only makes them harder to bear. Blaming others is therapeutic, although Dr. Yee would disagree with that. He believes that pain is blame and anger and depression internalized, trapped in the branches of our nervous system, and the stimulation of acupuncture shakes free these clots. Sometimes Dr. Yee doesn't even need needles. Sometimes he can do it with his bare hands.

I am trying to take responsibility for my problems. For instance, I no longer refer to the accident as *the* accident. I refer to it as *my* accident. Last fall I was driving home from New Haven after attending a symposium on Eva Le Gallienne and the Civic Repertory Theater.

Actually, I wasn't driving home after the symposium; I was driving home after the dinner that followed the symposium at which I had drunk at least a bottle of red wine. At some point between Greenwich and Danbury I realized I was driving into, not alongside, the concrete divider. The last thing I remember thinking was, Good, at least I'm not hurting anyone else. But I did. A young man named Hector Guzman Jimenez stopped his car on the shoulder and tried to cross the lanes of traffic and help me out of my burning car. He was hit and killed by a woman named Cornelia Hamelin. She broke six ribs and punctured a lung and needed major facial reconstructive surgery. I broke a lot of things, too, and was badly burned. And I have this pain.

Like many people who are deeply and mysteriously spiritual, Dr. Yee has an odd propensity toward kitsch: on the wall of his bathroom hangs a framed needlepoint sampler, on which the words THIS IS NOT THE ONLY WORLD are surrounded by flowered garlands and what appear to be windmills. Or perhaps Celtic crosses. And on top of the toilet tank, a beautiful plastic flamenco dancer conceals two extra rolls of toilet paper beneath her voluminous sateen skirt.

I can hear Caleb lurking in the waiting room, apparently waiting for me so he can say good-bye (antagonistically). But he gives up and leaves. I step out of the bathroom hesitantly, in case I am mistaken. I wouldn't put it past Caleb to fake his exit and trap me.

Dr. Yee is standing just inside his open office door. He watches my timid emergence. "You okay?" he asks.

"Yes," I say.

I follow him into his office. "I heard an awful story last night," I say.

"Please, no talking," says Dr. Yee. "Just quiet."

So I'm quiet. While he washes his hands, I undress and lie down on the table. A trace of Caleb's warmth lingers. Perhaps his smell, too. One of our rules is that neither Phillip nor I is allowed to sleep with anyone in our own apartment. We do not "host." We "travel." But like many rules, I think this one has been broken, because the warm scent of Dr. Yee's table seems familiar.

When Dr. Yee touches me, when he lightly places his warm clean hands on the center of my scarred back, I start to cry.

"The pain is bad for you?" Dr. Yee asks.

I tell him yes.

Of course I don't mention my scars in my profile. I'm talking about my physical scars, the ones from getting burned in my accident, not my emotional scars. They are pretty much assumed. But at some point before I actually meet someone, I do mention that my body is scarred. I used to say *badly* scarred until I met a man who, when he saw me naked, told me I wasn't badly scarred, just scarred. But of course he had problems of his own. All he wanted was someone to hold him while he lay on his bed, listened to *Appalachian Spring,* and wept. Another man was very nice about it all as well, and even though we did have sex—if a blow job in the foyer counts as sex—all he wanted was someone to admire his impressive collection of cold-painted Vienna Bronze reptiles. Another man longed only to be used as a footstool, and I could spend countless evenings with couples that just want someone to watch them, even if—especially if, I sadly suppose—that someone is a masturbating stranger.

Outside, as I'm walking up along the Bowery, people look odd to me. Not deformed, exactly, but certainly malformed: their heads rise out of their bodies in a weird way, their necks and jaws thrust heroically forward like figureheads on old ships. And of course, with the help of cell phones, they're all arguing with themselves. I often feel disoriented when I leave Dr. Yee's office. I don't feel pain, but things look strange. Gradually the world shifts back into its correctly familiar focus, and inexorably the pain that Dr. Yee has persuaded my body to forget, returns.

I've walked up the Bowery as far as CBGB but of course it's not

CBGB anymore. It's some men's clothing store where I can't even afford to look, the psychic cost is too debilitating. But I stand outside anyway.

I came to CBGB my first night in New York, in 1979. I remember it perfectly: a band called Donna Parker at Camp Cherrydale. I was starting an internship at the Public Theater the next morning. Joseph Papp was alive. I was illegally subletting an apartment on the ninth floor of the Westbeth overlooking the Hudson River with two friends from college. I met Paul, my first lover, that night. We went back to his apartment in the East Village and made love on his futon. Paul and I were together until he died in 1984. He was the first man I knew who died from the plague. And the youngest, too: twenty-five. RIP.

It comes to me, slowly, as I stand there on the hot sidewalk in front of what isn't CBGB anymore, that I've reached the end of my life in New York. It's come full circle, and I haven't got the strength or patience or money or a thousand other necessary things to continue.

Before I moved in with Phillip eight years ago, I had a rent-controlled apartment in Washington Heights, but I let it go. It's not that I thought we would last forever, Phillip and me, I just thought the other end would be different from this. I can't even afford to move to Brooklyn now. I'll have to move someplace far away, some-place no one really wants to live. Or no one like me. I can get a job teaching theater history. I still check the job listings: you'd be sur-prised how many Podunk community colleges have theater history programs. You'd think they'd have caught on by now as to the futility of it all, but they haven't. I've taught before and I'm quite good at it but I never got tenure on account of my drinking. I was always very open about it: I wasn't one of those professors with a bottle of scotch squirreled away in a file drawer, I had a little tea trolley bar in my office and a minifridge stocked with champagne in case there was ever anything to celebrate, which of course there always was. Or if I can't find a job teaching I can always be one of those middle-aged men working in Starbucks or Kinko's in Wichita or Eau Claire. They have well-trimmed beards and reading glasses on a lanyard around their thick necks and wear sweater vests and crepe-soled shoes. They're usually the manager and are very proud of how clean and orderly their shop is; they're not afraid to pitch in and wipe down tables or fill the creamers or change the toner or unjam jams and they think of themselves as mentors to a staff of tattooed slackers who despise them. I can be that.

Maybe it isn't a curse, Ramona's story. Maybe it's simply a warning. Not a hot potato but an amulet.

There was this insufferably lovely couple living on my floor, in the back apartment, facing the garden, Ramona said. He was an architect or something and looked British even though he wasn't and had that wonderful premature gray hair and shoes, not premature gray shoes, just wonderful shoes, usually suede and the color of ginger or lichen and she was lovely too, her name was Marie—his was Simon. She was a textile designer or a haberdasher or something creative and gentle like that and they were always pleasant and quiet and listening to classical music and they had a tortoise about as big as a dinner plate named Consuelo and whenever I saw them, which was almost every day, at least one of them, they would be perfectly charming in a reserved, nonintrusive way, as if they knew we lived too close to one another to actually be friendly. It's the top floor, you know, a walk-up, just the hallway and the two doors, 5F which is me and 5R which is them. Was them. Now it's some prissy adolescent hedge-fund manager who asked me not to park my bike in the hallway. Anyway, one day I see her, Marie, and she looks terrible. It's her hair I notice: she has this wonderful hair, very curly and hennaed and always a bit of a mess, you know, some pinned up and most falling down, but an exquisite mess, an artful mess, but this day when I see her it's just a mess, there's nothing artful or exquisite about it, in fact it's dirty and there might even be some food or something in it and she's pale and gaunt and is wearing sweatpants and before I can stop myself I ask her if she's okay, or what's wrong, or something like that and she looked at me sort of vaguely, but tragically vaguely, if you know what I mean, lost, lost, and said, Oh, you know, sometimes it's all too much, and I said, I know, I know, but are you okay, and she said, I'm fine, thanks, I've just got this pain. And I said, Pain? What pain? And she said, It's nothing really, just pain, it comes and goes or something like that. And then I don't see her again. I saw her looking awful taking her garbage down to the street in pain and I never saw her again. And then about a week later I come in and Simon's at the mailbox sort of tugging his mail out from it in an uncharacteristically hostile way and he just nods at me, he doesn't say hello or something charming, he just nods, and I look down and see that he's wearing those hideous plastic shoes that look like jellies on steroids, what are they called?

Crocs, somebody said.

Oh my God, yes: Crocs. He's wearing Crocs. Orange Crocs. They might even be fake Crocs. Bargain Crocs. So he yanks all his mail out of the box and starts upstairs, and I wait a minute before I follow him, because he obviously isn't in the mood for company, even polite, distanced company, so I wait and then I follow him and when I get up to the fifth floor he's standing in front of his door, very close to it, almost leaning his forehead against it but not quite, and the mail has dropped at his feet and I think he might be crying. Crying! I don't know what to do. I mean, what would you do? Simon, beautiful, elegant Simon, in orange mock-Crocs, crying. I pass by him and gently unlock my door and push it open but I can't go in and leave him there, I know that, I know that in some way he must want me, or need me, or he wouldn't be standing there outside the door, he'd be standing inside the door, right? So I say, Are you okay? And of course I remember saying the same thing, or something like it, to Marie just a few days before in the same spot, her coming out of the apartment with the garbage and with food in her hair. And pain. He doesn't say anything for a moment but I know he heard me, I know he knows I'm there, so I just wait. I close my door and we stand there, him in front of his door and me in front of mine. And then he turns away from his door and I see that he was crying and he says in an odd, adversarial way, You don't know? And I say, No, know what? and he says, Marie is dead. She killed herself last week. I don't say anything. I mean, what can you say? I'm shocked. Stunned. I say, Oh my God, I'm so sorry, or something lame like that, and then I unlock my door again and push it open and say, Would you like to come in? Would you like a drink or something? And I hold the door wide open, wide wide open, as if the opener it is the better, and he sets his briefcase down against his door very tenderly as if it's a pet and walks past me into my apartment and I follow him and turn on the lights and point to the couch as if it's not obvious and tell him to sit down and go into the kitchen and pour two vodkas and bring them back to the living room and I see that he's kind of looking around the room, at the books and the paintings and I think, Oh good, he hasn't lost his other-people's-apartments curiosity, and I give him one vodka and sit down next to him with the other. I don't say anything. I sip my vodka and he sips his and continues to look around and then after a moment he looks at me and says, Did she ever talk to you about the bag? The bag? I say. No. What bag? The Gristedes bag, he says. A yellow Gristedes bag. You know those bags? Of course, I say. Well, he says, last fall when the leaves fell off the tree outside our bedroom window, I think it's an ailanthus tree, one of those weed trees, you know. A Tree of Heaven, I say and I only knew that because of Jeff, do you remember Jeff, he was that guy I dated who always needed to know more about anything than you did? And Simon looks at me blankly and I say, I think they're called Trees of Heaven, and he says, Oh, well, there's one outside our bedroom window and when the leaves came off it last fall Marie saw this Gristedes bag caught in its branches, and for some reason it bothered her, she loved the view out the window, at the treetop in the summer with the green leaves, shaking, and in the winter with the bare branches, it grew up as tall as our window and there it was and she loved it, but she hated this bag. It drove her crazy. It was like a tangle or something in a knot she couldn't untangle. She had me go around the block to the people on Charles whose backyard the tree was in and ask them if they could get rid of the bag but of course they thought I was crazy, I mean it was crazy, but Marie didn't understand. She called 311, you know the city hotline or whatever, to report a bag in a tree and insisted they come remove it. She called the fire department. It was like something personal, something horrible that was ruining her life. This fucking bag in a tree. She got so she didn't want to sleep in the bedroom because she didn't want to see the bag in the tree. Even with the curtains closed it bothered her, just knowing it was there. During the winter it got less yellow and shredded a little but it hung on, nothing, not wind or rain or snow, nothing freed it, not sleet nor the darkness of night. He finished his vodka and I went into the kitchen and got the bottle and came back and poured us both a little more. After a moment he said, I know it was not just that but that's how it seemed, it seemed to be all about the bag. I know there were other things and the bag was just a symbol, something she could focus on, obsess on. I brought a bunch of rocks back from the beach and tried to toss them out the window into the bag, I thought I might be able to fill it with rocks so it would come loose, fall, but I couldn't get the rocks to land in the bag. It hung upside down. He stopped talking and cried a little, wet and choking, like men cry. But he seemed like a boy then, when he cried. Like a little boy.

Ramona said, Simon didn't tell me the rest of the story but the next day the woman in 3R did. It had happened a few days ago, early in the afternoon, when everyone was at work, she said. Marie unscrewed a broom pole from a broom and attached an opened wire hanger to the end of it and leaned out the window and tried to hook the bag, and then she must have apparently sat on the windowsill to lean farther out and fallen and no one found her until Simon came home and saw the open window and looked down into the courtyard, and the bag was gone, she had reached out far enough to free it.

A young man emerges from the air-conditioned gloom of the store that isn't CBGB anymore. He's carrying two shopping bags, one in each hand. He has that air about him that shopping is important, hard work. A rep tie is threaded through the loops of his tight white jeans. Don't tell me ties are belts once again.

He stands there for a moment. I think he must be looking for a taxi, but then I recognize the strange face reflected in his mirrored sunglasses. He is looking at me.

"Are you okay?" he asks.

"What?" I say.

"You don't look too good," he says. "You shouldn't be standing in the sun. Here." He puts down his shopping bags and maneuvers me over into the shade beside the store. "I think you're dehydrated. You need something to drink. Stay here."

He walks to the corner and buys a bottle of water from a pretzel-and-hot-dog cart. I look down into his shopping bags. Clothes swaddled in tissue paper. Luxurious cotton shirts with their arms folded and pinned behind their backs.

He returns and hands me the bottle of water. "Drink this," he says. "And stay out of the sun for a while."

"Thanks," I say.

"Take care," he says. He picks up his bags and disappears around the corner.

The bottle of water feels very cold and beautiful in my hand. I hold it up to my forehead, my cheeks. I unscrew the cap and drink the water.

I wish he had not been kind. It makes it harder to leave New York, kindness like that. And it is hard enough already. Or maybe it will be easy, a huge relief, like quitting the gym.

Ted Sanders

*Obit*

THE BOY WHO falls asleep to
the story of the bear will
grow old and wordlessly die. In
the end, he will die across his
pancakes, coughing up blood
in a restaurant in a distant
town, blood freckling the arms
and throat of his latest wife, the
table, the dark stone floor
where bright ice and dark water
from his spilled glass will also
fall. All of these events will
occur, and more. But the boy
who will become this man is
still young. He still lives in the
yellow house where he was
conceived. He was conceived as
the sun shone over spruce trees
into the front bedroom, onto

the face that would become his mother's, not far from the hall where the dog slept then, dreaming beneath the soft sounds falling through the open darkwood door.

The woman who lay in the buttress of sun slanted against the front window of the yellow house will explicitly recall her memories of that experience, of that day. She will continue to believe in these recollections steadfastly, long after the man that lay with her then has died. She will continue to believe in them even though, as she knows, there were a number of instances in the yellow house over the surrounding days which could, practically speaking, have been the act which led to conception.

The step that will never be fixed—the middle step on the short stairs of the front porch—will upend beneath the foot of the man as he comes to the yellow house on another sunny day, not so far off. He will, by then, have nearly for-

gotten what it is like to consider this house his own. The
boy—who from his bedroom
window at the front of the
house will have watched his
father come up the walk,
through the shadow of the
spruce tree—will hear the snap
of bone. Neither man will ever
forget this sound.

The dog that will die unseen in
the winter—far from home,
where the gate will have blown
open in the snow—will be
named after the dog that slept
in the hall in the yellow house.
The boy, grown into a man,
will have named this new dog.
He will remember the old dog,
the one who lay in the hall and
dreamt of berries and beasts,
the sound of his owner's voice.
This dog, the first, dies beneath
the kitchen table, his feet stirring, as the bear's story is being
told.

The woman who will die in a
hospital bed late into the
night—senseless and mute on
morphine, breathing slow and
shallow while her family,

The man who will wake in the
night to the implausible pain of
his own stopped heart will
remember—as he is fold-
ing to his knees in the dark—

around her and in and out of the room, waits for her to die—once lay in another bed wishboned around the man, watching a basket-colored sun make its urchin shapes through the spruce tree in the front yard. The man, moving above her, over her—with rigid arms and fisted shoulders, feeling the cool intermittent press of her breasts against his ribs—looked into the mottled sheet of sun that lay across the woman's face and the rumpled head of the bed. He considered, then, the wide hazel irises of the woman's eyes, eyes drawn to the window, out into the sky over the front yard. The man believed at that moment that he would remember this sight of her: the sun across her skin, falling between her just-open lips where a fine mindless shape was curling, her skin lit and blooming, her carved arms raised around her head like a harp's arms, as if the delicate gesture unfolding through them were being sung wordlessly into sight in her face. The woman will survive this understanding.

. . .

standing outside the room of the boy, listening to the still-young woman he once married sing to the boy a song a bear might sing. In the shadowed hall, he imagines the glint of peppermint. And the woman—the woman who will die in a dim hospital room, the mother of the boy who will die in a restaurant, the wife of this man who will die beside a bed in which a different woman will lie—this woman sings the bear's song to the boy, to the visiting man in the dark hall, to herself.

This man, who will later break his leg on the front step, will eventually marry a childless woman who is unable to conceive. To the boy, the new woman smells like the earth around trees, or honey and medicine, or wellwater. She will come to love the boy, will love the man he will become, will love the boy's child in turn. Years later, after the death of the father, this new woman will listen as the boy's mother recounts the moment the boy was conceived. The woman

The bear who lives in the woods licks peppermints from the palm of the old woman. From the steps of her porch each morning, the old woman feeds the peppermints to the bear—one after another after another—in order to keep him tame. The bear has no home that the old woman knows of. When the old woman walks to the white stream above the lake, the bear walks with her, and there as the old woman sits and watches, the bear slaps fish onto the bank. The bear eats his fill, and the old woman returns home, taking one fish or two with her, bent like silver moons inside her basket—all she can carry. She cooks the fish over a fire, gives silent thanks to the bear. Late each night, at bedtime, the bear returns. He sits at the bottom of the porch steps and sings to the old woman as she falls asleep. The bear sings deep and strong, a song of thankfulness and want. This is how the story ends.

The boy who will retell the story of the bear learns it from his mother. She tells him the who smells like wellwater will hear the sight of the sun's spread across dusty glass, the spread of warmth up the insides of raised arms, the rumble of low sounds made by the husband, the sight of the sun itself—and she will know from her own memory the tree through which the sun shone, the window through which the sun must have fallen, though in her mind the room has always belonged to the boy. She will imagine, correctly or incorrectly, the sounds made by the man on that day.

The treehouse that will never be built will be described many times. A hackberry tree stands in the yard where the man lives alone, where he will later pretend to introduce his son to the woman who smells like wellwater, though in fact they have already met. The leaves of the hackberry tree are perennially pocked with galls, and just over the man's head, high above the boy's, the tree's fingers open into a gesture of grasping, and the man imagines out loud to the boy the treehouse he

story at night in his bed beside the window, and she describes the whiteness of the peppermints given by the old woman, the gleam of the fish taken from the stream, and she sings the bear's wordless song to the boy, letting the bear's song press the boy to sleep—the boy who as a man will die in front of strangers, coughing blood onto his food. The boy dreams of the bear's song, fertile, low, and wide; he will dream of the song as a man. He will tell this story to his own child, will mistake it for remedy, will elect to fail to sing the song.

The song that will be sung instead to the boy's child is sad and sweet. The boy knows the song, likes the song, but the young woman who will sing it to his child will sing an extra verse the boy will have never before heard—not a verse so much as a small chorus, with a quicker cadence than the rest of the gentle song, a song which is not a lullaby, nor even the bear's song, but which has a lullaby's earnest swoon, and the extra verse sung by the woman will feel to the boy, for years, like

believes he could build for them there. The boy tells his mother. The man mentions it to his new wife. The man and the boy discuss the treehouse occasionally at bedtime, with ambitious talk of trapdoors, rope ladders, spyholes. The man, eventually, will be survived by the possibilities of the treehouse; the boy will describe it, much later, to the young woman he believes he does not love.

The young woman who will sing to the boy's child will never know that the boy himself dislikes the extra verse. It is a verse he would never have otherwise heard. But the woman will sing just as she is sung to. Her grandfather sings her this song, and she will sing it to the boy and his child in the car, on the way to the hospital, the day before the boy's mother will die. She will sing it to the mother herself, deep in the last full night. Long after, elsewhere, this woman will die in a different car, will be survived by a dif-

being startled from half sleep. The boy will come to believe that he does not love the woman who sings this song.

Hesitantly, suspiciously, the man who fathered the boy will ask the woman he once married about the circumstances surrounding the conception of their son. He will, by then, have forgotten things the woman will continue to remember.

ferent man to whom she will also have sung this song.

The tree under which a stranger's daughter will later play—kneeling into the bed of brown needles, pressing a hashwork of white and red grooves into her skin, peeling malleable bulbs of sap from the bark and murmuring to herself—is the same tree that stands aside the front walk, limbs nodded deep over the half-wanted patio furniture tilting loose-legged and flaking in the shade. It is the same tree through which the sun for years has fallen, making its way to the window of the front bedroom of the yellow house, the house the man has already left behind.

The bear in the story told to the boy does not enjoy the taste of peppermint. He licks the old woman's palms, slaps fish to the shore for her, but while he is drawn to the whiteness of the peppermints, he imagines himself wounded by their bite. This truth reveals itself near the story's end, but the mother will never reveal it to her son, his father, the dog in the hall. She will have no cause to reveal it because the story,

The boy's child will never know the yellow house. He will never firmly believe in his memories of the woman who once sang there. He will know different houses, different songs. He will know different mothers. He will know the bear's story, but not his song. Nonetheless he will die in sadness, far from the girl he will never learn not to love.

in the mother's telling, fails to end. Instead, it is survived by this tune, by the sad braided rumble of the bear's voice.

· · ·

Neither the man nor the boy nor any of the women loved by them each will ever notice that the bear's story, as told by the boy's mother, does not return from song. They will fail to suspect the things that will befall the bear, the old woman. Nonetheless they, and others they love in turn, will sing songs to themselves which resemble the bear's song. They, and others, will encounter and remember days full of voice. They will weep, celebrants and mourners; they will share breath with lovers, possessed by moments of unassailable faith; children will croon inaudibly over busy new hands; dogs will dream and mutter, safe in warm houses, paws trembling; bones will mend; trees will seek sun. These things will grow and turn bare. And after all there will be survivors.

Damon Galgut

*The Lover*

N O PARTICULAR INTENTION brings him to Zimbabwe, all those years ago. He simply decides one morning to leave and gets on a bus that same night. He has it in mind to travel around for two weeks and then go back.

What is he looking for. He himself doesn't know. Looking back at him through time, he has become partly a stranger, feeling things utterly lost to me now. And yet I can explain him better than my present self, he is buried under my skin. His life is unfocused and directionless, he has not made a home for himself. All his few belongings are in storage and he has spent months wandering around from one spare room to another. It has begun to feel as if he's never lived in any other way, nor will he ever settle down. He can't seem to connect properly with the world. He feels this not as a failure of the world but as a massive failing in himself, he would like to change it but doesn't know how. In his clearest moments he thinks that he has lost the ability to love, people or places or things, most of all the person and place and thing that he is. Without love nothing has value, nothing can be made to matter very much.

In this state travel isn't celebration but a kind of mourning, a way of dissipating yourself. So I move around from one place to another, not driven by curiosity but by the bored anguish of staying still. He spends a few days in Harare, then goes down to Bulawayo. He does the obligatory things required of visitors, he goes to the Matopos and sees the grave of Cecil John Rhodes, but he can't produce the necessary awe or ideological disdain, he would rather be somewhere else. If I was with somebody, he thinks, with somebody I loved, then I could love the place and even the grave too, I would be happy to be here.

He takes the overnight train to Victoria Falls. He lies in his bunk, hearing the breathing of strangers stacked above and below him, and through the window sees villages and sidings flow in out of the dark, the outlines of people and cattle and leaves stamped out in silhouette against the lonely light, then flowing backward again, out of sight into the past. Why is he happiest in moments like these, the watcher hiding in the dark. He doesn't want the sun to rise or this particular journey to end.

In the morning they come to the end of the line. He gets out with his single bag and walks to the campsite. Even early in the day the air is heavy and humid, green leaves burn with a brilliant glow. There are other travelers all around, most are younger than himself. He pitches his tent in the middle of the camp and goes down to look at the falls.

It is incredible to see the volume and power of so much water endlessly dropping into the abyss, but part of him is elsewhere, somewhere higher up and to the right, looking down at an angle not only on the falls but on himself there, among the crowds. This part of him, the part that watches, has been here for a while now, and it never quite goes away, over the next few days it looks at him keeping busy, strolling through the streets from one curio shop to another, going for long walks in the surrounding bush, it observes with amazement when he goes white-water rafting on the river, it sees him lying in the open next to his tent to keep cool at night, staring up into the shattered windscreen of the sky. And though he seems content, though he talks to people and smiles, the part that watches isn't fooled, it knows he wants to move on.

On the third or fourth day he goes for a swim at one of the hotel pools. Afterwards he sits near the bar to have a drink and his attention is slowly drawn to a group of young people nearby. They have their backpacks with them, they are about to depart. They're a strange mixture, a bit uneasy with each other, a plump Englishman with his girlfriend, a blond Danish man, two younger dark girls who sit close together, not speaking. He recognizes a burly Irishwoman who went rafting with him two days ago, and goes over to speak to her. Where are you off to.

Malawi. We're going through Zambia. Maybe she sees something in my face, because after a moment she adds, do you want to come along.

I sit thinking for a few moments, then say, I'll be right back.

He runs madly from the hotel to the campsite and takes down his tent. When he gets back he sits among his new companions, panting, feeling edgy with doubt. Why is he doing this. He has always been impulsive, the more irrational the urge the more compelling it is. An impulse has brought him to Zimbabwe in the first place, now a second impulse will take him farther.

Soon afterward the man they're waiting for, an Australian called Richard, arrives, and they stir themselves to leave. With the others he loads his bag onto the back of an open van and climbs up. They have paid somebody to drive them to the other side of the border, to the station. It's getting dark when they arrive. They are late and the queue for tickets is long, they can only get third-class seats, sitting amongst a crowd in an open carriage in which all the lights are broken. Almost before they can find a place the train lurches and starts to move.

There is a moment when any real journey begins. Sometimes it happens as you leave your house, sometimes it's a long way from home.

In the dark there is the sound of breaking glass and somebody cries out. They have been traveling for perhaps an hour, the darkness in

the carriage is total, but now somebody lights a match. In the gutter-
ing glow he sees a hellish scene, on one of the seats farther down a
man clutches his bloodied face, a pool of blood on the floor around
him, rocking from side to side with the violent motion of the train.
Everybody shrinks away, the light goes out. What's happening, the
Irish girl says.

What's happening is that somebody has thrown a rock through
the window. Almost immediately it comes again, the smashing glass,
the cry, but this time nobody is hurt, the cry is one of fear. They are
all afraid, and with good reason, because every time the train passes
some town or settlement there is the noise, the cry, or the deep thud-
ding sound of the rock hitting the outside of the train. Everybody sits
with their heads down and their arms over their heads.

Late in the night the ordeal winds down. Inside the train the
mood becomes lighter, people who would otherwise never have spoken strike up conversations. Somebody takes out bandages for those
who've been hurt. At the far end of the carriage are three women traveling with little babies, their window has been broken and the wind is
howling through, do you mind, they ask, if we come and sit with
you. Not at all. He is with the Irishwoman on a seat, the rest of their
group is elsewhere, they move up to make space. Now the dark smells
warm and yeasty, there is a sucking and gurgling all around. The
women are traveling to Lusaka for a church conference on female
emancipation, they have left their husbands behind, but a couple of
them are holding a child and the other woman has triplets. She is sitting opposite me, I can see her in the passing lights from outside.
Now a weird scenario begins. The triplets are all identically dressed in
white bunny suits, she starts to breast-feed them two at a time. The
third one she hands to me, would you mind, no not at all, he holds
the murmuring weight in his hands. Occasionally she changes them
over, he hands on a little bunny-suited baby and receives an exact
copy in exchange, this seems to go on for hours. Sometimes one of
her nipples comes free, a baby cries, then she says, please could you,
the Irishwoman leans over to rearrange her breast, sucking starts

again. The women talk softly to the white travelers and among themselves, and sometimes they sing hymns.

By the next morning his head is fractured with fatigue and swirling with bizarre images. Under the cold red sky of dawn Lusaka is another surreal sight, shantytowns sprouting between the buildings, tin and plastic and cardboard hemmed in by brick and glass. They climb out among crowds onto the platform. The three women say good-bye and go off with their freight of babies to discuss their liberation. While he waits for the group to gather he looks off to one side and sees, farther down the train, at the second-class compartments, another little group of white travelers disembarking. Three of them, a woman and two men. He watches, but the crowds block them off.

They walk to the bus station through streets filled with early light and litter blowing aimlessly. Somebody has a map and knows which way to go. Even at this hour, five or six in the morning, the place is full of people, standing idly and staring. They are the focus of much ribald curiosity, he's glad he's not alone. On one corner an enormous bearded man steps forward and, with the perfunctory disinterest with which one might weigh fruit, squeezes the Irishwoman's left breast in his hand. She hits his fingers away. You not in America now, the man shouts after them, I fuck you all up.

The bus station is a mad chaos of engines and people under a metal roof, but they eventually find their bus. When they get on, the first people he sees are the three white travelers from the train, sitting in a row, very quietly looking ahead of them, and as he passes they don't look up. The woman and the one man are young, in their early twenties, and the other man is older, perhaps his own age.

He takes a seat at the very back of the bus, at the window. The rest of his group is scattered around. He hasn't interacted or spoken with them much, and at the moment he's more interested in the other three travelers a few rows ahead, he can see the backs of their heads. Who are they, how do they fit together.

It takes eight hours to reach the border. They disembark into the main square of a little town, where taxi drivers clamor to take them to the actual border post. While they're negotiating a price he sees from the corner of his eye the three travelers get into a separate car and leave. They're not at the border post when he gets there, they must have gone through. There is a press of people, a long wait, by the time their passports have been stamped and the taxi has driven them on through the ten kilometers or so of no-man's-land it is getting dark.

The Malawian border post is a white building under trees. When he goes in some kind of dispute is in progress. An official in a white uniform is shouting at the three travelers, who look confused, you must have a visa. The older man, the one his own age, is trying to explain. His English is good, but hesitant and heavily accented. The embassy told us, he says. The embassy told you the wrong thing, the uniformed official shouts, you must have a visa. What must we do. Go back to Lusaka. They look at him and then confer among themselves. The official has lost interest, he turns to the new arrivals, give me your passports. South Africans don't need visas, he is stamped through. I pause for a second, then go up to the three. Where are you from.

I am French. It's the older man speaking. They are from Switzerland. He points to the other two, whose faces are now as neutral as masks, not understanding or not wanting to talk.

Do you want me to speak to him for you.

No. It's okay. Thank you. He has thick curly hair and round glasses and a serious expression which is impassive, or perhaps merely resigned. The younger man has from up close a beauty that is almost shocking, red lips and high cheekbones and a long fringe of hair. His brown eyes won't meet my gaze.

What will you do now.

I don't know. He shrugs.

They languish for a few days in Lilongwe, a featureless town full of white expatriates and jacaranda trees, killing time while somebody in their party tries to organize a visa to go somewhere. He is bored and frustrated, and by now he is irritated with the other travelers in the group. They are completely content to sit around drinking beer for hours, they go out in search of loud music at night, and some of them show an unpleasant disdain for the poverty they encounter. The two young women in particular, who turn out to be Swedish, have stopped being silent and go on in loud voices about their terrible trip through Zambia. The rocks, oh, it was just horrible, and the bus station, oh, it was so dirty, it smelled, oh, disgusting. The shortcomings and squalor of the continent have let them down personally, it never seems to occur to them that the conditions they find horrible and disgusting are not part of a set that will be struck when they have gone offstage.

But things improve a little when they get to the lake. It's the destination he's had in mind since leaving Zimbabwe, everything he's ever heard about Malawi has been centered on that body of water running up half the length of the country. Take a look at him there a few days later, standing on the beach at Cape Maclear. He is staring at the water with an amazed expression, as if he can't believe how beautiful it is. Light glitters on the tilting surface, the blond mountains seem almost colorless next to the intense blue, a cluster of islands rises up a kilometer from the shore. A wooden canoe passes slowly in perfect profile, like a hieroglyph.

As the day goes on his wonder only grows, the water is smooth and warm to swim in, under the surface are schools of brightly colored tropical fish, there is nothing to do except lie on the sand in the sun and watch fishermen repairing their nets. The pace of everything here is slow and unhurried, the only sound of an engine is from the occasional car on the dirt road high up.

Even the local people take up their appointed place in this version of paradise, they are happy to drop everything when called and go out fishing for these foreign visitors, or prepare a meal on the beach for them in the evening and clean up when they're gone. They will row you out to the islands for the price of a cool drink, or go running for miles over the hot sand to fetch some of the famous Malawi cob, even carving you a wooden pipe to smoke it in. When they're not needed they simply fade into the background, going back to their natural tasks, supplying peaceful lines of smoke from the picturesque huts they live in, or heading across your line of vision at an appropriate moment in the distance.

Only someone cold and hard of heart could fail to succumb to these temptations, the idea of traveling, of going away, is an attempt to escape time, mostly the attempt is futile, but not here, the little waves lap at the shores just as they always have done, the rhythms of daily life are dictated by the larger ones of nature, the sun or moon for example, something has lasted here from the mythical place before history set itself in motion, ticking like a bomb. It would be easy to just stop and not start again, and indeed a lot of people have done that, you can see them if you take a little walk, here and there at various points on the beach are gatherings that haven't moved in months. Talk to them and they'll tell you about themselves, Stan from Bristol, Jürgen from Stuttgart, Shlomo from Tel Aviv, they've been here half a year, a year, two years, they all have the glazed half-shaven look of lethargy, or is it dope. This is the best place in the world, they say, stick around you'll see, you can survive on next to nothing, a bit of money sent from home once in a while, we'll go back again one day of course but not just yet.

And already after a day, two days, three, the massive gravity of inertia sets in, the effort of walking from your room to the water is already more than it seems necessary to expend. Swim, sleep, smoke. The people he came here with can't believe their luck. This is the real Africa to them, the one they came from Europe to find, not the fake expensive one dished up to them at Victoria Falls, or the dangerous frightening one that tried to hurt them on the train. In this place each of them is at the center of the universe, and at the same time is nowhere, surely this is what it means to be spiritually fulfilled, they are having a religious experience.

And at first he himself partakes of it, look at him now, lying on the beach and then getting up and stumbling to the water for a swim. Later when he's too hot he goes back to his room to sleep, or retreats to the bar for a drink. When a joint is passed around he puffs along with everybody else, his face relaxes into the same befuddled grin that makes everyone around him look stupid. He's as hedonistic as the rest of them. Towards evening he wanders with some of the others in the group, they are all talking and laughing like old friends, to a clearing behind the village where some bearded itinerant hippie is offering sunset flights in an ultralight. Although he won't go up he watches Richard ascend for a long looping meandering cruise above the lake, and the gentle suspension of the little machine in the last light contains something of the unreal weightlessness of being here.

But the truth is that even in the first sybaritic day or two there is that same blue thread of uneasiness in him, no amount of heat or marijuana will quite sedate the restlessness. He is outside the group, observing. They have been around each other now for long enough for connections and tensions to develop, they all carry on like old companions. Everybody is called by nicknames, there is a lot of laughter and joking. But he's the odd one out here, he keeps a distance between himself and them, no matter how friendly they are. Once when all of them are walking on the beach he listens to a conversation behind him, one of the Swedish girls is talking to the Danish man, how did you like South Africa when you were there, oh, he says in reply, the country was beautiful, if only all the South Africans weren't so fucked-up. Then everyone becomes aware of him at once and silence falls, of all of them he is the only one smiling, but inwardly.

Then one day someone in their party has this wonderful idea, let's hire a boat and go out to that island for the day. One of the local men is conscripted to row them there for a small fee, over which the plump Englishman haggles, he will let them use his goggles and flippers to go snorkeling. These are among the few things he owns, the boat and oars, the mask and flippers, but while he rows he talks earnestly about how he is saving to go to medical school in South Africa, he would like to be a doctor. He's a young man of twenty-three with a wide gentle face and a body toned and hardened by fishing for a living. Nobody else in the party is interested in speaking to him, but he tells me later, on the island, about how they go night fishing, rowing for miles and miles into the far deep center of the lake, each boat with a torch burning in the prow, and how they row back at dawn weighed down by a pyramid of fish. Would you take me with you one night, I would like to see that. Yes I will take you.

Through glass the bottom of the lake is the surface of an alien planet, huge boulders are piled on each other in the sunlit depths, glowing fish float and dart like birds. The day is long and languid and everybody is happy when at last they climb into the boat to be rowed back again. But their oarsman is looking around, worried. What's the matter. One of the flippers has gone. The visitors sigh and chatter in the boat, while I get out to help him look. The price of the flipper is worth maybe a week or two of fishing to this man. They search in the shallow water, between the crevices in the rocks. Hurry up, one of the Swedish girls calls crossly, we're waiting for you. But now the anger finally touches the surface of his tongue, you get out of there, he cries, his voice rising, get out of there and help us look. One of you has lost the flipper, we're not going back till you find it again. There is muttering and resentment, let him buy a new one, but they all troop out onto the shore and pretend to cast around. In the end the flipper is found and everybody gets back into the boat and in a little while the frivolous conversation resumes, but he knows that his outburst has confirmed what they suspect, he is not the same as them, he is a fucked-up South African.

Something has changed for him now, he finds it difficult to make innocent conversation with these people. The next day he goes off alone on a long walk down the beach. At the far end, where the local village is, where the tourists never go, is a rocky headland, he thinks he would like to climb round it. But when he gets there he discovers that people have shat among the rocks, everywhere he tries to climb he finds old smelly turds and wreaths of paper. He can imagine the shrill voices of the Swedish girls, oh how disgusting, and it is, but now another notion comes to him, that if people are using these rocks for a toilet it's because they don't have an alternative. He climbs back down, his head hurting, his feet in pain on the hot sand. Nearby there is some kind of marina for wealthy expatriates, expensive yachts lift their silken sails like standards, but he passes it by and goes into the village. He tells himself he's doing it for the cool of the shade between the huts, but really a curiosity drives him. On the long hot walk back to his room he sees properly for the first time the ragged clothes on the smiling children, the bare interiors of the smoky huts with their two or three pieces of broken furniture, the skeletal dogs slinking away at his approach, and for the first time he chooses to understand why people who live here, whose country this is, might want to run errands for these foreign visitors passing through, and catch fish and cook for them, and clean up after them. It may only be the heat but his headache is very bad, and through the haze of pain the beautiful landscape has receded and broken into disparate elements, the water here, the mountain there, the horizon in another place again, and all of these into their constituent parts too, a series of shapes and textures and lines that have nothing to do with him.

When he gets back the Irish girl is sitting outside her room in the courtyard, smoking a cigarette. I'm feeling upset, she tells him, I just lost my temper with somebody, I think I was a bit extreme. The person she lost her temper with is an old man who works at the guesthouse, she paid him, she says, to do her washing for her, but when he'd finished he hung it up on the line and neglected to take it down and fold it. Is it too much to expect, she wonders aloud, when you pay somebody to do your washing that they should fold it when it's dry. She smiles and asks, Did I go too far.

He can't contain it anymore, the anger that fueled his little outburst yesterday is now a rage. Yes, he tells her, you went too far. She looks startled and confused. But why. Because he's an old man maybe three times your age. Because he lives here, this is his home, and you're a visitor. Because you're lucky enough to have the money to pay this old man to wash your clothes, your dirty underwear, while you lie around on the beach, you ought to feel ashamed of yourself instead of being so certain that you're right.

He says all of this without raising his voice but he sounds choked and vehement, he himself is startled at how furious he is. She blinks and seems about to cry, such anger for such a little thing, but his anger is not just at her or even at the others in their party, the hottest part of it is for himself. I am as guilty as any of them, I too am passing through, I too have luck and money, all my self-righteousness will not absolve me. After she has gone scurrying off he sits in the twilight outside his room, while his anger cools into misery. Even before she comes back to tell him that she went to the old man and apologized, so everything is all right now, he knows that the spell is broken and he can't be one of the lotus-eaters anymore, he has to move on, move on.

He leaves the next morning early, as the sun is coming up. Everything is fixed and still in the glassy air, the mountains of Mozambique are visible across the turquoise water of the lake. Talking to the man at the front desk of the guesthouse last night, he learned that a ferry will be leaving from Monkey Bay this morning, going up the whole length of the lake. This sounds good to him, he'll travel north to some other town where nobody knows him. He waits up on the dirt road for the bus.

When he gets to Monkey Bay the ferry is already at the dock, a rusting agglomeration of metal listing badly to one side. He buys a ticket to Nkhata Bay, halfway up the lake. There is a small crowd of passengers, mostly local people with crates and boxes. When the boat starts to move he goes and stands at the rail to watch the shore sliding past, feeling good in the cool early morning on the water. After an hour or so the ferry moves in toward the shore again and docks at Salima, where passengers get off and on. He waits till they move out into the middle of the lake again before he starts to wander around. The boat is a whole little world on its own, with passages and stairs and limits and rules, and a slowly increasing population. He stops to watch a crowd pressing in on the hatch where food is served. There are limbs and feet and faces moving, all anonymous and tangled, but when he glances to one side they are standing there in front of him. The three travelers from the bus. Where have you been.

They have been back to Lusaka to get their visas. They have had a terrible time. They managed to get a lift with a local man, who was very keen to take them in his car. It turned out that somebody had been using this car to sleep in the bush and had been murdered in it two nights before, so that the backseat was covered in dried blood on which two of them had to perch for the whole long drive. They got to Lusaka on Friday afternoon to discover that the Malawian embassy was closed till Monday, so they sat around in a hotel room to wait. Now they have their visas and are not stopping to linger, they are trying to get up to Tanzania as soon as they can, from where they are hoping to find a boat that will take them back to Europe. Two of them, the two men, have been traveling in Africa for a long time, nine months or more, and they are keen to get home.

All this he finds out in little bits and pieces through the day. Soon after he meets up with them, they come out to join him on the front deck. The boat is filling up at every stop and the only way to claim a place is to put your bag down somewhere. Sitting in the sun, chatting idly, he discovers that the Swiss travelers are twins. Their names are Alice and Jerome. The Frenchman, Christian, is the only one at all fluent in English, it's through him that most conversation goes. He tells me that he and Jerome met each other in Mauritania and went on from there through Senegal, Guinea, and Mali to the Ivory Coast, from where they flew to South Africa. They were there a couple of months, in which time Alice had joined them, and now they're on their way home.

Jerome listens attentively to this account, and now and then he interjects in French with a question or a comment. But when I ask him something, his face stiffens in confusion and he turns to the others for help.

He doesn't understand, Christian says. Ask me.

So the question has to be repeated to Christian, who translates it, and then translates the reply. The same happens in reverse when Jerome questions me, they look at each other, but speak to Christian. This gives the whole conversation a weird formality, through which no personal quality can break. He can never ask what he would like to, what is your relationship with Christian, what bond has kept you going all the way from West Africa. Once the most basic facts have been exchanged there seems nothing more to say.

Later in the day a wind comes up and the surface of the lake turns choppy. Then the ship starts to pitch and roll, drawing a thin line of queasiness under everything. When the sun goes down it becomes suddenly very cold. He is on the other side of the raised middle section of the deck to them, lying head-to-head with Jerome, and as he settles himself for the night he rolls his eyes up and finds Jerome in exactly the same position, looking back, and for a long arrested moment we hold each other's gaze, before we both look away and try to sleep.

In fact he doesn't sleep much, the boat is lurching and the deck is hard and uncomfortable. Dangling above them is a huge metal hook on a crane and all his latent uneasiness becomes focused on this hook, what if it comes loose, what if it falls, he keeps waking from jagged dreams to see that dark shape punched out on the sky. The night is starry and huge, despite this one concentration of dread at the very center of it, above him.

In the morning all the bodies stagger up stiffly from the deck, yawning and rubbing their necks. They dock at Nkhata Bay soon afterward. By now the heat is already building and he doesn't envy them the long voyage to the north, they will only arrive tomorrow. He says good-bye on the deck and this time he knows he won't see them again. He gets off in a dense press of bodies, the ship's horn bellows mournfully, when he's clear of the crowd he turns back to look but he can't see them.

He shoulders his pack and sets out in the hot sun, heading to a guesthouse ten kilometers out of town. The road climbs up and down among hills, the vegetation is lush and green. By the time he finds the place a few hours have gone by. The setting is lovely, a series of communal bamboo houses on stilts along the edge of the beach. He lays out his sleeping bag at one end of a row of others and changes into shorts and goes out for a swim. He leaves his towel on the beach and heads far out into the lake, the waves are strong and rough here, by the time he comes back to shore he feels replenished and renewed.

Jerome, Alice, and Christian are standing next to my towel, grinning. Hello, they say. It's us again.

They changed their minds at the last moment and decided to get off the boat. They thought they would rest here for a day or two and then continue overland. They are staying in a bungalow at the far end of the beach, half-hidden among trees.

He spends that day with them on the beach. All their towels are laid out in a row, they drift in and out of the water or sprawl in the sun. He gives himself completely to the pagan pleasures of idleness and heat, what wasn't possible for him with the other travelers down south is perfectly possible here, but underneath his tan he feels troubled. The way in which this mysterious threesome has threaded through his journey bothers him, there's almost the shape of a design to it, in which none of them has a say. This little reunion, for instance, it's purely by chance that they've also come to stay at this place, if they'd taken a room in town they would probably not have seen each other again. Or perhaps he wants to see it like this, it's only human, after all, to look for a hint of destiny where love or longing is concerned.

He is never alone with Jerome. Once or twice, when Christian has gone off to swim and Alice gets up to join him, it seems he and

Jerome will be the only ones left there on the sand. But it doesn't happen. Christian appears at the last moment, coming up dripping and panting from the lake, throwing himself down on his towel. But if he's laying claim to the younger man he doesn't show it, in fact it's Christian who suggests, sometime in that day or in the one following, that he come along with them to Tanzania. If you feel like it, why not, it will be fun. All of them seem pleased at the thought, there is no resentment or reluctance. Well, he says, I might, let me think about that.

He does have to think about it, the answer isn't simple. Apart from the complications of the situation, which will only thicken and grow, there are practical questions to be considered, he meant only to visit Zimbabwe, now he's in Malawi, does he want to go on to Tanzania. While he tries to make up his mind, he passes the days with the three of them on the lake edge. It is an idle time, the substance of it made of warmth and moving liquid and grains of sand, everything standing still and at the same time pouring and flowing. At the center of it, the only solid object, is Jerome, lying on his side, skin beaded with water, or throwing his hair back out of his eyes, or diving into the waves. He has become relaxed with me now, the questions he sometimes flings out through Christian have become more personal in nature. What do you do. Where do you live.

But even here he is outside the group, looking in. In the way the three of them talk and joke and gesture there is also the weight of a private history that will always be impervious to him. Things have happened between them that he can never be party to, so that their lives have become subtly joined. Even if he could speak French he could never close up this gap. This sets him apart, making his loneliness resound in him with a high thin note, like the lingering sound of a bell.

In the evenings they eat their meals together in the restaurant at the top of the hill, after which they say good night and go their separate ways. Then he sits alone on the top step outside the hut and watches the lights of canoes in a long row far out. Lightning flares above the lake, like the signature of God.

On the evening of the second day, or is it the third, when they say good night on the beach Christian mentions in an offhand way that they will be leaving in the morning. They are taking a bus up to Karonga in the north, and going to Tanzania the next day. Almost as an afterthought he adds, have you decided, are you interested in coming.

He finds himself taking the same tone, his voice surprising him by its flatness. Hmm, he says, yes, I think I will come with you. I'll go as far as the border and see if they'll let me in.

In the crowd waiting for the bus the next morning is another white traveler, a thin man with black hair and an unconvincing mustache, wearing jeans and a purple shirt. After a while he comes sauntering over.

Where are you going.

To Tanzania.

Ah. Me too. He smiles toothily under his mustache. Me, I am from Santiago. In Chile.

They shake hands. The newcomer's name is Roderigo, he's on his way up to Kenya. This man has the melancholy of certain travelers who want to cling, and though nobody feels especially drawn to him they allow him to drift into the group.

By the time they get to Karonga, far to the north, they are all quiet and withdrawn, the air is smoky with twilight. The bus station is at the edge of town and they have to walk in with their packs along the drab main road. They take a while to find a place to stay. Karonga is nothing like the villages down south, it's big and unappealing with that quality of border towns, of transitoriness and traffic and a slightly scuffed danger, even though the border is still sixty kilometers away. In the end they find rooms in an inn on an untarred back street, the place is made of concrete and filthy inside, the bathrooms furred over with mold. The ugliness stirs a sadness in him, which grows when he is left in one room on his own.

He has always had a dread of crossing borders, he doesn't like to leave what's known and safe for the blank space beyond, in which anything can happen. Everything at times of transition takes on a symbolic weight and power. But this too is why he travels. The world you're moving through flows into another one inside, nothing stays divided anymore, this stands for that, weather for mood, landscape for feeling, for every object there is a corresponding inner gesture, everything turns into metaphor. The border is a line on a map, but also drawn inside himself somewhere.

But in the morning everything is different, even the mud streets have a sort of rough charm. They hitch a lift to the border and go through the Malawian formalities together. Then they walk across a long bridge over a choked green riverbed to the immigration post on the other side.

It's only now that he starts to really consider what might happen. Although he said airily that he'd see if they would let him in it didn't seriously occur to him that they might not. But now, as the little cluster of sheds draws closer, with a boom across the road on the far side, a faint premonition prickles in his palms, maybe this won't turn out as he hopes. And once they have entered the first wooden shed, and all the others have been stamped through by the dapper little man behind his counter, his passport is taken from him and in the pause that follows, the sudden stillness of the hand as it reaches for the ink, he knows what's coming. Where is your visa. I didn't know I needed one. You do.

That is all. The passport is folded closed and returned to him.

What can I do.

The little man shrugs. He is neat and compact and clean, his chin impeccably shaven. Nothing you can do.

Isn't there a consulate somewhere.

Not in Malawi.

He turns away to tend to other people, people flowing in and out of the border, people who don't need visas.

The little group gathers sadly outside. Cicadas are shrieking on some impossible frequency, like a gang of mad dentists drilling in the treetops. The metal roof is humming in the heat. They feel bad on his behalf, he can see it in their faces, but he doesn't want to meet their eyes. He sits down on a step to wait while they go next door to the health office and customs. He can't quite believe this is happening. In a sudden flurry of emotion he gets up, goes back inside.

I heard of somebody who visited Tanzania, he says. A South African. He didn't need a visa.

Why this particular memory comes to me now I don't know, but the man's eyebrows go up. And what did he pay, he says, for this stamp.

He is stupefied. He doesn't know what the man paid, he doesn't know what it has to do with anything. He shakes his head.

Then I can't help you.

Again he turns away to help somebody else. I am vibrating with anguish and alarm, he waits for the little man to finish, please, he says, please.

I told you. I can't help you.

Everything that he desires in the world at this moment lies in a space beyond this obtuse and efficient public servant whom he will do anything, anything, to overthrow. What is your name, he says.

You want my name. The man shakes his head and sighs, his face has yet to yield up an expression, he pulls a black ledger across the counter toward him and opens it. Your passport, please.

Now hope flickers briefly, he saw the names of the others inscribed in a big book too, he gives over his passport. When his name and number have been written down he asks, what is that for.

You have been refused entry, the little man says, giving his passport back to him, this is the list of names of people who may not enter Tanzania.

What is your name, he says, you can't treat me like this. He hears the idiocy of the threat even as he makes it, who would he report this man to and for what, there is nothing he can do, in the world of metaphor and in the real world too he has arrived at a line he cannot cross. He goes back out into the sun, where the others are waiting, commiserative, did you talk to him again, what did he say. No, it's no good, I can't come with you. They stand around in the aimless awkwardness of sympathy, but already they're casting their eyes toward the road and rocking from foot to foot, it's past the middle of the day.

We'd better go, Christian says. I'm sorry.

They write down each other's addresses. The only piece of paper he has is an old bank statement, now years later as I write this it lies in front of me on my desk, folded and creased and grubby, carrying its little cargo of names, its different sets of handwriting, some kind of impression of that instant pushed into the paper and fixed there.

He walks with them to the boom across the road. He may not go farther than this. On the other side are flocks of young boys on bicycles, waiting to ferry passengers the six kilometers to the nearest town, where other transport begins. This is where they have to say good-bye. He looks down at his shoes. He finds it difficult to speak.

Have a good journey, he says eventually.

Where will you go now.

I think I'll go home. I've had enough.

Jerome says, you will come in Switzerland, yes.

The last word is a question, he answers with a nod, yes I will.

Then they are gone, climbing onto the bikes, wobbling tentatively into motion and speeding away, such a surreal departure, he stands staring but none of them look back. Roderigo's shirt is the last vivid trace of them, the flag of the usurper, the stranger who came to take his place. Meanwhile other boys on bikes are crowding around him, blocking his view, let me take you sir you want a lift me sir me. No, he says, I'm not going with them. He looks down the road a last time, then shoulders his bag and turns. The bridge is long and lonely in the midday heat. He walks.

. . .

When he gets back to the Malawian side he finds himself dealing with the same white-uniformed official who stamped him through. There is a second or two of confusion before the man works it out, weren't you here half an hour ago.

Yes, they won't let me through. They say I need a visa. I don't have one.

The man looks at his passport, looks at him, then beckons him closer. Offer him money, he says.

What.

That's what he wants. A little bit of money.

He stares back at the man, beginning to understand the conversation he had on the other side of the bridge. That cryptic statement, what did he pay for this stamp, suddenly makes sense, how could he not have seen. I am a fool, he thinks, and not only because of that.

I was nasty to him, he says. Things turned unpleasant.

But this man is losing interest too, he opens his palms and shrugs. I go back outside and stand in the sun for a long suspended moment while various possibilities arc past and return. With every second Jerome and Alice and Christian are getting farther and farther away. Then suddenly he is running over the bridge, his pack jouncing on his back. When he comes to the shed he is pouring sweat and panting, please, he says, there is something I remembered.

The little man seems unsurprised to see him. His attention is on the starched cuffs of his shirt.

The South African I told you about. The one who got the stamp. I just remembered what he paid.

No. The tidy little head shakes sadly. Your name is in the book. When your name is in the book it can't come out.

Twenty dollars.

No.

Thirty.

I thought you wanted my name. I thought you wanted to report me.

I made a mistake. I was upset. I'm very sorry about it. I apologize.

You were rude to me. It is a pity. You said you wanted my name.

I said I was sorry.

I am also sorry. It is not possible.

The circular discussion goes on and on. He feels as if he is doing battle with some mythical doorkeeper whom he has to overcome, but he doesn't have the right weapons or words. After a while another man comes in, also in uniform, but slovenly and unkempt, chewing a stick between his teeth. Hello hello hello, he says, what's the problem here.

No problem. We're just talking.

I'm the boss here, talk to me.

He looks warily at the new man. He has a gun and handcuffs on his belt and the sort of hearty bonhomie that might conceal a zealous devotion to duty. I ought to be careful, but there isn't time. I don't have a visa, but I need to get into Tanzania. Can you help me.

Now a long discussion ensues between these two officials, in which the black book is opened and examined, his passport is perused, much deliberation goes back and forth. Every word of their two encounters, it seems, is being repeated and examined. At the end of this process the boss man starts to upbraid him. You have been rude to my friend. You have upset him.

I apologized to him. I said I was sorry.

Say it again.

My friend, I'm sorry for being rude. I wasn't thinking.

That's better, the boss man says. Now everybody is polite.

His name, indelibly inscribed in the great black book, is crossed out. All things are possible again. Now that the door is opening at last, he is frantic to catch up. But neither of these two men is prepared to rush, they must see to the details at their own leisurely pace. The boss in particular wants to explain the ethics of this transaction to him, if you want a man to break the law, he says, if you want him to risk his job, then you must make it worthwhile for this man.

Forty dollars makes it worthwhile.

In the end both of them come to see him off, standing at the boom like a pair of friendly relatives, waving. Have a nice time. Instantly the flocks of bicycle boys are around him, me sir, take me. He chooses one who looks sturdy and strong. I have to try to catch my friends, I'll pay you double if you go as fast as you can. Yes sir, very fast. He climbs on, they go toiling down the road.

It was Christian's plan, he knows, to catch a bus to Mbeya, a town about three hours away, from where there is a train to Dar es Salaam tonight. He has to find them before they leave, in the big city he will never see them again. He still has hopes that they might be waiting to catch the bus. Faster, he calls to the pedaling boy, can't you go faster. The scene feels bizarre. There are bicycles going in both directions, some with passengers, some without. The road goes up and down between green rolling hills, the sun beats down. The boy works frantically, pouring sweat, and every now and then turns his head to blow a jet of snot out of his nose. Sorry, he calls back over his shoulder. Don't be sorry, just go faster.

But when they come to the first little town the roadside is bare and deserted. He gets down and looks around, as if they might be hiding nearby. Where are my friends, he asks, but the boy shakes his head and grins. The friends of this peculiar man are no concern of his.

So he waits for the next bus to come. It's as if he's come to a place outside time, in which only he feels its lack. He paces up and down, he throws pebbles at a tree, he counts ants going into a hole in the ground, all this to summon time again. When the interval is over, perhaps an hour and a half has passed. There is a little crowd swelling next to the road by then and everybody clambers on board the bus at once. He ends up without a seat and has to hang on to roof racks in the aisle. Outside there is a mountainous green countryside quilted with tea plantations. Banana trees clap their broad leaves in applause.

It's a full three hours or more before the road begins to descend from this high hilly country and the edges of Mbeya accrete around him. By now the sun is setting and in the dwindling light all he can see are low, sinister buildings, made mostly of mud, crouching close to the ground. He climbs down at the edge of a crowded street swirling with fumes. He asks somebody nearby if they know where the station is, somebody else overhears him and repeats it to somebody else, and he finds himself escorted to a group of men loitering nearby. He saw them when he first got off the bus, an expressionless and hard-looking bunch wearing caps and dark glasses, exuding menace. One of them says that he will take him to the station for five dollars. He hesitates for a few seconds in renewed panic, he's afraid of this man in dark glasses whose car, he sees, has dark windows too, is he really going to drive off into these anonymous streets walled in by so much dark glass. But he's come this far and he doesn't know what else to do.

The man drives very fast in complete silence and then pulls up in front of a long building that is completely in darkness. By now it's night. There is a chain on the front door and not a living soul in sight. Five dollars, the man says.

I want you to wait for me. I might need a lift somewhere else.

The man waits, brooding and watchful, while he fumbles his way up and down the length of the building, calling and knocking. Eventually he finds a window behind which a light is burning. He raps and raps on the glass until somebody comes, peering out suspiciously at him.

Yes.

Excuse me. Is there a train to Dar es Salaam tonight.

Not tonight. In the morning. It's dangerous around here. You should go back into town. Come in the morning.

He returns to the car and his surly driver, could you drive me into town. I'll give you another five dollars.

The man takes him to a hotel close to the point at which he got off the bus. You're lucky, the woman at the desk tells him, you've got the last room. But he doesn't feel lucky at all as he sits on the edge of the bed, staring at the various shades of brown and beige that surround him. He can't remember when he last felt so alone.

He decides that he will return to the station in the morning. If he doesn't find them there he will go back home. With this much resolved he tries to sleep, but he tosses and turns, he wakes continually into his strange surroundings to stare at a weird patch of light on the wall. At dawn he dresses and leaves the key in the door.

Opposite the hotel is an open patch of ground where the taxi rank is. As he comes to the bottom of the driveway he sees Jerome and Christian getting into a taxi. He stops dead still and then he starts to run.

The reunion is delighted all round, lots of clamor and slapping of shoulders. In the space of five minutes the whole world has changed shape, this town that looked mean and threatening to him is suddenly full of vibrancy and life. When they get to the station, this building too is no longer the empty darkened mausoleum of last night, it's been transformed into a crowded public space filled with clamor and commotion. The only bad news is that the train has been delayed, it will be a couple of hours before they leave.

While they wait he goes for a long walk with Roderigo into the surrounding streets to find something to drink. A rusted Coca-Cola sign takes them into the dusty inner courtyard of a house, where they are served under a faded beach umbrella at a plastic table while chickens peck around their feet. Roderigo is still wearing his purple shirt, a gaudy scarf tied around his neck. While we sip our drinks he tells me a story about my country. Before he went to work in Mozambique, he says, he stayed in South Africa for a few weeks, living in a hostel in Johannesburg. One day a young American traveler arrived and was put into the same room with him and they became friendly. On the second or third night Roderigo and this American went out drinking and landed up in a bar in Yeoville very late and very drunk. Roderigo wanted to go home to bed, but the American had started speaking to a black man he'd just met, who invited him to go somewhere else for another drink. The American was full of sentiment and goodwill about the country, talking to Roderigo about racial harmony and the healing of the past. He went away with his new friend and he never came back.

Roderigo went to the police to report him missing and a week later he was called to say that they'd found a body and would he come to identify it. The last time he saw his friend was through a window at the morgue. He'd been found stabbed in the back outside a big block of flats in the city, lying in the gutter. A day or two later a man in the building was arrested, who confessed to killing him for his watch and forty rand. Soon afterward Roderigo left for Mozambique.

Why he tells this story I don't know, but there seems to be some kind of accusation in it. They finish their drinks in silence and go slowly back to the station. By now it's almost midday and the train is due to leave.

An hour or two into the journey they hear for the first time that Tanzania is about to hold its first multiparty elections in two days' time. The newspapers are full of stories of possible violence and upheaval, the rumors on the train are edged with nervousness. But none of this touches them, there is a new festive feeling amongst them all, as if they're going to a party.

But he lies awake that night for a long time after the others have drifted off, listening to the slow sound of breathing all around, the throbbing of the tracks. He worries about what he is going to do with himself when they leave in a few days, he will be alone in Tanzania in a politically unstable time, without a visa, with the prospect of retracing his route. Returning along the same path in any journey is depressing, but he especially fears how he might feel on this occasion.

The part of him that watches himself is still here too, not ecstatic or afraid. This part hovers in its usual detachment, looking down with wry amusement at the sleepless figure in the bunk. It sees all the complexities of the situation he's in and murmurs sardonically into his ear, you see where you have landed yourself, you intended to visit Zimbabwe for a few days and now you find yourself weeks later on a train to Dar es Salaam. Happy and unhappy, he falls asleep in the end and dreams about, no, I don't remember his dreams.

In the morning they are in a different landscape, out of the soft green hills and moving across a flat plain of bushveld. As they get closer to the coast they leave behind the yellow grass and thorn trees, now there is greenery outside again, the lush and verdant green of the tropics. The air is humid and hot, smelling of salt.

They arrive close to midday. There is no warning or announcement, the train simply comes to a stop at a siding and people get off. From here they can see the city a little distance away, clustered against the sky. They wonder where they might find a taxi, but a passing couple offers them a lift. The man is driving a new Range Rover and, while he negotiates the traffic, he tells them that he and his wife are both diplomats. He points to the little groups of people that are everywhere visible on the pavements, crouched down around radios on the ground, they are listening to reports on the elections, he says, there's been trouble on Zanzibar. What sort of trouble. Zanzibar voted two days ago, ahead of the rest of the country, now the results there have been announced but some of the parties have rejected them, there has been some fighting, some people throwing stones. And what about everywhere else, is there going to be trouble too. I don't think so, the man says, there's a lot of talk but nobody's going to do anything.

The couple drive them to a cheap hotel near the harbor, where they manage to get two rooms. Alice and Jerome and Christian are in one, Roderigo and I in the other. Everybody by now is becoming irritated by Roderigo, he is endlessly dissatisfied with everything and strident about announcing it. The prices of things are too high, the service is too poor, nothing measures up to his standards. Under his garish exterior he is endlessly fretful and unhappy. Now his anxiety is focused on the question of money. Back in Mbeya, it turns out, they discovered they had a problem. Aside from me, the others are all traveling with Visa cards, which no bank or business will accept here. It is ridiculous, Roderigo fumes, who has heard of such a thing, what a terrible and backward place this is.

On the train Christian has already borrowed some money from me, in Dar es Salaam he is sure they will be able to make a plan. Now they all set off to try to find a place where they can draw money. He trails along in their wake, looking around at the city, while they go from one bank to another. But it's the same story, none of them accept Visa cards. Some banks say that the card will not be usable anywhere and others tell them that certain banks will take it, just not this one. It's a long hot search. They have walked for blocks and are starting to feel dispirited and low when they are told to try one last place. This is up three flights of stairs in a narrow building close to their hotel. The bank is behind two massive wooden doors, outside which, in the dim stairwell, a guard lounges at a desk, wearing dark glasses. I'll wait here, he says, and sits down on the stairs. Christian and Alice and Roderigo go in through the wooden doors and suddenly he is left outside with Jerome.

This is the first time they've ever been alone together. Now that the moment has come so unexpectedly, he doesn't know what to do with it. He is sitting on the stairs, facing the guard, while Jerome moves up and down the darkened vestibule, looking uneasy. Then he turns and very quickly comes over to sit next to me on the step. Only the speed at which he does this betrays how nervous he is. He takes hold of my arm in his hand.

With great difficulty, finding the words, he says, you want come in Switzerland with me.

I am astounded. Nothing has prepared the way for this question. My palms are sweating, my heart is hammering, but from the swirling behind my forehead only one question, the most stupid and irrelevant one possible, comes winding out, but what, I say, what will I do there.

You can work, he says.

Then the doors of the bank open, the others come out, he and Jerome pull away from each other, and they are never alone again.

It's no good, Christian says. They won't take the card.

It's like being struck by lightning. Or like being pushed over an edge, on which, he now realizes, he's been balanced for days. Nothing is quite the same as before. When he follows the others down the stairs and out into the street he is looking at everything through a strange pane of glass, which both distorts and clarifies the world.

By now it's too late to go on searching, all the banks are closing for the day. But by now it's also clear that there's no solution to the problem. In the morning they will go to the French embassy, perhaps they will get help and advice there.

The rest of the day passes aimlessly, they go to the hotel next door to theirs to swim, they lie around, they talk. From Jerome there is not the slightest trace of the strange feverishness that gripped him on the stairs. That night I go with them to the front desk of an expensive hotel nearby to phone. Alice and Jerome want to call their mother at home, it's been months since they spoke to her. It takes a long time to make the connection, they have to wait and wait in that vast echoey foyer, but then, while he listens to this half of a conversation around the world, *ah Maman, il est si bon d'entendre ta voix,* the syllables of a language he doesn't understand convey an intimacy and affection that he does, and he can half imagine this other life they come from, far to the north, which he's been invited to join. Should I go. Can I. His own life has narrowed to a fork, at which he dithers in an indecisive rapture.

He doesn't have to decide now, there is always tomorrow, tomorrow. But in the morning nothing has changed. He goes with them to the embassy to ask advice. We will lend you money, the people at the embassy say, go up to Kenya where you'll be able to use your card. There is a brief discussion but in fact there is no choice, without money there's nothing more they can do. They will go to Kenya the next morning. He knows already that they will ask him, they know already what he will say. Yes, I will come to Kenya with you.

I don't remember what they do the rest of that day. The next memory he has is of waking up in the middle of the night with the beam of a lighthouse flaring intermittently across the ceiling and the sound of Roderigo furtively masturbating under the sheets.

The next day is the election, but from the dusty windows of the bus the city looks the same as it did yesterday. It takes more than an hour to drive through the intricate alleys and little streets near the bus station. The complicated shop fronts with their myriad steps and tiny windows put him in mind of the innards of some enormous animal, through which they're creeping like a germ.

But once they're free of the city the bus accelerates to alarming speed. The road runs up in sight of the coast, across a broad green plain the flat water continually reappears, tiny villages and settlements flash past, palm trees lagoons mangroves all the detritus of the tropics. It's only when they get to the border post that he becomes anxious, what if they notice he has no visa. But he is out almost faster than the others, an exit stamp planted like a bruise next to the entry stamp he bought a few days ago.

As they drive into Kenya it's dark already and a steady drizzle starts to fall. Nearing Mombasa, there are more and more people at the side of the road. The final approach is by ferry, on which they move across open water to the city, he stands outside at the rail and watches the yellow lights through the rain. The hotel they find is the most depressing one yet, two flights of stairs climb to their floor, the whole place seems made of untreated concrete, in the middle of each room a ceiling fan shudders and turns. The building doubles as a bordello, the floors underneath them are occupied by prostitutes who hang around in the foyer and on the pavement in front, hello my darling are you looking for me kssk kssk. They are in two rooms again, he and Roderigo apart from the rest, but a narrow balcony outside connects them. From this balcony there is a view across the street to a similar building facing them, in the different rooms of which they can see various sex acts in progress, each in its little lit cube.

. . .

This time the invitation doesn't come from Jerome, but from Alice. At lunch the next day there is a little moment of seriousness at the table, would you like to come with us, we have found a cheap flight to Athens. My mother has a house in a little village in Greece. We are going there for a few weeks before we go home.

He looks to Jerome, who says, come. But there is no echo of the last invitation on the stairs, this is a formal offer he could easily turn down.

And then, he says. After Greece. What will I do. Let me tell you later.

He goes walking through the old city, between high and fantastic facades, movement has always been a substitute for thought and he would like to stop thinking now. Wandering around, he finds himself in an antique shop full of cool dark air and Oriental carpets and brass lamps, his eye slides off this material world until a human figure pulls it back. Where are you from. The man is in his fifties, white, with a big lined face and a lugubrious air. He has an improbable English accent, very overdone. South Africa, goodness me, how did you get up here. Through Malawi, my word, I'm off to Malawi in a few days. Look around, yes please, be my guest. What did you say your name was.

For some reason this lanky expat stays in his mind, even when he gets back to the hotel, in all this grimy and half-decayed city he is the only other person, aside from his companions, who knows my name. He sits on the balcony as it gets dark, staring out into the hot rainy street, where a taxi pulls up and a prostitute gets out, one of the brightly dressed women from downstairs, along with a bearded white man his own age. They kiss lingeringly next to the car, their tongues flicker in the humid air, then the man gets back into the taxi and glides away.

They all go out that night to eat, and because this is the last real night of traveling they go somewhere a little more expensive than usual, it's as if they're celebrating but the mood around the table is glum. The others are weighed down by different thoughts, the end of nine months in Africa, maybe, the prospect of going home. But somewhere in the intermittent bits of conversation the question does come up again, have you decided what to do. No, not yet, in the morning.

That night he hardly sleeps. He throws himself around on the bed, he stares up at the fan as it turns and turns, he keeps getting up and wandering out onto the balcony and then wandering back again. His brain is boiling over, he can't make it cool down.

In the morning everybody is up early. There is a lot of commotion and activity, and it's a while before Jerome comes in to ask with raised eyebrows, good decision.

He shakes his head, his voice won't come out properly. I must go back.

Jerome doesn't answer, but his face goes tight.

So the journey ends with four little words. Nobody argues with him, they are all caught up with what they have to do, sorting through their things and packing their bags. He doesn't want to sit around watching, so he tells Christian he's going out for a walk.

We must go by ten.

I'll be back by then.

He goes out through the crowded streets, he wanders without any plan clear to himself, but he's not surprised when he finds himself back at the dark antique shop. The seedy expat is there again, balanced with a cup of coffee on a pile of carpets. I was here yesterday, I tell him.

Oh yes, he says vaguely.

You told me you were going to Malawi in a few days. I wondered whether you might want a companion on the trip.

At this the dark eyes lighten a little, oh yes, he says, that would be good. Why don't you come by tomorrow and we can make plans. What is your name again.

Damon. My name is Damon.

The man repeats his name. He goes back to the hotel by half past nine, but there's no sign of them. At first he assumes they're out somewhere having breakfast, but then it dawns on him that they've gone. When Christian said ten he must've meant the time at which the bus actually left, they are at the bus station by now.

He thinks he must hurry over to say good-bye. But by the time he's downstairs again another conviction comes slowly over him. Isn't it better this way, let them go quietly without seeing them. So he starts to wander through the streets again, but in the wrong direction, away from the bus station, looking at people, at shops, at any detail he passes that might distract his mind. He can already feel the next few days stretching away in these aimless and awful walks of his, there is nothing more sordid than having to use up time.

But then suddenly he is off, running the other way through the crowds. Where does this movement come from, taking even him by surprise, he is looking for a taxi but none appears. He arrives at the bus station with only minutes to spare and then he has to look for the bus. When he finds it the engine is already running, a man at the door tells him there's still space. Go in, get a seat, I give you a ticket now. No, no, I want to say good-bye to my friends.

They all get off, assembling at the edge of the road with a dejected air, none of them quite looking at each other. He would like to say something, the perfect single word that contains how he feels, but there isn't any such word. Instead he says nothing, he makes half gestures that die before he can complete them, he shakes his head and sighs.

Good-bye, he says.

You will come in Switzerland, yes, Jerome says again.

All of this is spoken flatly, there is no trace of feeling in the whole little scene, and by now the driver is hooting impatiently at them. We have to go, Christian says. Yes, I say, good-bye. He leans forward and grips Jerome by the upper arm and squeezes hard. I promise you, he tells him, I will see you again.

Good-bye.

He and Alice smile at each other, then she turns and goes up the steps. Roderigo reaches out to embrace him, good-bye my friend take care of yourself, the odd one out is the most effusive of all.

He walks slowly back through the racket and chaos. It hasn't dawned on him yet what's happened. When he gets back to the hotel he pays the proprietor downstairs for another night, and while he's fumbling through his wallet for change he feels a furtive hand tugging at his fly. He jumps back in fright, the hand belongs to one of the prostitutes, her vivid lips smile at him in the gloom. I'm just trying to help you, she says.

I don't need help.

The vehemence of his tone is startling, she makes an ooing noise to mock him, he breaks away and goes up the stairs. Somehow this incident has set his feelings free, a thin column of grief rises in him like mercury. He goes into his room and stares around, then goes out along the balcony to their room. It's all as it was, the three beds, the fan turning listlessly overhead. He sits down on the edge of a chair. There are bits of paper crumpled on the floor, envelopes, notes, pages from a book, which they dropped while cleaning out their bags, and these solitary white scraps, drifting in the wind from the fan, are sadder to him than anything else that's happened.

Jerome, if I can't make you live in words, if you are only the dim evocation of a face under a fringe of hair, and the others too, Alice and Christian and Roderigo, if you are names without a nature, it's not because I don't remember, no, the opposite is true, you are remembered in me as an endless stirring and turning. But it's for this precisely that you must forgive me, because in every story of obsession there is only one character, only one plot. I am writing about myself alone, it's all I know, and for this reason I have always failed in every love, which is to say at the very heart of my life.

He sits in the empty room, crying.


He's not prepared for quite how bad the next few days turn out to be. He spends a lot of time lying on his back on the bed, staring up at the fan on the ceiling. Then he suddenly can't take it anymore and jumps up and goes out into the streets, striding along as if he has a purpose and a destination, but these walks always peter out at some point, often in an alley at the edge of the sea, where he stares into the haze, at a dhow going past.

Meanwhile he prepares for his return, he goes to the consulate and gets a proper visa for Tanzania. He also returns to the antique shop a couple of times. The expat, whose name is Charles, is always vague about his plans, but he insists that, yes, he will be going to Malawi. He just wants to wait a day or two, he says, till this election thing is over in Tanzania, you can never be sure, you know, this is Africa after all. The third time he goes back, Charles is more animated than usual. We can leave the day after tomorrow, he says, how does that suit you. There is only one thing, I stay out of town, come and spend the day there tomorrow. And listen, sorry, what is your name again.

He is there in the morning and they drive out soon after in Charles's battered van. They go back on the ferry and along the road to the coast. He spends his last day in Kenya at a resort on the beach, Charles lives nearby with his family.

This is also the day on which the others are leaving Kenya, he knows the time of their flight. So at two that afternoon, while he stands on a deserted beach of glimmering white sand, gazing out into an ocean that stretches in gradations of deepening color towards a line of surf that marks the reef far out, he looks at his watch and feels their departure almost as a physical change in himself. His heart missing a beat, say. You are going down the runway, you are lifting into the air, you are banking slowly to the north and moving away, away.

It's about now that he realizes he has made a mistake. It's only a couple of days later, but already his decision is senseless, he sees clearly what he's going back to in South Africa, the same state of nothing, the drifting from place to place. Never has this condition so obviously been what it is, an absence of love.

But it isn't too late. What rises in him now is an urge to make the largest and most dramatic gesture of all, he will chase them not for a few hundred kilometers but halfway across the world. He spends the afternoon walking up and down the beach, crossing and recrossing his own tracks between the palm trees, while he works out what to do. It's entirely possible. He must get back down to South Africa as quickly as he can, he must scrape some money together, he must fly to Greece in a few days. On the piece of paper from the Tanzanian border he has Jerome's home number, where his mother is. He must phone her and find out where they are, how to get to this holiday house. He will make his way there from Athens, he will arrive one night out of the dark, out of the recent past, with his hands open, smiling. It's me again, I came here to find you.

He's still knotted up when he and Charles set off the next morning. Charles is wearing shorts and sandals and a big straw hat on his head. He is a good-looking man in a loose, big-boned sort of way, but if you study him closely you begin to see the signs of decay. His nails are dirty, he has nicotine stains on his teeth, around his eyes the lines are as deep and dark as old bruises. There is something in his spirit that resembles an overripe fruit, soft and pulpy at the center. Just before they get to the border he pulls over in a cane field and lights up a huge joint. To calm me down, he says, before I deal with these bastards.

It turns out he's smuggling twenty thousand dollars' worth of Afghan rugs under two oil drums in the back. These are destined, he tells afterwards, for one or another official at the American embassy in Dar es Salaam, they are one of the reasons he's making this trip. Charles sweats and trembles like a junkie as they go across the border, but afterwards he affects a bored composure. No problem if they were found, he says breezily, a quick fifty dollars and they'll look the other way. I know these chaps, I speak the lingo.

It's his plan, he says, to try to sleep over at the place he's delivering the rugs. When they arrive at Dar es Salaam in the evening he takes them to a vast house in one of the more exclusive suburbs, with a metal fence and a security guard outside. It's the residence of some high-up official in the embassy, a plump middle-aged woman with glasses who comes out to meet them, smiling broadly.

She agrees to let them stay over, and he finds himself in a luxurious bedroom, drapes and thick carpets and a bathroom tiled to the ceiling. It's unreal to him, but not as unreal as dinner that night, which they eat with the Romanian ambassador to Tanzania. For some bizarre reason there is a portrait of Lenin on the wall and the ambassador makes a sign of the cross in self-defense when he sees it. I am silent under the weight of this surreal situation, and glad to be alone in bed not long after. In the passage outside his door a radio crackles and burps all night, leaking American voices talking in code.

The next day they drive to Mbeya and put up in a hotel. Since leaving Kenya Charles hasn't called him anything, but that night, in the bar, he hears him saying, Noel, Noel, and when he looks around Charles is speaking to me. Why he's fixed on this name it's hard to tell, but I feel too weary to correct him. By this time there is a high level of irritation between them and being called Noel is just part of the deal.

By the next day, when they enter Malawi, the irritation is teetering on the edge of argument. When they miss a turning somewhere Charles starts to berate him, you're supposed to be watching the road signs, Noel, and he has to force himself to stay silent. Later Charles expatiates on what lies beneath the Malawians' smiles, they're pretending to be innocent but they're a crafty lot. Don't be fooled, Noel, I've got their number.

It's time to move on and the next morning, when they get to the lake, he says good-bye. Charles is alarmed, why don't you hang around for a while, he doesn't want to be left alone with the crafty Malawians, but I shake my head. In two days he can be back at home, his mind wanders constantly northward, to Greece. Oh all right, Charles mutters defeatedly, go then. But write your address in my book, in case I ever come to Cape Town.

I hesitate with the book in hand, not knowing what to write. But after a moment he prints his new name, Noel, and an old telephone number, he will never hear from Charles again.

From here the return journey goes swiftly, Noel jumps from one bus to another, only pausing to overnight in Blantyre. In another two days he is back in South Africa, in Pretoria. It has taken him six days to get back from Mombasa, half the length of the continent.

But now something happens to him. The whole way home he has thought of nothing but what it is he wants to do, he has been consumed by the desire to get to Greece. Now back among familiar things again, the objects and faces that are the icons of his usual life, a kind of apathy comes over him. It's as if he's in shock. Did I really do that, he thinks to himself, did I really go chasing them all that way. And instead of rushing out in a continuation of his old momentum to book tickets and make plans, he finds himself sitting in the sun, brooding about what's happened. He feels even less sure than before about the meaning of it all.

By imperceptible degrees, then, he accepts the notion that the journey is over, and that he's back where he started. The story of Jerome is one he's lived through before, it is the story of what never happened, the story of traveling a long way while standing still.

Four months later he goes to Europe. On a bright morning with the first trace of warmth in the air, he arrives by train in Switzerland. He has written to say he's coming and from Germany, a few days before, he made a call. Jerome was not at home and when Alice came to the phone she sounded startled but happy. Yes, she said, please come to visit, we are waiting for you. But now, as the train slides and turns through the mountains, emerging at last into the bright open sky over the lake, he has a faint memory again of the fear that gripped him in Africa. He stands at the window, looking at the houses and little streets flashing past at the edge of the water, and feels doubt like a coldness in him.

He sits next to the lake for a long time, thinking. The water is silvery-gray in color, with hardly a crease on its surface, and on the other side, far away, mountains rise to sharp and jagged crests. Now that he has waited so long and come so far, he is in no hurry to arrive. He would like this moment to suspend itself indefinitely, so that he need never stir himself again.

But as the afternoon goes on he takes up his pack and walks back along the lake, in the direction from which the train came. The path narrows and goes under trees, past jetties. There are swans gliding in the water, supported on their own reflections. After half an hour he comes to a little street running up away from the water, and its name is the one written on that scrap of paper from Malawi.

The house is a largish one, set back from the corner, with a garden behind it. He knocks and after a while there are footsteps and the door opens. Hello, we have been waiting for you. Jerome's mother has short hair and a wide welcoming smile, come in, come in. She seems genuinely pleased to see him, she holds out her hand. My name is Catherine.

While they shake hands they look appraisingly at each other. He has no idea what she has been told about him or what she expects. Jerome has just come home, she tells him, it is a surprise. He was supposed to come only tomorrow. He will be so glad to see you. She calls to a young girl hovering nearby, go and find Jerome.

While they wait they go to sit on a stone veranda behind the house. In the garden there is a tree, a swing, and through a screen of leaves at the bottom, a view of the water. Alice comes out, smiling. There is the awkward happiness of hello, hello, how are you, looking at each other while they also look away.

When Jerome comes out he is wearing a blue military uniform and his hair is cut brutally short. They shake hands, smiling shyly, under the eyes of his mother and Alice. Ah hello yes excellent. Jerome, I'm glad to see you. The dialogue and the gestures are tinny and false, like some kind of bright paper wrapped around the meaning of the moment.

They all settle down uneasily around the outdoor table. The girl who was sent off to find Jerome is his younger sister. She is fourteen or fifteen with a chubby, cheerful face. An older sister arrives soon afterwards. Conversation flickers back and forth, returning continually to him, he can sense how curious they are about him. But at the same time he is also an observer, watching Jerome in this circle of women, while the light fades away.

Why don't you go for a walk, Catherine says. Before supper.

He goes with Jerome across the grass to a gate at the bottom of the garden. Through a narrow alley to the road. They stand on a little curved bridge that goes over a river, alone again for the first time since that minute or two outside the wooden doors of the bank.

But everything is different now. The artificial awkwardness of that first moment up at the house continues, they don't know what to say to each other.

So this is where you live.

Yes. Yes.

It's beautiful here.

Ah. Yes. I like.

Is it hard to be back.

Yes. Yes. He leans forward on the railing, his mouth works to find the words. In my head I am traveling, traveling.

I know what you mean.

Jerome is doing a session of military service, he is only home for the weekend. While he's here they share his room, the visitor sleeps on a mattress on the floor. Although this section of the house is apart from the rest, a separate little flat on its own, they are never away from the rest of the family. It's pleasant to sit in the sun behind the house, talking with Catherine, or wander to the shops with Alice or one of the other sisters. Jerome is always kind and solicitous, he invites him wherever he goes and introduces him to his friends, and he lets himself be taken along on outings and play the part of a contented guest.

On the Sunday, Jerome's father comes to visit. He has lived apart from them, at the other end of the lake, for some years now, and in the family his departure has left the lingering trace of a loss. So on this day, when they make a fire to cook in the yard, and knock a ball back and forth over a net, there is a feeling of completion and unity among them, to which I can only be a witness. He sits on the swing, pushing himself to and fro, watching as if from a great distance this scene that in Africa would be unimaginable to him.

He has come to like all of them, so when Jerome leaves again that night, going by train to some military base at the other end of the country, he is not alarmed at being left with his family. The week passes quickly and on the next weekend Jerome is back again, but if he was hoping that the gap of five days would change something between them, it doesn't happen. They are pleasant and polite with each other, but their interaction has something of the quality of a letter which Jerome sent him, the studied and careful presentation of words that have been translated and copied from a dictionary. He isn't himself, he is a guarded version of his own nature, nor does he recognize in the cropped hair and military terseness of the person whose room he shares the soft and gentle young man he traveled with four months ago.

There are hints, perhaps, that it might be possible to move past this state. Jerome makes some tentative conversation about plans he has for the future, how, when he's finished with this stint in the army, he would like to travel overland down to Greece. But this will only be in a couple of months from now. The possibility of another shared journey floats in the air, both of them consider it, but neither of them has the courage to say anything more.

He knows already that he must move on. On the night before Jerome gets back that next weekend, he takes a walk along the water. Mist is rolling in from the other side, smudging the outlines of the little boats at their moorings. When he comes to a jetty that projects a long way into the lake he walks out on the wooden planks to the end. From here there is no shore anymore, no edge to anything he can see. He is adrift in the white mist, with the water slapping softly below, cold air rolling across his face. He leans on the railing and stares into the whiteness and thinks about everything that's happened.

When Jerome returns this time, he finds a moment to let him know, I will be going on Monday. To London. I can't stay here forever. I'm sure your family must be getting tired of me.

No, no. Jerome is vehement in his protest. You can stay.

He shakes his head gently and smiles, I have to go, I can't keep standing still.

Later Jerome comes back to him again, bringing a friend who lives a few houses away. This friend speaks fluent English and has come along, he says, to translate.

Jerome says you must stay.

No, really. Tell him thank you. But I can't. Maybe I will come back.

When, Jerome says.

Later. When I've gone traveling for a while.

And it's true, he tells himself, maybe he will come back. There is always another time, next month, next year, when things will be different.

But after these flickers of feeling, that last weekend is much like the others. Jerome is friendly but distant, he makes no special effort to talk or be alone. At one point he says, we talk with Christian, yes, and picks up the phone. But the number just rings and rings. Jerome says, later, and puts it down again, but they never do try later.

On the Sunday evening when Alice drives her brother to the station, he goes along to say good-bye. Jerome is in uniform again, with all his buttons gleaming, his black shoes reflecting the light. He is proud of how he looks, although he pretends that he isn't. They all go into the bar together to wait. There are two friends of his there, also in uniform, with whom he'll be traveling, there are introductions and handshakes and murmured pleasantries all round.

You go tomorrow, Jerome says at last.

Yes.

But you come again later.

Maybe.

One of the friends says something and all of them stand up. Sorry. We must to go.

In the end they shake hands again, smiling formally, amongst all the artificial surfaces and military buttons shining like eyes. They have never been more distant, or polite. In the morning his actual departure will be an echo of this one. He has already left, or perhaps he never arrived.

He goes to London, but the same restlessness comes over him there, and he goes on somewhere else. And somewhere else again. Five months later he finds himself in a strange country, at the edge of a strange town, with dusk coming down. He is watching people drifting into a funfair on the other side of an overgrown expanse of ground. Circus music drifts towards him faintly over the weeds and in the gathering gloom at the base of a high green volcano he sees the lights of a Ferris wheel go round and round and round.

He doesn't know why, but this scene is like a mirror in which he sees himself. Not his face, or his past, but who he is. He feels a melancholy as soft and colorless as wind, and for the first time since he started traveling he thinks that he would like to stop. Stay in one place, never move again.

Then he is in London again, on his way back home. He is only here for a week, after which he will fly to Amsterdam and then, five days later, to South Africa.

He phones Jerome from a booth in the street. He doesn't know exactly why he's making this call, except that he promised he would, and he's unsure of whether to go back to visit them again. Before he can even mention the idea Jerome has put it to him, come, come, please. This time, even through the thin vein of the telephone line, he can hear the urgency of the invitation.

I have to think, he says, I have no money.

My family, it's okay, no money.

Also no time. I have only four days before I go. Maybe, all right, I'll see. I'll phone you from Amsterdam.

But before he gets to Amsterdam he has already made up his mind not to go. It's true that he has little money and time, but these are not the reasons for his decision. The memory of the last visit is still strong in his mind, he has carried it with him all the way on his travels, and he fears that the same thing will happen again. He will arrive, he will be made very welcome, he will spend a day or two in placidity and comfort, but the silence and distance between them, which they have incubated somehow since the first day they met in Africa, will amplify and grow, even as they become nicer to each other. This isn't what he wants, it is very deeply what he doesn't want, although it has taken this short conversation on the telephone for him to realize how unhappy that first visit made him.

So he goes down to Paris instead and stumbles aimlessly around the streets, wandering into shops and out again, sitting on benches. He's aware that he's engaged again in that most squalid of activities, using up time, but the journey hasn't ended where he wanted it to, it has frayed out instead into endless ambiguities and nuances, like a path that divides and divides endlessly, growing fainter all the time.

There are moments, it's true, in those three or four days, when a longing to go back to Switzerland comes over him like a pang, it's only a few hours on the train, he could do it on a whim, but then he remembers how he came back this way last time, emptiness weighing him down like a black suitcase chained to his wrist.

When he passes a public telephone now and then he remembers that he promised to call, but he can't do it yet, not yet. There would be a discussion again on the line, the push and pull of their broken attempts to communicate, and he might give in, in spite of himself.

So he leaves it to what is the very last moment, when he is at the airport in Amsterdam, with his bag checked in, waiting to board. There are crowds of people under the fluorescent lights, clutching packets from the duty-free shops, and outside, through the plate-glass windows, the weird unnatural shapes of aircraft in rows. He makes the call from a bank of public phones, jostled from either side by elbows and foreign syllables. He hopes that Jerome won't be home.

Catherine answers the phone and recognizes his voice before he's said his name. Hello, are you coming back to visit us.

No, I'm sorry, I can't. I'm at the airport right now.

Ahh. She sounds disappointed. What a pity, we were hoping, Jerome was hoping.

I know, I'm sorry about it. He starts to babble the excuses about money and time, but his tongue is tripping him up. Another time, he says, and now he means it, there will be another time to make this right.

Another time, she agrees, do you want to talk to Jerome, and though his money is fast running out he knows he must.

There is a brief conversation in the background before Jerome comes on, in his voice he knows already. Ah, but why.

No money, he says again, no time.

Come. Come.

It's too late. I'm at the airport. I'll make it up to you, he says, I promise. Another time.

Yes, I want. Traveling. Next year.

Where.

I don't know. Africa. Possibly.

That will be wonderful, he says. It sounds as if he's been invited, although the words, as always, haven't been said. Jerome, I have to go. The money.

I don't understand.

And then the phone goes dead. He hangs up slowly, wondering whether to ring again, but he's said what he has to say, and anyway he has to leave. Another time.

Friends who live in London have bought a house in the country three hours from Cape Town, and when I was passing through they offered the use of this place to stay in. If you think you would like it, it's going to be standing empty, it would be nice to have somebody keeping an eye.

He said he would think about it but the next day, just before leaving London, he phoned to accept. It felt in some way like a providential offer. He has no other place to return to, and he knows he can't go back to the way he was living before, the endless moving around, the rootlessness. So the idea of this house, far away from all the old familiar sites, is like a fresh beginning, the possibility of home.

The move isn't easy, he has to take all his things out of storage and hire vans to load everything up and conscript friends to help him drive. The house, when he gets there, is like nowhere he's ever lived before. It's rustic and rough, with a thatched roof and concrete floors and a windmill turning outside the bedroom window. His friends help him unload and then drive back to Cape Town almost immediately, leaving him alone amongst the piles and piles of boxes.

That first night he sits on the back step, looking out across a backyard choked with weeds to the occasional lights of trucks on the single road that passes the town. He watches the moon come up over the stony tops of the valley and gets gently drunk on sherry and wonders what he's done to himself now.

But over the next few days, as he sweeps and cleans and unpacks the boxes and puts his possessions into place, he starts to feel better about where he is. It doesn't belong to him, but he lives here, he doesn't need to leave unless he wants to. And as the shapes of the rooms and the noises of the roof become familiar, a sort of intimacy develops between him and the place, they put out tendrils and grow into each other. This process deepens as his life overflows outdoors, he starts pulling up the weeds in the garden, he digs furrows and lets water run to the fruit trees and the rosebushes, and when old dead branches begin to sprout buds and leaves, and then bright bursts of color, he feels as if it's happening inside himself.

By then the little town and even the landscape around it are also connected to him, there is no interruption between him and the world, he isn't separate anymore from what he sees. When he goes out the front door now it isn't to catch a bus, or to find another hotel, he walks into the mountains and then he comes back home again. Home. Sometimes he stops on whatever dirt road he's followed today and looks back down the valley to the town, and then he always picks out the tiny roof under which he will be sleeping tonight.

He doesn't feel like a traveler anymore, it's hard to imagine that he ever thought of himself that way, and when he finally settles himself to write a letter to Jerome it's like a stranger willing up the words. He tells about where he is and what it's like to be here, and says that he hopes Jerome will come to visit him one day.

A week after he sends the letter an envelope arrives from Switzerland. He doesn't recognize the handwriting, but the stamp is clearly visible, and it's with a sense of excitement that he sits down to read. When he opens the envelope his own letter falls out, like a piece of the past returned to his hands. The single stiff card that accompanies it says, *Dear Sir, I'm very sorry to break the death of Jerome to you. He died on the twenty-sixth of November in an accident of motorbike. His mother asked me to send you your letter back.* The signature at the bottom is that of a stranger, and even as he sits at the epicenter of this soundless white explosion, that separate watchful part of his brain is back again, reading over his shoulder, trying to decipher the name, aware of all the oddities of language, working out when it happened. One week to the day after I got back home.

A journey is a gesture inscribed in space, it vanishes even as it's made. You go from one place to another place, and on to somewhere else again, and already behind you there is no trace that you were ever there. The roads you went down yesterday are full of different people now, none of them know who you are. In the room you slept in last night a stranger lies in the bed. Dust covers over your footprints, the marks of your fingers are wiped off the door, from the floor and table the bits and pieces of evidence that you might have dropped are swept up and thrown away and they never come back again. The very air closes behind you like water and soon your presence, which felt so weighty and permanent, has completely gone. Things happen once only and are never repeated, never return. Except in memory.

He sits for a long time at the table, not seeing, not hearing anything. When he feels strong enough to move he gets up very slowly and locks the house and goes out, walking into the world. His body feels old and through the dark lens on his eyes everything he knows looks strange and unfamiliar, as if he's lost in a country he's never visited before.

George Bradley

## *An East Egg Update*

I T HAPPENED IN a place called Plandome, a village on the north
shore of Long Island occupying the low ground at the south end of
Manhasset Bay, a village he was not old enough to know had existed
in its present condition for little more than ten years, as what had
been the area's large estates were sold and subdivided after World
War II to create a bedroom community for New York's booming
population of young professionals, the comfortable homes, set each
on a half acre, initially intended as middle-class housing since they
lay at what was once considered a far distance from the city, if not
so far that skyscrapers were not visible in clear weather from a promi-
nence nearby, lay at the second-to-last stop on a direct railroad
line, although as the suburbs of New York marched inexorably outward, ripples in a demographic pond, to an hour's commute, an hour
and a half, two hours, in time this neighborhood a mere forty
minutes from Manhattan would become expensive once again,
the province once more of the wealthy, though now their shelter and
no longer their indulgence, the which in turn had moved ever east-
ward, to the Hamptons, to Amagansett, and all the way to Montauk,

while this site had ceased to be one of riotous misbehavior, no longer an address of festive dissipation as it had been following the first war, in the twenties, that decade thirty years earlier which Fitzgerald had chosen as the moment of the tidy morality tale he set in the West Egg and East Egg of Great Neck and Sands Point, between which now lay Plandome, a name the boy was too young to parse, being barely old enough to spell three- and four-letter words and certainly not old enough to recognize that there must exist meaning in any nomenclature, too young to understand that the name of his native place, while perhaps originating in the classical education of a seventeenth-century gentleman for whom *domus plana* signified a house on the plain, had more recently appealed to the speculators of the Plandome Land Co. as a subliminal marketing device, its sound suggesting, albeit real estate agents could be counted on to provide more elegant explanations, the phrase "planned home," the development's very syllables its selling point, its calling card, its pitch.

His mother had not needed to wake him on that weekday, for he was still of an age when mornings arrive as joyful opportunity, and he had bounded from his bed to watch his father, laconic always and today more taciturn than ever, shower in the tub of the upstairs guest bathroom, thereby leaving the master bath to the uses of his wife, and then shave at the porcelain pedestal sink, towel himself dry, and harness himself in the businessman's uniform of white oxford-cloth shirt, gray flannel suit, and brown wingtip shoes, the boy gazing with interest as his father paused to adjust a narrow red-and-blue striped necktie in the unfogged reflection of the hall mirror, and because the boy's mother had taken longer than usual to dress herself that morning, it fell uncustomarily to the father to help the child, with an intimacy the two of them would never share in later life, not even when the older man lay dying and his middle-aged son attended his bedside and tried to ease his exit, but now that unhurried death was forty years in the future, and it was the parent's duty to help the child into a T-shirt and shorts and a pair of white socks that climbed almost halfway up the boy's thin shanks, which were still a few years away from appearing awkwardly long, to assist in buckling the boy's red leather shoes, which resembled the sandals he would wear sometimes at leisure as an adult, but which were children's wear in that era and sold in assorted miniature sizes at a store called Buster Brown, and finally to run a small comb taken from the breast pocket of the pin-striped suit through the boy's short and still blond hair and, picking him up easily, carry him down the stairs to the kitchen where the boy's mother had hurried to make breakfast, two poached eggs on toast with a glass of orange juice and a cup of percolated coffee for her husband and a bowl of Raisin Bran strengthened with wheat germ and further sweetened with sugar for the son she kissed on the top of the head, who ate hungrily and noticed her kiss his stoic father directly and he thought a touch too long on the mouth.

After breakfast the family took the family car, the boy's mother at the wheel of the green Nash wagon, sitting on its plush upholstery behind the divided windshield and operating the manual gearshift on its steering column which offered three possibilities forward, its "three on the tree" rather than the "four on the floor" of a subsequent sports car the boy would inherit from his father when it came his turn to drive, the father now staring out the passenger window and the boy comfortable between his parents, the three of them close together on the broad bench seat as the wife drove the husband the few blocks to Plandome station, a station much smaller than the end-of-the-line building in nearby Port Washington, this stop no more than a siding with a shelter against bad weather, a platform where their car arrived early on this morning and did not wait, so that the man would be left standing longer than usual beside the track and be seen there silhouetted against the sky by the boy pulling away in the car below, a tall graceful figure dressed even on a mild spring day in a gray fedora and the raincoat he wore as a topcoat and carrying a briefcase in one hand and the folded *Herald Tribune* he would soon be reading in the other, who had patted his son and had been preparing to climb from the car when the boy's mother had turned to call her husband by name, Ty, which was the boy's name also, Tyler, though he knew himself at that age as Tykie, "Ty, I don't want to be alone afterwards," and his father had leaned over him and kissed one of her high cheekbones and smoothed her dark red hair and said, "I know, I'll call if I can do anything about it," though he perhaps knew already that he could not, a man steady in the event of shipwreck or kamikaze attack but shy of human interaction, who left them then, mother and child, to continue on their way to the kindergarten the boy had been attending for several hours five days a week ever since September.

The son described the antic plot of a televised cartoon to his mother while the car they drove described three-quarters of a circle around a pond separated by a brief causeway from the body of Manhasset Bay, which causeway crossed, they skirted the larger expanse, the steep hills of Port Washington quickly rising on their right and the bay only here and there to be glimpsed through the landscaped planting of the waterfront houses on their left, until the road climbed suddenly, turning abruptly inland and again sharply left as they entered Port Washington's business district and started a gentle descent towards the harbor and town dock, and they were already within sight of a bait-and-tackle shop and Louie's Seafood restaurant when the ground flattened out into what had at one time been the estuary of a stream, the streambed now interred in a culvert running underneath a collection of small houses, in one of which, identifiable by a brightly colored sign reading, LITTLEST WHALE, lay their destination, a school arranged in three rooms of a private home that engaged to socialize four- and five-year-olds if fully toilet trained, the schoolhouse a simple slate-blue Cape with picture windows that looked across the heavily traveled road to a boatyard and to the yacht club where the boy would before long begin to sail, unquestioningly, the activity as natural as learning to play hockey on the ice of Minnesota, since children were in those years still expected to occupy themselves out-of-doors and since Manhasset Bay and Long Island Sound composed the outdoors that was available, and when their station wagon came to a halt his mother, dressed in a silk blouse and pleated skirt and wearing heels, as was not her habit, who stood five-foot-eight and was tall for a woman of her day, got out with the boy to walk him the short distance to the door, as was not her habit, saying as they went, "I have somewhere I have to be this morning, honey, so Mrs. Skinner will pick you up and take you to the playground. You play awhile with Nori, and I'll meet you there by lunch," and entered inside with her son to inform the two young women who shared the home and taught the school, signing a piece of paper on a clipboard as they requested and waving as she left to the child already running towards the house's fenced backyard, there to add his eager voice to the cries of others arrived before him, the assembled offspring greeting a fresh day with the untamed energy of healthy animals.

The boy did not play often with the Skinner girl, whose given name was Eleanor, an appellation assigned in honor, or at least in echo, of her mother's name of Helen, although in the 1960s, swept by the cultural transformations of that decade, she would legally change her name to Aquilegia, explaining it as the Latin word for her favorite flower and angrily insisting that her family refer to her as such, or at least as Legia, even if her friends tended to call her Ack, and although she would legally change it again in the 1970s, swept by the personal transformation of religious conviction, to Abishag and thenceforward be known as Abbie, not without some remorse, or at least some mercy, seeing as she would one day name her own daughter Elena in evident recompense to her elderly mother otherwise without namesake, though that stratagem, too, would fail when the granddaughter legally changed her name to Melody in an unsuccessful attempt to make her way in musical theater and afterwards kept the new name as equally appropriate when she married and made her home in Great Neck and began teaching music to students in junior high, so that Helen would at last depart this world unhonored, or at least un-echoed, leaving neither an Elena nor an Eleanor, or even a Nori, the affectionate convenience to which the latter of these ultimately abjured designations had been shortened in childhood and the name the girl would always bear in the mind of her classmate Tyler Keane, who would be well acquainted with her all his life, would attend her wedding and her daughter's wedding and no doubt attend her funeral as well if she did not first attend his own, and who would always feel an affinity for Nori Skinner, though she felt no affinity for him, sensing already in kindergarten that he was an oddity and would never fit comfortably into any social group, feeling the anomaly in him, so that she did not this day or any other run to him upon arrival or stand near him to recite the Pledge or gesticulate along with him during the undemanding calisthenics the teachers led the children through, did not sing nursery rhymes with him or lie beside him on a bath mat for their fifteen-minute nap or rise to share her snack with him or sit next to him to hear a story read concerning a black baby obtaining butter from melted tigers, and on that morning Nori had not giggled in his vicinity or whispered behind his back or said anything at all to him until Helen Skinner arrived at eleven o'clock sharp to sign the clipboard as the boy's mother had done before and grasp both children by the hand to lead them to the Skinners' Chevrolet, at which point Nori turned to Tykie and said, "You're not supposed to come with us."

The girl was mistaken, however, for on that day it had been planned that Tykie and Nori play, as Mrs. Skinner explained to the unbelted children bouncing in the big sedan's backseat, in the process addressing herself mostly to the boy and treating him with polite affection, so much so that the girl looked at him with unconcealed distaste and aimed several kicks in his direction before he drew his ankles out of range, even though the boy had done nothing to elicit the woman's elaborate attention and had on no prior occasion received it, familiar with Mrs. Skinner simply as a family friend and only in later years to understand that she and his mother had not settled accidentally in the same part of Long Island but instead had sought each other out since they were friends already, former roommates at a Seven Sisters college, serious and like-minded women who had conceived intellectual aims before they conceived children, who had read philosophy and put on plays and contributed to literary publications and only then graduated to marry handsome officers, a navy commander, an artillery captain, the veterans returning from the masculine extreme of war, down-to-earth young men who had experienced all they would ever need of excitement and wished only to make their private peace now that a general armistice had been declared, who valued stability above imagination, security more than adventure, who having occupied the rubble of what was once Berlin, having walked the littered plain that had only recently been Hiroshima, would in reaction labor to create in America's suburbia their shelter from the wider world's fatality and caprice, though of course those evils would follow them into their Plandomes and Port Washingtons; as they follow humans everywhere, visiting even these dogged men working at their self-appointed task and afflicting their restless women, too, their girlish wives deferring personal aspirations while preoccupied with child care, since almost no one in that era attempted, as many of their daughters would a generation after, to combine parenting with a career, these mothers instead fully busy with the babies the men arrived from overseas intent to get, young women devoted first to family and only later resolved to take time for themselves, or some of them at any rate, the most energetic and alive, the determined ones who would hold out until their sons and daughters were fully grown before turning to projects of their own, often to the surprise and not infrequently the consternation of husbands by then just starting to relax, their houses paid, their kids through college, their individual level of worldly success finally ascertained, men at that point ready merely to drink their scotch and play their golf who found that the women on whose assistance they were long accustomed to depend suddenly had little time for them, their former helpmates now unaccountably eager to enter local politics or institute a charity, unpredictably decided on opening a gallery or starting a lecture series or, in what would be Helen Skinner's case, running a used-book store, the active wives in middle age patently relieved to recover larger interests, clearly pleased to set aside the duties that had been the basis of their marriage and leave behind the years in which their highest goal was to nurture others, their biggest achievement to locate an available babysitter, their greatest utility to refer another woman to the right hairdresser or dentist or doctor, to stand in for a friend by retrieving her child from kindergarten.

It did not take long to drive the five short blocks from the Littlest Whale to the Main Street Public School, a huge mass of dark brick symmetrically constructed in palatial style around a courtyard that had been roofed over, a three-story dormered building so impressive for its architecture and for the commanding ground on which it stood, several acres at the highest point of the bluff formed where the ground rising above Manhasset Bay levels off in a plateau, that when the time eventually arrived for necessary renovations the edifice would be deemed too grand, or at any rate too costly, for children's occupancy and instead be converted to mature purpose, undergoing a transformation wherein a theater and studio space and attractive condominium apartments would be fashioned from the run-down rooms that in the 1950s still accommodated pupils in grades one through six, and with the school so close at hand, it was not quite eleven-fifteen and the elementary students had not yet been let out for lunch when Tykie and Nori began to run about the playground on the back side of the building, a gravel plain sequestered from the traffic on Main Street by a ten-foot chain-link fence and studded with a metal glyptoteca of juvenile diversions, a jungle gym and whirligig, chinning bars and monkey bars, a shinning pole and slide, stations of amusement assembled from sections of a lead-alloy pipe that would one day lead to lawsuits and be judged too unsafe for children's use and therefore be replaced by elaborate structures built of pressure-treated lumber that would in turn be deemed too toxic and so prompt other lawsuits, and on that gravel plain and among those leaden bars the boy and girl would race about for no more than half an hour before his mother came, an interval that in their self-consumed activity did not seem long to them but no doubt did to a solitary adult, for the playground was all but deserted at that hour, its only other occupants a pair of large black women sitting on a slatted bench and intermittently rocking the perambulators that contained the white babies in their charge, the two domestics greeting the unknown mother politely but making no room for her on their bench or in their Caribbean-accented conversation, so that Helen sat on a bench nearby and tried to concentrate on *Partisan Review* while her daughter, who felt no affinity for the boy with whom she was now expected to play, as she would be expected to play with him the following year in this very elementary school and thereafter to tolerate him in middle school and invite him to her parties in high school and greet him on college breaks and summer vacations and accept him with good grace on each of the many occasions he would be in her family home, pushed him and ran swiftly off, dancing out of his reach, darting easily from his outstretched hands, for she was quicker than he and more coordinated and would always be so, even when her body swelled to womanly proportions, always by far the better athlete, casually, easily, without the least tomboyish effort, although the boy would in adolescence practice all social sports assiduously and yet without the least distinction, never to excel in those endeavors, and so on that day, when the girl did not pretend to enjoy his presence, she literally ran circles around him, tapping him on the back and scampering ahead of him up the slide, tagging him on the chest and skipping away around the seesaw, resenting him openly on that day as she would be irritated by him covertly for years to come, until in later life, when the boy had achieved his small measure of reputation, had been reviewed and interviewed and awarded his one or two prizes, she would discover herself, if not proud, at least not displeased by their long association, but such developments were decades off, and on that day Nori Skinner stepped up behind him and whispered in his ear, for the girl had older siblings, "You're a suckfuck," and ran away, and as he ran to catch her she slowed down long enough to repeat, "You're a suckfuck," and ran off again, and though he did not understand the words, being an only child and only five, he knew enough of childhood etiquette to answer, "No I'm not, you are," and again the girl said, "You're a suckfuck," which was precocious language but not unheard-of on a playground at that age, and then, but the girl had older siblings, she said something that was truly unusual, words more extravagant in their aggression and deliberate offense, "Your mom's a suckfuck, too," and there his mother was, sitting beside her best friend and staring at her son.

The boy and girl ran over, seeing the adults, only to be brought up short, repulsed as if by some magnetic field, held at a distance by the expressions on their parents' faces, the boy's mother apparently angry, her mouth tight, her eyes intense, the girl's mother grimacing, and as the children approached the girl's mother was saying, "Of course I will, of course," and as they stood stopped in their tracks she brought her hands up to cover her distress, crying out, "Oh, Beth, how could they just say it to you like that," and the boy's mother did not answer the question, if it was a question, but instead stood up and stretched one arm in gesture to her son and said, "Tell your Aunt Helen thank you," and, frightened, the boy did as instructed, though he did not know what he was thanking her for and had never addressed the woman by that name previously, and evidently his Aunt Helen was too discomposed to reply, for she did not say anything back, keeping her face covered, and after a moment his mother said, "I'll call you," and stepped forward to take the boy's hand, and the two of them, mother and child, walked to the station wagon she had temporarily parked by an expired meter on Main Street, and there, after sitting motionless for a few moments behind the wheel, she said, "Listen to what your Aunt Helen says," and then turned the key in the ignition and let the clutch out once the motor caught, and although they often went home from the playground by driving the length of Main Street up to the post office and then along Port Washington Boulevard as far as the turnoff at Stonytown Road, this time, perhaps because she had just arrived that way, coming from an office complex near the Long Island Expressway, or perhaps because the car was already pointed west and she had no thought of reversing direction, when the car was in gear his mother continued straight ahead, over the brow of the hill, the little harbor soon coming into view, and then stepped on the clutch again, letting momentum carry them as they started to drift downward.

Leaving the elementary school, they followed the arc of lower Main Street as it wound around St. Stephen's Church, where the boy attended Bible class each Sunday while his parents took what comfort they could in the faith of their fathers, and they continued to descend, past the intersection where Shore Road diverges to the strand and the adjacent millpond where villagers once ground flour to make their daily bread, moving onward and arriving in sight of the bay, and where Main Street angles almost ninety degrees to run south and become Plandome Road, they passed the parking lot on the town dock, though they did not stop that morning, as they often did, to watch the motorboats filling up with an excursion's worth of gas or gaze a little while at the bright sails farther off and estimate the wind by whether there were whitecaps out near the Sound, the attendant in the kiosk soon learning to wave the car through, recognizing the green eyes and full head of auburn hair that the boy's mother had never reduced to a housewife's bob, "Sure, lady, as long as you like," but they did not stop that day, driving on instead and coming shortly to the Littlest Whale again and the boatyard across from it and again to the yacht club where the boy would as a teenager crew for family friends, racing on the era's wooden boats, the big Resolutes and MBOs, Manhasset Bay One designs, and where he would come to take genteel meals on summer evenings with his father and step-mother, and then with a succession of his father's widowed lady friends after the quiet man had divorced his second wife, dining under a striped awning as the declining sun sank behind Great Neck and Kings Point and sent raking rays to backlight the sloops and schooners that returned to hail the launches nosing among the moorings to bring the sailors ashore, and through those long meals on that panoramic terrace he would listen for the club's brass cannon to be fired at the instant of sunset, its ceremonial report signaling that another increment of daylight had been fully portioned out, but it was not now summer, and he was not yet old enough to dine with grown-ups, and his mother and he were retracing their morning route, and because the parent responded to the child's questions either briefly or not at all, the way an adolescent might answer an adult, they proceeded most of the way in silence, this time leaving the heights of Port Washington on their left before recrossing the little causeway and circling Leeds Pond and arriving at Plandome and the brick gateposts and cement driveway of their house, where his mother sat again for a few moments with the engine spent, as she had sat motionless a short while on Main Street before beginning the quick run home.

The boy's mother sat looking through the windshield at their house, a faux château in white stucco with a gray roof and black shutters, a house where letters would be waiting below the mail slot in the red front door, where lunch needed to be served and dinner prepared, where there were bedrooms to be made up and a living room to neaten, where the books she never got around to reading could be reshelved in the newly added den, and at last she stretched her fingers that had held the wheel and took a deliberate breath and turned to her son, saying, "Tell me about school, honey. What did you learn today?" and the boy, who learned many things that day, but few that he could identify at the time, a verbally agile child who had not that morning added anything to his growing vocabulary at school, where the instructive monosyllables were still imparted by Dick and Jane and not yet by red or blue fish, and who had of course not to date acquired any of the difficult words his parents were learning to use, flowery terms with their calices in educated English and their roots in ancient Greek, *prognosis, myelosarcoma,* five years old and an eager absorber of language, the boy said what came to mind, "Nori Skinner's a suckfuck," and the sound of the blow landing by his ear as his mother slapped him hard on the cheek was a shock in itself, so that he burst immediately into tears, weeping even before he felt the sting and smart, and then his mother was crying, too, sobbing as she swept him into her arms, hugging him close, shaking, rocking, continuing to cry long after he had stopped, his face wet with her hot tears, and in later years when Tyler Keane tried to recall his mother, who died before he turned six, the only memory he could be confident was truly his own and not the composite of stories told by his Aunt Helen or by her husband, the man he called his Uncle Frank, the only image he knew for certain was not an extrapolation of the photographs that his unhappy father could not bear to see displayed and that the boy found as a teenager in a box at the back of a closet, the one recollection he was sure he had not in some way concocted was that slap and the shudder of teary embrace that followed, because even though the past into which we are ceaselessly borne is the landscape we necessarily inhabit, the present too fleeting to be lived in and the future no more than theory, a hypothesis ultimately untested, even though the myriad details of bygone experience seem to swim around us always, flowing, swirling, an immersion tending on us every instant, shaping our subconscious as waves define a shore, still, in comparison to so much incident, weighed against the sheer magnitude of prior circumstance, we remember almost nothing of our lives, and out of all that ocean of lapsed particulars what we do recall, mostly and most vividly, is pain.

# Ron Rash

## *Into the Gorge*

H IS GREAT-AUNT HAD been born on this land, lived on it eight
decades, knew it as well as she knew her husband and children.
That was what she'd always claimed. She could tell you to the week
when the first dogwood blossom would brighten the ridge, the first
blackberry darken enough to harvest. Then her mind had wandered
into a place she could not follow, taking with it all the people she
knew, their names and connections, whether they lived or whether
they'd died. But her body lingered, shed of an inner being, empty as
a cicada husk.

Knowledge of the land was the one memory that refused to dissolve. During his great-aunt's last year, Jesse would step off the school
bus and see her hoeing a field behind her farmhouse, breaking
ground for a crop she never sowed, but the rows were always straight,
right-depthed. Her nephew, Jesse's father, worked in an adjoining
field. The first few times, Jesse's father had taken the hoe from her
hands, led her back to her house, but she'd soon be back in the field.
After a while neighbors and kin just let her hoe. They brought meals
and checked on her as often as they could. Jesse always walked
rapidly past her field edge. His great-aunt never looked up, her gaze

fixed on the hoe blade and the dark soil it raised and churned, but he had always feared she might raise her eyes one day, acknowledge him, though what she might want to convey to him, Jesse could not say.

Then one March day she disappeared. The men in the community searched all afternoon and into evening, and as the temperature dropped and sleet crackled around them like static, the men rippled farther outward, lighting lanterns and moving into the gorge. Jesse watched from his family's pasture, the lantern flames growing smaller, soon disappearing and reappearing like fox fire, crossing the creek that held the speckled trout he fished for, then on past the ginseng patch he helped his father harvest. Going deeper into land that had been in the family for over two hundred years, toward the original homestead, the place she'd been born.

They found her at dawn, her white hair cauled with ice, her back leaned against a tree as if waiting for the searchers to arrive. But that was not the strangest thing. She was completely unclothed, her gingham dress and undergarments cast around her, shoes and bonnet found up the ridge. Years later Jesse read in a magazine that people dying of hypothermia did such a thing, believing heat, not the cold, was killing them. Back then woods had been communal, NO TRESPASSING signs an affront, but after his great-aunt's death, neighbors soon found places other than the gorge to hunt and fish, gather blackberries and galax. Her ghost was still down there, many came to believe, including Jesse's own father, who never returned to harvest the ginseng he'd planted and tended. When the park service made an offer on the family's old homestead, Jesse's father and aunts sold. That was in 1958, and the government paid sixty dollars an acre. Now, fifty years later, Jesse studied Sampson Ridge, where bulldozers razed woods for another gated community. He wondered how much those sixty acres were worth. Easily a million dollars.

But what would he do with that much money if he had it? His house and twenty acres were paid for, as was his truck. The tobacco lease earned less each year but still enough for a widower with grown children who were able to support themselves. Enough as long as he didn't have to go to the hospital or his truck didn't throw a rod. He needed some extra money put away for that. Not a million, but some.

So two autumns ago Jesse had gone into the gorge, following the old logging road to the homestead, then up the ridge's shadowy north face, where his father had seeded and harvested his ginseng patch. Plants were still there, evidently untouched for half a century. Some of the plants rose to Jesse's waist. There was more ginseng than his father could have dreamed of, a hillside spangled with bright yellow leaves, enough roots to bulge Jesse's knapsack. Afterward, he'd carefully replanted the seeds just as his father had done, then walked out of the gorge, past the iron gate that kept vehicles off the logging road. A tin marker nailed to a nearby tree said, U.S. FOREST SERVICE.

Now another autumn had come. A wet autumn, which was good for the plants, as Jesse had verified three days ago when he'd checked them. Once again he gathered the knapsack and trowel from the woodshed. He also took the .32 rimfire from his bedroom drawer. It was late in the year for snakes, but after days of rain the afternoon was warm and sunny enough to bring a rattler or copperhead out to sun.

He followed the old logging road into the gorge, the green knapsack slung over his shoulder, the pistol in the outside pouch. Jesse's arthritic knees ached as he made the descent. They would ache more that night, even after rubbing liniment on them. He wondered how many more autumns he'd be able to make the trip. Till he was seventy, Jesse figured, giving himself three more years. The ground was slippery from all the rain, and he walked slowly. A broken ankle or leg would be a serious thing this far from help, but it was more than that. He wanted to enter the gorge respectfully.

When he got in sight of the homestead, the land leveled out but the ground grew soggier. He saw the boot prints he'd left three days earlier. Then he saw another set, coming up the logging road from the other direction. Boot prints, as well, but smaller. He looked around, not just up the road but toward the homestead and edge of the woods. He saw no one, so he kneeled down, his joints creaking as he did so.

The prints appeared at least a day old, maybe more. They stopped on the logging road where they met Jesse's, then veered toward the homestead. Jesse got up and looked around again before walking through the withered broomsedge and joe-pye weed. He passed a cairn of stones that once had been a chimney, a dry well covered with a slab of tin so rusty it served as more warning than safeguard. The boot prints were no longer discernible but he knew where they'd end. Led the son of a bitch right to it, he told himself, and wondered how he could have been stupid enough to walk the road on a rainy morning. But when he got to the ridge, the plants were still there, the soil around them undisturbed. Probably just a hiker or a bird-watcher, Jesse figured, that or some punk looking to poach someone's marijuana, not knowing the ginseng was worth even more. Either way, he'd been damn lucky.

Jesse lifted the trowel from the knapsack and got on his knees. The plants had more color than three days ago, the berries a deeper red, the leaves bright as polished gold. It always amazed him that such radiance could grow in soil the sun rarely touched, like finding rubies and sapphires on the gloomy walls of a cave. He worked with care but with haste. The first time he'd returned here, two years earlier, he'd felt a sudden coolness, a slight lessening of light, as if a cloud had passed over the sun. But when he'd looked up the sky was cloudless. Imagination, he'd told himself then, but it had made him work faster, with no pauses to rest.

Jesse jabbed the trowel into loamy soil, probing inward with care so as not to cut the root, slowly bringing it to light. The root was a big one, six inches long, tendrils sprouting from the core like clay renderings of human limbs. Jesse scraped away dirt from the root and placed it in the knapsack. Just as carefully, he buried the seeds to insure another harvest. As he crawled a few feet left to unearth another plant, he felt the moist dirt seeping its way through the knees of his blue jeans. He liked being this close to the earth, smelling it, feeling it on his hands and under his nails, the same feeling as when he planted his tobacco sprigs in the spring. A song he'd heard on the radio drifted into his head, a woman wanting to burn down a whole town. He let the tune play on, tried to fill in the refrain as he pressed the trowel into the earth.

"You can lay that trowel down," a voice behind Jesse said. "Then raise your hands."

He turned and saw a man in gray pants and shirt with a U.S. Forest Service patch on the shoulder. Short blond hair, dark eyes. A young man, probably not even thirty. A pistol filled his right hand and it was pointed at Jesse.

"Raise your hands," the younger man said again, louder this time. "Don't get up."

Jesse did as he was told. The park ranger came closer, picked up the knapsack, and stepped away. Jesse watched as he opened the compartment with the ginseng root, then the smaller pouch. The ranger held the .32 in his open palm. The gun had belonged to Jesse's grandfather and father before it was passed on to Jesse. The ranger inspected it as he might an arrowhead or spear point.

"That's just for the snakes," Jesse said.

"Possession of a firearm is illegal in the park," the ranger replied. "You've broken two laws, federal laws. You'll be getting some jail time for this." He looked like he might say more, then seemed to decide against it.

"This ain't right," Jesse said, lowering his arms. "My daddy planted the seeds for this patch. That ginseng wouldn't even be here if it wasn't for him. And that gun, if I was poaching I'd have a rifle or shotgun."

What was happening didn't seem quite real. The world, the very ground he stood on, felt altered, more distant, as if he were watching himself on videotape or in a movie. Jesse almost expected somebody, though he couldn't say who, to come out of the woods with a camera in hand, laughing about the joke they'd all just played on him. The

ranger placed the .32 in the knapsack and set his own pistol in its hol-
ster. He unclipped the walkie-talkie from his belt, pressed a button,
and spoke.

"He did come back, and I've got him."

A staticky voice responded, the words indiscernible to Jesse.

"No, he's too old to be much trouble," the ranger said. "We'll be
waiting on the logging road."

The ranger pressed a button and placed the walkie-talkie back on
his belt. Jesse read the name on the silver name tag: "Barry Wilson."

"You any kin to the Wilsons over on Balsum Mountain?"

"No," the younger man said. "I grew up in Charlotte."

The walkie-talkie crackled and the ranger picked it up, said okay,
and placed it back on his belt.

"Call Sheriff Atwood," Jesse said. "He'll tell you I've never been in
any trouble before. Never, not even a speeding ticket."

"This isn't his jurisdiction."

"Can't you just forget this?" Jesse asked. "It ain't like I was growing
marijuana. There's plenty that do in this park. I know that for a fact.
That's worse than what I done."

The ranger smiled. "We'll get them eventually, old man, but their
bulbs burn brighter than yours. They're not stupid enough to leave us
footprints leading to their crops."

The ranger slung the knapsack over his shoulder.

"You've got no right to talk to me like that," Jesse said.

There was still plenty of distance between them, but the ranger
looked like he contemplated another step back.

"If you're going to give me trouble, I'll just go ahead and cuff
you now."

Jesse almost told the younger man to come on and try, but he
made himself look at the ground, get himself under control before he
spoke. "No, I ain't going to give you any trouble," he finally said, raising his eyes.

The ranger nodded toward the logging road. "After you, then."

Jesse moved past him, stepping through the broomsedge, past the ruined chimney, the ranger to his right, two steps behind. Jesse veered slightly to his left, moving nearer to the old well. He paused and glanced back at the ranger.

"That trowel of mine, I ought to get it."

The ranger paused, as well, was about to reply when Jesse took a quick side step and with two hands shoved the ranger toward the well. The ranger didn't fall until one foot, then the other went through the rotten tin. He didn't go all the way through, just up to his arms, his fingernails scraping the tin for leverage. The ranger's hands found purchase, one on a hank of broomsedge, the other on the metal's firmer edging. He began pulling himself out, wincing as the rusty tin tore cloth and skin. He looked at Jesse, who stood above him.

"You've really fucked up now," the ranger gasped.

Jesse bent down and reached not for the younger man's hand but his shoulder. He pushed hard. The ranger's hands clutched only air as he fell back through the rotten metal. There was a simultaneous thump and snap of bone as he hit the well's dry floor. Seconds passed but no other sound rose from the darkness.

The knapsack lay at the edge of the well, and Jesse snatched it up. He ran, not toward his farmhouse, but into the woods. He did not look back again but bear-crawled through the ginseng patch and up the ridge, his breaths loud pants. Trees thickened around him, oaks and poplars, some hemlocks. The soil was thin and moist, and he slipped several times. He stopped halfway up the ridge, his heart battering against his chest like something snared. When it finally calmed, he heard a vehicle coming up the logging road and saw a pale green forest service jeep. A man and a woman got out. Both wore forest service uniforms, pistols holstered to their waists.

Jesse went on up the ridge, passing through another patch of ginseng, probable descendants from his father's original seedlings. He moved on. The sooner he got to the ridge crest, the sooner he could make his way across it toward the gorge head. His legs were leaden now, his breaths never quite enough. The extra pounds he'd put on the last few years were a swaying gut-sack draped over his belt. His mind went dizzy, and he slipped and skidded a few yards downhill. For a while he lay still, his body sprawled on the slanted earth, his arms and legs flung outward. Jesse felt the leaves cushioning the back of his head, an acorn nudging against a shoulder blade. Above him, oak branches appeared not just to rise toward but to pierce a darkening sky. He remembered the fairy tale about a giant beanstalk and imagined how convenient it would be simply to climb off into the clouds.

Several minutes passed before Jesse tried to regain his feet. He turned his head so that one ear touched the ground, as if listening for the faintest footfall of pursuit. It seemed so wrong to be sixty-seven years old and running away from someone. Not just wrong, but impossible in the world he'd known up until this moment. Old age was supposed to give you some dignity, at the very least, some respect. He remembered the night the searchers brought his great-aunt out of the gorge. The men had stripped off their heavy coats to cover her body and had taken turns carrying her. They had been silent and somber as they came into the yard.

Even after the women had taken the corpse into the farmhouse to be washed and dressed, the men stayed on his great-aunt's porch. Some smoked hand-rolled cigarettes, others cudded their jaws with tobacco. Jesse had sat on the lowest porch step and listened, knowing the men would forget he was there. They did not talk of how they'd found his great-aunt or the times she'd wandered from her house to the garden. The men spoke instead of a woman who could tell you tomorrow's weather by looking at the evening sky, a godly woman who'd taught Sunday school into her seventies. They told stories about her in a quiet, reverent way, as if now that she was dead, she'd become again who she truly was.

Jesse rose slowly. He hadn't twisted an ankle or broken an arm and that seemed the first bit of luck since he'd walked into the gorge. He made his way on up the slant land. Once on the ridge crest he sat down. His legs were so weak he clutched a maple sapling to ease himself to the ground. He looked below, and through the trees he saw an orange-and-white rescue squad van at the homestead. The park ranger was on a stretcher, and two men were carrying him toward the van's open doors. Jesse was too far away to tell the ranger's condition, or even if the man were alive.

At the least a broken arm or leg, he knew, and tried to think of an injury that could make things all right, maybe a concussion or shock from pain enough to make the ranger forget what Jesse looked like. Jesse tried not to think about whether the snapped bone was in the back or neck.

The back door of the van closed from within, and the vehicle turned onto the logging road. The siren was off, but the beacon cast wide swipes of red into the day's waning light, making the trees look as if they'd been drenched in blood. The woman ranger scoured the hillside with binoculars, sweeping without pause over where Jesse sat. Another green forest service truck drove up, two more rangers spilling out. Then Sheriff Atwood's car, as silent as the ambulance.

The sun lay behind Clingmans Dome now, and he knew that waiting any longer would only make it harder to see. He got up slowly and moved in a stupor of exhaustion, feet stumbling over roots and rocks, swaying like a drunk. When he got far enough, he'd be able to come down the ridge, ascend the narrow gorge mouth. But he was so tired now he didn't know how he could go any farther without resting. His knees felt like they grated bone on bone, popping and crackling each time they bent or twisted. He panted and wheezed and imagined his lungs an accordion that never unfolded enough.

"Old" and "a fool." That's what the ranger had called Jesse. An old man no doubt. His body told him so every morning when he awoke to a litany of aches. The liniment he applied to his joints and muscles each morning and night made him think of himself as a creaky, rust-corroded machine that had to be oiled and warmed up before it could sputter to life. Maybe a fool, as well, he acknowledged, for who other than a fool could have gotten into such a fix?

Jesse found a felled oak and sat down, a mistake because he couldn't imagine summoning the energy to rise. He looked through the trees and saw that Sheriff Atwood's car was gone, but the ranger truck and jeep were still there. Only one person lingered by the homestead and Jesse knew the rest searched the woods for him. He listened a few more moments but heard only a crow cawing farther up the ridge. He took the ginseng from the knapsack and threw it into the thick woods below him, just in case they came to his house and searched. It might still be all right, Jesse told himself softly. At least he'd had the good sense to pick up the knapsack, so they couldn't trace the pistol back to him, no fingerprints either. Even if the ranger identified him, wouldn't it just be his word against his?

Jesse contemplated ridding himself of the knapsack and pistol, as well, knowing there'd be no better place to prevent their ever being found. He tossed only the knapsack down the ridge. The gun had belonged to his father, and even if they found it in his house, they'd have no proof it was the one the ranger had seen.

Night fell fast now, darkness webbing the gaps between tree trunks and branches. Below him, high-beam flashlights flickered on to probe the gathering dark. Jesse remembered two weeks after his great-aunt's burial, Graham Sutherland had come out of the gorge shaking and chalk-faced, not able to tell what had happened until Jesse's father gave him a draft of whiskey. Graham had been fishing near the old homestead and glimpsed something on the far bank, there for just a moment then gone. A warm afternoon, the second day of spring, but the air in the gorge had become cold and damp. Graham had seen her then, moving through the trees, her arms out-stretched. "Beseeching me," Graham had told them. "Not speaking, but letting that cold and damp touch my very bones so I'd feel what she felt." He'd paused and raised his cup for more whiskey. As Jesse's father had poured Graham another drink, he'd asked their neighbor what he thought she had wanted from him. "She wanted me to stay with her down there," Graham had said. "She didn't want to be alone."

Jesse arose and moved on until he came to where he could make his descent and meet the logging road on its uphill grade. A flashlight moved below him, its holder merged with the dark. The light bobbed as if on a river's current, a river running uphill all the way to the iron gate that marked the end of forest service land. The searchers were closer to him now, no more than a hundred yards. The light turned away, bobbed and swayed back down the logging road. Someone shouted, and the disparate lights gathered like sparks of a fire returning to their source. Then headlights and engines came to life. Two sets of red taillights dimmed and soon disappeared.

Jesse made his way down the slope, one hand close to the ground to break his falls. Branches slapped his face. He butted up against trees, but at least it was downhill. Once on level land Jesse let minutes pass as he listened for footsteps or a cough on the logging road, someone left behind to trick him into coming out. After a while a rind of white moon and a few sparse stars settled overhead, enough light for him to make out a human form.

Jesse moved quietly up the logging road. Get back in the house and you'll be all right, he told himself. He came to the iron gate and slipped under. It struck him only then that someone might be waiting. He went to the right and came to the pasture edge. He studied the house. No lights were on, as he'd left it, but he remained outside the barbed wire fence, eventually able to see the front porch as he moved up the pasture, his fingers lightly brushing the sagging wire and dulled barbs.

Someone sat on the steps. Jesse looked past the porch and driveway, saw the squad car parked on the road. Soon a pickup came down the road and parked beside the squad car. Two men got out, lowered the tailgate, and a torrent of bloodhounds poured from the truck bed. The dogs barked and whined as the men buckled on their leashes.

Jesse followed the fence back toward the gorge. Everything suddenly was unmoored, not quite real. He paused and clasped his hand around one of the fence's thorns, felt the rusty metal pierce his palm.

Pain jarred him from what seemed a waking dream. He needed time to think, to trace back all of what had happened, the same way he might untangle a fishing line on a reel. Maybe then find a way out of the trouble. He came to the end of the pasture and slipped back under the gate.

The moon had disappeared but enough stars yet flickered for a little light. Jesse followed the land's downward tilt, the same way he'd come hours before, going in circles. The ground was leveling out when he heard the hounds coming in his direction, flashlights waving behind them. Jesse could make out the outline of the homestead's ruined chimney. As he moved closer, the chimney solidified, grew darker than the dark around it, as if an unlit passageway into some greater darkness.

Jesse took the .32 from his pocket and let the pistol's weight settle in his hand. Throw it far as you can so they won't find it. He turned his body to face the woods then hesitated, even now reluctant to give up the heirloom. He hurled the pistol, almost falling to the ground with the effort, but the weapon only went a few feet before thunking against a tree. It landed close by, probably on the road itself or the homestead's open ground, but Jesse couldn't tell exactly where. The hounds came moiling into the gorge, flashlights dipping and swaying behind them. Jesse headed into the far woods toward the creek, thinking maybe the hounds would lose his scent if he waded through the water. Then he could circle back and find the gun.

He did not see the creek but fell off a bank into it. He got up and waded downstream, his boots quickly soggy with water. But it worked. There was soon a confusion of yapping and howling, the flashlights no longer moving toward him but instead sweeping the woods from one still point. He fell and something sharp tore into his shoulder.

Jesse stepped from the creek and sat down to wring his socks and pour water from the boots. As he did, he remembered his boot prints, how they led right down the logging road from his house. The law had ways of matching boots to a print, and not just a certain foot size and make of a boot. He'd seen on a TV show how they could match the worn part of the sole to a print. He took off the boots and socks, stuffed the socks inside the boots and threw them at the dark. Like the gun, they did not go far before hitting something solid.

It took him a long time to find his way back to the logging trail. Once out of the woods Jesse saw that the stars had thickened and the road was easily seen. He followed it until he was in sight of the homestead. The hounds and the men hunting him had gathered between the homestead and the iron gate. The pistol lay somewhere near them, perhaps found already. The dogs were restless, yelping and whining to get back onto the trail, but the searchers had evidently decided to wait until morning to continue. They huddled together, and though Jesse was too far away to hear them, he knew they talked to help the time pass. Perhaps they had coffee and food with them. Jesse suddenly realized he was thirsty, so thirsty it seemed as if his throat was lined with sandpaper. He thought about going back to the creek and drinking from it, but he was too weary.

Dew wet his bare feet as he passed the far edge of the homestead and went to the woods' edge where the ginseng was. He sat down, and in a few minutes felt the night's chill envelop him. A frost warning, the radio had said. He thought of his great-aunt taking off her clothes and how, despite the scientific explanation, her unclothing had always seemed to Jesse a final abdication of everything she'd once been.

He looked toward the eastern sky. It seemed he'd been running a week's worth of nights, but he saw the stars hadn't begun to pale. The first pink smudges on the far ridgeline were a while away, perhaps hours. The night would linger long enough for what would come or not come. He waited.

John Edgar Wideman

# *Microstories*

## RAIN

NEVER ENDING RAIN had seemed the truth forever until the day he'd been born, and rain stopped the very next day and no rain since. No one he'd spoken to had much to say about rain. Nothing good to say. They were glad it was finished. Envied his freedom from what rain had imposed on their lives. Why was he so curious about something people assured him had been no fun. Worse than no fun. Some people would shake their heads to suggest he harbored an unhealthy obsession. Why this worrying after rain. If he had known rain, they said, if he'd been there, he'd shut up about rain, they warned or advised or teased or just turned away to end a conversation they could not stomach. None of them, not a single soul yet, understood his need to recover what he'd missed, rain falling for the final time the day he'd been born, the rain other people had forgotten or had no desire to recall, and him with a million questions, a million dreams, tears once when he couldn't explain his yearning to the only person who had ever seemed really curious, but how could he describe to her something lost, and worse, lost irrevocably, before he had experienced it, how could he express his loss because what was rain, after all, what could he say except the next to nothing others had told him about rain that had never missed a day before he arrived and would start again, he was sure (and this might be the unbearable part), the instant he left.

## DIVORCE

He is dressing for his grown-up daughter. How strange, he thinks, peering into his closet. To be picking this and discarding that as if he's going to a wedding or funeral. Since when (how long, how long) is meeting her an occasion. A date. The peacock dashiki to give her a laugh. The good suit to offend her. Bell-bottom jeans she'll smirk at or, worse, ignore. As if he can predict the consequences of his choices in her eyes. As if he knows what they'll talk about in the restaurant she's chosen. The waiter setting down a cup of coffee that rattles in its saucer, spotting the white blaze of tablecloth before they can even begin. Not the waiter's fault. Nobody's fault, really, that their table happens to be at the foot of a mountain range with jagged peaks looming above them, obdurate and unimpeachable as annular rings of a tree. The crack, the fissure begins under there, under the stony folds of mountains stacking up, stacking up. Too much weight, too many years. The earth shudders, dances the rug under the poor, pompadoured waiter's feet. *Sorry . . . sorry . . .* he faintly warbles . . . *excuse me,* a canary dying of what's to come.

## THIRTEEN

Now comes the thirteen story. Thirteen the day of my son's birth. Lucky. Unlucky. How could it happen. On the thirteenth, one fifteen-year-old kills another. The chance of that one particular thing happening small as a single breath in the universe. The universe the size of the chance against the possibility of that moment undoing itself, never happening, going away. With two Arizona lawyers, my son, his mother I'd stopped loving, and me in it, the car speeds south to north, Phoenix to Flagstaff. I'm driving, listening to one lawyer speak when the other, suffering unbeknownst to us from his own lonely addiction, interjects something about too bad it's not *Massachusetts,* which he pronounces *Massa-two-sits,* before he resumes staring out the window. Arizona wants to start executing juveniles, the other lawyer continues. The state's looking for the right kid to kill. A black kid would suit them perfectly. Plea bargaining our only chance to save your son's life.

Years before I'm able to sit through this ride again, before I can speak to anyone about Arizona's jails full of Mexicans and Indians, the zigzag mountain peaks stitching sky to earth, sumptuous oil spills of sunset, one sudden burst of rain battering dry plains like sheets of tears. On the last night of a Western tour, returning from the Grand Canyon, a group of fifteen-year-olds stay at an Arizona motel. Next morning my son's roommate found stabbed to death. My son missing. For days presumed dead, tortured, buried by some madman in the Arizona desert or mountains. Then my son calls home. We fly to Arizona to turn him in. Plead. Life the best we can hope for. After long silence Freddie Jackson's "You Are My Lady," my son's favorite song, on the car radio. One note breaks me down. Like one shooting-star mote of plaque can explode a brain. One instant of insanity explodes two boys' lives. Sheets of tears. You only get one chance. That's all a father gets with a son. A child's life in your hands once. That's it. Once. He was born in New Jersey and I took classes to assist at his birth, but some clown passed out the day before, so on the thirteenth the delivery room off-limits for fathers and I missed the moment the earth cracked and she squeezed out his bloody head.

## AT&T

They employ the same robot in prisons three thousand miles apart to inform you that you have a collect phone call from an inmate. Each time he wonders if part of the astronomical charge for a five-minute call from a prison includes a bill for forty or so seconds of the lady robot's time announcing, interrupting, signing off. Once he'd responded to her, imitating her recorded voice, the robot cadence and tone she'd taught him. Proposed marriage. Why not. Two could live as comfortably as one on the enormous profits she must reap participating how many goddamn times a day coast to coast and everywhere in between in the misery of conversations between the incarcerated and those not. If you can get away with it, why not charge a rate fifty, a hundred times more than what the unincarcerated pay to speak to one another. Are you still there, darling, he'd asked her after he said, I love you, and she didn't respond. Then he said, No . . . no, it's okay, you don't have to answer. You don't need to tell me your name and I won't tell you mine. After all, if we meet in the street, you, me, my brothers and sons and fathers when they're free, who'd want to remember all this.

## FAT LIVER

The campaign for attaining a higher level of enlightenment goes well. *Hurrah. Hurrah. No more foie gras.* A silly banner, she admits. And maybe a silly cause. Who gives a crap if it becomes a crime to force-feed ducks and geese, a crime to package and sell their agony, she asks herself. Imagines bloated black kids with tubes down their throats fed buckets of KFC, rivers of Orange Crush, tons of Big Macs. Imagines the iron maws of prisons pried open, dark bodies crammed in. Sees America's bare, fat ass upturned in the air, oil pumping in like an enema. Imagines her fellow citizens' fuzzy heads bobbing like baby birds in a nest, every beak propped open by a funnel, the grinning president stuffing them with lies, terror, disinformation, war. Maybe she'll skip the foie gras victory march and victory party this afternoon.

*Ring. Ring.* That must be Sarah calling. Or perhaps Samuel. Though a bit early for him. Either one, it will break her heart to answer. No, I'm staying home this afternoon. No, our chance for a life together is over. No. No. Please don't call me ever again. The disappointed faces of Sarah and Samuel blend. Separate tales for each one collapse into one long, sad story. *Ring. Ring.* She realizes she's crying and that her mouth's open. The phone with a million miles of AT&T cable spooled behind it pushing through her lips, filling her to bursting.

## WAR STORIES

I have a friend, a kind of friend anyway, I talked with only once, and that once we'd seemed simpatico. I learned a lot from a story he'd written about things men carried when they fought in Vietnam. Years have passed and I've lost track of him, so to speak. I need to talk with him now because I'm trying to understand the war here in America, the worst war, in spite of mounting casualties in wars abroad, this war filling prisons, filling pockets, emptying schools, minds, hearts, a war keeping people locked down at home, no foreign enemies to defeat, just ourselves defeated by fear of one another, a war incarcerating us all in killing fields, where the only rule is feed on the bodies of fellow inmates or surely they will feed on yours. What do combatants carry in this war, in this civil strife waged within stone walls, in glass cages, barbed-wire-enclosed ghettos of poverty and wealth, behind the lines, between the lines. Can friend be distinguished from foe by what they wear. By the way they walk, how they talk. Their words, their silence. A war different, though not entirely unlike others in Afghanistan, Iraq, and soon Iran or wherever else folly incites us to land our young men and women with whatever they will carry into battle this time and carry when they return like chickens Malcolm warned always come home to roost. Not separate wars, really. No more separate than different colors of skin that provide logic and cover for war. No more separate than the color of my skin from yours, my friend, if we could meet again and talk about carrying the things we carry, about what torments me, an old man ashamed of this country I assume you still live in, too.

## HOME FROM COLLEGE

She counts her mother's missing fingers. Two more gone to the disease. Wonders if the rumor reaching her at school of toes rotting inside those ratty bedroom slippers is true. When she's away and scared, she counts the missing parts of her mother, and the count always equals one. One mother. She smiles and counts again. One. The magic answer calms her each time she figures out how many mothers she has left, just to be sure, just to make sure. One. One mother minus two fingers equals what. One. Take away ten toes. Still never equals less than one. Until a day no absent parts to count. No more lost fingers or toes. No sad little round potbelly looks like it's full to bursting, tiny as it is, because her mother, skinny as a string, keeps no food down. Nothing gone away to count. Just the pink, slinky robe that always reminds her of the silvery one she was never allowed to suck her thumb with the silky tail of sleeping on her mother's lap. No missing poke of knee or nipple under the pink robe draped flat over the couch arm next to the kitchen door, the couch end where her mother settles each morning. Nothing new to minus. Only a girl standing beside an empty couch who would, if she could, subtract one from herself, count a missing part that starts the count again.

## GIBLETS

Clara's dog Giblets had four legs. One leg for each day of the week. Now, Clara Johnson understood as well as you understand that each week the Lord sends got seven days, but Clara's memories are not your memories. Once upon a time, every Friday and Saturday and Sunday of every week were holy days in her mama's house, and Clara'd get her ass kicked often and terribly, bloodied by any comb or switch or board or cord her mother could lay her hands on, because Clara never could satisfy her mama by being as good as she was s'posed to be from the hour they started till those three days of church and praying and singing and sitting still as stone were over. So as soon as Clara out on her own she amputated the merciless days. Her weeks four days long with no scars, no beatings, no screaming, no cringing in a dark corner. Go away, goddamn church, and she never missed one of the cruel three days she cut out of her week, not once, never, just like Giblets after one long howl just lay there quiet and didn't miss his leg she chopped off when Tyrone from over at Mason's lounge told her a church he'd heard about commenced its holy days on Thursdays.

## AUTOMATIC

They stole my money, my father says. I know exactly what you mean, man, I could have responded, but don't want to get him started on the frozen poem of frustration and rage he can't help reciting, stanza by stanza, because the thieves won't send him the prizes their letters declare he's won. I've come to take away his car keys. Or rather do what our worried family has decided, Ask for his car keys. We'd tried before. No way, José, he let us know. Me and that old girl automatic. Drive this whole city blindfold. Today it's as if he knew before I knocked, someone would be coming by and there would be less of him left as soon as he opened his door, so he's reminding me, whatever my good intentions, that I'm also just like those others who'd lied, stripped, and stolen from him his entire life and aren't finished yet, vultures circling closer and closer, withholding his prizes, picking his bones clean because an old black man too tired to shoo them off anymore. His quick mind leaving him fast but thank goodness my father no pack rat. Until the end his apartment fairly neat. He keeps only the final letters in their boldly colored, big-print envelopes guaranteeing a Corvette or condo in Acapulco or million in cash megaprize. Beside his bed and on the kitchen table large stacks of these lying motherfuckers that taunt and obsess him, his last chance, a glorious grand finale promised, though how and when not precisely spelled out in the fine print. He never quite figures out the voices on the other end of his daily 800 calls are robots. Curses the menus white women's voices chirp. His response to my request he surrender his keys gentler. A slightly puzzled glance, a smile breaking my heart, *No, Daddy, no. Don't do it,* I'm crying out helplessly, silently, as he passes me the keys.

## MESSAGE

A message in red letters on the back of a jogger's T-shirt passed by too quickly for me to memorize exactly. Something about George Bush going too far in his search for terrorists and WMDs. A punch line sniggering that Bush could have stayed home and found the terrorist he was looking for in the mirror. I liked it. The message clever, I thought, and jacked the idea for my new line of black-lettered T-shirts: America went way too far looking for slaves. Plenty niggers in the mirror for sale.

## NORTHSTAR

She said I find the idea of anal sex quite un-sexy, and he dropped the subject. A tube of lubricating cream that had appeared magically on the perforated seat of an antique, wire-legged stool that served as a bedside table disappeared. How come men think they can make up the rules to liberate women, she'd asked before the subject dropped. Two weeks later when it happens, on his knees hunched over her in the dark bedroom, he's alone. Alone as the last person alive on earth and wonders if that's how a fugitive slave might have felt the first night free, racing through black forests and swamps following the Northstar, and remembers a dinner party in her brother's garden, the moon and a solitary star shining high above the patio table where everybody's happy drinking and eating, then the two of them walking around a corner of the house, beyond the arc of light cast by a fat candle burning in a crystal globe on the tabletop, the sky full of stars, the quiet amazingly deep though they'd moved only a few steps from the others, and there he'd taken her hand and wanted to say, I'm sorry. I didn't mean to upset you. Just forget I ever brought up that business because it's not something that really matters, all that matters is how much we love each other, but he couldn't reassure her without bringing up the dropped subject, so didn't speak, and now on his knees, pressed against her in this even quieter darkness, gooey mess all over his hands, his presumptions melted, him too sloppy and droopy, alone, scared to move an inch forward or back, would she ever forgive him, would he ever forgive her.

## PARTY

I go up to Aunt May's wheelchair. She gives me her crinkly hand and I take it. Why are you sprouting warts and whiskers, I want to ask her, looking down to find Aunt May's tiny green eyes twinkling in the folds of her moon face, the same pitted, pale flesh of the hand my pale hand squeezes, not too hard, not testing for bones I'm very curious about. Are they brittle or soupy-soft or sea-changed altogether to foam like is stuffed inside cloth animals to hold their shape. Draped by bead necklaces that dangle to her waist, her hips snug in a sequined flapper dress hemmed with fringe that starts at her knees and almost touches the silver buckles of her shoes, May smiles at me from a sepia-toned photo. No. That's not true. May smiles here, now, during this celebration of her eighty-third birthday, although unbeknownst to everybody at the party (and everyone at the party in the old photo) the surgeon forgot a metal clip in May's gut last week that's festering and will kill her next Christmas Eve. Not one party and then another and another. It's all one big party. Life ain't nothing but a party, May grins at me after I sugar her cheek, dance her hand, the fringe swish, swishing, brushing my trouser leg as she swirls out, spins, spools in, jitterbugging, camel walking, fox trotting, buzzard lope. My, my, Miss May. Oh-blah-dee. Watch out, girl. You have only eighty-three years or eight months or eight seconds to live before the party's over and the flashbulb freezes you forever, the sepia photo's close-up portions the color of batter I used to lick from my finger after swiping it around the mixing bowl when my grandmother, your cousin, your fine running partner, light, bright, and almost white as you, May, finished pouring her cake in a pan, set the pan in the oven to bake, and turned me loose on that bowl. Don't miss none, she'd grin. Get it all, Mr. Doot.

## PARIS MORNING

One, two, three, four birds flutter up and perch on top of a Paris apartment building. Birds the color of stains where the whitish, pill-box plain structure bleeds at its seams, corners, along the edge of its flat roof on which the birds stay just a few moments before dropping like stones past five or six upper stories, then treetops he can see from a window above the kitchen sink. The blank-walled, massive, squared unloveliness of the building squatting where it squats, the birds land-ing precisely when and where they land, staying precisely as long as they stay, tell time exactly as the church bells that morning when he'd awakened, and doesn't that mean all eternity has been waiting for those birds to rise up and putter, each on its appointed spot, each hopping about no more, no less than its allotted number of hops along the razor edge of rooftop, every second accounted for, poised, primed to happen, must align itself ahead or behind the appearance of a flight of birds the dirt color of almost transparent shadows, four creatures gathering to touch down together on top of a whitish build-ing with its meager, barred terraces, deeply recessed windows, tiny heads and breasts all he could see of the birds until they swoop off riding invisible ropes like mountain climbers rappelling, swiftly gone, another eternity passing or the same one passing once again before the birds, attuned to some simple fixed design, like seasons changing or clock hands recycling, would alight again precisely as he'd glimpsed them alighting just an instant ago, except meanwhile gears and pulleys, streaming particles of light and bundles of light tearing one another apart or fumbling under one another's clothes inside dark rooms of the apartment building across the way, have transformed in the twinkling of an eye, the one, two, three, four birds and every other possible bird and each and every concrete block stacked, cemented together to form the structure atop which the birds jiggle a moment, all of that and the universes containing it crumbled to dust then nothing then starting over and starting to crumble again during an unfathomable interval between two iron links in the chain of being, the stroke of one moment connected to the next stroke, and if he misses the next one where would he be then.

## HAIKU

Toward the end of his life, a time he resided in France in self-imposed exile from America, the negro novelist Richard Wright chose the Japanese form haiku, an unrhymed poem of three lines, seventeen syllables, as his principal means for speaking what burned inside him, the fire he needed to express through some artistic medium or another each day till he died. Thousands of haikus, and the thought of him working hour after hour, a tired colored man from Mississippi, fifty-two years old, world famous once then nearly forgotten by his countrymen, trying again, one more time, to squeeze himself into or out of a tiny, arbitrary allotment of syllables dictated by a tradition conceived by dead strangers in a faraway land, poor Richard Wright in Paris hunched over a sheet of paper midwifing or executing himself within the walls of a prison built without reference to the dimensions required by anyone whose life arched gigantically like Richard Wright's from slavery in the South almost to men on the moon, the idea of this warrior and hero falling upon his own sword on a battlefield chosen, rigged so Richard Wright's struggle doomed before it began, the still multiplying and heartbreaking ironies I perceive in the man's last, quiet, solitary efforts—counting one, two, three . . . five, six, seven, up and back like salsa dancers, or however, whatever you do, pacing, measuring your cage in order to do the thing he'd ended up doing, haiku, it makes me want to cry, but also sit back, shout in wonder.

## WRITING

All the years I never learned to write. Stop. Start. A man on a bicycle passes down Essex Street in the rain. Gray. Green. Don't go back. You won't write it any better. More. You can only write more or less. That's all. A man in a greenish gray slicker pedals down Essex in a slashing downpour. Leaves behind a pale brushstroke of color that pulsates, coming and going as you stare into empty slants of rain. A flash of color left behind. Where is the man. Where gone. What on his mind. The color not there really. Splashed and gone that quick. A bit of wishful thinking. A melancholy painting on air. Do not go back. It doesn't get better. Only more. Less. The years not written do not wait to be written. Wait nowhere. No. An unwritten story is one that never happens. A story is never until after the writing. Before is pipe dream. Something lost you wish you hadn't or wish you had. Gone before it got here. There is no world full of unwritten stories waiting to be written. Not even one. To hang people's hopes on, the hope that their story will be revealed one day, worth something, true, even if no one else can see it or touch it, a beautiful story like in that girl's sad eyes on the subway, her life story real as anyone's, as real as yours, her eyes say to me, a story no one has written, desperate to be written. Never will be. Rain blurs the image of a man steadfastly slashing down Essex Street on his bike through driving rain, rain whose force and weight any second will disintegrate the gray sheet of paper on which the figure's drawn, a man huddled under a gray-green slicker who doesn't know he's about to disappear and take his world with him. Except for a stroke of gray-green hovering in my eyes like it did the day we crossed the dunes and suddenly, for a moment, between steep hills of sand I saw framed in the distance what I thought might be a sliver of the sea we'd come so far to find.

## PASSING ON

Why couldn't he choose. Blue suit or brown suit. Throughout a long life, he'd endeavored to make sense of life, and now, almost overnight it seemed, the small bit of sense he'd struggled to grasp had turned to nonsense. Even the toys his grandkids played with mocked him, beeping, ringing, squealing, flashing products of a new dispensation he'd never fathom. Only prickly pride remained, pride in how he dressed, how he spoke the language, pride he hoped would allow him a dignified passage through final disappointments and fickleness. Unbending pride a barely disguised admission he's been defeated by that world he no longer pretends to understand and refuses to acknowledge except as brutal intervention, as disorder and intimidation constructed to humiliate him personally, pride wearing so thin he's trying to recall skills his father had taught him. Not a list of the meager skills themselves—not shaving, not tying a tie—but evidence of intimate exchange. Traces of the manner in which, through which, his father might have said, Here are some things I know, some things I am, and I want you to know them and I hope they will serve you well. In other words he was attempting to remember any occasion when or if his father had granted him permission to enter that unknown world which intersected only rarely, unpredictably with a home his father shared with a wife and children. Who was his father. How was it possible to be the man his father was. Did anything that man ever say suggest a son would be welcome in the other spaces he occupied. Closure what he had learned from his father. The absolute abandonment of shutting down, disappearing. Cover-ups. Erasing all tracks. Eluding pursuit. Were those the skills. Teaching the shame of bearing an inexhaustible bag of useless tricks he knew better than to pass on.

## TROUBLE

The man in the second place gives him a card and directions to a third place but the third place isn't the right one either, and he listens to a more complicated set of directions for reaching another place, which will be the fourth place if he's remembering correctly what's happened already this morning with car trouble in a strange town, and various strangers who seem quite willing to be helpful even to the extent of drawing maps on scratch paper or repeating numerous times their instructions, listening intently, patient with him as he explains his problem or the car's problem, and he requires their patience because for some reason this morning he feels like he's speaking a second language, one he's not very good at, one you might as well say he's forgotten how to speak, it's that bad, he's reduced to a kind of baby talk, pidgin, grunt, point translation of words he's unsure of in his original language, whatever it is, if he owns one, and wonders if he possesses the car's papers, his papers, the papers for whatever lumpy, large thing it is he has no word for but suddenly recalls stuffing last night hurriedly into the car's trunk, papers tucked away, locked somewhere safely inside the car, papers explaining everything he can't say so that if or when he ever reaches the fourth place or fifth or however many places it's going to take, someone will understand him, believe him, fix the problem.

## BREATH

Sometimes you feel so close it's like we're cheek-to-cheek sucking the breath of life from the same hole.

    In a few hours the early flight to Pittsburgh because my mom's life hanging by a thread. Thunder and lightning you're sleeping through cracks the bedroom's dark ceiling like an egg. About four a.m. I need to get up. Drawing a deep breath, careful as always to avoid stress on the vulnerable base of my spine when I shift my weight in bed, I slide

my butt toward the far edge, raise the covers, and pivot on one hip-
bone to a sitting position, letting my legs fold over the bed's side to
find the floor, still holding my breath as I get both feet steady under
me and slowly stand, hoping I didn't bounce the mattress, waiting to
hear the steady pulse of your sleep before I exhale.

In the kitchen a yellowish cloud presses against the window. A
cloud oddly lit and colored it seems by a source within itself. A kind
of fog or dust or smoke that's opaque, unsettling, until I understand
the color must come from security lights glaring below in the courtyard. It's snow. Big flakes not falling in orderly rows, a dervishing
mob that swirls, lifts, goes limp, noiselessly spatters the glass. Snow
obscuring the usual view greeting me when I'm up at crazy hours to
relieve an old man's panicked kidneys or just up, up and wondering
why, staring at blank, black windows of a hulking building that mirrors the twenty-story bulk of ours, up prowling instead of asleep in
the peace I hope you're still enjoying, peace I wish upon the entire
world, peace I should know better by now than to look for through a
window, the peace I listen for beside you in the whispering of our
tangled breaths.

Alice Munro

*Some Women*

I AM AMAZED SOMETIMES to think how old I am. I can remember
when the streets of the town I lived in were sprinkled with water to
lay the dust in summer, and when girls wore waist cinchers and
crinolines that could stand up by themselves, and when there was
nothing much to be done about things like polio and leukemia.
Some people who got polio got better, crippled or not, but people
with leukemia went to bed, and, after some weeks' or months'
decline in a tragic atmosphere, they died.

It was because of such a case that I got my first job, in the summer
holidays, when I was thirteen.

Old Mrs. Crozier lived on the other side of town. Her stepson,
Bruce, who was usually called Young Mr. Crozier, had come safely
home from the war, where he had been a fighter pilot, had gone to
college and studied history, and got married, and now he had
leukemia. He and his wife were staying with Old Mrs. Crozier. The
wife, Sylvia, taught summer school two afternoons a week at the college where they had met, some forty miles away. I was hired to look
after Young Mr. Crozier while she wasn't there. He was in bed in the
front-corner bedroom upstairs, and he could still get to the bathroom

by himself. All I had to do was bring him fresh water and pull the shades up or down and see what he wanted when he rang the little bell on his bedside table.

Usually what he wanted was to have the fan moved. He liked the breeze it created but was disturbed by the noise. So he'd want the fan in the room for a while and then he'd want it out in the hall, but close to his open door.

When my mother heard about this, she wondered why they hadn't put him in a bed downstairs, where they surely had high ceilings and he would have been cooler.

I told her that they did not have any bedrooms downstairs.

"Well, my heavens, couldn't they fix one up? Temporarily?"

That showed how little she knew about the Crozier household and the rule of Old Mrs. Crozier. Old Mrs. Crozier walked with a cane. She made one ominous-sounding journey up the stairs to see her stepson on the afternoons that I was there, and I suppose no more than that on the afternoons when I was not. But the idea of a bedroom downstairs would have outraged her as much as the notion of a toilet in the parlor. Fortunately, there was already a toilet downstairs, behind the kitchen, but I was sure that, if the upstairs one had been the only one, she would have made the laborious climb as often as necessary, rather than pursue a change so radical and unnerving.

My mother was thinking of going into the antique business, so she was very interested in the inside of the Crozier house, which was old and far grander than ours. She did get in, once, my very first afternoon there. I was in the kitchen, and I stood petrified, hearing her yoo-hoo and my own merrily called name. Then her perfunctory knock, her steps on the kitchen stairs. And Old Mrs. Crozier stumping out from the sunroom.

My mother said that she had just dropped by to see how her daughter was getting along. "She's all right," Old Mrs. Crozier said, standing in the hall doorway, blocking the view of antiques. My mother made a few more mortifying remarks and took herself off.

That night, she said that Old Mrs. Crozier had no manners, because she was only a second wife, picked up on a business trip to Detroit, which was why she smoked and dyed her hair black as tar and put on lipstick like a smear of jam. She was not even the mother of the invalid upstairs. She did not have the brains to be. (We were having one of our fights then, this one relating to her visit, but that is neither here nor there.)

The way Old Mrs. Crozier saw it, I must have seemed just as intrusive as my mother, just as cheerily self-regarding. Shortly after I began working there, I went into the back parlor and opened the bookcase and took stock of the Harvard Classics set out in a perfect row. Most of them discouraged me, but I took out one that looked like it might be fiction, despite its foreign title, *I Promessi Sposi*. It was fiction all right, and it was in English.

I must have had the idea then that all books were free, wherever you found them. Like water from a public tap.

When Old Mrs. Crozier saw me with the book, she asked where I had got it and what I was doing with it. From the bookcase, I said, and I had brought it upstairs to read. The thing that most perplexed her seemed to be that I had got it downstairs but brought it upstairs. The reading part she appeared to let go, as if such an activity were too alien for her to contemplate. Finally, she said that if I wanted a book I should bring one from home.

Of course, there were books in the sickroom. Reading seemed to be acceptable there. But they were mostly open and facedown, as if Mr. Crozier just read a little here and there, then put them aside. And their titles did not tempt me. *Civilization on Trial. The Great Conspiracy Against Russia.*

My grandmother had warned me that if I could help it I should not touch anything that the patient had touched, because of germs, and I should always keep a cloth between my fingers and his water glass.

My mother said that leukemia did not come from germs.

"So what does it come from?" my grandmother said.

"The medical men don't know."

"Hunh."

It was Young Mrs. Crozier who picked me up and drove me home, though the distance across town was not far. She was a tall, thin, fair-haired woman with a variable complexion. Sometimes there were patches of red on her cheeks as if she had scratched them. Word had been passed that she was older than her husband, that he had been her student at college. My mother said that nobody seemed to have gotten around to figuring out that, since he was a war veteran, he could easily have been her student without that making her older. People were just down on her because she had gotten an education.

Another thing they said was that she should have stayed home and looked after him, as she had promised in the marriage ceremony, instead of going out to teach. My mother again defended her, saying that it was only two afternoons a week and she had to keep up her profession, seeing as how she would be on her own soon enough. And if she didn't get out of the old lady's way once in a while wouldn't you think she'd go crazy? My mother always defended women who worked, and my grandmother always got after her for it.

One day I tried a conversation with Young Mrs. Crozier, Sylvia. She was the only college graduate I knew. Except for her husband, of course, and he had stopped counting.

"Did Toynbee write history books?"

"Beg pardon? Oh. Yes."

None of us mattered to her—not me, or her critics or her defenders. We were no more than bugs on a lamp shade.

As for Old Mrs. Crozier, all she really cared about was her flower garden. She had a man who came and helped her; he was about her age, but more limber than she was. His name was Hervey. He lived on our street, and, in fact, it was through him that she had heard about me as a possible employee. At home, he only gossiped and grew weeds, but here he plucked and mulched and fussed, while she followed him around, leaning on her stick and shaded by her big straw hat. Sometimes she sat on a bench, still commenting and giving orders, and smoking a cigarette. Early on, I dared to go between the perfect hedges to ask if she or her helper would like a glass of water, and she cried out, "Mind my borders!" before saying no.

Flowers were never brought into the house. Some poppies had escaped and were growing wild beyond the hedge, almost on the road, so I asked if I could pick a bouquet to brighten the sickroom.

"They'd only die," Mrs. Crozier said, not seeming to realize that this remark had a double edge to it, under the circumstances.

Certain suggestions or notions would make the muscles of her lean spotty face quiver, her eyes go sharp and black, and her mouth work as if there were a despicable taste in it. She could stop you in your tracks then, like a savage thornbush.

The two days a week that I worked were not consecutive. Let us say they were Tuesdays and Thursdays. The first day, I was alone with the sick man and Old Mrs. Crozier. The second day, somebody arrived whom I had not been told about. I was sitting upstairs when I heard a car in the driveway, and someone running briskly up the back steps and entering the kitchen without knocking. Then the person called, "Dorothy," which I had not known was Old Mrs. Crozier's name. The voice was a woman's or a girl's, and it was bold and teasing all at once.

I ran down the back stairs, saying, "I think she's in the sunroom."

"Holy Toledo! Who are you?"

I told her who I was and what I was doing there, and the young woman said that her name was Roxanne.

"I'm the masseuse."

I didn't like being caught by a word I didn't know. I didn't say anything, but she saw how things were.

"Got you stumped, eh? I give massages. You ever heard of that?"

Now she was unpacking the bag she had with her. Various pads and cloths and flat velour-covered brushes appeared.

"I'll need some hot water to warm these up," she said. "You can heat me some in the kettle." (The Crozier house was grand, but there was still only cold water on tap, as in my house at home.)

Roxanne had sized me up, apparently, as somebody who was willing to take orders—especially, perhaps, orders given in such a coaxing voice. And she was right, though she may not have guessed that my willingness had more to do with my own curiosity than with her charm.

She was tanned, although it was still early in the summer, and her pageboy hair had a copper sheen—something that you could get easily from a bottle nowadays but that was unusual and enviable then. Brown eyes, a dimple in one cheek—she did so much smiling and joking that you never got a good enough look at her to say whether she was really pretty, or how old she was.

I was impressed by the way her rump curved out handsomely to the back, instead of spreading to the sides.

I learned quickly that she was new in town, married to the mechanic at the Esso station, and that she had two little boys, one four years old and one three. ("It took me a while to figure out what was causing them," she said, with one of her conspiratorial twinkles.)

In Hamilton, where they used to live, she had trained to be a masseuse and it had turned out to be just the sort of thing she'd always had a knack for.

"*Dor*-thee?"

"She's in the sunroom," I told her again.

"I know, I'm just kidding her. Now, maybe you don't know about getting a massage, but when you get one you got to take off all your clothes. Not such a problem when you're young, but when you're older, you know, you can get all embarrassed."

She was wrong about one thing, at least as far as I was concerned.

About its not being a problem to take off all your clothes when you're young.

"So maybe you should skedaddle. You're supposed to be upstairs anyway, aren't you?"

This time I took the front staircase, while she was busy with the hot water. That way I got a glance in through the open door of the sunroom—which was not much of a sunroom at all, having its windows on three sides all filled up with the fat leaves of catalpa trees. There I saw Old Mrs. Crozier stretched out on a daybed, on her stomach, her face turned away from me, absolutely naked. A skinny streak of pale flesh. The usually covered length of her body didn't look as old as the parts of her that were daily exposed—her freckled, dark-veined hands and forearms, her brown-blotched cheeks. The skin of her back and legs was yellow-white, like wood freshly stripped of its bark.

I sat on the top step and listened to the sounds of the massage. Thumps and grunts. Roxanne's voice bossy now, cheerful but full of exhortation.

"Stiff knot here. Oh, brother. I'm going to have to whack you one. Just kidding. Aw, come on, just loosen up for me. You know, you got nice skin here. Small of your back—what do they say? It's like a baby's bum. Now I gotta bear down a bit—you're going to feel it here. Take away the tension. Good girl."

Old Mrs. Crozier was making little yelps. Sounds of complaint and gratitude. It went on for quite a while, and I got bored. I went back to reading some old *Canadian Home Journals* that I had found in a cabinet. I read recipes and checked on old-time fashions till I heard Roxanne say, "Now I'll just clean this stuff up and we'll go on upstairs, like you said."

Upstairs. I slid the magazines back into their place in the cabinet that my mother would have coveted, and went into Mr. Crozier's room. He was asleep, or at least he had his eyes closed. I moved the fan a few inches and smoothed his cover and went and stood by the window, twiddling with the blind.

Sure enough, there came a noise on the back stairs, Old Mrs. Crozier with her slow and threatening cane steps, Roxanne running ahead and calling, "Look out, look out, wherever you are. We're coming to get you, wherever you are."

Mr. Crozier had his eyes open now. Behind his usual weariness was a faint expression of alarm. But before he could pretend to be asleep again Roxanne burst into the room.

"So here's where you're hiding. I just told your stepmom I thought it was about time I got introduced to you."

Mr. Crozier said, "How do you do, Roxanne?"

"How did you know my name?"

"Word gets around."

"Fresh fellow you got here," Roxanne said to Old Mrs. Crozier, who now came stumping into the room.

"Stop fooling around with that blind," Old Mrs. Crozier said to me. "Go and fetch me a drink of cool water, if you want something to do. Not cold, just cool."

"You're a mess," Roxanne said to Mr. Crozier. "Who gave you that shave and when was it?"

"A few days ago," he said. "I handle it myself as well as I can."

"That's what I thought," Roxanne said. And to me, "When you're getting her water, how'd you like to heat some more up for me and I'll undertake to give him a decent shave?"

Shaving him became a regular thing, once a week, following the massage. Roxanne told Mr. Crozier that first day not to worry. "I'm not going to pound on you like you must have heard me doing to Dorothy-doodle downstairs. Before I got my massage training I used to be a nurse. Well, a nurse's aide. One of the ones who do all the work and then the nurses come around and boss you. Anyway, I learned how to make people comfortable."

Dorothy-doodle? Mr. Crozier grinned. But the odd thing was that Old Mrs. Crozier grinned, too.

Roxanne shaved him deftly. She sponged his face and neck and torso and arms and hands. She pulled his sheets around, somehow managing not to disturb him, and she punched and rearranged his pillows. Talking all the while, pure nonsense.

"Dorothy, you're a liar. You said you had a sick man upstairs, and I walk in here and I think, Where's the sick man? I don't see a sick man around here. Do I?"

Mr. Crozier said, "What would you say I am, then?"

"Recovering. That's what I would say. I don't mean you should be up and running around, I'm not so stupid as all that. I know you need your bed rest. But I say recovering. Nobody who was sick like you're supposed to be ever looked as good as what you do."

I thought this flirtatious prattle insulting. Mr. Crozier looked terrible. A tall man whose ribs showed like those of a famine survivor when she sponged him, whose head was partly bald, and whose skin looked as if it had the texture of a plucked chicken's, his neck corded like an old man's. Whenever I had waited on him in any way I had avoided looking at him. Though this was not really because he was sick and ugly. It was because he was dying. I would have felt a similar reticence even if he had been angelically handsome. I was aware of an atmosphere of death in the house, which grew thicker as you approached his room, and he was at the center of it, like the Host the Catholics kept in the box so powerfully called the tabernacle. He was the one stricken, marked out from everybody else, and here was Roxanne trespassing on his ground with her jokes and her swagger and her notions of entertainment.

On her second visit, she asked him what he did all day.

"Read sometimes. Sleep."

And how did he sleep at night?

"If I can't sleep I lie awake. Think. Sometimes read."

"Doesn't that disturb your wife?"

"She sleeps in the back bedroom."

"Uh-huh. You need some entertainment."

"Are you going to sing and dance for me?"

I saw Old Mrs. Crozier look aside with her odd involuntary grin.

"Don't you get cheeky," Roxanne said. "Are you up to cards?"

"I hate cards."

"Well, have you got Chinese checkers in the house?"

Roxanne directed this question at Old Mrs. Crozier, who first said she had no idea, then wondered if there might be a board in a drawer of the dining room buffet.

So I was sent down to look and came back with the board and a jar of marbles.

Roxanne set the game up over Mr. Crozier's legs, and she and I and Mr. Crozier played, Old Mrs. Crozier saying that she had never understood the game or been able to keep her marbles straight. (To my surprise, she seemed to offer this as a joke.) Roxanne might squeal when she made a move or groan whenever somebody jumped over one of her marbles, but she was careful never to disturb the patient. She held her body still and set her marbles down like feathers. I tried to do the same, because she would widen her eyes warningly at me if I didn't. All without losing her dimple.

I remembered Young Mrs. Crozier, Sylvia, saying to me in the car that her husband did not welcome conversation. It tired him out, she told me, and when he was tired he could become irritable. So I thought, If ever there was a time for him to become irritable, it's now. Being forced to play a silly game on his deathbed, when you could feel his fever in the sheets.

But Sylvia must have been wrong. He had developed greater patience and courtesy than she was perhaps aware of. With inferior people—Roxanne was surely an inferior person—he made himself tolerant, gentle. When likely all he wanted to do was lie there and meditate on the pathways of his life and gear up for his future.

Roxanne patted the sweat off his forehead, saying, "Don't get excited. You haven't won yet!"

"Roxanne," he said. "Roxanne. Do you know whose name that was, Roxanne?"

"Hmm?" she said, and I broke in. I couldn't help it.

"It was Alexander the Great's wife's name." My head was a magpie's nest lined with such bright scraps of information.

"Is that so?" Roxanne said. "And who is that supposed to be? Great Alexander?"

I realized something when I looked at Mr. Crozier at that moment. Something shocking, saddening.

He *liked* her not knowing. Her ignorance was a pleasure that melted on his tongue, like a lick of toffee.

On the first day, she had worn shorts, as I did, but the next time and always after that Roxanne wore a dress of some stiff and shiny light green material. You could hear it rustle as she ran up the stairs. She brought a fleecy pad for Mr. Crozier, so that he would not develop bedsores. She was dissatisfied with the arrangement of his bedclothes, always had to put them to rights. But however she scolded her movements never irritated him, and she made him admit to feeling more comfortable afterward.

She was never at a loss. Sometimes she came equipped with riddles. Or jokes. Some of the jokes were what my mother would have called smutty and would not have allowed around our house, except when they came from certain of my father's relatives, who had practically no other kind of conversation.

These jokes usually started off with serious-sounding but absurd questions.

*Did you hear about the nun who went shopping for a meat grinder?*

*Did you hear what the bride and groom went and ordered for dessert on their wedding night?*

The answers always came with a double meaning, so that whoever told the joke could pretend to be shocked and accuse the listener of having a dirty mind.

And after she had got everybody used to her telling these jokes Roxanne went on to the sort of joke I didn't believe my mother knew existed, often involving sex with sheep or hens or milking machines.

"Isn't that awful?" she always said at the finish. She said she wouldn't know this stuff if her husband didn't bring it home from the garage.

The fact that Old Mrs. Crozier snickered disturbed me as much as the jokes themselves. I wondered if she didn't actually get the jokes but simply enjoyed listening to whatever Roxanne said. She sat there with that chewed-in yet absentminded smile on her face, as if she'd been given a present that she knew she'd like, even though she hadn't got the wrapping off it yet.

Mr. Crozier didn't laugh, but he never laughed, really. He raised his eyebrows, pretending to disapprove, as if he found Roxanne outrageous but endearing all the same. I tried to tell myself that this was just good manners, or gratitude for her efforts, whatever they might be.

I myself made sure to laugh so that Roxanne would not put me down as an innocent prig.

The other thing she did to keep things lively was tell us about her life—how she had come down from some lost little town in northern Ontario to Toronto to visit her older sister, when she was only four-teen, then got a job at Eaton's, first cleaning up in the cafeteria, then being noticed by one of the managers, because she worked fast and was always cheerful, and suddenly finding herself a salesgirl in the glove department. (She made this sound like being discovered by Warner Bros.) And who should have come in one day but Barbara Ann Scott, the skating star, who bought a pair of elbow-length white kid gloves.

Meanwhile, Roxanne's sister had so many boyfriends that she'd flip a coin to see whom she'd go out with almost every night, and she employed Roxanne to meet the rejects regretfully at the front door of the rooming house where they lived, while she herself and her pick of the night sneaked out the back. Roxanne said that maybe that was how she had developed such a gift of gab. And pretty soon some of the boys she had met this way were taking her out, instead of her sis-ter. They did not know her real age.

"I had me a ball," she said.

I began to understand that there were certain talkers—certain girls—whom people liked to listen to, not because of what they, the girls, had to say but because of the delight they took in saying it. A delight in themselves, a shine on their faces, a conviction that whatever they were telling was remarkable and that they themselves could not help but give pleasure. There might be other people— people like me—who didn't concede this, but that was their loss. And people like me would never be the audience these girls were after, anyway.

Mr. Crozier sat propped up on his pillows and looked for all the world as if he were happy. Happy just to close his eyes and let her talk, then open his eyes and find her still there, like a chocolate bunny on Easter morning. And then with his eyes open follow every twitch of her candy lips and sway of her sumptuous bottom.

The time Roxanne spent upstairs was as long as the time she spent downstairs, giving the massage. I wondered if she was being paid. If she wasn't, how could she afford to stay so long? And who could be paying her but Old Mrs. Crozier?

Why?

To keep her stepson happy and comfortable? To keep herself entertained in a curious way?

One afternoon, when Roxanne had gone downstairs, Mr. Crozier said that he felt thirstier than usual. I went to get him some more water from the pitcher that was always in the refrigerator. Roxanne was packing up to go home.

"I never meant to stay so late," she said. "I wouldn't want to run into that schoolteacher."

I didn't understand for a moment.

"You know. *Syl-vi-a.* She's not crazy about me, either, is she? She ever mention me when she drives you home?"

I said that Sylvia had never mentioned Roxanne to me during any of our drives.

"Dorothy says she doesn't know how to handle him. She says I make him a lot happier than what she does. Dorothy says that. I wouldn't be surprised if she even told her that to her face."

I thought of how Sylvia ran upstairs to her husband's room every afternoon when she got home, before even speaking to me or her mother-in-law, her face flushed with eagerness and desperation. I wanted to say something about that—I wanted to defend her—but I didn't know how. And people as confident as Roxanne often seemed to get the better of me.

"You sure she never says anything about me?"

I said again that she didn't. "She's tired when she gets home."

"Yeah. Everybody's tired. Some just learn to act like they aren't."

I did say something then, to balk her. "I quite like her."

"You *qwat* like her?" Roxanne mocked.

Playfully, sharply, she jerked at a strand of the bangs I had recently cut for myself.

"You ought to do something decent with your hair."

*Dorothy says.*

If Roxanne wanted admiration, which was her nature, what was it that Old Mrs. Crozier wanted? I had a feeling that there was mischief stirring, but I could not pin it down. Maybe it was just a desire to have Roxanne, her liveliness, in the house, double time?

Midsummer passed. Water was low in the wells. The sprinkler truck stopped coming and some stores put up sheets of what looked like yellow cellophane in their windows to keep their goods from fading. Leaves were spotty, the grass dry.

Old Mrs. Crozier kept her garden man hoeing, day after day. That's what you do in dry weather, hoe and hoe to bring up any moisture that you can find in the ground underneath.

Summer school at the college would end after the second week of August, and then Sylvia Crozier would be home every day.

Mr. Crozier still seemed glad to see Roxanne, but he often fell asleep. He could drift off without letting his head fall back, during one of her jokes or anecdotes. Then after a moment he would wake up again and ask where he was.

"Right here, you sleepy noodle. You're supposed to be paying attention to me. I should bat you one. Or how about I try tickling you instead?"

Anybody could see how he was failing. There were hollows in his cheeks like an old man's, and the light shone through the tops of his ears, as if they were not flesh but plastic. (Though we didn't say plastic then; we said celluloid.)

My last day of work, Sylvia's last day of teaching, was a massage day. Sylvia had to leave for the college early, because of some ceremony, so I walked across town, arriving when Roxanne was already there. She and Old Mrs. Crozier were in the kitchen, and they both looked at me as if they had forgotten I was coming, as if I had interrupted them.

"I ordered them specially," Old Mrs. Crozier said.

She must have been talking about the macaroons sitting in the baker's box on the table.

"Yeah, but I told you," Roxanne said. "I can't eat that stuff. Not no way no how."

"I sent Hervey down to the bakeshop to get them."

"Okay, let Hervey eat them. I'm not kidding—I break out something awful."

"I thought we'd have a treat," Old Mrs. Crozier said. "Seeing it's the last day we've got before—"

"Last day before she parks her butt here permanently? Yeah, I know. Doesn't help to have me breaking out like a spotted hyena."

Who was it whose butt was parked permanently?

Sylvia's. Sylvia.

Old Mrs. Crozier was wearing a beautiful black silk wrapper, with water lilies and geese on it. She said, "No chance of having anything special with her around. You'll see. You won't be able to even get to see him with her around."

"So let's get going and get some time today. Don't bother about this stuff. It's not your fault. I know you got it to be nice."

"'I know you got it to be nice,'" Old Mrs. Crozier imitated in a mean, mincing voice, and then they both looked at me, and Roxanne said, "Pitcher's where it always is."

I took Mr. Crozier's water out of the fridge. It occurred to me that they could offer me one of the golden macaroons sitting in the box, but apparently it did not occur to them.

I'd expected Mr. Crozier to be lying back on the pillows with his eyes closed, but he was wide awake.

"I've been waiting," he said, and took a breath. "For you to get here," he said. "I want to ask you—do something for me. Will you?"

I said sure.

"Keep it a secret?"

I had been worried that he might ask me to help him to the commode that had recently appeared in his room, but surely that would not have to be a secret.

He told me to go to the bureau across from his bed and open the left-hand drawer, and see if I could find a key there.

I did so. I found a large, heavy, old-fashioned key.

He wanted me to go out of his room and shut the door and lock it. Then hide the key in a safe place, perhaps in the pocket of my shorts.

I was not to tell anybody what I had done.

I was not to let anybody know I had the key until his wife came home, and then I was to give it to her privately. Did I understand?

Okay.

He thanked me.

Okay.

All the time he was talking to me there was a film of sweat on his face and his eyes were as bright as if Roxanne were in the room.

"Nobody is to get in."

"Nobody is to get in," I repeated.

"Not my stepmother or—Roxanne. Just my wife."

I locked the door from the outside and put the key in my pocket. But then I was afraid that it could be seen through the light cotton material, so I went downstairs and into the back parlor and hid it between the pages of *I Promessi Sposi*. I knew that Roxanne and Old Mrs. Crozier would not hear me, because the massage was going on, and Roxanne was using her professional voice.

"I got my work cut out for me getting these knots out of you today."

And I heard Old Mrs. Crozier's voice, full of her new displeasure.

". . . punching harder than you normally do."

"Well, I gotta."

I was headed upstairs when a further thought came to me.

If he had locked the door himself—which was evidently what he wanted the others to think—and I had been sitting on the top step as usual, I would certainly have heard him and called out and roused the others in the house. So I went back down and sat on the bottom step of the front stairs, a position from which I could conceivably not have heard a thing.

The massage seemed to be brisk and businesslike today; Roxanne was evidently not making jokes. Pretty soon I could hear her running up the back stairs.

She stopped. She said, "Hey, Bruce."

Bruce.

She rattled the knob of the door.

"Bruce."

Then she must have put her mouth to the keyhole, so that he would hear but nobody else would. I could not make out exactly what she was saying, but I could tell that she was pleading. First teasing, then pleading. After a while she sounded as if she were saying her prayers.

When she gave that up, she started pounding on the door with her fists, not too hard but urgently.

Eventually, she stopped that, too.

"Come on," she said in a firmer voice. "If you got to the door to lock it, you can get there to open it up."

Nothing happened. She came and looked over the banister and saw me.

"Did you take Mr. Crozier's water into his room?"

I said yes.

"So his door wasn't locked or anything then?"

No.

"Did he say anything to you?"

"He just said thanks."

"Well, he's got his door locked and I can't get him to answer."

I heard Old Mrs. Crozier's stick reaching the top of the back stairs.

"What's the commotion up here?"

"He's locked hisself in and I can't get him to answer me."

"What do you mean, locked himself in? Likely the door's stuck. Wind blew it shut and it stuck."

There was no wind that day.

"Try it yourself," Roxanne said. "It's locked."

"I wasn't aware there was a key to this door," Old Mrs. Crozier said, as if her not being aware could negate the fact. Then, perfunctorily, she tried the knob and said, "Well. It'd appear to be locked."

He had counted on this, I thought. That they would not suspect me, that they would assume that he was in charge. And in fact he was.

"We have to get in," Roxanne said. She gave the door a kick.

"Stop that," Old Mrs. Crozier said. "Do you want to wreck the door? You couldn't get through it, anyway—it's solid oak. Every door in this house is solid oak."

"Then we have to call the police."

There was a pause.

"They could get up to the window," Roxanne said.

Old Mrs. Crozier drew in her breath and spoke decisively. "You don't know what you are saying. I won't have the police in this house. I won't have them climbing all over my walls like caterpillars."

"We don't know what he could be doing in there."

"Well, then, that's up to him. Isn't it?"

Another pause.

Now steps—Roxanne's—retreating to the back staircase.

"Yes. You'd better just take yourself away before you forget whose house this is."

Roxanne was going down the stairs. A couple of stomps of the stick went after her, then stopped.

"And don't get the idea you'll go to the constable behind my back. He's not going to take his orders from you. Who gives the orders around here, anyway? It's certainly not you. You understand me?"

Very soon I heard the kitchen door slam shut. And then Roxanne's car start.

I was no more worried about the police than Old Mrs. Crozier was. The police in our town meant Constable McClarty, who came to the school to warn us about sledding on the streets in winter and swimming in the millrace in summer, both of which we continued to do. It was ridiculous to think of him climbing up a ladder or lecturing Mr. Crozier through a locked door.

He would tell Roxanne to mind her own business and let the Croziers mind theirs.

It was not ridiculous, however, to think of Old Mrs. Crozier giving orders, and I thought she might do so now that Roxanne—whom she apparently did not like anymore—was gone. But although I heard her go back to Mr. Crozier's door and stand there, she did not even rattle the knob. She just said one thing.

"Stronger than you'd think," she muttered. Then made her way downstairs. The usual punishing noises with her steady stick.

I waited awhile and then I went out to the kitchen. Old Mrs. Crozier wasn't there. She wasn't in either parlor or in the dining room or the sunroom. I got up my nerve and knocked on the toilet door, then opened it, and she was not there, either. Then I looked out the window over the kitchen sink and I saw her straw hat moving slowly along the cedar hedge. She was out in the garden in the heat, stumping along between her flower beds.

I was not worried by the thought that seemed to have troubled Roxanne. I did not even stop to consider it, because I believed that it would be quite absurd for a person with only a short time to live to commit suicide.

All the same, I was nervous. I ate two of the macaroons that were still sitting on the kitchen table. I ate them hoping that pleasure would bring back normalcy, but I barely tasted them. Then I shoved the box into the refrigerator so that I would not hope to turn the trick by eating more.

Old Mrs. Crozier was still outside when Sylvia got home.

I retrieved the key from between the pages of the book as soon as I heard the car and I told Sylvia quickly what had happened, leaving out most of the fuss. She would not have waited to listen to it, anyway. She went running upstairs.

I stood at the bottom of the stairs to hear what I could hear.

Nothing. Nothing.

Then Sylvia's voice, surprised but in no way desperate, and too low for me to make out what she was saying. Within about five minutes she was downstairs, saying that it was time to get me home. She was flushed, as if the spots on her cheeks had spread all over her face, and she looked shocked, but unable to resist her happiness.

Then, "Oh. Where is Mother Crozier?"

"In the flower garden, I think."

"Well, I suppose I'd better speak to her, just for a moment."

After she had done that, she no longer looked quite so happy.

"I suppose you know," she said as she backed out the car. "I suppose you can imagine Mother Crozier is upset. Not that I am blaming you. It was very good and loyal of you. Doing what Mr. Crozier asked you to do. You weren't scared of anything happening, were you?"

I said no. Then I said, "I think Roxanne was."

"Mrs. Hoy? Yes. That's too bad."

As we were driving down what was known as Crozier's Hill, she said, "I don't think he wanted to frighten them. You know, when you're sick, sick for a long time, you can get not to appreciate other people's feelings. You can get turned against people even when they're doing what they can to help you. Mrs. Crozier and Mrs. Hoy were certainly trying their best. But Mr. Crozier just didn't feel that he wanted them around anymore today. He'd just had enough of them. You understand?"

She did not seem to know that she was smiling when she said this. Mrs. Hoy.

Had I ever heard that name before?

And spoken so gently and respectfully, yet with light-years of condescension.

Did I believe what Sylvia had said?

I believed that it was what he had told her.

I did see Roxanne again that day. I saw her just as Sylvia was introducing me to this new name. Mrs. Hoy.

She—Roxanne—was in her car and she had stopped at the first cross street at the bottom of Crozier's Hill to watch us drive by. I didn't turn to look at her, because it was all too confusing, with Sylvia talking to me.

Of course, Sylvia would not have known whose car that was. She wouldn't have known that Roxanne must have been waiting to see what was going on, driving around the block all the time since she had left the Croziers' house.

Roxanne would have recognized Sylvia's car, though. She would have noticed me. She would have known that things were all right, from the kindly serious faintly smiling way that Sylvia was talking to me.

She didn't turn the corner and drive back up the hill to the Croziers' house. Oh, no. She drove across the street—I watched in the sideview mirror—toward the east part of town, where the wartime houses had been put up. That was where she lived.

"Feel the breeze," Sylvia said. "Maybe those clouds are going to bring us rain."

The clouds were high and white, glaring. They looked nothing like rain clouds, and there was a breeze only because we were in a moving car with the windows rolled down.

I understood pretty well the winning and losing that had taken place between Sylvia and Roxanne, but it was strange to think of the almost obliterated prize, Mr. Crozier—and to think that he could have had the will to make a decision, even to deprive himself, so late in his life. The carnality at death's door—or the true love, for that matter—was something I wanted to shake off back then, just as I would shake caterpillars off my sleeve.

Sylvia took Mr. Crozier away to a rented cottage on the lake, where he died sometime before the leaves were off.

The Hoy family moved on, as mechanics' families often did.

My mother struggled with a crippling disease, which put an end to all her moneymaking dreams.

Dorothy Crozier had a stroke, but recovered, and famously bought Halloween candy for the children whose older brothers and sisters she had ordered from her door.

I grew up, and old.

Lore Segal

# Making Good

D R. SAMUEL ROSEN believed in the circle. They rearranged their chairs and Gretel, one of the Viennese visitors, volunteered to go first: "I am Gretel Mindel. You are Margot Groszbart. Dr. Samuel Rosen. Father Sebastian Gotthalt—" Here Dr. Rosen held up his hand to say, "How about just Gretel, Margot, Sam . . . ? It's hard to learn twelve new names." Father Sebastian had brought the six Viennese to New York to meet with the six Viennese-born New Yorkers whom Dr. Rosen had found—not without difficulty—for five intensive days of bridge building. Father Sebastian believed in bridges.

Gretel started over: "I am Gretel. You are Margot. Dr. Sam. Father Sebastian. Bob and Ruth. Erich. Steffi. And your name is . . . ?"

"My name is Konrad," said the eldest of the Viennese—thin, elegant, and tremulous like a man after a heavy illness. Margot Groszbart, one of the New Yorkers, observed his high, narrow nose—an alp of a nose. Margot liked to say the one thing she missed was the mountains.

Konrad Hohenstauf's papery brown lips parted as if reluctantly: "Gretel. Margot. Sam. Father Sebastian. Bob. Ruth. Erich. Steffi.

And you are?" He looked past—not at—Shoshannah Goldberg, who sat next to him. If looking at Shoshannah was hard it was impossible *not* to look and try to figure what was wrong—beside the inward-turning left eye, the abbreviated leg, and frozen shoulder—with the way she was held together.

Shoshannah forgot the name of the forgettable Erich Radezki, a pink young Viennese with a round chin and soft round cheeks. Erich got as far as Jakob Kohn, a New Yorker with a Kaiser Franz Joseph mustache. Gretel, on her second turn, was first to remember everybody's name and close the circle.

Dr. Sam wanted input. "Questions? Suggestions? Anything anybody would like to share?"

"Yes, I," Gretel responded. "This morning I walked into this room and was surprised with myself that I believed that you all . . . that all you in New York would know each other. I mean I felt surprised why I believed this." Gretel addressed herself to Margot Groszbart. During their first American breakfast of sugared doughnuts and bad coffee, Gretel had failed to get close enough to talk to the elderly pianist whom she had seen in performance from the back of a Vienna concert hall. Across the room, in New York, Margot Groszbart looked to have retained a lot of black in her hair. Her eyes had a snap; they had lighted briefly on Gretel Mindel before continuing to rove the room. Gretel understood that she had made no impression on the elderly Jewish musician.

Margot Groszbart was surprised at herself too. After not responding to Dr. Rosen's repeated and particular invitation that she join the workshop, she found herself on the phone postponing a visit to her daughter in Los Angeles in order to attend it. Rachel said, "Last time you were here, you told Jack's mother you were proposing to worry about current genocides. You weren't going to keep doing the Holocaust." "I know," Margot had said, "I know, but it's so fascinating— six of us stuck in a room with six of them. And, unlike your Brooklyn-born mother-in-law, I do not walk around in a state of chronic Holocaust anger." "Why don't you?" Rachel asked her. "Don't know," Margot had answered. "I don't seem to have the chronic-anger gene." Rachel had refrained from questioning her mother's chronic anger toward her mother-in-law and said only, "Come the next week, then, and tell us how it went."

And so here, on this Monday morning, Margot Groszbart sat on a bottom-chilling metal folding chair in the windowless basement meeting room that Dr. Rosen had rented from the local reform synagogue. The upright in the corner had the jolly, debauched look of a barroom piano. Here, for the next five days, she was going to build bridges with the children and children's children of the Hitler generation.

Dr. Sam, building on Gretel's input, said, "Isn't that what we have come together *for*? To tell each other what maybe we don't even know that we are thinking?"

"What don't we know that we are thinking?" Ruth Schapiro said. Margot began to feel as if she had always known this old, pretty woman with her neat ankles, nice blue suit, hair nicely kept, the kind of red that gets redder with each passing year. Bob Schapiro looked toward his wife. She said, "We know what we are thinking."

"And will you share it with us?" Dr. Sam asked. Bob Schapiro looked at Dr. Sam. Ruth Schapiro said, "The six million."

Konrad Hohenstauf looked at the floor, lifted his pointed, tremulous fingers to cover his mouth, and murmured, "Ach, what I have done . . . ?"

To fill the ensuing pause, Margot said, "I have a question. How is it that all of you speak such efficient English?" The Austrians demurred. "Well, you seem to get said what you want to say." During breakfast Margot had given up the attempt to activate her rusty childhood German, first in conversation with the baby-faced Erich, then with Father Sebastian, a powerful, red-haired man who looked at Margot out of intelligent eyes. Neither of the two young men had been about to give up the opportunity of practicing his English.

Margot said, "Why could I never get my American daughter to learn German?"

"You want her to learn German?" asked Ruth Schapiro.

Dr. Sam was master of his own Socratic method. When the input for which he had asked turned the conversation off course, he knew an exercise to fetch it home. He went around the circle and had them free-associate with their given names, which they did until a boy appeared with a great cardboard box of Cokes and brown paper bags of kosher lunches.

The circle is not a natural configuration for a roomful of strangers. The young Austrians—Erich, Steffi, and Gretel—took their lunch bags and went out to discover the New York neighborhood; Dr. Sam and Father Sebastian went off together to talk workshop business. The others disposed themselves about the ugly room, the elderly folk—Austrians and Jews—headed for the chairs set out around small tables that Dr. Sam planned to use when he broke the bridge builders into working units. Margot, who had been widowed for decades, watched Bob and Ruth Schapiro share their lunch bags wordlessly, as she imagined them sharing a lifetime of breakfasts, lunches, and suppers. At another table Konrad Hohenstauf supported his chin on the handle of his cane and seemed to sleep. Plump young Jenny Birnbaum, the only bridge builder born in the New World, spread her coat on the floor, curled up, and really slept, while Jakob Kohn, the Jewish stage-Viennese—shirtsleeved, beer bellied, mustachioed—lit a pipe and walked to and fro.

Margot's lifelong and daily discipline as a performer translated doing nothing into guilt. She had sacrificed a week's practice and felt that she should use her time talking to people. She could not remember having heard the voice of the unusually tall Austrian woman in the plum-colored turban, who sat close enough for conversation but had her back and shoulders hunched against the room. It had become oppressively hot. A midday lassitude fixed Margot onto her chair.

For the afternoon session Dr. Sam had them go around the circle and speculate on the name they would have given themselves if they'd been their own parents. Konrad Hohenstauf asked to be permitted to pass and passed again when they were asked to complete Gretel's sentence "When I came into this room, I thought . . ." going counterclockwise.

On Tuesday morning Dr. Sam handed out blank sheets of paper and crayons, saying, "Don't think, draw."

Gretel followed Margot to one of the little tables. She said, "I heard you play in the Akademie Theater. *Wunderbar.*" Margot gave Gretel Mindel her professional smile. People made a mistake thinking this a prosperous opening for conversation. A decent, "Well, thank you," returned the ball to the flatterer, who had nowhere to go with it except on and on. Margot, aware of the girl's eagerness, did not return it. These Viennese young women knew how to dress, Margot thought. In black on black with the hair left to look slept-in and not the least makeup to cover a rather sallow complexion, Gretel Mindel was, in her way, a beauty. While talking with the undersexed Erich and the courteous Father Sebastian, Margot had recognized a familiar chill. She experienced it now, sitting across from Gretel Mindel. Margot took it for granted that *she* must radiate toward the Austrians a reciprocally alien heat. Margot gave a laugh. Gretel raised her hopeful face.

Margot said, "I'm looking forward to getting Dr. Samuel's goat."

"His goat, please?"

"I'm going to irritate Dr. Sam by telling him my racial theory based on an incompatibility of body temperatures."

"It is a joke?" Gretel Mindel asked.

"Yes, yes," Margot said, and had, once more, surprised herself: Why was she making herself interesting to the Austrian girl? Margot said, "Asking me to draw something is like asking me to say something. My head goes empty."

"I know! I know it!" cried the girl. "I know it exactly! Mine also!"

Gretel Mindel now searched her mind for some other human oddity that she and a Jewish pianist might discover to have in common. Gretel asked Margot if she, on entering the room yesterday morning, had thought of the Viennese as a cohort. "Were you surprised we did not even know each other's names?"

Margot said, "No, I was thinking how I never walk into a room full of new people without a drop of the heart: I look around, I think 'Is *this* all the world has available?' My folks as well as yours."

Gretel laughed nicely. "I always look if there will be an available man."

The two women glanced across the room where the rosy Erich and the slender, stylish Steffi sat on the floor side by side bent over their drawings. It reminded Margot and Gretel to take up their crayons.

"In my age group," Margot said, "there is Bob." Bob Schapiro was a heavy man in a brown suit. He wore a yarmulke.

Gretel said, "But not available."

"Well," said Margot, "there's always—what *is* the name of the fellow who did something he won't say?"

"Konrad Hohenstauf," said Gretel. She drew silently for a while before she asked, "It is permitted to make jokes?"

Margot said, "My daughter's American-born mother-in-law thinks it's sacrilege, but I refuse to think of the Holocaust as a sacred event."

Gretel kept drawing.

Margot wasn't sure she agreed with what she had just said and felt uncomfortable having said it to the Austrian girl. She was drawing a train that started on the left edge of her paper and traveled off the right edge. She made a row of windows and drew a face in each window.

Gretel said, "I have made a Munch." In the foreground she had drawn the back view of a lollipop-shaped human form facing the back of another lollipop in the middle distance. "But your heart does not drop at Dr. Samuel?" she said.

"It doesn't?" Margot said.

They both looked in the direction of a pleasant incongruity—stout Dr. Sam, with the drama of his full beard, sat on the floor. His sad, hot eyes above their sack of flesh were fixed on the paper before him: Dr. Samuel was drawing. Father Sebastian sat next to him, drawing.

Gretel said, "*Der Dr. Sam schaut so lieb aus.* How to say this in English?"

"You can't. English won't let someone 'look dear.' You can say he has a look of sweetness."

"Yes, I think that is what he has! Don't you think he has it?" Gretel urged Margot.

Margot said, "Bet you somewhere under the mess of coats behind the piano there's a guitar."

Gretel and Margot took their lunch bags to the little green community garden across from the synagogue. It was a windy blue day, barely warm enough to sit. "Who is the woman in the turban?" Margot asked Gretel.

"Peppi Huber. We think she doesn't understand English."

"Did she come all the way to New York to sit and not understand?"

"That we were wondering also."

Margot asked Gretel where *she* had learned her English.

"I was six months at the University of Texas."

They waved to Konrad walking by with his cane, and to Shoshannah limping beside him. Shoshannah waved back. Gretel told Margot that her grandmother had taken her to the Akademie to hear Margot play. "You played *Das Wohltemperierte clavier*," Gretel said.

"So I did." Margot ate her sandwich and tried to calculate Gretel's grandmother's age in 1938, but did not ask Gretel. There exists an embarrassment—a species of shyness—between the party of the murderers and the murdered. From a tooth-whitening ad in her dentist's office, Margot had learned which of the facial muscles operate the human smile. These muscles appeared to have frozen the area around Gretel Mindel's mouth. She said, "My grandmother liked to tell that she was the youngest district SS youth leader. There comes Dr. Sam." Crossing the street toward the synagogue, Gretel frowned and said, "But you like Dr. Sam."

"I do. I do like him! How can you not like Dr. Sam Rosen! What I don't care for are his exercises to force-feed intimacy and pressure-cook healing."

"Better than not cooking!" cried Gretel Mindel. "Here you and I are talking."

"So we are," Margot said.

In the afternoon session they went around the circle to explain their drawings. Ruth Schapiro said, "Bob doesn't draw." Across his paper he had printed, "MARCH 12, 1938," the date of Hitler's annexation of Austria, in black capitals. Ruth had drawn a Magen David on a blue-white-blue background.

Konrad had removed the paper sleeve from a black crayon and rolled the crayon on its side from the top to the bottom of his paper.

Jakob Kohn had drawn an adorable pair of lederhosen. He said, "You can take the Jew out of Vienna but you can't take Vienna out of the Jew."

Shoshannah's picture depended on explanation: "This is supposed to be a soldier," she said. "I don't know how to draw a kneeling person, but he is kneeling down planting something. I think maybe he went AWOL and got a job on a farm."

"Went AWOL from which army?" Ruth Schapiro asked.

Shoshannah didn't know. "Someone maybe stole his uniform or he bartered it for food?"

"But was he an Ally or was he a Nazi?"

"How would we even know? This white thing with the red is the bloody bandage round his head. In the background these are supposed to be burned-out farms. Here are the puffs of smoke from guns. We didn't know if we were behind the front line or ahead, or if the war was over and they weren't telling us. Maybe they didn't know. They were marching us south, as it turned out, and we saw this soldier kneeling. He was planting things. See the row of green? Anyway, Dr. Sam said to draw something."

Bob Schapiro stared at Shoshannah. Ruth Schapiro said, "What has this to do with the murder of the six million?"

Margot peered around the room. The Austrians were looking straight before them except for Konrad, who looked at the floor. He covered his mouth.

Shoshannah's drawing started a debate that lasted the four remaining days: Shoshannah held that a head wound is a head wound is a head wound, while Ruth argued that you have to know if it was the head of a soldier who had killed or a soldier who had liberated Jews.

Erich said, "My father died of a head wound in Russia," but he said it in German to Steffi, later, when they were walking back to the hotel.

Jenny Birnbaum had drawn three skeletons—her grandparents and a baby uncle on her mother's side.

The Austrians looked straight before them.

Margot's turn. "The faces in the windows of the train are Jewish children leaving Vienna. This is my Mutti waving."

Ruth Schapiro asked Margot, "Did your parents get out?"

"No. When they invited me to play at the Akademie, I went to the Resistance Archive. My parents were numbers 987 and 988 out of 1,030 on the train leaving Vienna on June 14, 1942, original destination Izbica, detoured to Trawniki."

"Bob and I don't go to Vienna," Ruth Schapiro said.

The Austrians kept looking straight ahead. Margot thought, Where are they *supposed* to look? What do we want them to do with their eyes?

Dr. Sam had drawn a circle of people dancing the hora. Father Sebastian had drawn a bridge over a lot of troubled-looking water.

That evening produced the guitar. Dr. Sam taught the Austrians to sing the Hatikvah. They sang *"Ach, du lieber Augustin."*

"You don't sing?" Gretel asked Margot.

"I'm willing, but my mouth is not." Margot's mouth would not open to sing the Hatikvah; it would not sing, "Oh, say can you see . . ." It refused to sing anything communally, from which Margot Groszbart chose to deduce that if birth had made her an Aryan in Vienna in 1938, she would not have sung the *"Horst Wessel Lied,"* or raised her arm and opened her mouth to shout, *"Heil Hitler."*

At lunchtime on Wednesday, Margot told Gretel she was staying in to talk to people and found her path blocked by the plum-colored turban. *"I' will Ihna 'was sagen.* I want to say something to you." Margot followed the tall woman back to one of the little tables. They sat down. The turban approached Margot's face. Speaking in Margot's childhood Viennese German, the woman said, "There was no anti-Semitism in Vienna before they accused Waldheim." She held Margot's eyes. "This time it is the Jews." She waited, her face so close it blurred in Margot's vision.

In her childhood German, Margot said, "Is it possible you don't recognize the same old line?"

"I know. I know that. I do, but this time it is true." The turban intensely waited.

Margot said, "I cannot have this argument with you," got up, and, seeing the Schapiros by the coffee urn, walked over to talk with them. Ruth Schapiro said, "We heard you play––Bob, what was it we heard Margot Groszbart play? Wonderful."

Bob Schapiro said, "Wonderful."

"Thank you," Margot said. She told them her encounter with the purple turban, and Ruth said, "So? She's an anti-Semite. What else is new?" Margot looked back. Peppi continued to sit; her head appeared to be sinking in the direction of her lap. Margot said, "She is, but I think she was waiting for me to argue her out of it. That's what she came to New York for. She's no longer comfortable being an anti-Semite."

"An anti-Semite is an anti-Semite. What's to argue?" Ruth Schapiro said.

"What made the two of you come to the workshop?" Margot asked them.

"Dr. Rosen begged us. He was afraid no Jews would come."

Margot took her cup of coffee to chat with young Steffi. Steffi was a graphic designer. Her mother, it turned out, had gone to Margot's old district *Volksschule*. Margot reported the Waldheim conversation to Steffi, who looked disgusted and said, "*Na, die is 'a anti-Semit.* That one is an anti-Semite." Steffi wanted Margot to tell her all the anti-Semitic remarks she remembered from her school days in Vienna and was disappointed—was disbelieving—when Margot couldn't recall any.

In the afternoon, Dr. Sam paired them off to interview each other. Steffi and Bob Schapiro, Ruth and Father Sebastian, Shoshannah Goldberg and Konrad Hohenstauf. One had to wonder in what language the American schoolgirl, Jenny Bernstein, and the plum-colored turban were going to interview each other; the beardless young Erich and the historically mustachioed Jakob might hit it off.

Gretel Mindel asked to be with Margot. A premature nostalgia made her bag the table at which they had drawn pictures together. Gretel was wanting to confess. Gretel's SS grandmother had led a cadre to Poland. It was her job to establish the "Jew houses," in which deportees could be held over till their transportation to the final destination. She would give a Polish farm family twenty-four hours to load what they could onto a wagon and get out of the area. Gretel's grandmother boasted of never having had to use her whip.

Gretel asked about Margot's Mutti, who had waved from the platform. Margot experienced a reluctance, but said, "All right, here's something I remember: When I was a bad child and hadn't put my toys away, my Mutti would be angry and not look at me and not talk to me. So long as my Mutti was not talking and not looking, I couldn't play, couldn't do anything. I would follow her around the apartment saying, *'Sei wieder gut! Sei wieder gut!'*—something else, by the way, that doesn't translate into English. You can't say, 'Be good again!'"

"'Stop being angry,'" suggested Gretel. "'Forgive me!'"

Margot said, "Anyway, I would keep walking behind her saying, *'Sei wieder gut!'* till she relented or, more probably, forgot."

The next morning they sat in their circle to report on each other's stories. Shoshannah related only her faithful promise not to tell what Konrad had told her. Using her right hand to lift the inoperative left arm, she laid her hand on Konrad's wrist and said, "You were only eight years old."

Margot gave a straightforward account of Gretel's grandmother's Nazi career. "She never had to use her whip," she concluded.

It was in recounting Margot's story of walking after her Mutti that Gretel experienced that shock of understanding something one has merely known: the Mutti whom the little Margot had followed around the Vienna apartment was the Mutti who had put her on the train was the Mutti who had been put on the train for the east from where she had not returned. Gretel sobbed aloud.

At the lunch hour Margot got her coat and walked out of the door, universally irritated by the freshness of Gretel Mindel's emotion; by the mileage Konrad Hohenstauf was getting out of what he wasn't telling; by the hurt hunch of Peppi Huber's shoulders; by the Schapiros' single incorruptible idea, and Sam Rosen's incorruptible goodwill. She hailed a taxi. Margot opened the door to the calm of her handsome apartment, finished yesterday's soup, skimmed the *Times,* failed to reach her daughter on the telephone, sat at the piano, and practiced for fifteen minutes before getting into a taxi so as not to be late for the afternoon session.

. . .

On their last day, Gretel, Steffi, and Erich took Margot to lunch in the little restaurant they had discovered. When the conversation relaxed into German they forgot she wasn't one of them. Steffi was a good mimic: she appeared to blow herself up to Bob Schapiro size and said, "Sixmillionsixmillionsixmillion."

Erich said, "Did you see Ruth let the cuff of her sleeve fall open, to show the numbers on her wrist?"

"And you think that was impolite of her?" asked Margot.

Steffi said, *"Na, aber die is' ja immer so hochnäsig."*

"Interesting," Margot said to Gretel beside her. *"Hochnäsig* translates, literally, into 'high-nosed.' Both languages place the seat of arrogance in the nose. You know the English expression 'being snotty'?" They had lost Steffi and Erich to a conversation of their own.

Gretel had been studying Margot and now said, "You don't think we have the right to say Ruth Schapiro does anything wrong?"

"I think you're wrong about her being '*hochnäsig*': it's not that she looks 'down her nose' at you; it's that there is no way for her to look. What is the right way for Ruth Schapiro, with the numbers on her wrist, to look at you?"

But Gretel said, "That was not what I asked. You think *we* don't have the right to criticize *you*."

"You're right," Margot said, "I don't grant you that right. Notice," she added, "that you and I are now saying the things for which Dr. Sam has no exercises." She turned to her table companions and asked them, "What did *you* come for?"

"I know the answer," Gretel bitterly said. "We came for you to console us for having been terrible."

Margot laid an affectionate hand on the girl's wrist.

Margot had agreed to give a final brief recital. The upright had not only the look but the timbre of a barroom piano. She played the first prelude and fugue of the *Well-tempered Clavichord* with a smile in the direction of Gretel Mindel, who, as the day advanced, had become tearful. The windowless meeting room had been transformed and the little tables arranged into one long table covered with a cloth for a last supper. During the kosher chicken with vegetable garnish, Father Sebastian rose to announce that he and Dr. Sam planned another such workshop next year, under the auspices of his church. He hoped that the New York bridge builders would come to Vienna and participate.

"I will," Shoshannah said.

"I want my mom to go," young Jenny said.

"By next year," Jakob Kohn said, "I am thinking I may have my own apartment in Vienna."

"Bob and I will be in Jerusalem," Ruth Schapiro said.

"Come! Come to the workshop!" Gretel said to Margot. "Come and you can stay with me."

"Thank you," Margot said, "but I don't know that I'll be going to Vienna again."

Gretel went with Margot to help her find her coat. "Forgive me!" she said.

"What for?" asked Margot. "I don't know that you've done anything wrong."

Gretel held Margot's coat, watched Margot put her arms into the sleeves and button the buttons, and felt time running out. She said, "I go to Jerusalem also, for six months. I want to learn Hebrew!"

"Do you?" Margot said. "I've forgotten mine." Here came the big red-haired Father Sebastian to say good-bye and to reinforce the invitation to Vienna. Margot shook his hand. Margot shook hands with Erich and embraced Steffi. "Good-bye, young Jenny. Good-bye Schapiros!" She embraced them. "Good-bye Shoshannah, Jakob." Everybody was shaking hands with everybody except for Konrad Hohenstauf, who had not come to join in the adieus by the door, or the plum-colored turban, who must have left without anybody noticing. Margot took Dr. Rosen's hand. "This has been quite something else. Good-bye."

*"Sei wieder gut!"* Gretel called through the door after Margot Groszbart.

It came to Margot that she had not said good-bye to Gretel Mindel, and she meant to—thought she was going to—turn around and wave to her, but she was already halfway across the road and she kept walking.

# Reading *The PEN/O. Henry Prize Stories 2010*

## The Jurors on Their Favorites

*Our jurors read* The PEN/O. Henry Prize Stories *in a blind manuscript, that is, each story was in the same type and format with no attribution of the magazine that published it or the author's name. They also wrote their essays without knowledge of the author's name or that of the magazine. On occasion, the name of the author was inserted later into the essay for the sake of style.*
—LF

**Junot Díaz on "A Spoiled Man" by Daniyal Mueenuddin**
What a superb story. What a gift.

I cannot stress enough what a marvel this story is. From the title onward the author displays a courteous offhand ferocity unlike any I've ever encountered. The writing is clear, kind, disarming. The rhythms are classic, Chekhovian. But what awaits is the reason I got into this art game in the first place.

Enter Rezak, an old, lonely man on the edge of Islamabad, on the edge of summer-home privilege, on the edge of, basically, everything, trying to make himself "useful" as the string runs out on the last days of his life. The writer puts my man in a box, in a literal box, and so with understated self-conscious panache we get, "Opening the heavy padlock, he lifted the door hatch and climbed in. . . . Tiny red lights, run off an electrical connection drawn from the poultry sheds, were strung all over the ceiling and warmed the chamber. He could sit but not stand inside, and had covered the floor with a cotton mattress, which gave off a ripe animal odor, deeply comforting to him."

Here is marginalized third-world living in a single devastating half sentence: "He could sit but not stand."

And not far from where Rezak's box squats stands the Harounis' weekend digs. Home to Harouni—American-educated Pakistani who has come into money and is probably making some of his own now—and his game American wife.

From this primal situation you could spin a million tales, but Daniyal Mueenuddin spins what I would argue is the best one. So casually terrifying and so irrefutably true I finished "A Spoiled Man" with my heart blown out.

I've always thought that it is the curse-lure of short stories that they can be perfect and the curse-lure of novels that they cannot. Here in my mind is a story that nears perfection. In a matter of pages, Daniyal Mueenuddin not only charts the downfall of one humble man's heart; he also draws back the gnostic veil that often obscures the truth about our world: that it is in fact multiple worlds existing in one another's midst. Daniyal Mueenuddin does so with such economy and so patent a lack of fanfare you wouldn't be blamed for thinking it an accident.

For in part this is what this sublime story is kinda-sorta about: worlds. The fact that we, all of us, live in a terrible concatenation of often mutually exclusive but nevertheless articulated worlds. Often ignorant of one another, governed by a cruel economy that dictates who gets seen, who remains unseen, who can remain ignorant of the other worlds, who cannot and who can be devoured by the world above, despite all intentions, with nary a good-bye. Strategically, Daniyal Mueenuddin allows us to inhabit all the various characters in the drama, from upright Rezak to Sonya, the American wife, and reminds us, with one shocking reversal, that it is the very way this ecology of worlds is structured that makes the kind of fall that Rezak suffers not only probable, but inevitable.

I'm putting this all in head terms, not doing a good job describing this story's power, its nuance, its sudden dark turn. How could I?

Cetaceans, I read recently, have muscles that allow them to shape the lenses of their eyes so they can see equally well above water as below. They can, in other words, see in two worlds. We humans are not so biologically fortunate. It is only art that can shape our eyes to see all our various worlds, only art that reminds us at times gently, at times forcefully, of what we are and what we've let ourselves become. Stories like "A Spoiled Man" are the subtle knife that cuts open the membranes that hold the worlds apart and allows us not only to see into our other worlds but for a moment to reside there as well. What more could we ask from art? From a short story? From a writer?

Junot Díaz was born in 1968 in the Dominican Republic and raised in New Jersey. He is the author of *Drown* and *The Brief Wondrous Life of Oscar Wao,* which won the John Sargent, Sr., First Novel Prize; the National Book Critics Circle Award; the Anisfield-Wolf Book Award; and the 2008 Pulitzer Prize. Díaz has been awarded the Eugene McDermott Award, a fellowship from the Guggenheim Foundation, a Lila Acheson Wallace Reader's Digest Award, the 2002 PEN/Malamud Award, the 2003 U.S./Japan Creative Artist Fellowship from the National Endowment for the Arts, a fellowship at the Radcliffe Institute for Advanced Study at Harvard University, and the Rome Prize from the American Academy of Arts and Letters. He is the fiction editor at the *Boston Review* and the Rudge (1948), and Nancy Allen Professor at the Massachusetts Institute of Technology. He lives in Cambridge, Massachusetts.

### Paula Fox on "Oh, Death" by James Lasdun

Short stories bring readers news of people, places, the often inexplicable vagaries of life, the search for meaning or the threat of meaninglessness, crises and events characters themselves find incomprehensible. My reading of the stories in *The PEN/O. Henry Prize Stories 2010* took me to places I'd never been, Nigeria, Malaysia, Pakistan, a Greek prison island, a South American city, and areas of the United States of which I have scant knowledge.

How does one determine the "best" stories? All are human efforts to grasp the truths of experience, of life. Even when stories fail, all of them convey the mystery that lies at the center of human existence. Chekhov and Flannery O'Connor were artists, one great, the other very good. When I read their stories, I am sometimes puzzled about which writer I would apply the word *great* to.

Storytelling, as far as is known, began millennia ago—a tribe gathered around a fire in the night, a storyteller standing before it, telling a tale that would illuminate and teach.

Of course, there is the entertainment of storytelling, the charm, the knowledge, the comedy. And perhaps as significant, a temporary vacation from the reader's own troubles. Reading these stories made me feel more hopeful about this world, reminding me that there's far more variation in life than I ever imagined!

All the stories I read in *The PEN/O. Henry Prize Stories 2010* said something of value about the way we live, often showed the frequent cruelty or indifference with which we treat others in the same boat—lifeboat!

Some of the stories in the present collection had outstanding characters but barely a story, others were reports of events, interesting enough but rather like reading newspaper reports. I chose the following seven for their fulfilling aspects of good writing: "Oh, Death" by James Lasdun, "Into the Gorge" by Ron Rash, "Sheep May Safely Graze" by Jess Row, "The Bridge" by Daniel Alarcón, "Them Old Cowboy Songs" by Annie Proulx, "Visitation" by Brad Watson, and "Some Women" by Alice Munro. I also recommend "The Headstrong Historian" by Chimamanda Ngozi Adichie, "A Spoiled Man" by Daniyal Mueenuddin, and "Birch Memorial" by Preeta Samarasan.

Of all these, my favorite was "Oh, Death" by James Lasdun.

Told by a compassionate narrator, "Oh, Death" is the story of Rick, a man easily aroused to anger. The writing is supple and subtle. This reader had the sense of a voice speaking simply but eloquently of events filled with dramatic tensions, yet the reader did not have to make that partially conscious adjustment between print and inner comprehension. This is the one story, I found, that has the Chekhovian quality of being a human voice, not words on a page—not always a virtue in writing but essential to the quality of "Oh, Death."

Paula Fox was born in 1923 and has been writing since she was in her early twenties. Since her first novel, *Poor George* (1967), and first book for children, *Maurice's Room* (1966), she's published books for young people, as well as novels, such as *Desperate Characters* and *The Widow's Children,* and short stories for which she's twice been awarded an O. Henry Prize (2005 and 2006). Her memoirs are *Borrowed Finery* and *The Coldest Winter: A Stringer in Liberated Europe.* Fox lives in Brooklyn, New York.

## Yiyun Li on "The Woman of the House" by William Trevor

A while ago I reread *A Farewell to Arms,* and reencountered a line that greatly impressed me when I first read the novel at nineteen: "The world breaks everyone and afterward many are strong at the broken places. But those that will not break it kills." Though what resonated more in the rereading, which had eluded me when I was younger, was a character's observation of small people who did not occupy the main stage in Hemingway's books. "That is why the peasant has wisdom," said the character, "because he is defeated from the start."

I enjoyed reading the stories in *The PEN/O. Henry Prize Stories 2010.* Many of the characters' struggles against what has come to break them—nature, history, love, hope, kinship, loneliness—stayed with me. A few stories kept me awake at night, but, as a longtime admirer of William Trevor's work, I was pleased to discover that "The Woman of the House" was one of his.

Like many of Trevor's stories, "The Woman of the House" explores the subdued and sometimes neglected dramas in the lives of those characters who have not much to start with nor much to end up with. The roaming brothers—called Gypsies though they were not—harbored the hope "that there might somewhere be a life that was more than they yet knew" yet "their immediate purpose" was about survival. The crippled man, unable to go outdoors for years, wanted two fresh coats of paint for his house, which he would not see with his eyes. Martina, the crippled man's cousin and lodging with him as a caretaker by arrangement, "had once known what she wanted, but she wasn't so sure about that anymore." Silence prevailed in the story: the brothers chose not to understand English when it was convenient, and between themselves they communicated more with their eyes than with language; Martina, listening to old-time music played on the wireless, was told that the music was terrible by the crippled man, yet she chose not to comment on that. "The ancient Dodge was part of Martina's circumstances, to be tolerated because it was necessary"—and indeed other things were tolerated by her, too, out of necessity: the probing hands of the local grocer which had in time become a memory; the small cash stowed away more for the joy of a secret than any solid hope it provided; the repeated queries of the crippled man on the origin of her name, the cruelty unsaid yet felt; the rain that drenched her dress and ran down between her breasts, cold as death itself.

Death, in the end, remained unexplained—the brothers suspected that Martina had killed the crippled man—because it was hardly a drama worth dwelling upon, either by them or by the world. "The woman's history was not theirs to know, even though they now were part of it themselves. Their circumstances made them that, as hers made her what she'd become." When the brothers roamed on in their journey, and the woman lived on among still lifes in the house, what was felt by the readers, and would continue being felt by them, was the weight of time.

Yiyun Li was born in Beijing in 1972, and came to the United States in 1996. Her stories and essays have been published in *The New Yorker, Best American Short Stories, The O. Henry Prize Stories 2008,* and elsewhere. She has received fellowships and awards from the Lannan Foundation and the Whiting Foundation. Her debut collection, *A Thousand Years of Good Prayers,* won the Frank O'Connor International Short Story Award, PEN/Hemingway Award, Guardian First Book Award, and California Book Award for first fiction; it was also short-listed for the Kiriyama Prize and the Orange Prize for New Writers. In 2007, she was selected by *Granta* as one of the 21 Best Young American Novelists under 35. Her latest book is a novel, *The Vagrants.* She teaches at University of California, Davis, and lives in Oakland, California.

# Writing *The PEN/O. Henry Prize Stories 2010*

## The Writers on Their Work

**Chimamanda Ngozi Adichie, "The Headstrong Historian"**
My father talks often about his grandmother, a wonderfully fierce, outspoken woman. I fell in love with her memory and knew I would one day write about her in my fiction. Then, as a graduate student at Yale, I sat in a class and listened to a professor say, rather flippantly, that European colonialism in Africa had hurt people who had lost their lands but not necessarily people who had simply been governed. I remember reacting very viscerally to this idea of loss defined narrowly in material terms. I have always felt that the great tragedy of colonialism is not that Europeans stole a people's resources, but that the enterprise came with metaphysical losses that continue to be inherited generation after generation. That moment in class became the trigger to write about my great-grandmother—many of the details of Nwamgba are based on her life—but also about the complicated history of colonialism, and how Western education was irretrievably tied to religion. I also wanted to challenge some of the stock ideas about the role of women in precolonial Igboland. Women were, in general, more powerful, more flexible, in their political and economic roles before the arrival of Victorian Christianity. I wrote the

first draft of the story in a kind of frenzied, exhilarating rush, and I like to think that my great-grandmother was watching.

Chimamanda Ngozi Adichie was born in Nigeria in 1977. She is a 2008 MacArthur Foundation fellow. Her first novel, *Purple Hibiscus,* won the Commonwealth Writers' Prize, and her second novel, *Half of a Yellow Sun,* won the Orange Prize. Her work has been translated into thirty languages. She divides her time between the United States and Nigeria.

### Daniel Alarcón, "The Bridge"

This story began with the central anecdote—a toppled pedestrian bridge, a blind person, an accident. This part is all real. A friend of mine had covered this event when he was a reporter at a daily paper in Lima. This most basic version of the story was told one night, and it immediately became special to me, one of those that contains, at its core, some dimly illuminated truth, the sort of event that neatly encapsulates much of what is heartrending and tragicomic about daily life in the city I love so much. It seemed so weighty, so full of meaning, I couldn't stop thinking about it. At first, I had included this event—briefly mentioned it—within the novel I'm currently writing, but when I took a step back, I felt it simply had too much to offer to be background. So I took it out, and decided to see where it led me. I was looking specifically for a narrator who was both distant, able to relate the central incident with detached equanimity, and also uniquely and fully tied to the events and to the deceased couple, a voice connected to these victims, who must in the course of the story question the very nature of this connection. Beyond that, I had no fixed sense of where the story was going, where it might end, or whom the narrator might meet along the way, which, I've found, is the most exciting way to write.

Daniel Alarcón was born in Lima, Peru, in 1977. He is associate editor of *Etiqueta Negra,* an award-winning monthly magazine published in his native city. He is the author of *Lost City Radio,* which won the 2008 PEN/USA Novel Award. His most recent story collection, *El rey siempre está por encima del pueblo,* has been published throughout Latin America. He lives in Oakland, California.

### Kirstin Allio, "Clothed, Female Figure"

This story started with the impulse to preserve memory, and composing often felt like collaging. For example, a dingy, rent-controlled, air-shaft apartment in New York where I showed up after my last dance class of the day to babysit. I was eighteen, like Leah. One of the accompanists at the school where I studied was a square Soviet woman with heartbreakingly formal hair in the style of Anna Akhmatova. Or, a holiday I once sat out, the Mediterranean visible through a keyhole in dusky olive bushes: my baby son apparently had a case of the mysterious, medieval-sounding "sestina." After a while, and a lot of colors and patterns butting up against one another, the "meaning" of the story surfaced. This one is about the spectrum of maternal love. I wanted to say, steering clear of sentiment, that motherhood can end up being *all of it.*

Kirstin Allio was born in Maine in 1974. Her novel, *Garner,* was a finalist for the Los Angeles Times Book Prize for First Fiction. She also received the National Book Foundation's "5 Under 35" Award. Her short stories have appeared in a variety of publications. She lives in Seattle, Washington.

### Natalie Bakopoulos, "Fresco, Byzantine"

When doing research for my novel in progress, set in Athens, Greece, during the military dictatorship (1967–1974), I came across an interesting tidbit about frescoes that were painted in an island church by political prisoners who were held nearby. I couldn't get the idea out of my mind, so I began to work on a short story that imagined two characters doing such a thing. I also couldn't stop thinking of a line from the film *Before Night Falls* about the Cuban poet Reinaldo

Arenas: "People who make art are dangerous to any dictatorship. They create beauty and beauty is the enemy. . . . Artists are counter-revolutionaries." The conditions in many of these island prison camps were truly abhorrent, and the amount of suffering experienced is almost beyond my realm of thought. Yet I didn't want to write a story simply portraying such. Instead, I wanted to imagine prisoners dealing with such conditions but also going on with daily life as best they could in a new environment. To invent another context, one of escape, seems to me an artistic instinct: real-life stories abound of art being created under the most horrifying circumstances.

But "Fresco, Byzantine" is also a love story. Certain love affairs might also be a kind of artistic urge: the need, for whatever reason, to create a new, shared perspective, a new way of being in the world, one that when returned to the harshness of reality can fail and leave its players, like Nefeli and Vagelis, blinking into the light. Mihalis, in a way, represents the moral judgment we place on ourselves and others, a sort of judgment that might be rooted simply in an envy that arises from watching others break rules that we're too afraid to break ourselves.

Natalie Bakopoulos was born in 1972 in Dearborn, Michigan. She received her MFA in fiction from the University of Michigan. An early draft of her novel in progress won an Avery and Jule Hopwood Award and a Platsis Prize for Work on the Greek Legacy, both administered through the University of Michigan. Her short fiction has appeared in *Ninth Letter* and *Tin House*. Bakopoulos lives in Ann Arbor, Michigan.

## Wendell Berry, "Stand by Me"

My story comes from many years of thinking about World War II and its impact on such small places as my imagined town of Port William and its neighborhood. I first wrote about the Coulter family in 1954. I first wrote about the death of Tom Coulter in my novel *A Place on Earth,* which was begun in 1960, and the subject has come up again in my stories and novels from time to time. And finally, by long thought and what I can only call inspiration, I finally was able to write the story of Tom Coulter from the point of view of his uncle.

Wendell Berry was born in Newcastle, Kentucky, in 1934. He is an essayist, poet, and fiction writer, and has received fellowships from the Guggenheim, Lannan, and Rockefeller foundations and the National Endowment for the Arts, and also the T. S. Eliot Award, the Aitken Taylor Award, and the John Hay Award of the Orion Society. His latest book of prose is *Bringing It to the Table,* a collection of essays on farming and food, and his latest collection of poems is *Leavings.* Berry lives with his family on a farm in his native Henry County, Kentucky.

### George Bradley, "An East Egg Update"

The story was occasioned by the confluence of memory and hearsay, as I think most art is. The setting is one I recall from my youth, but the central event is someone else's remembered pain. An acquaintance told me that his sole recollection of his mother was a slap in the face, and the story started there. It started there, and I made it end there, but the body of it is a fabrication . . . not that all its readers have been happy to believe as much. People who ought to know better (some screenwriters and movie directors, now and then a novelist, even the occasional poet) have endorsed the myth that art depends immediately on circumstance, that the artist is a stenographer to incident, that life takes place and the author's job is to jot down what occurred. Call it the *Shakespeare in Love* fallacy. But to make a fiction, one composes—i.e., combines and arranges—elements of invention: a tale heard or overheard, a few troublesome or merely persistent memories, a harbored wish, an encountered name, a bit of pure fantasy. And then one looks at the result and sort of kicks it all in the direction of art.

"An East Egg Update" is not, then, a "true story." I don't believe there are any such things—all our experience comes mediated by the quality of our perceptions, our cast of mind—and if there were, I don't believe they would be inherently worth any more than the narrative of our ideas.

George Bradley was born in 1953 in Roslyn, New York. His volumes of poetry are *Terms to Be Met, Of the Knowledge of Good and Evil, The Fire Fetched Down,* and *Some Assembly Required,* and his work has appeared in *The New Yorker, The Paris Review, The New Republic,* and elsewhere. He was the Yale Younger Poet for 1985, and is editor of *The Yale Younger Poets Anthology.* He lives in Chester, Connecticut.

## Peter Cameron, "The End of My Life in New York"

Over the course of my writing career, I've morphed from an almost exclusive short-story writer into an almost exclusive novelist. I don't know exactly why or how this happened, but it's been increasingly difficult for me to find ideas for stories; the few ideas I do get nowadays all seem better suited for novels. I enjoy writing novels (well, sometimes) but I miss the particular pleasures and satisfactions that come from writing stories: it's a more intense, concentrated creative experience. So every once in a while I try to write a story, and since the writer Iris Owens once told me that she didn't believe in writer's block because all you needed was *one* sentence, the first sentence, and there you go, I occasionally try to come up with opening sentences, this being easier than coming up with complete ideas for stories. The first sentence of "The End of My Life in New York" is one of the very few sentences that grew up to be a short story, although it took a very long time to do this: for many years it languished on my hard drive, like one of those adult children who live in their parents' basement.

Peter Cameron was born in Pompton Plains, New Jersey, in 1959. He is the author of two collections of stories (*One Way or Another* and *Far-flung*) and five novels (*Leap Year, The Weekend, Andorra, The City of Your Final Destination,* and *Someday This Pain Will Be Useful to You*). His short fiction has been published in many magazines and journals, including *The New Yorker, Rolling Stone, The Paris Review, The Kenyon Review, The New England Review,* and *The Yale Review.* He is the recipient of fellowships from the National Endowment for the Arts and the John S. Guggenheim Foundation, and has worked on all of his books at the MacDowell Colony and Yaddo. He has taught at Columbia University, Sarah Lawrence College, and the New School, and worked administratively for different nonprofit organizations (the Trust for Public Land and Lambda Legal Defense and Education Fund). Cameron lives in New York City.

### Damon Galgut, "The Lover"

This story is an account of a real journey I made in 1995. By the time I sat down to write about it, several years had gone by and I could no longer recall everything with clarity. The straining to remember became as much a part of the story as the details of the journey and at a certain point it struck me that all memory is a kind of fiction. Hence the switch between first and third person, because in memory one is both a "he" and an "I" and at some moments even an "it." The journey involved is, of course, not just the physical one. It was my project in writing to tell the truth as honestly as I could recall it, about everybody's behavior, including my own, and not to let anybody off the hook. The result is something that includes fiction and memoir, travel narrative and confession, but doesn't fit comfortably into any one of those genres.

Damon Galgut was born in 1963 in Pretoria, South Africa. His first novel, *A Sinless Season,* appeared when he was seventeen years old. For several years he studied and taught drama at the University of Cape Town. His books include *Small Circle of Beings, The Beautiful Screamings of Pigs,* and *The Quarry,* which was made into a feature film in 1998. His novel *The Good Doctor* was short-listed for the Man

Booker Prize, the IMPAC Dublin Literary Award, and won the Commonwealth Writers' Prize for Africa. His latest novel, *The Impostor,* appeared in 2008. Galgut lives in Cape Town.

### James Lasdun, "Oh, Death"

This story was based on a real event. Much of the narrative around the event is invented, but the essential feelings driving it are as true to the strong emotions the event itself aroused in me as I could make them. One element I brought in as a way of giving expression to these emotions was the music—the "mountain music"—that the narrator has become infatuated with. I hope something of the wild energy and pathos, the joy and melancholy, of that music has found its way into the story.

James Lasdun was born in London in 1958. He has published several books of fiction, including *The Horned Man,* and three collections of poetry, including *Landscape with Chainsaw.* His story "The Siege" was made into the film *Besieged* by Bernardo Bertolucci. Another story, "An Anxious Man," was the inaugural winner of the BBC National Short Story Award (2006). His latest collection of short stories, *It's Beginning to Hurt,* was published in 2009. He lives in upstate New York.

### Daniyal Mueenuddin, "A Spoiled Man"

In the 1960s my parents bought a piece of land on a steep hillside, forty-five minutes up into the foothills of the Karakoram, up from Islamabad along the old British road to Srinagar. My mother designed and built a house, and this became our weekend retreat, cooler than the plains because of the elevation, a rock-built house surrounded by pine trees and terraced fields. The people in that area—*paharis,* mountain people—are notorious for their whinging, cringing character, their faithlessness, their duplicity, their pettiness and feuding. One weekend morning an old man came to see my father, a *pahari,* a small landowner from the area. He explained that he was unmarried and childless—could he have been gay? I wonder, yet another story—and that he feared his cousins were planning to murder him for the sake of the fine little orchard he owned just up the road from our house, with a stream running through it, apple trees, poplars. I happened to be riding my bicycle around in the lawn where my father had received this caller—and the old man pointed to me and said, "My cousins won't kill for what they can't get. I'll put the land into your son's name, if you'll protect me and pay me a life-time pension." And so, at the age of five, I became the owner of Ali Khan's land—that was the old man's name—and he became one of my familiars, a benefactor, with his flowing beard, his scratchy waist-coats, his ruddy cheeks, and his heavy walking stick on which he lumbered up to the teahouse every morning to sit and watch the buses come and go up to Kashmir, down to the plains. My father, of course, had thought that the old man would soon breathe his last, but he lived to a positively biblical age, enjoying the pension that my father had granted him, living in his orchard, tending the apple trees.

Throughout my childhood I would be taken to the Ali Khan land, and I now remember with a shiver of nostalgia the atmosphere there—the cool dirt floor in his windowless room, the jutting earthen terrace where he sat, looking out into the valley below, the river a thousand feet below, the cunning irrigation system that blocked the stream and flooded the lush grass growing between his apple trees, the tea that he would make, with goat's milk, clotted, and the smell of smoke from the fire that burned in his single room and of the goats that he kept, the soughing of the trees over the stream, his cracked blunt hands. Ali Khan is buried in his orchard, and I sometimes visit his grave. Some part of his spirit is memorialized in this story.

Daniyal Mueenuddin was born in Glendale, California, in 1963, and brought up in Lahore, Pakistan, and Elroy, Wisconsin. He is a gradu-ate of Dartmouth College, Yale Law School, and the MFA program at the University of Arizona, and his stories have appeared in *The New Yorker*, *Granta*, *Zoetrope*, and *The Best American Short Stories*

*2008.* His debut collection of linked stories, *In Other Rooms, Other Wonders,* was a finalist for the National Book Award in 2009, and was selected as one of the best books of the year by *Time, The Economist, Publishers Weekly, The New York Times,* the *Guardian,* and a number of other publications. For several years he practiced law in New York. He is now based on a farm in Pakistan's southern Punjab.

### Alice Munro, "Some Women"

The inspiration came, I think, from the tradition of dirty jokes in families quite prudish in behavior. Also important to the story is the delight men take in cheerfully uneducated women (this might be waning).

Alice Munro was born in 1931, grew up in Wingham, Ontario, and attended the University of Western Ontario. She has published eleven collections of stories—*Dance of the Happy Shades; Something I've Been Meaning to Tell You; The Beggar Maid; The Moons of Jupiter; The Progress of Love; Friend of My Youth; Open Secrets; The Love of a Good Woman; Hateship, Friendship, Courtship, Loveship, Marriage; Runaway;* and *The View from Castle Rock*—as well as a novel, *Lives of Girls and Women,* and *Selected Stories.* During her distinguished career, she has been the recipient of many awards and prizes, including three of Canada's Governor General's Literary Awards and two of its Giller Prizes, the Rea Award for the Short Story, the Lannan Literary Award, England's W. H. Smith Book Award, and the U.S.'s National Book Critics Circle Award. Her stories have appeared in *The New Yorker, The Atlantic Monthly, The Paris Review,* and other publications, and her collections have been translated into thirteen languages. She lives in Clinton, Ontario, near Lake Huron.

### Annie Proulx, "Them Old Cowboy Songs"

The idea for this story, one in the final collection of Wyoming stories, *Fine Just the Way It Is,* was to oppose the myth that hard work and riding out rough times—staples of frontier settler stories—would result in success and the foundation of a family ranch dynasty. Some people failed, and this is such a story. But the story was also an excuse for me to use two minor details that I've been saving for years: the variety of whiskey brands on the western frontier, and old cowboy songs which I find moving and plangent. My parents collected old bottles, and at my mother's death I donated their collection to the Shelburne Museum in Vermont. Obviously I have some interest in antique bottles, though without any desire to collect them. I have books, tapes, CDs, and sheet music of old C&W (cowboy-and-western) songs. The old name for these songs—"heart songs"—I used in a story collection focused on Vermont hill farms years ago. Most of the stories in *Fine Just the Way It Is* concern Wyoming women.

Annie Proulx was born in 1935 in Norwich, Connecticut. Her literary awards include the Dos Passos Prize, the National Book Award, the Irish Times International Fiction Prize, the PEN/Faulkner Award for Fiction, and the Pulitzer Prize. Her stories have won National Magazine awards and have been selected for *The O. Henry Prize Stories* several times before. Her works of fiction include a trio of story collections about Wyoming, *Close Range, Bad Dirt,* and *Fine Just the Way It Is.* Annie Proulx divides her time between an old sheep ranch in Wyoming and Albuquerque, New Mexico.

### Ron Rash, "Into the Gorge"

In the early 1930s, an elderly woman wandered off her mountain farm into a sparsely populated gorge called "The Dismal." My grandfather, her neighbor, led a search party into the gorge. Two days later they found her, sitting with her back against a tree as if waiting for them. I grew up hearing that story, and two years ago I matched that factual story with an image that had come to me of an older man running, though from what I did not know.

Ron Rash was born in 1953 and grew up in Boiling Springs, North Carolina. He is the author of four novels, *One Foot in Eden, Saints at the River, The World Made Straight,* and *Serena*; three collections of poems; and three collections of stories, among them *Chemistry and Other Stories*. Twice a finalist for the PEN/Faulkner Award, he is a previous recipient of the O. Henry Prize as well as National Endowment for the Arts fellowships in poetry and fiction. He teaches at Western Carolina University. Rash lives in Clemson, South Carolina.

## Jess Row, "Sheep May Safely Graze"

My relationship with Washington—the setting of "Sheep May Safely Graze"—is somewhat complicated. I was born and spent most of my childhood there; some of my earliest memories are of Rock Creek Park, the Mall, the reflecting pool, the Smithsonian, the National Cathedral. My father worked in the Department of Agriculture, and whenever I went to visit him I remember walking down a gray stone hallway smelling of Lysol that seemed to stretch into infinity. Then I would go into his office, where decaying, forgotten glasses of iced tea nestled among piles of papers and books taller than my head, and play with the cards from his punch-card IBM computer. That was my world; that was home. When you grow up around symbols part of you will always be incapable of thinking of them *as* symbols; they're simply the way things are.

In 2002 I traveled to Laos to do research on a novel set during the Vietnam War, and I saw on the Plain of Jars the giant bomb craters left when B-52 bombers discharged their payloads, sometimes in the dark, at random, after flying bombing missions over North Vietnam. I saw fences built of cluster-bomb canisters almost forty years old. Everywhere you go in Laos you see people who have lost limbs or eyes to exploding munitions, because, during that long-ago war, Laos was the most heavily bombed country on earth (I believe that since then it has been replaced by Iraq). At the time, the extent of U.S. involvement in Laos was a closely held secret, but hundreds or thousands of people in Washington knew exactly what was happening; they, too, went about their lives, playing tennis, picking up their kids from school, making cream-cheese-and-pimento canapés for cocktail parties. That, too, is simply the way things are.

In his famous essay *Das Unheimliche,* Freud invokes a German word with no exact equivalent in English; it's usually translated as "the uncanny," but *unheimlich* as I understand it more literally means "unhomely," or, as Freud puts it, "that class of the frightening which leads back to what is known of old and long familiar." When I return to Washington now I have a feeling that I can only classify as *unheimlich:* a kind of simultaneous recognition and revulsion. I have my memories, and also the feeling that I was entirely deceived. It sounds absurd and melodramatic to say so, but the city to me now seems covered in a kind of funereal dust, and everywhere I look I see faces immobilized by shame and wretchedness. That same feeling drove me to write "Sheep May Safely Graze." Here we have a man who can't manage his own emotions without turning them into a kind of vicious, private political theater, who has allowed grief and guilt to hollow him into a functional automaton. In Washington there is such a very thin line between altruism and violence. The most terrifying thing of all is that when I finished it, this story seemed entirely plausible, as if it had happened to someone I know, or, in another life, to me.

Jess Row was born in 1974 in Washington, D.C. After graduating from Yale in 1997, he taught English for two years as a Yale-China Fellow at the Chinese University of Hong Kong. He completed an MFA at the University of Michigan in 2001. His story collection *The Train to Lo Wu* was short-listed for the PEN/Hemingway Award and was a finalist for the Kiriyama Prize. In 2007 he was named a Best Young American Novelist by *Granta.* His stories have been anthologized twice in *The Best American Short Stories,* and he has received a Pushcart Prize, a National Endowment for the Arts fellowship in fiction, and a Whiting Writers' Award. His nonfiction and criticism have appeared in *Slate, The New York Times Book Review,* and elsewhere. An associate professor of English and Buddhist chaplain at the College of New Jersey, he also teaches in the MFA program at the Vermont College of Fine Arts.

### Preeta Samarasan, "Birch Memorial"

When I was about seven years old, I saw an old man bathing quite joyfully—obviously unperturbed by the stares and shouts of passersby—in a public fountain in my hometown, Ipoh. Over the next few years he became a fixture in that part of town. From the window of a bus, I once watched him loudly serenading an invisible listener with an air microphone, dressed in a little girl's dress he must have found at some rubbish dump. I never forgot that old man, or the way I could tell, even riding past him in a bus, that he lived in a hermetic alternate universe with its own inhabitants, its own history, its own geography, its own conventions.

Then, just a few years ago, I heard that the memorial statue of J. W. W. Birch—a very unpopular nineteenth-century representative of the British Empire in my home state—had been stolen from its place under the clock tower in Ipoh, and a new inscription added to the plaque to announce that the statue was "missing."

I'm not sure why these two details—the old man of long ago and the recent disappearance of the Birch statue—came together in my head, but they did, as disparate details often do, and seemed to demand to be woven into a single narrative.

Preeta Samarasan was born in Malaysia in 1976 and moved to the United States in 1992 to finish high school. She has an MA in musicology from the Eastman School of Music and an MFA in creative writing from the University of Michigan. In 2007, she won the Asian American Writers' Workshop/*Hyphen* magazine short-story contest. Her short fiction has appeared in *Hyphen, A Public Space, Asia Literary Review, Five Chapters, EGO Magazine,* and the anthology *Urban Odysseys: KL Stories.* Her novel is *Evening Is the Whole Day.* She lives in a small village in central France.

**Ted Sanders, "Obit"**

The impetus for "Obit" came in part because I'd heard an old man had died in a restaurant I used to work in, at table 21 against the back wall, and blood had been left behind on the scene for the owner and a busboy to dispose of, coughed up by the man as he sat and died in front of his wife. I remember wondering how dissimilar this dying was to any of the deaths the man had imagined for himself. Meanwhile, for some time, I'd been thinking about obituaries as a species of writing, and had been trying to excavate some discomfiting vein of distaste I had—that I still have—for the form. An obituary, I think, speaks a strange dialect of sadness—sadness that comes not simply from the apparent tragedies involved, but also from the obituary's own entrenched inability to convey anything meaningful about the nature of those tragedies. The obituary supplies us with names, dates, locations, maybe a few choice activities (a list that may or may not include the specifics of the dying itself), but leaves everything unexplicated. So much is lit upon, but nothing is illuminated. These conspicuous omissions diminish the very endeavor—that is, life—the obituary alleges to honor; the obituary does not, for instance, say anything about love. And because those limitations—the sterility, the terseness, the yawning implications—are the obituary's own most salient features, they have always seemed callous to me, and the practice is so ritualized that the callousness can come to feel like conspiracy. The whole custom feels a bit like serving an empty plate stained with the remnants of some already eaten meal. And the meal itself, the diner knows, was nothing short of everything. So that suggested a direction. I wandered into the thing hoping to summon up both the physical structure of the obituary and some of its crueler limitations. I can't, of course, say how clearly I'd refined such concerns at the time; I find that writing is often not much more than the act of allowing some half-unearthed dissatisfaction to speak obliquely for itself. I do know I fussed endlessly over the details of the story's structure, but whatever's worthy there now came together more the way an artifact of nature might, which is to say by force but not decree:

the outlines of characters emerged from the constraints of the prose, and eventually these paper shapes began to belong to one another—as if by echolocation—and in the end the entire structure of their delicate interactions managed, I hope and sometimes think, to briefly illuminate what any formal expression of grief must imply but never explore—which is to say again: everything.

Ted Sanders was born in 1969 in Illinois. His stories and essays have appeared in *Black Warrior Review, Georgia Review, Cincinnati Review, Gettysburg Review, Massachusetts Review,* and other journals. He teaches at the University of Illinois at Urbana-Champaign, and lives in Urbana, Illinois.

## Lore Segal, "Making Good"

Some years ago, two men of incorruptible goodwill, the late Isaac Zieman, a Jewish New York therapist, and Wolfgang Bornebusch, a German Lutheran pastor, held "workshops" here and in Germany that brought Jews and Germans together for a week of daylong concentrated interchange. It was my novelist's curiosity—not without massive misgivings—that made me join the New York workshop. My curiosity concerns the mutual relations, half a century after the events, of the party of the perpetrator and the party of the victim—German and Jew, white and black, colonial and colonized.

"Making Good" is a fiction. My workshop leader, Dr. Samuel Rosen, is no portrait of either of those two excellent men, and my irony is directed not at them but in illustration of my misgivings about the uses of confrontation. I have translated the original German contingent into fictional Austrians because my personal holocaust took place in my native Vienna before my parents put me on the children's transport to England.

I have been back to Vienna and have German friends whose feelings, actions, and politics I trust. Why do I breathe more freely when I'm out of there? Logic allows reconciliation, but the nerves are retentive, imprinted, won't let go. I don't recommend that it should be so; I found it was so in the act of writing "Making Good."

Lore Segal was born in Vienna, Austria, in 1928. In addition to several books for children, she is the author of the widely acclaimed novels *Other People's Houses, Her First American,* and *Shakespeare's Kitchen,* which was a finalist for the 2008 Pulitzer Prize for Fiction. A recipient of the American Academy of Arts and Letters Award in Literature, the Harold U. Ribalow Prize, the Carl Sandburg Literary Award, the Clifton Fadiman Medal, and a Guggenheim Fellowship, she has contributed to *The New Yorker,* among other publications. She has before been included in *The O. Henry Prize Stories.* Segal lives in New York City.

**William Trevor, "The Woman of the House"**
William Trevor was born in 1928 at Mitchelstown, County Cork, and spent his childhood in provincial Ireland. His novels include *Fools of Fortune, Felicia's Journey, The Story of Lucy Gault,* and *Love and Summer.* He is a renowned short-story writer and has published thirteen story collections, from *The Day We Got Drunk on Cake* to his most recent, *Cheating at Canasta.* Trevor lives in Devon, England.

**Brad Watson, "Visitation"**
I've made more than my share of mistakes in domestic affairs, and so I've spent a lot of time in motels with my younger son, Owen (sixteen), an exemplary travel companion who always helps to make my own experiences on the road easier and more pleasant than Loomis's experience in this story. We did spend some time in Southern California, but I loved visiting there with him, love the beaches and restaurants and of course the weather. Maybe I don't love I-5, but who does? Nevertheless, I wanted to write a story about the particular sense of loss that the "visitation" arrangement forces a divorced parent without custody to confront during visits. And I wanted to

evoke the sense of disorientation, even dissociation, that parents and children may feel when they spend their only time together in places and spaces which are, at worst, emotionally sterile, and at best merely accommodating in a bland and civil sort of way.

Brad Watson was born in 1955 in Meridian, Mississippi, and educated at Meridian Community College, Mississippi State University, and the University of Alabama. He has published two books, *Last Days of the Dog-Men* and *The Heaven of Mercury*. After working in journalism, advertising, and public relations in Alabama, he taught at the University of Alabama, Harvard University, the University of West Florida, the University of Mississippi, and the University of California, Irvine. Currently he's a member of the MFA faculty at the University of Wyoming. "Visitation" is included in his new book, *Aliens in the Prime of Their Lives*. Watson lives in Laramie, Wyoming.

### John Edgar Wideman, "Microstories"

Though I had tried short short fictions before, a request from *O* magazine got me thinking seriously about the idea that less could be more in a story—Oprah wanted a five-hundred-word story with all the conventional trappings of the conventional short story—so I contributed "Witness," and approximately one hundred twenty other short shorts followed.

John Edgar Wideman was born in 1941 in Washington, D.C. He is the author of more than twenty works of fiction and nonfiction, including the award-winning *Brothers and Keepers, Philadelphia Fire,* and most recently the story collection *God's Gym*. He is the recipient of two PEN/Faulkner awards as well as the Katherine Anne Porter Award from the American Academy of Arts and Letters, and has been nominated for the National Book Award. He teaches at Brown University. Wideman divides his time between New York City and France.

# Recommended Stories 2010

The task of picking the twenty PEN/O. Henry Prize Stories each year is at its most difficult at the end, when there are more than twenty admirable and interesting stories. Once the final choice is made, those remaining are our Recommended Stories, listed, along with the place of publication, in the hope that our readers will seek them out and enjoy them. Please go to our Web site, www .penohenryprizestories.com, for excerpts from the stories and information about the writers.

Luther Magnussen, "Work and Industry in the Northern Midwest," *The Yale Review*
Daniel Orozco, "Only Connect," *Ecotone*

# Publications Submitted

Because of production deadlines for the 2011 collection, it is essential that stories reach the series editor by May 1, 2010. If a finished magazine is unavailable before the deadline, magazine editors are welcome to submit scheduled stories in proof or manuscript. Work received after May 1, 2010, will be considered for *The PEN/O. Henry Prize Stories 2012*.

Stories may not be submitted by agents or writers.

Please see our Web site, www.penohenryprizestories.com, for more information about submission to *The PEN/O. Henry Prize Stories*.

The address for submission is:

Professor Laura Furman, The PEN/O. Henry Prize Stories
The University of Texas at Austin
English Department, B5000
1 University Station
Austin, TX 78712

The information listed below was up-to-date when *The PEN/O. Henry Prize Stories 2010* went to press. Inclusion in the listings does not constitute endorsement or recommendation.

**African American Review**
Saint Louis University
Humanities 317
3800 Lindell Boulevard
St. Louis, MO 63108
Joycelyn Moody, Editor in Chief
http://aar.slu.edu
Quarterly

**AGNI Magazine**
Boston University
236 Bay State Road
Boston, MA 02215
Sven Birkerts, Editor
agni@bu.edu
www.bu.edu/agni/
Semiannual

**Alaska Quarterly Review**
University of Alaska—Anchorage
3211 Providence Drive
Anchorage, AK 99508
Ronald Spatz, Editor
www.uaa.alaska.edu/aqr
Semiannual

**Alimentum**
PO Box 776
New York, NY 10163
Paulette Licitra and Peter Selgin,
    Editors
editor@alimentumjournal.com
www.alimentumjournal.com
Semiannual

**Alligator Juniper**
Prescott College
220 Grove Avenue
Prescott, AZ 86301
Melanie Bishop, Fiction Editor
aj@prescott.edu
www.prescott.edu/alligator
    _juniper
Annual

**American Letters &
Commentary**
Department of English
University of Texas at San
    Antonio
One UTSA Boulevard
San Antonio, TX 78749-0643
Catherine Kasper and David Ray
    Vance, Editors
AmerLetters@satx.rr.com
Annual

**American Literary Review**
PO Box 311307
University of North Texas
Denton, TX 76203-1307
John Tait, Editor
www.engl.unt.edu/alr
Semiannual

**The American Scholar**
Phi Beta Kappa Society
1606 New Hampshire
    Avenue NW

Washington, DC 20009
Robert Wilson, Editor
scholar@pbk.org
www.theamericanscholar.org
Quarterly

**American Short Fiction**
PO Box 301209
Austin, TX 78703
Jill Meyers, Editor
www.americanshortfiction.org
Quarterly

**Annalemma**
Chris Heavener, Editor
info@annalemma.net
http://annalemma.net

**Antioch Review**
PO Box 148
Yellow Springs, OH 45387-0148
Robert S. Fogarty, Editor
http://review.antioch.edu
Quarterly

**Apalachee Review**
PO Box 10469
Tallahassee, FL 32302
Michael Trammell, Editor
http://apalacheereview.org
Semiannual

**Arkansas Review: A Journal of Delta Studies**
Department of English and
    Philosophy
PO Box 1890
Arkansas State University
State University, AR 72467
Tom Williams, Editor
www.clt.astate.edu/arkreview
Triannual

**Ascent**
Concordia College
Department of English
901 S. Eighth Street
Moorhead, MN 56562
W. Scott Olsen, Editor
ascent@cord.edu
Triannual

**The Atlantic Monthly**
600 New Hampshire Ave, NW
Washington, DC 20037
C. Michael Curtis, Senior Fiction
    Editor
www.theatlantic.com
Monthly

**Avery Anthology**
Stephanie Firorelli, Adam
    Koehler, Andrew Palmer,
    Editors
submissions@averyanthology
    .org

www.averyanthology.org
Biannual

**Ballyhoo Stories**
PO Box 170
Prince Street Station
New York, NY 10012
Suzanne Pettypiece, Editor
editors@ballyhoostories.com
www.ballyhoostories.com
Annual

**Baltimore Review**
PO Box 36418
Towson, MD 21286
Susan Muaddi Darraj, Senior
    Editor
www.baltimorereview.org
Semiannual

**Barrelhouse**
Dave Housley, Editor
webmaster@barrelhousemag.com
www.barrelhousemag.com
Biannual

**Bat City Review**
Department of English
The University of Texas at Austin
1 University Station, B5000
Austin, TX 78712
Jenny Hanning, Editor
www.batcityreview.com

**Bateau**
PO Box 2335
Amherst, MA 01004
James Grinwis, Editor
info@bateaupress.org
www.bateaupress.org
Biannual

**Bellevue Literary Review**
Department of Medicine
NYU Langone Medical Center
550 First Avenue OBV-612
New York, NY 10016
Ronna Wineberg, J.D., Senior
    Fiction Editor
www.BLReview.org
Semiannual

**Black Clock**
California Institute of the Arts
24700 McBean Parkway
Valencia, CA 91355
Steve Erickson, Editor
submissions@blackclock.org
www.blackclock.org
Semiannual

**Black Warrior Review**
Box 862936
Tuscaloosa, AL 35486
Colleen Hollister, Fiction Editor
bwr@ua.edu
http://bwr.ua.edu/
Semiannual

**Bloodroot Literary Review**
PO Box 322
Thetford Center, VT 05075
"Do" Roberts, Editor
bloodroot@wildblue.net
www.bloodrootlm.com
Annual

**BOMB**
New Art Publications
80 Hanson Place
Suite 703
Brooklyn, NY 11217
Betsy Sussler, Editor in Chief
generalinquiries@bombsite.com
www.bombsite.com
Quarterly

**Boston Review**
35 Medford Street, Suite 302
Somerville, MA 02143
Deborah Chasman and Joshua
    Cohen, Editors
review@bostonreview.net
www.bostonreview.net
Published six times a year

**Boulevard Magazine**
6614 Clayton Road, PMB 325
Richmond Heights, MO 63117
Richard Burgin, Editor
www.boulevardmagazine.org
Triannual

**Brain, Child: The Magazine for Thinking Mothers**
PO Box 714
Lexington, VA 24450
Stephanie Wilkinson and Jennifer
    Niesslein, Editors
editor@brainchildmag.com
www.brainchildmag.com/
Quarterly

**Briar Cliff Review**
3303 Rebecca Street
PO Box 2100
Sioux City, IA 51104-2100
Tricia Currans-Sheehan, Editor
currans@briarcliff.edu
www.briarcliff.edu/bcreview
Annual

**Callaloo**
English Department
Texas A&M University
4227 TAMU
College Station, TX 77843-4227
Charles Henry Rowell, Editor
callaloo@tamu.edu
http://callaloo.tamu.edu
Quarterly

**Calyx, A Journal of Art and Literature by Women**
PO Box B
Corvallis, OR 97339
Beverly McFarland, Senior Editor

calyx@proaxis.com
www.calyxpress.org
Semiannual

**Canteen**
70 Washington Street, Suite 12H
Brooklyn, NY 11201
Sean Finney, Editor in Chief
info@canteenmag.com
www.canteenmag.com
Quarterly

**The Carolina Quarterly**
Greenlaw Hall, CB# 3520
University of North Carolina
Chapel Hill, NC 27599-3520
Matthew Luter, Fiction Editor
www.unc.edu/depts/cqonline
Triannual

**Chattahoochee Review**
2101 Womack Road
Dunwoody, GA 30338-4497
Marc Fitten, Editor
www.chattahoochee-review.org
Quarterly

**Chelsea**
PO Box 773
Cooper Station
New York, NY 10276-0773
Alfredo de Palchi, Editor
www.chelseamag.org
Semiannual

**Chicago Reader**
11 East Illinois
Chicago, IL 60611
Alison True, Editor
mail@chicagoreader.com
www.chicagoreader.com
Daily

**Chicago Review**
5801 S. Kenwood Avenue
Chicago, IL 60637
V. Joshua Adams, Editor
http://humanities.uchicago.edu/
    orgs/review
Quarterly

**Cimarron Review**
205 Morrill Hall
Oklahoma State University
Stillwater, OK 74078-4069
E. P. Walkiewicz, Editor
http://cimarronreview.okstate
    .edu
Quarterly

**Cincinnati Review**
University of Cincinnati
McMicken Hall, Room 369
PO Box 210069
Cincinnati, OH 45221-0069
Brock Clarke, Fiction
    Editor
www.cincinnatireview.com
Semiannual

**The Cold River Review**
PO Box 107
Acworth, NH 03601
riverrev@sover.net
Quarterly

**Colorado Review**
9105 Campus Delivery
Department of English
Colorado State University
Fort Collins, CO 80523
Stephanie G'Schwind, Editor
creview@colostate.edu
http://coloradoreview.colostate
    .edu
Triannual

**Commentary**
165 E. Fifty-sixth Street
New York, NY 10022
John Podhoretz, Editor
editorial@commentarymagazine
    .com
www.commentarymagazine
    .com
Monthly

**Concho River Review**
English Department
Angelo State University
PO Box 10894, ASU Station
San Angelo, TX 76909-0894
Mary Ellen Hartje, Editor
ME.hartje@angelo.edu

www.angelo.edu/dept/english/
    conchoriverreview.html
Semiannual

**Conclave: A Journal of Character**
7144 N. Harlem Avenue, #325
Chicago, IL 60631
Valya Dudycz Lupescu, Editor
editor@conclavejournal.com
www.conclavejournal.com
Annual

**Confrontation Magazine**
English Department
C. W. Post Campus, Long Island
    University
720 Northern Boulevard
Brookville, NY 11548
Martin Tucker, Editor in Chief
martin.tucker@liu.edu
www.liu.edu/confrontation
Semiannual

**Conjunctions**
21 E. Tenth Street
New York, NY 10003
Bradford Morrow, Editor
www.conjunctions.com
Semiannual

**Crab Orchard Review**
Southern Illinois University—
    Carbondale

1000 Faner Drive
Faner Hall 2380, Mail Code
    4503
Carbondale, IL 62901
Allison Joseph, Editor
http://craborchardreview.siuc.edu/
Semiannual

**Crazyhorse**
Department of English
College of Charleston
66 George Street
Charleston, SC 29424
Carol Ann Davis and Garrett
    Doherty, Editors
crazyhorse@cofc.edu
http://crazyhorse.cofc.edu
Semiannual

**Cream City Review**
Department of English
University of Wisconsin—
    Milwaukee
Box 413
Milwaukee, WI 53201
Jay Johnson and Phong Nguyen,
    Editors
www.creamcityreview.org
Semiannual

**Daedalus**
Norton's Woods
136 Irving Street

Cambridge, MA 02138
Phyllis S. Bendell, Managing
    Editor
daedalus@amacad.org
www.mitpressjournals.org/page/
    editorial/daed
Publication by invitation only.
    Quarterly.

**Dappled Things**
Mary Angelita Ruiz, Editor in
    Chief
dappledthings.editor@gmail.com
www.dappledthings.org
Quarterly

**Denver Quarterly**
Department of English
University of Denver
2000 E. Asbury
Denver, CO 80208
Bin Ramke, Editor
www.denverquarterly.com
Quarterly

**descant**
Department of English
Texas Christian University
TCU Box 297270
Fort Worth, TX 76129
Dave Kuhne, Editor
www.descant.tcu.edu
Annual

**Dossier**
244 DeKalb Avenue
Brooklyn, NY 11205
Thomas Yagoda, Literary Editor
www.dossierjournal.com
Semiannual

**Ecotone: reimagining place**
Department of Creative Writing
University of North Carolina—
  Wilmington
601 S. College Road
Wilmington, NC 28403-5938
Ben George, Editor
www.ecotonejournal.com
Quarterly

**Eleven Eleven Journal**
California College of the Arts
1111 Eighth Street
San Francisco, CA 94107
Hugh Behm-Steinberg, Faculty
  Editor
www.elevenelevenjournal.com
Biannual

**Epiphany**
71 Bedford Street
New York, NY 10014
Willard Cook, Editor
www.epiphanyzine.com
Semiannual

**Epoch**
251 Goldwin Smith Hall
Cornell University
Ithaca, NY 14853-3201
Michael Koch, Editor
www.arts.cornell.edu/english/
  epoch.html
Triannual

**Event**
Douglas College
PO Box 2503
New Westminster, BC V3L 5B2
  Canada
Rick Maddocks, Editor
http://event.douglas.bc.ca
Triannual

**Fantasy & Science Fiction**
PO Box 3447
Hoboken, NJ 07030
Gordon Van Gelder, Editor
www.sfsite.com/fsf/
Monthly

**The Farallon Review**
1017 L Street
Number 348
Sacramento, CA 95814
Tim Foley, Editor
editor@Farallonreview.com
www.Farallonreview.com

**Faultline**
Department of English
University of California—Irvine
Irvine, CA 92697-2650
Devin Becker and Max Winter,
    Editors
faultline@uci.edu
www.humanities.uci.edu/
    faultline
Annual

**FemSpec**
Batya Weinbaum, Editor
batyawein@aol.com
www.femspec.org
Biannual

**Fence Magazine**
Science Library 320
University at Albany
1400 Washington Avenue
Albany, NY 12222
Lynne Tillman, Fiction Editor
fence@albany.edu
www.fenceportal.org
Biannual

**Fiction**
Department of English
The City College of New York
Convent Avenue at 138th Street
New York, NY 10031
Mark Jay Mirsky, Editor in Chief
fictionmagazine@yahoo.com

www.fictioninc.com
Biannual

**The Fiddlehead**
Campus House, 11 Garland
    Court
UNB PO Box 4400
Fredericton, New Brunswick E3B
    5A3
Canada
Ross Leckie, Editor
fiddlehd@unb.ca
www.lib.unb.ca/Texts/Fiddlehead
Quarterly

**Fifth Wednesday Journal**
PO Box 4033
Lisle, IL 60532-9033
Vern Miller, Editor
www.fifthwednesdayjournal.com
Biannual

**First Line**
PO Box 250382
Plano, TX 75025-0382
David LaBounty, Editor
info@thefirstline.com
www.thefirstline.com
Quarterly

**Five Points**
Georgia State University
PO Box 3999
Atlanta, GA 30302-3999

David Bottoms and Megan
Sexton, Editors
http://www.webdelsol.com/Five
_Points
Triannual

**Florida Review**
Department of English
PO Box 161346
University of Central Florida
Orlando, FL 32816
Jocelyn Bartkevicius, Editor
www.flreview.com
Biannual

**Fugue**
University of Idaho
200 Brink Hall
PO Box 441102
Moscow, ID 83844-1102
Michael Lewis and Kendall Sand,
Editors
www.uidaho.edu/Fugue
Biannual

**Gargoyle**
3819 North Thirteenth Street
Arlington, VA 22201
Lucinda Ebersole and Richard
Peabody, Editors
gargoyle@gargoylemagazine.com
www.gargoylemagazine.com
Annual

**Georgia Review**
The University of Georgia
285 S. Jackson Street
Athens, GA 30602-9009
Stephen Corey, Editor
www.thegeorgiareview.com
Quarterly

**The Gettysburg Review**
Gettysburg College
Gettysburg, PA 17325-1491
Peter Stitt, Editor
www.gettysburgreview.com
Quarterly

**Glimmer Train**
1211 NW Glisan Street,
Suite 207
Portland, OR 97209
Susan Burmeister-Brown and
Linda B. Swanson-Davies,
Editors
www.glimmertrain.com
Quarterly

**Good Housekeeping**
Hearst Communications
300 West Fifty-seventh Street
New York, NY 10019
Laura Mathews, Literary Editor
www.goodhousekeeping.com
Monthly

**Grain**
PO Box 67
Saskatoon, Saskatchewan S7K 3KI
Canada
Sylvia Legris, Editor
grainmag@sasktel.net
www.grainmagazine.ca
Quarterly

**Granta**
12 Addison Avenue
London, UK W11 4QR
John Freeman, Editor
editorial@granta.com
www.granta.com
Quarterly

**Greensboro Review**
MFA Writing Program
3302 HHRA Building
University of North Carolina at
    Greensboro
Greensboro, NC 27402-6170
Jim Clark, Editor
www.greensbororeview.org
Biannual

**Gulf Coast**
Department of English
University of Houston
Houston, TX 77204-3013
Nick Flynn, Faculty Editor
www.gulfcoastmag.org
Biannual

**Happy**
46 St. Pauls Avenue
Jersey City, NJ 07306-1623
Bayard, Editor
bayardx@gmail.com
Quarterly

**Harper's Magazine**
666 Broadway
New York, NY 10012
Ben Metcalf, Literary Editor
www.harpers.org
Monthly

**Harpur Palate**
English Department
Binghamton University
P0 Box 6000
Binghamton, NY 13902
Barrett Bowlin and Kim Vose,
    Editors
http://harpurpalate.binghamton
    .edu
Biannual

**Harvard Review**
Lamont Library
Harvard University
Cambridge, MA 02138
Christina Thompson, Editor
harvard_review@harvard.edu
http://hcl.harvard.edu/
    harvardreview
Biannual

**Hayden's Ferry Review**
Box 875002
Arizona State University
Tempe, AZ 85287-5002
Beth Staples, Managing Editor
HFR@asu.edu
www.asu.edu/clas/pipercwcenter/
  publications/
  haydensferryreview/
Biannual

**Hemispheres**
Pace Communications
1301 Carolina Street
Greensboro, NC 27401
Randy Johnson, Editor
www.hemispheresmagazine
  .com
Monthly

**Hobart: another literary
journal**
PO Box 1658
Ann Arbor, MI 48106
Aaron Burch, Editor
www.hobartpulp.com
Biannual

**Hotel Amerika**
Columbia College, English
  Department
600 S. Michigan Avenue
Chicago, IL 60657
David Lazar, Editor

www.hotelamerika.net
Biannual

**H.O.W.**
112 Franklin Street, Fourth
  Floor
New York, NY 10013
Alison Weaver and Natasha
  Radojcic, Editors
www.HOWjournal.com
Biannual

**Hudson Review**
684 Park Avenue
New York, NY 10021
Paula Deitz, Editor
www.hudsonreview.com
Quarterly

**Hyphen: Asian America
Unabridged**
PO Box 192002
San Francisco, CA 94119
Harry Mok, Editor
editorial@hyphenmagazine.com
www.hyphenmagazine.com
Triannual

**Idaho Review**
Department of English
Boise State University
1910 University Drive
Boise, ID 83725
Mitch Wieland, Editor in Chief

http://www.boisestate.edu/the
  idahoreview/
Annual

**Image: A Journal of the Arts &
Religion**
3307 Third Avenue West
Seattle, WA 98119
Mary Kenagy Mitchell,
  Managing Editor
image@imagejournal.org
www.imagejournal.org
Quarterly

**Indiana Review**
Indiana University
Ballantine Hall 465
Bloomington, IN 47405-7103
Nina Mamikunian, Editor
inreview@indiana.edu
www.indiana.edu/~inreview/
Semiannual

**Iowa Review**
308 EPB
University of Iowa
Iowa City, IA 52242
David Hamilton, Editor
www.iowareview.org
Triannual

**Iron Horse Literary Review**
Department of English
Texas Tech University

Mail Stop 43091
Lubbock, TX 79409-3091
Leslie Jill Patterson, Editor in
  Chief
ironhorselitrev@yahoo.com
http://english.ttu.edu/IH/
Published six times a year

**Jabberwock Review**
Drawer E
Department of English
Mississippi State University
Mississippi State, MS 39762
Michael P. Kardos, Editor
www.msstate.edu/org/
  jabberwock
Biannual

**The Journal**
Ohio State University
Department of English
164 West Seventeenth Avenue
Columbus, OH 43210
Kathy Fagan and Michelle
  Herman, Editors
thejournal@osu.edu
http://english.osu.edu/research/
  journals/thejournal/
Biannual

**Juked**
110 Westridge Drive
Tallahassee, FL 32304
J. W. Wang, Editor

www.juked.com
Annual

**Kalliope: A Journal of Women's
Literature and Art**
Florida Community College at
 Jacksonville
11901 Beach Boulevard
Jacksonville, FL 32246
Margaret L. Clark, PhD, Editor
maclark@fccj.edu
Biannual

**Karamu**
English Department
Eastern Illinois University
600 Lincoln Avenue
Charleston, IL 61920
Olga Abella, Editor
www.eiu.edu/~english/karamu/
 index.html
Annual

**Kenyon Review**
Kenyon College
Finn House
102 W. Wiggin Street
Gambier, OH 43022
David H. Lynn, Editor
kenyonreview@kenyon.edu
www.kenyonreview.org
Quarterly

**The L Magazine**
20 Jay Street, Suite 207
Brooklyn, NY 11201
Jonny Diamond, Editor in Chief
editor@thelmagazine.com
www.thelmagazine.com
Annual fiction issue

**Lake Effect**
Penn State—Erie
4951 College Drive
Erie, PA 16563-1501
George Looney, Editor in Chief
www.behrend.psu.edu/lakeeffect
Annual

**The Land-Grant College
Review**
PO Box 1164
New York, NY 10159
Dave Koch and Josh Melrod,
 Editors
editors@lgcr.org
www.land-grantcollegereview
 .com/
Semiannual

**Laurel Review**
Green Tower Press, Department
 of English
Northwest Missouri State
 University
800 University Drive
Maryville, MO 64468-6001

John Gallaher, Editor
http://catpages.nwmissouri
.edu/m/tlr
Biannual

**Lilies and Cannonballs
Review**
PO Box 702
Bowling Green Station
New York, NY 10274-0702
Daniel Connor, Editor
info@liliesandcannonballs.com
www.liliesandcannonballs.com
Semiannual

**The Literary Review**
285 Madison Avenue
Madison, NJ 07940
Minna Proctor, Editor
tlr@fdu.edu
www.theliteraryreview.org
Quarterly

**The Long Story**
18 Eaton Street
Lawrence, MA 01843
R. P. Burnham, Editor
rpburnham@mac.com
http://homepage.mac.com/
rpburnham/longstory.html
Annual

**Louisiana Literature**
Box 10792

Southeastern Louisiana
University
Hammond, LA 70402
Jack Bedell, Editor
lalit@selu.edu
www.louisianaliterature.org/
press/
Semiannual

**Low Rent**
W. P. Hughes, Editor
Robert Liddell, Fiction Editor
fiction@lowrentmagazine.com
www.lowrentmagazine.com
Published six times a year

**Make: A Chicago Literary
Magazine**
PO Box 478353
Chicago, IL 60647
Sarah Dodson, Managing Editor
http://makemag.com
Biannual

**Malahat Review**
University of Victoria
PO Box 1700
STN CSC
Victoria, BC V8W 2Y2
Canada
John Barton, Editor
malahat@uvic.ca
www.malahatreview.ca
Quarterly

**Mānoa**
English Department
University of Hawai'i
1733 Donaghho Road
Honolulu, HI 96822
Frank Stewart, Editor
mjournal-l@hawaii.edu
http://manoajournal.hawaii.edu
Semiannual

**Massachusetts Review**
South College
University of Massachusetts
Amherst, MA 01003-7140
David Lenson, Editor
massrev@external.umass.edu
www.massreview.org
Quarterly

**McSweeney's Quarterly Concern**
849 Valencia Street
San Francisco, CA 94110
Dave Eggers, Editor
printsubmissions@mcsweeneys
   .net
www.mcsweeneys.net
Quarterly

**Meridian**
University of Virginia
PO Box 400145
Charlottesville, VA 22904-4145
Julia Hansen, Editor

www.readmeridian.org
Semiannual

**Michigan Quarterly Review**
University of Michigan
3574 Rackham Building
915 E. Washington Street
Ann Arbor, MI 48109-1070
Laurence Goldstein, Editor
MQR@umich.edu
www.umich.edu/~mqr
Quarterly

**Midstream**
633 Third Avenue, 21st Floor
New York, NY 10017-6706
Leo Haber, Editor
midstreamthf@aol.com
www.midstreamthf.com
Published six times a year

**Minnesota Review**
Department of English
Carnegie Mellon University
Pittsburgh, PA 15213
Jeffrey J. Williams, Editor
editors@theminnesotareview.org
www.theminnesotareview.org
Semiannual

**Minnetonka Review**
PO Box 386
Spring Park, MN 55384
Troy Ehlers, Editor in Chief

www.minnetonkareview.com
Semiannual

**MiPOesias**
Didi Menendez, Editor
www.mipoesias.com

**Mississippi Review**
The University of Southern
    Mississippi
118 College Drive
Box 5144
Hattiesburg, MS 39406
Frederick Barthelme, Editor
www.mississippireview.com
Semiannual

**Missouri Review**
357 McReynolds Hall
University of Missouri—
    Columbia
Columbia, MO 65211
Speer Morgan, Editor
www.missourireview.com
Quarterly

**Mused: The BellaOnline
Literary Review Magazine**
Melissa Knoblett-Aman, Senior
    Fiction Editor
www.bellaonline.com/review/

**Natural Bridge: A Journal of
Contemporary Literature**
Department of English
University of Missouri—St. Louis
One University Boulevard
St. Louis, MO 63121
Kenneth E. Harrison, Jr., Editor
natural@umsl.edu
www.umsl.edu/~natural
Semiannual

**Ne'er-Do-Well Literary
Magazine**
Sheila Ashdown, Editor
www.theneerdowell.com

**New Delta Review**
English Department
15 Allen Hall
Louisiana State University
Baton Rouge, LA 70803-5001
Shelby Goddard, Editor
www.lsu.edu/newdeltareview/
Semiannual

**New England Review**
Middlebury College
Middlebury, VT 05753
Stephen Donadio, Editor
nereview@middlebury.edu
www.nereview.com
Quarterly

**New Letters**
University of Missouri—Kansas
   City
5101 Rockhill Road
Kansas City, MO 64110
Robert Stewart, Editor in Chief
newletters@umkc.edu
www.newletters.org
Quarterly

**New Madrid**
Department of English
Murray State University
7C Faculty Hall
Murray, KY 42701-3341
Ann Neelon, Editor
www.murraystate.edu/
   newmadrid/
Biannual

**New Millennium Writings**
PO Box 2463
Knoxville, TN 37901
Don Williams, Editor
www.newmillenniumwritings
   .com
Annual

**New Ohio Review**
English Department
360 Ellis Hall
Ohio University
Athens, OH 45701

Jill Allyn Rosser, Editor
noreditors@ohio.edu
www.ohiou.edu/nor
Semiannual

**New Orleans Review**
Box 195
Loyola University
New Orleans, LA 70118
John Biguenet and Christopher
   Chambers, Editors
www.neworleansreview.org
Semiannual

**New Quarterly**
St. Jerome's University
290 Westmount Road North
Waterloo, Ontario N2L 3G3
Canada
Kim Jernigan, Editor
editor@tnq.ca
www.tnq.ca
Quarterly

**The New Yorker**
4 Times Square
New York, NY 10036
Deborah Treisman, Fiction
   Editor
fiction@newyorker.com
www.newyorker.com
Weekly

**Nimrod International Journal
of Prose and Poetry**
University of Tulsa
800 S. Tucker Drive
Tulsa, OK 74104
Francine Ringold, Editor in
    Chief
nimrod@utulsa.edu
www.utulsa.edu/nimrod
Semiannual

**Ninth Letter**
Department of English
University of Illinois, Urbana-
    Champaign
608 S. Wright Street
Urbana, IL 61801
Jodee Stanley, Editor
www.ninthletter.com
Semiannual

**Noon**
1324 Lexington Avenue
PMB 298
New York, NY 10128
Diane Williams, Editor
www.noonannual.com/
Annual

**North American Review**
University of Northern Iowa
1222 West Twenty-seventh Street
Cedar Falls, Iowa 50614-0516

Grant Tracey, Fiction Editor
nar@uni.edu
www.webdelsol.com/
    NorthAmReview/NAR
Published five times per year

**North Carolina Literary Review**
Department of English
2201 Bate Building
East Carolina University
Greenville, NC 27858-4353
Margaret Bauer, Editor
bauerm@ecu.edu
www.ecu.edu/nclr
Annual

**North Dakota Quarterly**
Merrifield Hall, Room 110
276 Centennial Drive, Stop 7209
Grand Forks, ND 58202-7209
Robert W. Lewis, Editor
ndq@und.edu
www.und.nodak.edu/org/ndq
Quarterly

**Northern New England Review**
Attn: Humanities Department
Franklin Pierce University
40 University Drive
Rindge, NH 03461
Edie Clark, Managing Editor
nner@franklinpierce.edu
Semiannual

**Northwest Review**
5243 University of Oregon
Eugene, OR 97403
Ehud Havazelet, Fiction Editor
www.uoregon.edu/~nwreview
Triannual

**Notre Dame Review**
840 Flanner Hall
Department of English
University of Notre Dame
Notre Dame, IN 46556
John Matthias and William
    O'Rourke, Editors
www.nd.edu/~ndr/review.htm
Semiannual

**Ocho**
www.mipoesias.com

**One Story**
The Old American Can Factory
232 Third Street, #A111
Brooklyn, NY 11215
Hannah Tinti, Editor
www.one-story.com
Published about every three
    weeks

**Open City**
270 Lafayette Street
Suite 1412
New York, NY 10012

Thomas Beller and Joanna Yas,
    Editors
editors@opencity.org
www.opencity.org
Triannual

**Opium Magazine**
144 A Diamond Street
Suite #2
Brooklyn, NY 11222
Todd Zuniga, Editor
todd@opiummagazine.com
www.opiummagazine.com
Semiannual

**Oranges & Sardines**
Didi Menendez, Editor in Chief
www.poetsandartists.com
Triannual

**Other Voices**
University of Illinois at Chicago
Department of English, MC162
601 South Morgan Street
Chicago, IL 60607-7120
Gina Frangello, Executive
    Editor
www.othervoicesmagazine.org
Semiannual

**Overtime**
PO Box 250382
Plano, TX 75025-0382

www.workerswritejournal.com/
overtime.htm
One–three times annually

**Oxford American**
201 Donaghey Avenue,
Main 107
Conway, AR 72035
Marc Smirnoff, Editor
oamag@oxfordamericanmag
.com
www.oxfordamericanmag.com
Quarterly

**Pakn Treger**
National Yiddish Book Center
Harry and Jeanette Weinberg
Building
1021 West Street
Amherst, MA 01002-3375
Nancy Sherman, Editor
pt2008@bikher.org
www.yiddishbookcenter.org/
+10527
Triannual

**Panhandler**
Department of English and
Foreign Languages
University of West Florida
11000 University Parkway
Pensacola, FL 32514
Jonathan Fink, Editor

jfink@uwf.edu
www.uwf.edu/panhandler
Annual

**The Paris Review**
62 White Street
New York, NY 10013
Nathaniel Rich, Fiction Editor
www.theparisreview.org
Quarterly

**Parting Gifts**
3413 Wilshire Drive
Greensboro, NC 27408
Robert Bixby, Editor
rbixby@earthlink.net
www.marchstreetpress.com
Semiannual

**Passages North**
Department of English
Northern Michigan University
1401 Presque Isle
Marquette, MI 49855
Kate Myers Hanson, Editor in
Chief
http://myweb.nmu.edu/~passages
Annual

**PEN/America**
PEN American Center
588 Broadway, Suite 303
New York, NY 10012

M. Mark, Editor
journal@pen.org
www.pen.org
Semiannual

**Phantasmagoria**
English Department
Century College
3300 Century Avenue North
White Bear Lake, MN 55110
Abigail Allen, Editor
Semiannual

**Phoebe: A Journal of
Literature and Art**
MSN 2C5
George Mason University
4400 University Drive
Fairfax, VA 22030-4444
Nat Foster, Editor
phoebe@gmu.edu
www.gmu.edu/pubs/phoebe
Semiannual

**Pilot Pocket Book**
PO Box 161, Station B
119 Spadina Avenue
Toronto, Ontario M5T 2T3
Canada
Reuben McLaughlin, Lee
    Sheppard, Bryan Belanger,
    Editors
editor@thepilotproject.ca

www.thepilotproject.ca
Semiannual

**The Pinch**
Department of English
University of Memphis
Memphis, TN 38152
Kristen Iversen, Editor
www.thepinchjournal.com
Semiannual

**Playboy**
730 Fifth Avenue
New York, NY 10019
Amy Grace Loyd, Literary Editor
aloyd@playboy.com
www.playboy.com
Monthly

**Pleiades**
Department of English and
    Philosophy
University of Central Missouri
Warrensburg, MO 64093
Wayne Miller and Kevin Prufer,
    Editors
pleiades@ucmo.edu
www.ucmo.edu/englphil/pleiades
Semiannual

**Ploughshares**
Emerson College
120 Boylston Street

Boston, MA 02116-4624
Ladette Randolph, Editor in
    Chief
pshares@emerson.edu
www.pshares.org
Triannual

**PMS poemmemoirstory**
HB 217
1530 Third Avenue South
Birmingham, AL 35294-1260
Minda Frost, Editor in Chief
http://pms-journal.org
Annual

**Post Road**
PO Box 400951
Cambridge, MA 02140
Ricco Siasoco, Managing Editor
fiction@postroadmag.com
www.postroadmag.com
Semiannual

**Potomac Review**
Montgomery College
Paul Peck Humanities Institute
51 Mannakee Street
Rockville, MD 20850
Julie Wakeman-Linn, Editor
www.montgomerycollege.edu/
    potomacreview
Semiannual

**Prairie Fire**
423-100 Arthur Street
Winnipeg, Manitoba R3B 1H3
Canada
Andris Taskans, Editor
prfire@mts.net
www.prairiefire.ca/
Quarterly

**Prairie Schooner**
201 Andrews Hall
University of Nebraska
Lincoln, NE 68588-0334
Hilda Raz, Editor in Chief
www.prairieschooner.unl.edu
Quarterly

**Prism International**
University of British Columbia
Buchanan E-462
1866 Main Mall
Vancouver, British Columbia
    V6T 1Z1
Canada
Michelle Miller, Fiction Editor
prism@interchange.ubc.ca
www.prismmagazine.ca
Quarterly

**Product**
University of Southern
    Mississippi
118 College Drive, #5144

Hattiesburg, MS 39406-0001
J. W. Wang, Editor
Annual

**A Public Space**
323 Dean Street
Brooklyn, New York 11217
Brigid Hughes, Editor
editors@apublicspace.org
www.apublicspace.org
Quarterly

**Puerto del Sol**
MSC 3E, New Mexico State
    University
PO Box 30001
Las Cruces, NM 88003-8001
Carmen Giménez Smith, Editor
    in Chief
www.puertodelsol.org
Semiannual

**Quarterly West**
University of Utah
255 South Central Campus
    Drive
Department of
    English/LNCO3500
Salt Lake City, UT 84112
Paul Ketzle and Brenda
    Sieczkowski, Editors
www.utah.edu/quarterlywest
Semiannual

**Raritan: A Quarterly Review**
Rutgers University
31 Mine Street
New Brunswick, NJ 08903
Jackson Lears, Editor in Chief
http://raritanquarterly.rutgers
    .edu
Quarterly

**Redivider**
Emerson College
120 Boylston Street
Boston, MA 02116
Matt Salesses, Editor in
    Chief
www.redividerjournal.org
Semiannual

**Red Rock Review**
English Department, J2A
College of Southern Nevada
3200 E. Cheyenne Avenue
North Las Vegas, NV 89030
Richard Logsdon, Senior
    Editor
Semiannual

**Reed Magazine**
Department of English
San Jose State University
One Washington Square
San Jose, CA 95192-0090
D. E. Kern, Senior Editor

reed@email.sjsu.edu
www.reedmag.org
Annual

**Relief: A Quarterly Christian Expression**
60 W. Terra Cotta, Suite B,
Unit 156
Crystal Lake, IL 60014-3548
Kimberly Culbertson, Editor in
Chief
www.reliefjournal.com
Quarterly

**River Styx**
3547 Olive Street, Ste. 107
St. Louis, MO 63103-1014
Richard Newman, Editor
www.riverstyx.org
Triannual

**Roanoke Review**
221 College Lane
Salem, VA 24153
Paul Hanstedt, Editor
review@roanoke.edu
Annual

**Rosebud Magazine**
N3310 Asje Road
Cambridge, WI 53523
Roderick Clark, Editor
www.rsbd.net
Triannual

**Ruminate**
140 North Roosevelt Avenue
Fort Collins, CO 80521
Brianna Van Dyke, Editor in
Chief
editor@ruminatemagazine.com
www.ruminatemagazine.com
Quarterly

**St. Anthony Messenger**
28 West Liberty Street
Cincinnati, OH 45202-6498
Pat McCloskey, O.F.M., Editor
StAnthony@AmericanCatholic
.org
www.AmericanCatholic.org
Monthly

**St. Petersburg Review**
Box 288
Concord, NH 03302
Elizabeth L. Hodges, Editor
editors@stpetersburgreview.com
www.stpetersburgreview.com
Annual

**Salamander**
English Department
Suffolk University
41 Temple Street
Boston, MA 02114
Jennifer Barber, Editor
www.salamandermag.org
Semiannual

**Salmagundi**
Skidmore College
Saratoga Springs, NY 12866
Robert Boyers, Editor in Chief
Quarterly

**Santa Monica Review**
Santa Monica College
1900 Pico Boulevard
Santa Monica, CA 90405
Andrew Tonkovich, Editor
antonkovi@uci.edu
www.smc.edu/sm_review
Semiannual

**Saranac Review**
CVH, Department of English
SUNY Plattsburgh
101 Broad Street
Plattsburgh, NY 12901
Linda Young, Editor
http://research.plattsburgh.edu/
    saranacreview
Annual

**Sensations Magazine**
PO Box 132
Lafayette, NJ 07848
David Messino, Editor
www.sensationsmag.com

**Seven Days**
PO Box 1164
Burlington, VT 05402-1164

Pamela Polston and Paula Routly,
    Editors
www.sevendaysvt.com
Weekly

**Sewanee Review**
University of the South
735 University Avenue
Sewanee, TN 37383-1000
George Core, Editor
www.sewanee.edu/sewanee
    _review
Quarterly

**Shenandoah**
Mattingly House
2 Lee Avenue
Washington and Lee University
Lexington, VA 24450-2116
R. T. Smith, Editor
shenandoah@wlu.edu
shenandoah.wlu.edu
Triannual

**Silent Voices**
PO Box 11180
Glendale, CA 91226
Peter A. Balaskas, Editor
exmachinapab@aol.com
www.exmachinapress.com
Annual

**Slice Magazine**
920 8th Avenue, Suite 1

Brooklyn, NY 11215
Shane Dixon Kavanaugh,
    Submissions Editor
editors@slicemagazine.org
www.slicemagazine.org
Semiannual

**Sonora Review**
English Department
University of Arizona
Tucson, AZ 85721
Astrid Duffy Slagle, Fiction
    Editor
sonora@email.arizona.edu
www.coh.arizona.edu/sonora
Semiannual

**South Carolina Review**
Center for Electronic and Digital
    Publishing
Clemson University
Strode Tower, Box 340522
Clemson, SC 29634-0522
Wayne Chapman, Editor
www.clemson.edu/caah/cedp/
    scrintro.htm
Semiannual

**South Dakota Review**
Department of English
University of South Dakota
414 E. Clark Street
Vermillion, SD 57069
Brian Bedard, Editor

sdreview@usd.edu
www.usd.edu/sdreview
Quarterly

**Southeast Review**
Department of English
Florida State University
Tallahassee, FL 32306
Jessica Pitchford, Editor
southeastreview@gmail.com
www.southeastreview.org
Semiannual

**Southern Humanities Review**
9088 Haley Center
Auburn University
Auburn, AL 36849
Dan R. Latimer and Virginia M.
    Kouidis, Editors
www.auburn.edu/shr
Quarterly

**Southern Indiana Review**
College of Liberal Arts
University of Southern Indiana
8600 University Boulevard
Evansville, IN 47712
Ron Mitchell, Editor
www.usi.edu/sir/
Semiannual

**Southern Review**
Louisiana State University
Old President's House

Baton Rouge, LA 70803-0001
Jeanne M. Leiby, Editor
www.lsu.edu/thesouthernreview
Quarterly

**Southwest Review**
Southern Methodist University
PO Box 750374
Dallas, TX 75275
Willard Spiegelman, Editor in
    Chief
www.smu.edu/southwestreview
Quarterly

**Spot Literary Magazine**
PO Box 3833
Palos Verdes Peninsula, CA
    90274
Susan Hansell, Editor
susan.hansell@gmail.com
www.spotlitmagazine.net/
Semiannual

**Subtropics**
Department of English,
    University of Florida
4008 Turlington Hall
PO Box 112075
Gainesville, FL 32611
David Leavitt, Editor
subtropics@english.ufl.edu
www.english.ufl.edu/
    subtropics
Triannual

**Sun Magazine**
107 N. Roberson Street
Chapel Hill, NC 27516
Sy Safransky, Editor
www.thesunmagazine.org
Monthly

**Sycamore Review**
Purdue University
Department of English
500 Oval Drive
West Lafayette, IN 47907-2038
Mehdi Okasi, Editor in Chief
sycamore@purdue.edu
www.sycamorereview.com
Semiannual

**Tampa Review**
University of Tampa
401 W. Kennedy Boulevard
Tampa, FL 33606-1490
Richard Mathews, Editor
utpress@ut.edu
http://utpress.ut.edu/
Semiannual

**Third Coast**
Department of English
Western Michigan University
Kalamazoo, MI 49008-5331
Daniel Toronto, Editor
editors@thirdcoastmagazine.com
www.thirdcoastmagazine.com
Semiannual

**Threepenny Review**
PO Box 9131
Berkeley, CA 94709
Wendy Lesser, Editor
www.threepennyreview.com
Quarterly

**Timber Creek Review**
PO Box 16542
Greensboro, NC 27416
John M. Freiermuth, Editor
Quarterly

**Tin House**
PO Box 10500
Portland, OR 97210
Win McCormack, Editor
  in Chief
www.tinhouse.com
Quarterly

**Transition Magazine**
104 Mount Auburn St.
3R
Cambridge, MA 02138
F. Abiola Irele and Tommie
  Shelby, Editors
transition@fas.harvard.edu
www.transitionmagazine.com
Triannual

**TriQuarterly**
Northwestern University
629 Noyes Street

Evanston, IL 60208
Susan Firestone Hahn, Editor
www.triquarterlyto-day
  .blogspot.com/
Triannual

**upstreet**
PO Box 105
Richmond, MA 01254-0105
Vivian Dorsel, Editor
www.upstreet-mag.org
Annual

**Virginia Quarterly Review**
1 West Range
PO Box 400223
Charlottesville, VA 22904
Ted Genoways, Editor
vqreview@vqronline.org
www.vqronline.org
Quarterly

**Watchword**
Watchword Press
PO Box 5755
Berkeley, CA 94705
Editorial Team
Liz@watchwordpress.org
www.watchwordpress.org
Semiannual

**Weber: The Contemporary
West**
Weber State University

1405 University Circle
Ogden, UT 84408-1408
Michael Wutz, Editor
weberjournal@weber.edu
www.weber.edu/weberjournal
Triquarterly

**West Branch**
Bucknell Hall
Bucknell University
Lewisburg, PA 17837
Paula Closson Buck, Editor
westbranch@bucknell.edu
www.bucknell.edu/westbranch
Semiannual

**Western Humanities Review**
University of Utah
English Department
255 S. Central Campus Drive,
    Room 3500
Salt Lake City, UT 84112-0494
Barry Weller, Editor
www.hum.utah.edu/whr
Triannual

**Whistling Shade**
PO Box 7084
Saint Paul, MN 55107
Anthony Telschow, Executive
    Editor
editor@whistlingshade.com
www.whistlingshade.com/
Quarterly

**Willow Springs**
Eastern Washington University
501 North Riverpoint Boulevard,
    Ste. 425
Spokane, WA 99202
Samuel Ligon, Editor
http://willowsprings.ewu.edu
Semiannual

**Witness Magazine**
Black Mountain Institute
University of Nevada, Las Vegas
Box 455085
Las Vegas, NV 89154-5085
Amber Withycombe, Editor
witness@unlv.edu
http://witness
    .blackmountaininstitute
    .org/
Annual

**WLA: War, Literature & the Arts**
Department of English
2354 Fairchild Drive, Ste.
    6D45
USAF Academy
Colorado Springs, CO 80840-
    6242
Donald Anderson, Editor
www.wlajournal.com
Semiannual

**Worcester Review**
1 Ekman Street
Worcester, MA 01607
Rodger Martin, Managing Editor
www.theworcesterreview.org/
Annual

**Words of Wisdom**
8969 UNCG Station
Greensboro, NC 27413
Mikhammad Bin Muhandis
    Abdel-Ishahara, Editor
Quarterly

**Workers Write!**
PO Box 250382
Plano, TX 75025-0382
David LaBounty, Editor
www.workerswritejournal.com
Annual

**Xavier Review**
110 Xavier University
New Orleans, LA 70125
Richard Collins, Editor
rcollins@xula.edu
www.xula.edu/review/
Semiannual

**xconnect: writers of the
information age**
PO Box 2317
Philadelphia, PA 19103

David E. Deifer, Editor
editors@xconnect.org
www.xconnect.org
Annual

**Yale Review**
PO Box 208243
Yale University
New Haven, CT 06520-8243
J. D. McClatchy, Editor
yalereview@aol.com
www.yale.edu/yalereview/
Quarterly

**Zoetrope: All-Story**
916 Kearny Street
San Francisco, CA 94133
Michael Ray, Editor
info@all-story.com
www.all-story.com
Quarterly

**Zone 3**
APSU Box 4565
Austin Peay State University
Clarksville, TN 37044
Blas Falconer and Barry
    Kitterman, Editors
www.apsu.edu/zone3
Semiannual

# Permissions

## Associate Member Registration

NAME: _____

ADDRESS: _____

CITY/STATE/ZIP: _____

TELEPHONE: _____

E-MAIL ADDRESS: _____

I AM A(N): ❑ WRITER  ❑ ACADEMIC  ❑ BOOKSELLER  ❑ EDITOR
❑ JOURNALIST  ❑ LIBRARIAN  ❑ PUBLISHER  ❑ TRANSLATOR  ❑ OTHER_____

❑ I AM INTERESTED IN VOLUNTEER OPPORTUNITIES WITH PEN.

❑ I ENCLOSE $40, MY ANNUAL ASSOCIATE MEMBERSHIP DUES.
         -- OR --
❑ I ENCLOSE $20, MY ANNUAL STUDENT ASSOCIATE MEMBERSHIP DUES.

❑ I ALSO ENCLOSE A TAX-DEDUCTIBLE CONTRIBUTION IN ADDITION TO MY DUES TO PROVIDE MUCH-NEEDED SUPPORT FOR THE *READERS AND WRITERS* PROGRAM AT PEN, WHICH ENCOURAGES LITERARY CULTURE THROUGH OUTREACH PROGRAMS AND LITERARY EVENTS, INCLUDING AUTHOR PANELS, WRITING AND READING WORKSHOPS FOR HIGH SCHOOL STUDENTS, AND THE WRITING INSTITUTE, WHICH INVITES TEENS TO INTERACT DIRECTLY WITH PROFESSIONAL WRITERS IN A SERIES OF WORKSHOPS. FOR MORE INFO, VISIT: WWW.PEN.ORG/READERSANDWRITERS.

❑ $50  ❑ $100  ❑ $500  ❑ $1,000 PRESIDENT'S CIRCLE
❑ OTHER $_____

TOTAL: $_____

(ALL CONTRIBUTIONS ABOVE THE BASIC DUES OF $40/$20 ARE TAX DEDUCTIBLE TO THE FULLEST EXTENT ALLOWED BY THE LAW.)

PLEASE MAKE YOUR CHECK PAYABLE TO **PEN AMERICAN CENTER.**

MAIL FORM AND CHECK TO:
PEN AMERICAN CENTER, MEMBERSHIP DEPARTMENT
588 BROADWAY, 303, NEW YORK, NY 10012.

TO PAY BY CREDIT CARD PLEASE VISIT **www.pen.org/join.**

Meet with Interesting People
Enjoy Stimulating Conversation
Discover Wonderful Books